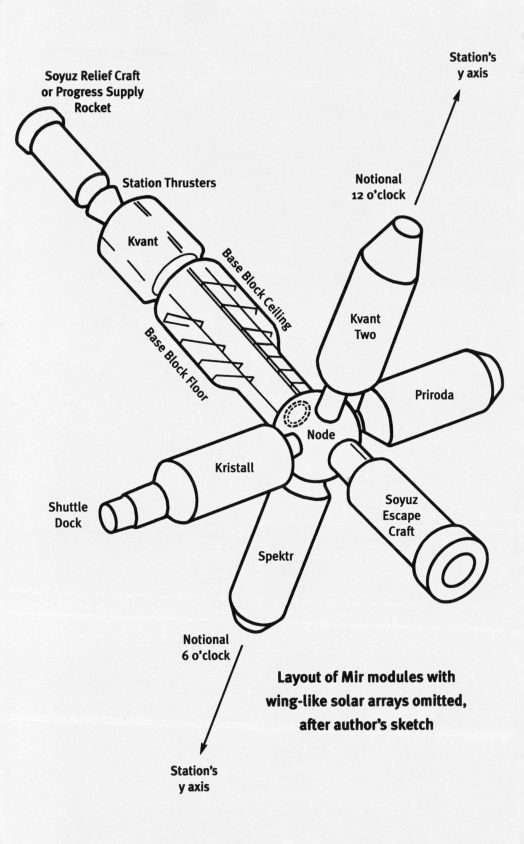

Soyuz Relief Craft or Progress Supply Rocket

Station Thrusters

Kvant

Base Block Ceiling

Base Block Floor

Station's y axis

Notional 12 o'clock

Kvant Two

Priroda

Node

Shuttle Dock

Kristall

Soyuz Escape Craft

Spektr

Notional 6 o'clock

Station's y axis

Layout of Mir modules with wing-like solar arrays omitted, after author's sketch

WAYSTATION TO THE STARS

WAYSTATION TO THE STARS

The Story of Mir, Michael and Me

Colin Foale

HEADLINE

First published in 1999 by
HEADLINE BOOK PUBLISHING

10 9 8 7 6 5 4 3 2 1

British Library Cataloguing in Publication Data

Foale, Colin
Waystation to the stars : the story of Mir, Michael & me
1. Foale, Michael 2. Mir (Space station) 3. Space flight
I. Title
629.4'42'092

ISBN 0 7472 7380 4

Edited by Jeff Howlett
Designed by Grahame Dudley

Typeset by Avon Dataset Ltd, Bidford-on-Avon, Warks

Printed and bound in Great Britain by
Mackays of Chatham PLC, Chatham, Kent

HEADLINE BOOK PUBLISHING
A division of Hodder Headline PLC
338 Euston Road
London NW1 3BH

Contents

To those men and women, of every nationality, who accept the dangers and discomforts, pride and exhilaration, of furthering the human dream to travel in space, and to all those who support them.

Acknowledgements

I am grateful for the use of library photographs and Mir status reports supplied by the Lyndon Johnson Space Center and used in this book, and for all the family's agreement to the use of relevant personal letters and e-mail.

My wife Mary never failed to give me enthusiastic encouragement in my writing of this account and she also did most of the typing from my written drafts. My daughter Susan was always ready with sound advice and accurate recall of family events. I am very grateful to both.

During the four-and-a-half months while Michael was enduring his bumpy Mir ride, we all much appreciated the moral support and timely information given to us by his astronaut friend, Captain Bill Readdy, USN, and also NASA's Stephen Vanderark and Kelly Curtis who were so prompt and effective with family support. I thank them, together with Michael's faithful and helpful 'ham' radio contacts, Dr David Larsen of California and Miles Mann of Massachusetts who selflessly patched us in to Mir, both for telephone and e-mail contact. I also record my deep admiration for the steadfast control and support sent to us by Michael's beautiful wife Rhonda during times which must have been personally very difficult for her.

My family's concern was understood by countless friends, both old and new, who were unhesitating in their expressions of support. I specially acknowledge the strength which I received from my old school friends at our 1997 reunion when the news of a Mir collision first broke, including that given subsequently by two who were unable to be present, Anne Reglar (née

Smith) who was too ill to attend and Doreen Kinder (née Braun). In particular I was grateful for the presence there of Aileen Button who had taught me English composition in the 1940s and whose company with us, on a later occasion in Cambridge, helped to soften one of the many Mir shocks.

The sympathetic interest of the media allowed us to know what was going on throughout and I am grateful for the help I received during the crises from the ITN, Sky and Anglia TV news desks, the Mason's Press Agency in Cambridge and for the invariable courtesy of individual reporters.

But it is of course Michael and his qualities that make this story, and I remember with undying affection his late brother Christopher who had so much to do with Michael's attitudes and development, and with our own too.

Foreword

Dear Dad,

It was a special feeling I had, when I put down your book, having turned the last page. It was as if I had had a chance to relive my whole experience on Mir once more. More than a year has passed since I landed back on earth, after spending the better part of five months on the space station. I should tell you immediately that you have written a book that brought back the sensations, sounds, incredible views and feeling of brotherhood I had with my Russian crew mates during my stay on Mir. Strangely disturbing for me, you even recount an event that I had already forgotten, about which I spoke to you via a ham contact during the flight. In such an extraordinarily action- and event-filled flight, I suppose I should not be so surprised that some less drastic events in my memory are harder now to recall, overwhelmed as they are by the severity of others, like the Progress collision and subsequent depressurization of Mir!

Inevitably, a son tends to look for a hero in his father, and your accounts of your adventures in the Royal Air Force as a pilot were the stuff of dreams to me as a small boy. Nobody should underestimate the value of good role models for young children, so that they are inspired and encouraged throughout childhood. Susan, Chris and I have all been especially fortunate having had you as such a role figure, balanced by our mother's calm and matter-of-fact intelligence throughout our family's life. I only wish Chris could have lived his life fully to share all our family's joys and tribulations.

....

With support and personal care from people on earth, it was easy to endure the difficulties we encountered in space. Of course Rhonda is my greatest darling, who never wavered in her upbeat, gentle chats and e-mails to me, never letting me feel the need to worry about her, regardless of the tension and uncertainty she must have felt, alone with Jenna and Ian at home.

When I reflect where I have come from, I started with a dream to fly in space, consciously looking for stepping stones to achieve my goals. I was very lucky to somehow achieve what I needed along that path.

During my flights on Mir, I learned many important lessons. One very poignant lesson for me was how important a family and its well-being is to a person. When I lived those long summer months on Mir, I appeared only rarely to my children as a brightly moving star crossing their evening skyline, above our home in Texas. Long-duration space flight, either in orbit around the earth, or on a journey to Mars, will always have significant costs for those of us who want to live our dreams and execute these endeavours when separated from the people we care about. But those same costs can result in fantastic benefits for the human spirit, inspiring our children to explore, to imagine new horizons, and to boldly solve our world's problems.

Dad, you have enthused me again. Rhonda now understands her British relatives a little more deeply, and our family has an excellent treasure to refer to in our archive, when we look back from the twenty-first century, to see how far we have come.

With love
Mike

Michael Foale
Houston, Texas, March 1999

....

Preface

ntil things began to go badly wrong on the Russian space station Mir, not many people in Britain had taken much notice of it. It had been there for eleven years. It briefly caught the world's attention when the break-up of the Soviet empire threw existing plans for crew retrieval and replacement into confusion and delay. The lonely figure of 'the last Soviet citizen', a man who had been launched by the USSR to Mir but who was eventually retrieved by Russia, caught the imagination.

But from 25 June 1997, the station was rarely out of the news. The NASA astronaut and two successive Russian crews had had to find the means to survive a series of unprecedented dangers in space. The NASA astronaut was my son Michael, dear to us and to his own family. It was he who, to use the media phrases of the time, was on Troubled Mir, Crisis-hit Mir, Mishap-stricken Mir. One leading scientist, commenting on this 'ageing Russian module', was said to urge that we stop playing Russian roulette with astronauts' lives. We knew our son well and we watched and listened, wrote to and received e-mails from him and occasionally spoke to him. It was due to his confidence and attitudes at each turn that we felt increasingly sure he would survive those 'tumultuous four months', to use another phrase of the time.

Michael was born and nurtured within the colourful and exciting bounds of my first career, in the Royal Air Force, wherever duty took us in England or overseas. His story is extraordinary by any standard and needs to be told. However, his continuing involvement at NASA prevents him from recounting it himself, and I have mustered the considerable temerity to do it instead. I tell myself that few can know him so well, and only his mother has known him longer. In describing the influences under which he moulded himself into the right stuff, I anticipate that I can happily touch on the host of stories and experiences with which I, as a dad, regaled my family at table on countless occasions. He would have heard them all. I publicly ask my loved ones' pardon if I was ever boring or repetitive, as I probably was. However, some of the reminiscences can still terrify *me*.

The story that follows is the result of our knowledge and respect for each other. It is amplified by our long conversations in easy chairs by the lighted Christmas tree over the family's post-mission stay at my home in Cambridge, when he often had me on the edge of my seat. The conversations continued over Hogmanay at his highland godfather's farmhouse in northern Scotland, and on the trains to and from there. I hope that he will like reading it, and will recognize us both. I ask nothing in return – perhaps he will consider attempting a filial biography after I am gone.

A House in the Sky

The six men were gathered at one end of a long, narrow room which was shaped like a cylinder, and was well lit and warm. From small speakers came the singing of a Russian pop star, longing for her lover. The music won, but only just, over the low, constant background whirr of atmosphere-controlling fans and hidden stabilizing gyros.

They were all in festive mood. Commander Valeri Korzun and his crewman, Aleksandr Kaleri, were in good spirits because their reliefs, Commander Vasily Tsibliyev and Sasha Lazutkin, had recently blazed a fiery trail in their Soyuz spacecraft from Baikonur, joining them to begin a twenty-day handover period. Korzun and Kaleri were glad to be going home after six months' weightless existence on their space station. The arrival of the Soyuz had temporarily doubled the number of the station's normal complement of three to six, and this in itself was a satisfying source of variety, however brief the overlap, and a cause for celebration.

Jerry Linenger, the quiet, thoughtful US Navy doctor and NASA 'paying guest' astronaut, had already completed the first month of the four which he would spend there conducting American scientific experiments. With the new crew had arrived the sixth member of the little gathering, German researcher Reinhold Ewald, who would remain as a 'paying guest' for the twenty-day handover period only.

They sat around a table amiably and comfortably in a normal 'on earth' way. It was difficult to spot that each was in fact quite weightless, and that without the restraining straps across their thighs and feet, they would readily float 'upwards' in reaction if they gave a good belly laugh. They happened to be the same way up, but for all six there was no real up or down. Russian, American and German food packs were sampled, they drank carefully through straws, and they relaxed, savouring each other's company.

Beyond the group at the table was the dark, circular hole which led to the Node and then to the departing crew's Soyuz return and escape craft, in which they and the German would soon leave for earth. At the opposite end of the long room, the cylinder narrowed, passing between the station's thruster engines, and led to the recently docked Soyuz which had brought up the new crew from Kazakhstan.

During a conversational pause, Commander Korzun looked at his watch and said, 'Time for another oxygen candle, I believe.' He looked meaningfully at the new crewman, Sasha Lazutkin.

The station's electronic oxygen generators could continuously support only three persons. When there was an overlap and six were on board, a supplementary supply was needed, and this was regularly provided by the burning of patent oxygen-producing canisters, called 'candles'. One candle, burning for twenty minutes, provided enough oxygen for one person for one day.

This was Sasha Lazutkin's first mission into space, and it would be well for him to become familiar with procedures as quickly as possible. Korzun gestured towards the narrowing end of the room where the metallic holder for the burning candle was situated, and Lazutkin happily allowed himself to float free of his restraints and pulled himself along a convenient bungee strung lengthwise towards the room's far end.

He removed a candle from storage and struck the canister's end to ignite it, as he had been trained to do, and placed it in its holder.

Immediately he cried out in alarm and pain, loud enough to be heard by the five men still at the table, who flashed anxious, enquiring faces towards him. He was pulling himself wildly back along the bungee, revealing to them what he was leaving so hurriedly.

....

The sight was shocking. An out-of-control flame, two feet long, was spurting from the canister while spots of molten metal were flying randomly from it to the surrounding walls, followed by thick, blackening and enveloping smoke. Any fire in the delicate atmospheric and constructional fabric of a space station was unthinkably dangerous. It threatened to destroy the crew's defence against the airless, pressureless, life-extinguishing nothingness outside, beyond its walls. It was worse even than an uncontrollable fire on a tiny yacht, alone in a great ocean, where there could still be the chance of rescue, however small.

In one movement, Commander Korzun shot from the table over the heads of the others towards an emergency fire extinguisher on the wall, grabbed it and dived to the room's narrowing end where the deadly flame continued to roar. He had to put the fire out quickly or evacuate the station. But each Soyuz could take only three men. If the fire was not stopped, the route to the docked Soyuz aft would be impassable. If he failed, at least three of them would die.

The five other men watched with horrified concentration as Korzun applied the fire extinguisher, his body hunched lengthwise in the confined space, now blocking their view of the source of the flame and smoke and leaving them unaware of the effect of his actions. At one stage he seemed to be lying so still in the narrowness of the passage and the increasing smoke that Linenger, as the medical man, grabbed Korzun's leg and shouted, 'Are you all right? Answer us!'

Korzun turned around in some irritation, his face black, as the smoke thickened and spread further into the room. Between his gasps for air he said, 'Get me more extinguishers!'

Two more extinguishers were quickly found and passed to him.

'Bring me an oxygen mask and goggles. All of you do the same. The smoke may be toxic.'

It took a long time for the canister holder to cool down before they could be sure that the fire was truly out. Smoke continued to issue from it for seven minutes. The fire had actually burned, they later decided, for only ninety seconds, but with its intensity and the fear that it might spread, it had seemed like an eternity. The three extinguishers were thought to have had little effect. The fire had lasted until it had burned itself and the 'candle' holder out. Miraculously, no collateral damage had been caused by the molten metal.

In Linenger's view, later expressed on the ground, this disturbing incident was never fully reported by Russian Ground Control, nor treated as being of particular significance, yet his own experience of it was that of a near disaster. Sasha Lazutkin says that it was profoundly frightening. The unfortunate American and his new Russian colleagues were to experience a further unsettling event a few weeks later. The new commander, Vasily Tsibliyev, was ordered by Ground Control to execute a previously unrehearsed manual docking of a supply vehicle (Progress).

A video camera had been mounted on the forward end of the Progress, providing Tsibliyev's TV monitor on Mir with a view as seen from Progress of its approach to the station. Tsibliyev was then manually to give approach and docking commands to the supply vessel up to its actual docking. The monitor failed to work properly, and the docking had to be abandoned. The result was the nerve-racking loss of the Progress. This incident was also reported by Russian Ground Control as of no international significance; it was a purely Russian matter which was being dealt with.

The directors at NASA badly wanted their Phase One programme of cooperation with the Russians to succeed, and were already planning to replace Linenger with Michael Foale. The Russians were careful not to do or say anything to deter the Americans from their resolve to continue. The Russians gained much-needed hard currency from the programme, and the Americans the equally valuable experience of long-term weightlessness for their astronauts, preparing for the start of the International Space Station (ISS) scheduled to begin launching in late 1998. Perhaps the Russians should have been more forthcoming. Perhaps the Americans should have been more inquisitive. For both countries, it was important that the programme succeed.

Tsibliyev had consulted an astrologer before the launch to this, his second space-station mission. She had not been entirely frank, and he had felt that she knew this mission was to be fraught with difficulties. Those first two months did nothing to relieve him of the darkness of his expectations.

Linenger had already decided that this would be his last space mission, and after his return to earth, he resigned from NASA at the end of 1997, glad to know that he would not see Mir, this Russian marvel in space, again.

....

Mir. It's a short Russian word meaning peace. Its brevity belies its significance. The space station was designed by Russian scientists during the Cold War. The first component in space, called the Base Block, was successfully rocketed, unmanned, into orbit around the earth in 1986, as the Cold War was finally coming to an end. It has circled the earth continuously ever since, once every 90 minutes, over 240 miles aloft. Its path is roughly north-east over the world on one side and south-west on the other, reaching in turn latitude 52 degrees north and then 52 degrees south.

The earth always has a daytime sun side and a night-time dark side as it rotates on its axis once every 24 hours. But Mir circles the rotating earth every 90 minutes, and so passes from daylight into darkness and back again sixteen times during the period of one 24-hour earth day. And because its path in space is stable, the rotation of the earth beneath it effectively moves Mir's geographical path steadily westwards, 22.5 degrees longitude on each silent pass across the earth's surface. In time, there is no part of the earth between 52 degrees north and 52 degrees south which is not flown over by Mir. This makes the station an unparalleled platform for observation of the planet's resources, an awareness of its sheer beauty, and the changes it suffers.

Americans call their spacemen and spacewomen astronauts. Russians call theirs cosmonauts. In the same way that human readiness to take risks brings a heightened conscious love of life, the shrugging off of earth and its gravity by flying in space brings a conscious and intense love of the home planet. Cosmonauts and astronauts alike are happy to spend many hours just watching the majesty of the earth in its infinite variation slide silently by. They are usually too busy to allow much time for such wonder, but it explains why so many return to earth without having read one word of the leisure reading they have thoughtfully taken with them.

Pilots of long-range aircraft sitting for hours at their controls experience much the same serene satisfaction, although at only a fraction of the orbital height. But even from a jumbo jet at a comparatively puny eight miles high, the shapes of islands, lakes and coastlines begin to resemble the familiar pages of an atlas. Only the map's colours, names and national borders are missing. My two early years on a fighter squadron in Egypt (1952–4) left the dark green shape of the Nile Delta against the gold of the surrounding desert etched indelibly on my mind. As is the north–south flow of the biblical River Jordan, running from Galilee to the Dead Sea, its surrounding hills green after winter rain, just like the map of Palestine so often drawn on the blackboard by my divinity teacher in our once-a-week lesson at school.

My father, a devout evangelical Christian, as indeed was my mother, was struck by my description of Palestine from the air. But both my loving parents were conscious of the risks inherent in military flying and the monotonous regularity of fatal crashes at the time. So they prayed for my safety (as often so did I) and sometimes ended their letters with a comforting biblical quotation. One that stuck in my mind throughout my flying career, and since, is Deuteronomy 33 v 27 – 'Underneath are the everlasting arms' – not a bad thought to have at times when the sheer *joie de vivre* of flying could put one in deadly danger. But as my friends who shared these experiences will readily agree, and God knows, none of this awareness ever deterred me from being as cheerful a sinner as they were, then or now.

There is something godlike about flying an aeroplane, with views of lands and seas which are endlessly varied, the artefacts of mankind diminished so as to give the pilot the feeling of a sublime overview. This was classically brought home to me when flying low over the snowy treetops of the home of the Greek gods, on the Mount Parnassus summit in ancient Aetolia. I throttled back the powerful jets and dipped to follow the mountain's downward slope and dark pines to Delphi, banked steeply over the temple of Apollo, and, on the azure coast of the Gulf of Corinth, passed over the tiny port of Itea. I would have made a suitably Jovian thunder-roll as I opened up over the Greek countryside towards Olympia and Sparta to the south. Not quite winged sandals, but Homer would have loved it – and been pleased to see how right he had originally got it.

But it is not all to do with looking down on earth, compassionately or angrily, as deities are traditionally expected to do. There are also the night skies which, even at orbital height, are barely closer than when seen from the earth's surface. But 240 miles above the cloud, vapour, dust and earth light, the impression of being surrounded by stars can be overwhelming. I once offered to an astronaut the thought that in orbit, one would have a much better view of the firmament and would see more stars.

....

He said, 'You don't just see more stars, you see *hundreds* of times more stars.'

For the astronaut, they become a fascination, at first because of the unexpected initial difficulty of identifying known and loved constellations, set now within the myriad new star lights, unwinking, not twinkling, demanding attention.

There is, of course, a fundamental difference between high-altitude jet aircraft flying and being in orbit, and that is the phenomenon of weight-lessness. This needs explaining for the benefit of the uninitiated, which includes most of us. An aeroplane does not fall to earth, unless the pilot wants it to, because the engines thrust it and its wings fast through the air to give lift, exactly balancing the earth's pull of gravity, which is the aircraft's weight. The air's dynamic lift supports the aircraft, and our seats in the aircraft support us. All of us still weigh the same. However, if an object should leave the aircraft in free fall to earth, it becomes weightless. If during its free fall the object is travelling *forward* fast enough, its free fall will always be taking place beyond the next horizon, over the far edge of the earth's ball. It falls around the earth. It is in orbit. Any person or thing within it will also experience weightlessness, floating about inside.

Weightlessness is difficult to simulate for training except in free fall. Spacewalk rehearsals are often done in a large water tank to give the participant the slow, floating feeling to be expected when doing actual, external space work. But it does not produce true weightlessness. If the astronaut puts his head down (and feet up) in the tank, he will still feel the blood run to his head, which would not happen in space, where no gravity affects the blood. Indeed, the only true earthly simulation is to be in a diving aircraft on a concave path relative to the earth, which lifts the participants from the aircraft floor as if in free fall, but it is difficult to produce periods of weightlessness for longer than thirty seconds because the aircraft must pull out of the quickly steepening dive. Astronauts in training in both America and Russia are given this taste of weightlessness in a large transport aircraft, its body empty of seats and the trainees sitting on the floor without restraint. The pilot starts a gradual steepening dive, lifting the occupants off the floor, floating in space, until he has to bring the aircraft back to the safety of level flight and the floaters sink, hopefully gently, to the floor once again. The

....

aircraft used in America is one of the older, out-of-service jet transports, like the first British transport jet, the Comet. For this, and other less savoury reasons, it is known throughout NASA as the Vomit Comet.

Mir's first and later additional component parts have all been rocketed upwards and along its required velocity path at such a final speed that, even when the rocket thrust ceases, the forward speed is enough to take the free fall beyond the next, and the next, horizon. There is virtually nothing at orbital heights to cause friction and therefore retardation. So, like a minuscule moon, Mir circles the earth without the need for propellant thrust to keep it going. However, all space vehicles do need some small thrusters to be able to rearrange their attitude on their axes or to nudge them into a suitable position to dock with another vessel or, ultimately, to slow them down to leave orbit and return to earth.

Any view of Mir gives the strong impression that it has been constructed piecemeal. That impression is right: it has. Its first part was the Base Block, a large metal cylinder 13 feet in diameter and some 40 feet long, equipped with instruments, a galley, an eating position, sleep positions and a space toilet. At one end, nominally known as 'aft', there are small thruster engines and a docking port for the arrival of a spacecraft carrying supplies or a crew change. At the other end, nominally 'forward', is a large hollow sphere, as wide as the Base Block, with five openable hatches. If one looked into the sphere from the Base Block (forward), one would see on the far side of the sphere one of these hatches leading to a docking port similar to the one aft of the Base Block. The other four hatches are spaced around the sphere at 90-degree angles to one another. The sphere is called the Node.

Two giant winglike structures stretch out from the Base Block cylinder, catching the sun's rays during each day portion of the orbit (day pass). The solar energy collected is converted to electrical power to charge the Base Block batteries. Heat, light, oxygen and water recycling depend on this power. This was how the station started.

Over the following ten years, five additional cylindrical modules were sent for docking and fixing to Mir. One, called Kvant, docked at the aft end of the Base Block, providing an in-line extension to the aft docking port. Four more in turn were docked to the Node sphere, in a cruciform pattern at the four hatches already described. Looking forward from the Base Block, these

....

are known clockwise as Kvant 2 (say, at twelve o'clock – one has to start somewhere), Kristall at three o'clock, Spektr at six o'clock and Priroda at nine o'clock. Most have solar arrays of their own, which makes any outside view of the whole station confusing.

If one could observe Mir in its current configuration while trying to ignore the confusion of the multiple winglike sets of solar arrays, one would see a long, cigar-shaped Base Block extended aft by Kvant. At the other, forward end is a cruciform set of smaller cylindrical modules fixed around the spherical Node. In the centre of this cross protrudes forward the Soyuz escape/return-to-earth craft, docked there by the new crew, after the previous crew's departure in theirs. At the opposite end, at old Kvant, also protruding, is docked from time to time another spacecraft, an unmanned supply and waste-disposal vessel called Progress.

The whole edifice, its solar arrays as fragile in appearance as insect wings, moves steadily and continuously along its line of orbit. Although weightless in space, it still has considerable mass, which on earth would weigh 130 tons. If one multiplies this by the speed at which it is travelling, some 17,500 miles per hour, one has a force value for its momentum, should the station be unfortunate enough to collide with a meteorite or another spacecraft or space debris, a fact which does not, for the human inhabitants of Mir, bear too much thinking about.

There have been men and women on Mir for over twelve years. While the Americans concentrated on the development and successful use of the space shuttle, a retrievable and reusable spaceship which, after two weeks in orbit, could glide to a runway on earth, the Russians concentrated on successful longer-term human occupation of space on a space station. Each emphasis has separate merits for research and no doubt each was perceived as also having separate military merit in the Cold War period. It has to be a reason for thankfulness by all the world's inhabitants that the two powers saw reason and advantage in bringing their lines of experience together in the US–Russian 'Phase One' cooperative programme. This has provided American astronauts with long-term space habitation experience and brought to Mir the advantage of periodic supply visits by the shuttle, additional to their Progress supply vehicles. It has also given the Russians much-needed foreign currency. The arrangement was an entirely appropriate introduction to the

....

International Space Station (ISS) project, which had its first launches in November and December 1998.

Any launch of a vessel which is required to reach orbital or escape speed is best done not too far from the equator, if advantage is to be taken of the earth's surface rotation speed relative to space. At the equator, this provides a start speed of over 1,000 mph in an easterly direction, reducing progressively to the north or south to zero at the poles. Both Russia and America, being northern hemisphere countries, have their launch sites as far south as their geographical limits permit.

The Russians lift their cosmonauts into orbital rendezvous with Mir by a remarkable rocket-launched vehicle called Soyuz, from Baikonur in Kazakhstan. The top end of the rocket, the Soyuz capsule, has seats for three cosmonauts, one of them the commander, who is provided with instrumentation and some manual controls, should the automatic system fail at any point. After the blast-off, the whole assembly accelerates towards an orbit which will take the manned capsule part-way to the Mir orbit. Then, with the use of its own thrusters, the Soyuz unites with Mir at the aft end dock, on Kvant. This is how the Russians deliver a relief crew to Mir, the old crew returning to earth in their own delivery Soyuz which would have originally brought them to Mir, and which would subsequently have been parked at the forward end on the Node. Unlike the shuttle, the Soyuz craft uses parachutes after descent and re-entry into earth's atmosphere, for a landing in Russia.

Space is a virtual vacuum. Where the sun shines, without an atmosphere, it can be unbearably hot, and in the darkness it is unbearably cold. There is no oxygen to breathe, and no air pressure such as we are used to on earth – fourteen pounds per square inch on every part of our bodies. We do not notice this pressure, since we have experienced it since conception and birth. But without it our blood would boil and we would quickly die.

The interior of a spaceship must therefore be organized to meet the physical needs of humans. The oxygen needed for breathing has to be supplied and replaced as it is used. The carbon dioxide in the expelled breath must be extracted from the ship's atmosphere to avoid a build-up which would otherwise, in time, smother the crew. Within the airtight interior, the atmosphere must be maintained at a pressure similar to that on earth. Water must be supplied, and where possible, recycled. Food, obviously, has to be

....

available. The interior must be heated and lit during the time the station's orbit is in darkness, and cooled when it is in sunlight. The controlling computers and communications systems need power. All of these functions are sustained, one way or another, by the electrical power delivered through the absorption of the sun's energy by the solar arrays.

The initial delivery and further provision of supplies, as well as some disposal of waste, is carried out during the regular visits of the unmanned Progress supply vessels, and has been supplemented during the Phase One programme by a US space shuttle every four to five months, during the delivery and retrieval of a NASA astronaut.

Should it be necessary for members of the crew to go outside the humanized environment of the space station's interior into the hostility of open space, their bodies need protection in order to survive. Such protection can be provided for a limited time by the wearing of a pressurized spacesuit, with its own integral oxygen supply, that is worn by astronauts doing exterior work in space during their so-called spacewalks, technically 'extra vehicular activity' (EVA). The spacesuit is really a mini, flexible spacecraft shaped like an astronaut. The average length of time spent outside the main craft is currently about six hours, the limit of the spacesuit's resources.

Weightlessness for crew members involves psychological factors as well as physical. It is possible for a crew member to find him- or herself floating in mid-module, as it were, just out of reach of any fixed object on the wall. In such a position it is extremely difficult to proceed in any direction. Without help, one could even be marooned; there is a tendency to resort to a vigorous swimming breaststroke or crawl, to no avail. Only one area, that of the Base Block leading to the Node, is so wide (thirteen feet) as to make such helplessness likely, so the cosmonauts have strung elasticized bungee ropes the length of the module and on into the Node, five feet apart, to use as handholds in order to move about. The ropes are vital, not just useful, and allow two individuals proceeding in opposite directions to float past each other, like boats, without interference. They are also useful for attaching objects to temporarily, while the hands are needed for something else. All the other modules, and in particular the hatch entry circles, are narrow enough for one wall or another to be within reach as a handhold or toehold.

The word 'wall' introduces the concept of a vertical dimension which, in weightless space, cannot physically exist, either up or down. Such terms can only be meaningful relative to the position that one crew member is in at any one time. Psychologically this needs attending to, particularly if it is considered beneficial, as it is, for crew members to get together socially at certain times during the day, such as mealtimes and regular communication periods with Ground Control (comm passes). So the Base Block has a designated 'floor', painted green, a 'ceiling', painted pale blue, and 'walls' in gentle pastel colours.

The commander has a seat positioned on the 'floor', at the forward end facing the consoles of his operations centre and desk. There are foot restraints to help him stay in place. Above his head, on the wall which he faces, is the circular opening to the Node and its five openings to the other modules. Behind his stool is a dinner table with stools or anchor points for all crew members, and a small personal drawer in the table for individual eating implements and food supplements. On the sides, vertical to the 'floor', are two sleeping recesses, where a body and its sleeping bag can be anchored during the eight sleeping hours per twenty-four permitted by Ground Control (11.30 pm to 7.30 am Moscow time). There is a galley for heating food and drink, and a wash area.

The important point about this largest central area is that it is where the whole crew, three normally but six during the twenty-one-day handover periods, will need to come together periodically and, for mutual comfort, to be all the same way up. The importance of uniform orientation when people are talking, thinking, eating or recreating together is instinctively understood by the crew. Spacemen are, after all, human. But when alone, a crew member can hang like a bat, or curl up into a ball alone, or jam himself on the 'floor', and, closing his eyes, know no difference in his position. However, weightlessness does bring on an initial physical symptom, which can bother astronauts for some days. It is a vague backache syndrome. It could be caused by the absence of gravitational compression on the vertebrae, or floating and traversing in a prone position with the head lifted to see ahead. Whatever it is, relief can often be found by regularly adopting a foetal position, curling up hard into a ball, stretching the vertebrae in the back and neck.

The station cannot be serviced regularly like a great jumbo jet. Instead,

....

many duplications and planned redundancies are introduced at the design stage, which can be activated as a replacement or back-up by a signal from the ground. Without this inbuilt resilience to problems or failures, there would be unacceptably heavy maintenance responsibilities put on valuable scientific crews, or unreasonably frequent requirements for them to hazard spacewalks outside. There are therefore many electrical circuits, motors, systems and their related computer controls, all designed to be responsive to ground-originated and -transmitted telemetric signals.

All of these systems are regularly monitored electronically by teams on the ground. Problem evaluation and decision-making is done by groups of experts in each field, working at their desks and consoles on shift, from the information received from telemetry or voice communications. All have the ability to talk to the Controller, who alone talks to the crew, or to each other, and, when necessary, to call a conference. This round-the-clock human input is known as Mission or Ground Control. In Russia it is called TSUP, pronounced 'tsoup'. Sometimes the staff of Ground Control are bound to feel that the astronauts are simply an extension of themselves in space, such is their concentration and dedication to the work. Apart from telemetric inputs to the station, their considerations and conclusions will also be expressed in the make-up of the loads on the regular supply vessels.

Valeri Korzun and Aleksandr Kaleri left the station to the new crew shortly after the fire in February 1997. The new commander, Vasily (Vassy) Tsibliyev, was forty-four years old, a fighter pilot and family man, somewhat withdrawn in personality, unassertive but pleasant and relaxed in style. His childhood had been spent on a collective farm, and he was pleased to have avoided a future on the land. This was Vasily Tsibliyev's second mission on Mir. The flight engineer, Aleksandr (Sasha) Lazutkin, was an employee of Energiya, the manufacturers of the space station. He was forty-one years old, married, and on his first mission. He was intelligent, light-hearted, dark-eyed and sported a moustache. He was quickly able to develop a rapport with strangers and did so enthusiastically, unlike Tsibliyev whose natural reserve was perhaps reinforced on this flight by his awareness of the terms of his contract and the responsibilities of command.

Later they both told Michael that they had actively looked forward to his arrival. His predecessor had not got on well with Valeri Korzun. Whether it was an inadequate grasp of the Russian language or too great a focus on his experiments was hard to say, but the net result was a general lack of communication and relationship. However, they gave him some benefit of the doubt, agreeing that Russian cosmonauts, all of whom were probably mad, were not the best social stimulus for a withdrawn American. So roll on Michael Foale, whom they had met at their training base in Star City, near Moscow, and who had taken the trouble to accompany them to Baikonur to watch their launch.

Michael had later sent them a polite message on Mir, saying how much he looked forward to joining them and how he hoped that he would not get in their way. They replied immediately, saying that he should be assured that he would be welcomed not just as a crewman but as a friend.

The fire episode was not repeated, but another less immediate problem became a background worry for months. This was an ethylene glycol leak, detectable by smell, from piping carrying the essential cooling system, which keeps station temperature levels within habitable limits during sunlight passes. It could not be switched off, and it was known that a person could only take so much of this poison per unit of time before serious damage to the body would occur. The detectors showed that the rate of emission was within human tolerance limits, but little was known of the cumulative effects. Also disturbing was the fact that much of the crew's drinking-water supply came from recycled humidity in the station's atmosphere; some of the moisture might have condensed on to surfaces which themselves could have accumulated the leaked ethylene glycol. There was a fear that this would dissolve in the condensate and contaminate the drinking water. So the laborious and time-consuming search for the leaks became an early priority for the new Russian crew, and virtually a daily chore.

Indeed, the fire and the unsolved leaks were major factors in putting doubts into NASA minds, in April 1997, as to the wisdom of continuing to send their astronauts to Mir at all.

The space shuttle Atlantis was scheduled to launch in mid-May from Cape Canaveral, as STS-84, to rendezvous with Mir and to retrieve Linenger. The nominated replacement, Dr Michael Foale, had been preparing for the mission for eighteen months, almost exclusively in Russia, where he had

....

been accompanied by his wife and two small children. In April he returned to Texas to await NASA's decision, but NASA was in no hurry. He was to be kept in doubt up to a late stage.

Michael, the Eldest of Three

I t must always be a revelation, sometimes a surprise, for a father to see what happens to his baby boy, but the passing years at least bring the benefit of indisputable hindsight. One of the first sounds that Michael was likely to have heard were the Meteor and Hunter jet aircraft operated by my fighter-attack training flight at Strubby in Lincolnshire, as they roared over the area adjacent to Louth and its maternity hospital. On 6 January 1957 I drove my wife Mary to the hospital from our rented home in Sutton-on-Sea in a hurry. The previous night had been humid and the car engine would not fire. I removed the plugs and dried them – it took only a few minutes, but Mary was anxious. We arrived at the hospital with just half an hour to spare. Michael was born without much hair, and what little there was looked sandy, even red, in the ward's light. When I got back to the airfield the wing commander in charge of flying (and therefore of me) telephoned me to ask for an update. The first words that I uttered about Michael were, 'Well, we have a boy.'

'Great, congratulations! How's Mary?'

'She's fine.' (Pause.) 'He has red hair.'

'Well.' (Longer pause.) 'You can't have everything.'

His hair turned out to be fair, his eyes blue. He was born into a family that was dominated by my career in the Royal Air Force. I was then the flight commander of a gunnery and rocket projectile training flight of fighters at the RAF flying college in Lincolnshire. His brother Christopher was born the following year, also fair and blue-eyed. They subsequently lived and breathed for years among the sights and sounds of operational airfields. Until Michael went away to boarding school at eleven, followed a year later by Christopher, the majority of their friends were likely to have air force, or other armed services, fathers. I suppose I always thought of my sons as potential air force pilots, and I never hesitated to tell them my RAF stories, adventurous or rueful, and sing them some of the songs.

My wife Mary is from Minneapolis. Her nationality was to be significant for Michael in later years. We first met in 1953, at the Usher Hall in Edinburgh. A performance of Elgar's 'Enigma Variations' had just ended, and we were both profoundly moved. I was in the middle of a tour of duty on a fighter squadron in Egypt, and had been detached to Britain for four months to attend a course in Yorkshire. My meeting with Mary at the Edinburgh Festival, and being in those familiar home-country environments, was a most satisfying contrast to the rigours of the Middle East. It provoked a need in me to tell of my many adventures of the past eighteen months, all youthful, many colourful, some nerve-racking. Against a background of Edinburgh and the Yorkshire Wolds, they were also exotic. Mary was an appreciative and interested listener, and contributed many gems of her own. This first convivial off-loading of memories became a habit and, later, part of our married life. Any children we might have were unlikely to be short of an oral family tradition, even line-shoots, as the RAF termed the more extravagant stories.

In the year between meeting Mary and finally returning to England for our wedding, I had flown a fighter reinforcement exercise to Cape Town, four aircraft in formation. This comprised eleven two- to three-hour flights and five night stops en route in each direction, from the top to the bottom of Africa, Egypt to the Cape. Africa was still colonial then, and we were greeted by English voices at every air traffic control centre we called on the radio, one of them out of breath from biking in a hurry to his remote control tower on hearing our engines approach – we were early, with a strong following wind. Another flood of potentially recountable memories.

From Michael's age of three-and-a-half to six we were all at Akrotiri in Cyprus, one of the busiest operational airfields in the RAF, with five resident

....

squadrons and many more visiting on attachment. Our two boys were bouncy little fair-haired figures, brown-skinned, happiest on the beach and in the water. I had sometimes encouraged Michael to jump from an object such as a table or low wall into my arms, as a confidence-builder. It was always, 'Are you ready? All right, jump.'

And he would jump, his arms wide, a smile on his face, to be caught by his trusty dad. Indeed, the media have made much of a photo of him at three, in mid-air, from a leap off the sofa in his pyjamas. His first experience of weightlessness, they said.

Came the day when I had preceded the family down some steps from the Limassol sea wall to the beach below.

'Are you ready, Dad?' sang out Michael's voice behind me. I turned to see him jumping confidently from the top of the wall, well above my head, a weightless smile on his face as he hurtled towards me. There was no time to say no, nor to explain that the force of momentum was mass times velocity, and he was accelerating. Neither of us was injured, but we both seemed to rise very slowly from a flattened posture on the beach. That was probably the last time we played that game.

I was thirty years old and confident in a way that single-seat fighter pilots tend to be – boring for those who do not share the privilege. In 1960 I took over command of a light bomber squadron of Canberra B2s, with ten crews of one pilot and two navigators each. An entirely new experience for me, which official logic only dictated because the Canberra had proved a poor conventional war substitute for the Vampire and Venom aircraft which it had replaced. It was forlornly hoped that a little fighter mentality in the commanding officer could change all that. It couldn't.

The Canberra's tactical inadequacy in a local, conventional war was, however, mitigated by its long range, considerably better than fighters, so helpful in peacetime for fostering and maintaining goodwill among allies. I was thus able to send individual aircraft on detachment or on Central Treaty Organization (CENTO) alliance exercises; to take the whole squadron to Turkey, Iran and Pakistan, or south over the Sudanese deserts to Khartoum, across the mountains of Ethiopia to southern Yemen (Aden), to the Persian Gulf sheikhdoms, to Kenya and the two Rhodesias. It was an agreeably large parish to visit.

Michael heard me telling the family and our guests of my detachments, such as those to the north-west frontier of Pakistan with its brown hills and wild, armed tribesmen, once a fighting training ground, often deadly, for young British army officers. I described the 'sugar-loaf' peak Damavand, gleaming white, east of the golden domes and minarets of Tehran, the thousands of miles of mountain and desert of North Africa and Arabia, the snows of Kilimanjaro and Mount Kenya and the great lakes of central Africa. He got used to my work taking me briefly away from our home at Akrotiri on these operational detachments, with more stories for the telling on my return.

Michael and Christopher became drearily familiar at an early age with the concept of accidental death – the base witnessed eleven fatalities during our time there: one aerial collision, one disappearance in the sea on an approach to the airfield at night, and one catastrophic failure on take-off. I was the first to arrive at the seven-hundred-metre-long burning swathe of vegetation and aircraft wreckage, quickly finding in the scrub the burned corpses of the five crew which had been scattered on impact. My emotion was not horror, only sadness, but I will never forget the smell.

At lunch Michael asked me what had happened. Everybody on the station had heard the crash explosion and had seen the black pall of smoke towering to a thousand feet.

'Yes, Dad, but what actually happened?' He was barely six, but looked straight at me with his question. Christopher, four, kept his eyes on his plate.

'Something went wrong on take-off, when the aircraft should have unstuck at about a hundred and twenty knots. It slammed back on to the rough ground beyond the runway and exploded into fragments.'

'Yes, but why?'

'We don't know yet, but the investigation has started. The cause will certainly be found.' He wanted to ask more, but sensed that I was reluctant to speculate.

There was also a further highly significant birth, that of our daughter Susan, which took place while I was away with the squadron in Tehran. I received the signal from Akrotiri too late for an immediate departure that night, but the squadron helped me to celebrate the event at our hotel. She soon grew dark hair, and her brown eyes were merry, matching her temperament.

....

I flew back to Akrotiri in haste and delight to welcome my new daughter into the family. By this time Michael was well over five years old, and had started at the station's infant school. He was an active boy, already showing determination to do well at swimming – he had just learned how – and his teachers said that he took his school classes seriously. He told Christopher about his experiences.

'Yes, Michael,' little Christopher said, 'but what do you actually do all day [until one pm]?'

'Well,' said Michael importantly but then somewhat self-consciously, 'we have lessons from teachers on how to write and add up. But we also have a lot of games to play. I think it's fun. Later this year you can start too, and you'll see.'

The arrival of a little sister only increased his awareness of being the eldest and the family's flag-bearer. Christopher had become more accustomed to being a year younger. He still tried hard to keep up, but in a light-hearted way. Both now had hair bleached almost white by the Mediterranean sun. Mary had been confined in the RAF hospital on the station, and was soon home in our nice cool house with its veranda looking towards the blue Troodos mountains. Susan, with her dark eyes and infectious chuckle, tended to be the family's centre of attention for a while, and Christopher quietly established himself, at four years old, as her primary interface (after her mother) with the outer world, a role he unobtrusively maintained towards adulthood.

Although Akrotiri was quite well lit, to help guard against possible hostile, lunatic-fringe intruders, our gardens were dark. We would often stand at the back of the house to look at the deep black of the clear Mediterranean night sky with its endless arrays of stars. Michael and Christopher would look too, and were usually silent with wonder until a shooting star streaked down, when two excited shouts seemed to be triggered simultaneously. They were never short of questions about sky, land or sea. Mary and I had never to be short of answers.

We returned to England a family of five, to live in Bracknell for two years.

A period followed on ground-staff duty for three years in Germany, where I was concerned with the NATO alliance and facing up to the perceived might of the Soviet Union in the Cold War. It was a hard, demanding life, with frequent late hours at the office. Family life was barely less full, as we had annual camping holidays each August and travelled to all the most colourful places within driving range this side of the Iron Curtain. Our official intelligence services strongly implied (but never committed themselves officially) that the Russians also went on holiday in August, so it was probably safe to go: intelligence easy to believe.

We trekked by car to the Swiss Alps (a memorable *Wow!* from Christopher when he saw his first alp looming out of the mist above the window's field of view), the Austrian Tyrol, the Italian Riviera and the Bay of Naples, the French Pyrenees and southern Spain. Michael's later references to Mir being a bit like a camping trip probably stem from this period, although I personally made no connection with him and space at the time. We always bought bed and breakfast while in transit, then pitched our nice big tent on a camping site at our destination. We snorkelled a lot in the sea and I bought a large, glamorous diving knife – quite unnecessary, but its aura of adventure (James Bond!) captivated the boys. They were growing up happily together, Michael scientific and deliberate, conscious of responsibilities and being the eldest. Christopher, only fourteen months younger, was steadily catching up. The gap was closing, and he was becoming more spontaneous and humorous. From an early age he loved laughter. Both remained well disposed towards their sisterly bundle of mischief, Susan, who loved them both. Susan recently told me that she and Christopher always held Michael a little in awe.

Halfway through our time in Germany, I built from a kit at our home in Rheindahlen a fourteen-foot sailing boat which we sailed, not very successfully, on the swift-flowing River Maas in Holland, and more success-fully in the Bay of Naples during a trip south (diving knife at the ready). While towing the boat behind on our return, I rashly took an educational diversion for the children's benefit across St Peter's Square in Rome, causing voluble consternation among the intercepting *polizia*. The evident anger and frank disbelief of the police that anyone could be so stupid as to drive through crowded St Peter's Square with a boat on a trailer provoked profuse and ultimately sincere apologies from me, and lasting teasing memories for the children in the back seat.

We drove a large Ford, and on long journeys we built up the floor of

....

the back to make a single platform so that the children could nap when they felt like it, especially on night drives. They were bonding strongly together, each with an individual and distinct contribution to make. Michael remained the natural leader, inventor, instigator. Susan was the bright, cheerful worshipful acolyte, utterly and gladly responsive. Christopher was the pervasive, steady and reliable link. Together they could create mayhem in the back, which, as driver, I could tolerate only up to a point, then I would shout for silence. This always produced the required result – for a while. Michael enjoyed his gentle ascendancy over Christopher, Christopher his over Susan, and Susan, eventually, over both.

Images abound. Walking in the shadow of Vesuvius, through the streets and houses which its eruption had suffocated with ash in Pompeii, Michael said, 'Look at all these old Roman bricks making the walls, quite a different size from those we're used to at home.'

'Yes,' said Ross Lambert, our Oxford historian friend, 'they are typical of the Roman period.'

'What size are they then?' asked Michael.

'Ten by five by two,' said Ross quickly – too quickly.

Michael had produced a small ruler from his pocket and measured a brick, then said loudly, 'No they are *not!*' Ross had the grace to chuckle guiltily.

Michael was eleven. His naive trust in adult knowledge and verity was probably irretrievably undermined. He was fortunate to experience it early. I told him later that Ross was undoubtedly preoccupied with the closure to tourists of the Pompeian chamber of delights, it being Sunday.

The little sandy beach at Lerici and the strong, late summer sun stay in our minds. A small rocky island lies a hundred metres out to sea in the shimmering waves. Michael is swimming strongly to the rock, Christopher is lagging but utterly determined to follow. He gets there, but he has taken a risk. I swim out to monitor his return.

On the snow-covered slopes of the Zugspitze at Ehrwald, the boys made good beginners' progress on their skis. Little Susan gamely tried also, at three and a half, complaining that the ground kept moving away. At two, in Minnesota, she had happily followed the boys leaping from a jetty into a forest lake, once she knew that she and her life jacket would quickly bob up

....

again. On the same lake, Christopher, aged six, learned to row. Three years later on the lake, Michael helped devise a mast and sail for the rowing dinghy – with some help from his uncle Jack, Mary's brother-in-law – and it worked.

One summer we made a visit to Mary's mother in Minneapolis, significant because Michael saw there at the annual state fair, and never forgot, the actual capsule that took the first American astronaut, John Glenn, into orbit in 1962. At the age of seventy-six, Glenn went into space again in 1998 in the shuttle, for weightless research into the care of the elderly. A brave and remarkable man.

In 1966, Christmas at home near the RAF headquarters in Germany was still a few months off. Mary and I discussed presents for the children. Michael was nine, Christopher eight and Susan four. We all lived together in a nice official house, walking distance away from my work at the head-quarters. Mary said, 'Michael is still very keen on model aeroplanes, but he also keeps talking about space and the American Gemini programme. He and Christopher have both shown interest in chemistry sets, and Susan's becoming clothes-conscious. She even showed me a picture of a trouser suit [then first becoming fashionable] in a magazine.'

I said that I too would talk to them. Michael responded earnestly without any need for thought, 'Dad, what I would really like is a rocket.'

'That,' I said, 'might be difficult, but I will look to see what's available – and possible.'

The upshot was that I found and bought a clever two-stage toy rocket, which worked on a water jet produced by pumped-in air pressure, sending the first stage to fifty feet and the second twice as high – when it worked. It was an enormous success. Michael and Chris loved playing with it together and also shared the chemistry set. Susan's big brown eyes had Daddy helplessly buying an expensive little navy-blue trouser suit, with brass buttons, from Harrods. Even though Mary received a beautiful new dress, she could not help envying four-year-old Susan her devastatingly smart suit. A few months later I healed the apparent breach with a very chic lovat tweed version for Mary, as shown on a model in *Country Life* magazine. Altogether a successful gift year, but historically it is the two-stage water rocket that put a permanent gleam in Michael's eye.

Michael and Christopher started at boarding school in England while

....

we were in Germany – they actually asked to go, having seen their returning contemporaries, with considerable and apparent aplomb, making their way down the aircraft steps of the official jet charter at the start of the school holidays.

Later came another island tour of duty, this time in Malta, where Michael took advantage of the RAF station's deep-sea diving club to learn to scuba-dive, and formally and finally took over the diving knife. All three children came to us wherever we were for all of their holidays, and we never stopped talking. I am sure that we communicated more under these circumstances than if they had been at home every day, all year – difficult to prove, but they agree. There were never any sullen silences.

I think I began to notice at this time that, when together, the strength of our children's companionship could act as a deterrent to other children who were attracted to the group. There was always interesting talk going on, and they were full of ideas. They did not deliberately keep their trio private and exclusive, nor was it a closed trio all the time. They understood each other so well, often without a word, that outsiders simply felt rather left out.

As the two boys grew, they were inseparable except for the brief periods when Michael preceded Christopher at their two boarding schools. By the time he was ten, Christopher had finally outgrown any private frustration at being younger than his clever brother, and was beginning to show his own fund of talent, leaning towards the humanities, music and art. He acted in school plays, sang in choirs, was interested in dancing and probably enjoyed a more relaxed personal life than Michael. He was also closer in spirit to Susan, although all three stayed good friends, with no jealousies. Christopher showed what he was made of by getting to scholarship level in his entrance exams for his senior school, something not achieved by Michael, and this made a welcome contribution towards costs.

Although not aspiring to scientific qualifications, he was quick to understand Michael's discoveries, enthusiasms and the subjects that drew his concentration, and became a marvellous intellectual foil to Michael's ideas. In return, Michael valued Christopher's preoccupation with the humanities, his relaxed common sense and balanced humour, as did we all.

It was during our first tour in Malta, from 1969 to 1970, that the Apollo programme's first lunar landing took place, when Michael was twelve,

Christopher eleven and Susan seven. We were glued to our TV set, as was the rest of the advanced world. In Malta, one had to use considerable ingenuity and exercise patience, because much of the UK commentary was loudly and simultaneously translated into Maltese. The children all looked as if they wanted to climb into the screen to hear the English in the background – so did I!

Michael made it clear on that day that he wanted to become an astronaut, following a test-pilot period in the RAF. I liked the idea, and wondered if Britain would join the American programme in time for him to participate.

3

Michael the Astronaut

I n retrospect, it seems that, from the age of seven, most things Michael did revolved around an ambition to travel in space. Even before his gift of a toy rocket, he had built make-believe rockets in our Bracknell garden, having read a children's book called *Michael Goes to the Moon*. After the age of thirteen and his move to the King's School, Canterbury, followed the next year by Christopher, it seemed that everything became focused on space.

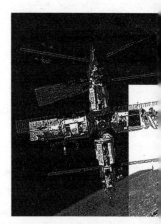

Until King's, Canterbury, Michael was primarily a father's boy. He listened carefully to what I said, enjoyed my humour without reservation and was the one who missed me most if I was away. After his first term at King's, he returned to our home on Wyton airfield for the Christmas holidays a changed boy. It was not just that his hair had been allowed to grow longer. He had become a little remote, more directed to himself and less towards me. After a few days I said, 'Michael, what is it, do you think, in your first term at King's that has been the greatest change for you?' I was trying to tempt him into some explanation of his new style.

He said, 'I have learned that my father is not right all the time, as I had once thought.'

I felt a bit helpless over this reply, and wondered over what in particular I had been found out. The teaching staff at King's were all of the highest quality, and it would be no wonder if in many areas they would surpass my knowledge. But surely not at the level on which I had so far been involved with Michael? I never found out what he meant, and I suspect he has long forgotten that he said it. It might have been something to do with his lack of knowledge of, and preparation for, the style of this great school, which was beyond my own experience as a grammar-school day boy. But this had not happened three years earlier when I visited him at his Devon prep school at the end of his first term there. Then he had already immersed himself in the school's wolf cub pack and had become senior sixer. He was proudly wearing his uniform and badges of rank for our sakes, an almost saintly smile on his face, knowing how pleased and proud we would be. But at King's it was different: perhaps, I told myself, it was simply the onset of adolescence, a time that always puts a son on a distinctly separate path from his father, when above all else a boy needs space, as I needed it too at his age.

I had been hurt by his remark, but my instinct that this was a natural process, not to be resented, was of course correct. But ruefully I knew that I had lost for ever my little boy. Now it was time to be glad for the wonderful thirteen years during which he had been able to allow me to feel like a fully involved dad.

While at King's, Michael concentrated on maths and physics and strove for standards that would help him to get into Cambridge, his next goal. Mary and I attended his last assembly at King's, when his wonderfully humane headmaster, Canon Newell, was awarding the regular school prizes for this and that subject. When the process had been completed, the headmaster surprised us all by saying that Michael Foale had come so close to winning so many prizes, but had always just missed, that this year he was awarding a special prize, just for him. This was the first sign that, far from being a narrow specialist, our Michael was emerging strongly as a universal man. He had a very broad grin on his face as he went up to receive his prize, and the award was loudly appreciated by the assembly – and Christopher.

He was awarded an exhibition to Queens' College, Cambridge, but elected to have a year off first to earn money towards his university maintenance, a loyal and thoughtful thing to do. As we were about to leave for Malta again, I asked him if he would let his Scottish godfather find summer work for him. Yes, he said, if it paid well. He was found a navvying job in

....

Morayshire on a road-bridge construction, where frankly he was given the most dangerous jobs, wielding a pneumatic drill on the parapet. Ever practical, he refused to begin until he had devised and constructed a rope safety harness to avoid slipping to injury or death. His Scottish laddie workmates spent their spare time and most of their money in the pubs. Michael cycled each weekend to the RAF station at Lossiemouth and joined the gliding club to begin his first flights, staying overnight at their hostel.

From my then job as station commander in Malta, I had to visit England for a few days in July 1975. I visited Canterbury to see Christopher acting in the lead role in a Greek play at the end of his final term, his first year without Michael. The play was performed on the lawns beside the cloisters and he shone in the sunlight, confident and well defined. We were able to talk in our frank way over supper before I had to depart. He had begun to teach himself piano and guitar, and was delighted to be reminded that we had a piano at our house in Malta, to which he would soon travel for the summer holidays. This was probably the first time I had seen him at school without Michael, and the memory is valuable. We got on so well together, and I had no comment to make on his resolve to get a Cambridge college to accept him to read classics. He knew that it would suit me if he made the RAF his career, but he gently convinced me that no decisions were needed yet.

'There really is no hurry, Dad, and so many things seem to be happening to me, even faster since Michael left school. There is so much on offer in this lovely world.'

In fact, a year or two later I knew that he was writing song lyrics and some music, one direction his creativity was taking. I gave up on the RAF. Back in Malta that summer I found Chris and Susan making a tape of a song Chris had written. The tune was gentle, persuasive, almost nostalgic, as of something lost.

In Cambridge, I met Michael, who proudly showed me around his new college, Queens'. I reminded him that when he was four he had run to the centre of King's College close and across the hallowed lawn, to be retrieved by a stony-faced porter.

'Perhaps,' he said, 'that's why it was Queens' who accepted me.'

A lazy right eye had failed him in the RAF University officer cadetship scheme, a system that gave full junior officer pay to an undergraduate in exchange for some career commitment. The eye would probably be self-correcting in time, they said (and it was), but I was not in fact disappointed for myself; perhaps Christopher was already influencing me to encourage my sons to go their own ways. However, Michael then astounded me by offering to go for a similar cadetship in the Royal Marines, so that he could still get the pay while up at Cambridge.

'After all,' he said, 'they do a lot of skiing in Norway.'

I said that we did not need the money that much, and the Marines, although admirable, were not, at least in Britain, a way to space. But I sincerely thanked him for the thought. I think it was from here that Michael saw that his best route to NASA was an academic one. Once at Cambridge, he worked even harder in his first three years to get a first in the natural sciences tripos exams. He was successful, and later gratefully accepted the invitation to study for a doctorate in astrophysics at the Cavendish Laboratory.

The studied independence from habitual parental concern and influence that Michael had adopted was not often seen by us while we lived outside Cambridge. I was therefore mildly shocked to see it in action on an occasion when Mary and I travelled to Cambridge to attend a lecture in which we knew Michael was also interested. We took our seats with the students in the lecture hall and the lecture began. A few minutes later we were conscious that a door had opened and closed, quietly, and that the curved rows of the desk surfaces in front of and behind us were rhythmically shaking. It was Michael, arriving late, having spotted us from the upper entrance, taking a short cut down to where we sat, walking from desktop to desktop, over heads, until he reached us and gracefully sat down. I was amazed. It was so outrageous, so quick, so silent, and it worked. I don't think the lecturer even blinked. I could not have done it. He had.

We were also surprised by a sight on a day's visit to Cambridge when going to the Mill, near the mill-race near Lammas Land. Two dapper, boatered figures with long golden hair were hiring themselves out to visitors to punt them upriver through the sunlit meadows to Grantchester. It was Michael and a King's School friend, Peter Stewart. The price was high but they were not short of takers, who were impressed by the genuine Cambridge product before their eyes. Michael looked at us with a very straight face and solemnly

....

read out from their noticeboard: '**CAMPUNTION**, THE ONLY WAY TO GO UPRIVER'.

Christopher went up to Cambridge the year after Michael to study classics at Selwyn College, maintaining for us all a now traditional family breadth of interest which we so much enjoyed. The boys kidded Susan, still at school, telling her that it was obviously now up to her to be good at everything, across the board.

Christopher had become a very attractive young man, his fair hair long and his puckish face and grin almost fey. He could easily have been a supernatural foundling, although we never told him so. He also earned what money he could during his year off as a petrol-pump attendant in Bristol, living with his godfather, the Revd Ray Price, who, with his family, had a living at Mangotsfield. He had taken part much more in music and drama while at school than Michael had, and in the latter's absence in his final year, developed more surely his own individual style of gentle wit, forgiving manner and readiness to help.

During a phone call from Bristol he said, 'My petrol station was robbed yesterday. I think the two men would have mugged me, but I remained quietly polite and showed them how to open the cash till, instead of breaking it. While they took everything, I memorized exactly how they looked and the car they were using, and phoned the police as soon as they left. They were arrested a few hours later still with the money. I felt rather sorry for them.'

He was more of a community person than Michael ever was, and was able to guide his elder brother in many ways. Michael listened and took note. At Cambridge, Christopher met a lovely girl called Lynn, who was studying at Newnham College, and we were delighted to see them become very close.

'Will you marry her?' I asked, in my usual direct way.

'We might,' he answered, going ever so slightly pink, but with a delighted grin at the thought.

One night when Mary and I were attending the Trinity College May Ball, we had arranged to meet the boys at three am at Queens' College for a pre-dawn punt down the Cam. We were ten minutes early. Christopher was right on time. We boarded the Queens' punt and began to drift elegantly downriver, only to become conscious of a fast punt overtaking us, vigorously poled by Michael. As he was in charge of the Queens' punts, he had somewhat

....

arbitrarily hijacked a docile freshman's party. When alongside us, he cheerfully handed the pole back to his reluctant host, who had probably wanted to go upriver, with thanks. He deftly took over from Christopher, saying hello. It was all done with the same easy, graceful unassailability as the lecture hall interlude. There seemed to be much that I was not familiar with about our Michael.

At the end of his second year, Christopher moved into theology and comparative religion, graduating a year after Michael in June 1979. He had not tried for nor achieved a first, but, unlike Michael, who stopped college rowing during his finals year, Christopher kept on to the end and was awarded his 'oar' for both the Lent and May 'bumps'. In his first year he had been light enough in weight to be a winning cox, and thus his later rowing successes and concomitant increased shoulder breadth were remarkable. He shrugged off his respectable but not brilliant lower-second result with the words, 'After all, I *am* now a Cambridge man.' He smiled happily, unabashedly accepting his own self-indulgence.

Michael's readiness to argue cleverly had increased, not always to my liking. In fact, he seemed to welcome argument as a way of feeling his strength. I was immeasurably helped in our attempts to avoid conflict by Christopher, who showed none of these confrontational needs, and who often poured oil on troubled waters. Christopher never rebelled as such, but simply did what he wanted to do quietly, indeed as I like to think that I had always done, and in addition lightened every occasion with his humour.

Susan remembers these years vividly, my arguments with Michael and her arguments with Mary. Christopher would engineer a quiet time when, all three together, Michael could air his bitterness at my 'blindness' or Susan at Mary's 'injustices'. A scenic example of this took place in 1978 at the same Minnesota woodland lake previously mentioned. Michael had just been awarded his first-class honours degree. He could do no wrong. I was in the mental exercise of a possible career change. We all agreed that we should again convert the rowing boat, properly this time, into a sailing craft, using a birch tree for the mast, lee-boards for the keel and some tough plastic sheeting for the sails. I wanted to try the graceful, romantic lateen or dhow rig, seen by me so often on the Nile or East African coast. Michael, knowing that for general purposes the Bermuda rig had been shown to be the most efficient,

....

found the lateen idea archaic and ridiculous. Apparently we fought for days. Susan remembers how Christopher, in the evening, suggested a long dusk row across the lake for the three of them. In fact, they rowed into the middle of the lake, stopped and talked together in their well-tried therapeutic way.

'I cannot do it, I will not do it,' said Michael. 'It's stupid to make an outmoded rig, particularly as the Bermuda is simpler.' (It was.)

'I would have thought you could have bent a little, to avoid this impasse,' said Susan.

Christopher smiled indulgently. He said, 'We have six days of our holiday here left. Dad is clearly in need of distraction from his London duties, and has his heart set on trying a dhow rig. I think if he manages it, one sail at sunset, like the silhouettes he saw on the Nile, would be enough to satisfy him. Why don't we do all we can to help him achieve this quickly, then we'll have enough time to convert it to a Bermuda rig afterwards.' Initially there were objections because Michael was set on 'winning', but Christopher's view prevailed. We designed and built both rigs.

I thoughtfully recall that the three of them were not the only ones to use the solitude of the lake's centre for reflection. I was so irritated by Michael's intransigence one evening that I walked to the lake shore, peeled off, entered the water and swam away steadily for over an hour. When I turned to swim back, I realized it had grown dark. There were lights far away from a few cabins, but which one was ours? I swam in their general direction for about forty-five minutes – at least it would be land – then saw our raft moored two hundred metres out where we dived. There was Susan, watching and looking for me, crying. She thought I had drowned. I climbed out on to the raft, and after a few moments of tender and subdued exchanges, we swam to the jetty and towards the lighted cabin windows. She probably does not know how utterly comforting and reassuring it was, for me at the time, to find her waiting there.

Susan had recently completed her GCE exams at Westwood School, and was now an outgoing girl of sixteen. As we had begun a period of RAF service in England, she decided that she would prefer to live at home with us for her two years of sixth-form study, and she applied for a place at the local Huntingdon comprehensive school as a day girl. She was accepted, but never went. King's School, Canterbury, had recently begun to take girls in the sixth form. Susan had previously shown no interest in this option, saying that she looked forward to a more normal life than continuing as a boarder at her girls' school. Then Michael stepped in with his brand-new Cambridge first, and told her how much he owed to King's. Susan changed her mind, and we got her a place there. Christopher also advised her on how to cope with King's. Neither had prepared her for her first day's assembly. A hymn was announced, the organ played, and five hundred boys' voices soared in song. After five years at a girls' school, Susan found herself almost buckling at the knees at such a concentrated male presence. Five hundred new, additional brothers – or whatever.

Michael undertook paid supervision of undergraduates at Queens' College during his three postgraduate study years, using every penny he earned to buy himself light-aircraft flying lessons at Marshall's Airport, which brought him his private pilot's licence. He used his Malta deep-sea diving experience to work voluntarily as a diver on many cold autumn weekends, as late as November, wearing only a wetsuit, on the underwater excavation and recovery of the Elizabethan ship, the *Mary Rose*, off Portsmouth harbour. He showed me a cut on his finger caused by its having inadvertently entered a long-drowned Elizabethan's eye socket. He proposed to lead diving expeditions looking for sunken Mycenaean walls in the southern Peloponnese at Plitra. Challenging and enjoyable adventures, yes, but they were also consciously geared to show that he was the 'right stuff' to achieve his ambitions.

A year passed at King's School, Queens' College and Selwyn. We attended the graduation ceremonies of Christopher and his Cambridge year in July 1979. Then, a few weeks later, came a shocking accident.

Michael and Christopher and Michael's then girlfriend Catherine were together in a car on their way to southern Greece. Michael was to lead an archaeological diving expedition under the auspices of the Cambridge University Underwater Exploration Group. They had left England in plenty of time to travel at a leisurely pace across Europe before joining their colleagues in Greece, stopping to camp at night.

A careening lorry in Yugoslavia lurched across the centre line of a mountain road on a blind bend, hitting Michael's car head-on, killing Catherine and our so special Christopher. By a miracle Michael survived. Devastated,

....

Mary, Susan and I flew to Zagreb to bring him home, and to begin our collective and individual recovery. It says much for the love and resilience of us all and of golden friends that over the years we did recover; but we will never forget either Christopher or Catherine. Why should we?

Michael was our main worry. In many ways his work at the Cavendish Laboratory, with the sympathetic help of his supervisor, the director, Professor Sir Alan Cook, got him over the worst, first year when the wounds of grief were most painful and the shock and outrage unabated. But time does begin to heal, as all we Foales know at first hand. Michael spent more time with us, since we had moved into Cambridge. He also began to realize that the tragedy had removed the source of any reservations he might have had about leaving England in pursuit of a space career, now based necessarily in the USA. We, his family, already made regular visits. Unwillingly, unexpectedly, but surely he was now really on his own, and would follow his own beacons – the stars.

Mary and I welcomed this increased clarity of focus which obviously helped him, and therefore the rest of us, on the steady road to recovery. He was able to concentrate, through the pain of his loss, on the research that was to earn him a Cambridge PhD. His subject was 'The far ultraviolet spectroscopy of some molecules of astrophysical interest'. He remained an active member of Queens' College, rowing for them occasionally and increasing his diving and flying skills. Any post-adolescent desire for confrontation and argument for argument's sake had gone. He came to our home frequently, enjoying ours and Susan's company, when she was there, as a basic family salve to his undoubted wounds, and we too were helped by him. Slowly we began to laugh again, at life and all its perennial absurdities – and glories.

Our move to Cambridge came in late 1979. RAF postings had already introduced us to East Anglia, and with both boys at Cambridge University, Mary the librarian of the computer laboratory and me casting about for a change in occupation, it seemed the right time to move. We are still in this beautiful city with its silent lawns in college closes, its pinnacles and spires, its slow brown river and weeping willows, mill-race and arching bridges. We are familiar with its pubs and restaurants, coffee houses and bookshops, lecture halls and undergraduates and long May Ball nights. Even the many tourists are quite well behaved.

A year earlier I had begun to toy with the idea of leaving the RAF prematurely for a change of direction. I asked Michael what he thought, whether he would mind.

'Dad, I think you should leave. You've been with them long enough and should try something new.'

His forthright response surprised me. I had not known that he had given the subject any thought. It actually helped me to decide to leave my life of the past thirty years when I did, but I have since wondered if he had any personal reason for his view. At the time he had just been awarded his first from Queens' in the natural sciences tripos, and the world was at his feet. He had had to accommodate the looming figure of a station commander father in the background, and now the arguably more substantial figure of air rank. He might have shrunk from the possibility of having to contend with a knighted air marshal (as I think Mary already had). I have never asked him as it was irrelevant: I wanted the change.

In the event, the change and the move to Cambridge coincided with our loss of Christopher. From our Cambridge base we got used to our new situation, Mary perhaps helped by her daily work at the computer laboratory, I suddenly lonely for the RAF I had left. At the end of 1979 I made contact with the archaeological department of the Greek government with a view to getting their agreement to another expedition, the Cambridge element again to be led by Michael, to replace the one tragically curtailed in 1979. It seemed only right. Mary and I travelled to Athens and Plitra in March 1980 to cement the final arrangements for Michael and his colleagues to dive later that year, having many useful discussions with the director of underwater archaeology Dr Papathanosopoulos. Christopher and his close friend Lynn had visited several classical sites in Greece the previous summer, and we retraced some of his journeys too, to those beautiful, lonely places.

On the way back we ran into some of my old friends from Yorkshire Television with whom I had worked as Director of Public Relations in the RAF. I subsequently spent time helping them with aviation advice while looking for a good, well-paid captain of industry post. Some of the earlier anticipated post-service euphoria of perceiving limitless personal horizons was happily beginning to return as the shock of the accident receded. Unexpectedly, however, thoughts of occupying a senior management post

....

began to lose their glitter when the University showed interest in giving me the opportunity to manage a small department: aerial photography, primarily of classical and historical subjects. I would also have, for my exclusive use, a light twin-engined aircraft to fly – heady stuff for a fifty-one-year-old retired air commodore who had not flown professionally for six years. Hardly believing my luck, I buckled down to getting the civilian licences.

A wonderful college beyond King's Parade, St Catharine's, gave me membership, with dining rights at their high table. The fellows still welcome me, where conversation is multicoloured, light but deeply informed, and nobody is afraid of silences. Individuals think before they speak and are patient for a response. There can be little in this world as civilized and precious as dinner at a Cambridge high table, in the company of the fellows.

Christopher's old college, Selwyn, was where the founder of the aerial photography department had for years held a college fellowship, and from which he had retired as deputy master. Some of the fellowship had attended Christopher's funeral in 1979, and I have been privileged to retain a close and warm connection too within this college, which Chris had enjoyed so much up to his death.

Michael, meanwhile, took the first step towards his own new career when he flew to Houston in 1982, told people at NASA that he was a Cambridge PhD in astrophysics, had dual nationality and wanted to be an astronaut. There were no immediate vacancies at NASA for a scientist at his level, but the nearby McDonnell Douglas company quickly scooped him up into their orbital navigation research unit. This immediately had the somewhat unfamiliar effect of making him solvent; in quick succession over the next few years he acquired an apartment, a car, further flying practice, even a helicopter licence, which could only enhance his 'right stuff' image. His apartment was in Clear Lake, near the Johnson Space Center, where he hoped eventually to work.

Soon, Michael was offered a ground appointment in NASA as a payload officer. He felt that he had reached the next step. In 1984, he sold his first apartment (to us, actually – we probably paid too much) and bought another more to his liking, right on the shore of Clear Lake itself, where he could walk twenty paces on to his sailboard for a sunset windsurf in the warm Texas breezes after work, as far as the Hilton Hotel and back. The peace of solitary windsurfing appealed to him, and he could be alone with his thoughts. He had girlfriends, and I met some of them, all intelligent and attractive, but he seemed to want to avoid getting too serious with anyone. It was the year that Mary had decided to follow my earlier (1977) RAF footsteps to visit China with a widowed friend from New York. While she was away, I flew to Texas for a holiday with Michael. By then he had acquired a fifth share in an aeroplane, a little single-engine Grumman North American Tiger Cub, and he booked it for us during my week's holiday.

He said, 'Where would you like to go, Dad?'

I said, 'As we are in or near the Wild West already, why don't we take a quick tour of Texas, Arizona, New Mexico, Colorado and then home?'

He said, 'It's funny you should say that, because that's exactly what I would like to do.'

He showed me maps of a possible route, with intermediary refuelling stops, to El Paso, Sedona, Grand Canyon, Flagstaff, Santa Fe, Colorado Springs and back to Clear Lake. It involved two two-hour flights each day, followed by cold beer and Western steaks each night and sometimes a swim in the motel pool. We probably ate in the 'wrong' places. Mexican eyebrows were raised in the off-beat restaurant on the Rio Grande at El Paso, maybe Hispanic surprise at the two naive gringos trespassing. We took it in turns to fly. When over the foothills of the Rockies, I kept my eyes open for emergency landing areas in case the single engine failed – a habit of mine, but with no real point. Only the rivers might have given us a chance, and they were neither straight nor tranquil. It was Michael who did the landing on the sloping mesa of Sedona's runway (land uphill, take off downhill, regardless of the wind), rather like approaching a sloping aircraft carrier. We explored the vastness of the Grand Canyon, flying below the rim, which is now illegal and should have been then, for good reason: the down draughts could make it impossible to climb out again.

I had had an earlier foretaste of this problem when I was flying in Wales. One of the first flights I had made for Cambridge University was a photographic sortie to Snowdonia, to take reasonably close low-level shots of the rim and slopes of a sinisterly named feature called the Devil's Kitchen, a semi-enclosed crater. It was a bright, breezy day. For years, all my low-level flying had been in operational RAF aircraft with powerful jet engines, which,

....

when the throttle was opened, would thrust you up at a good steep angle to avoid hitting a fast-approaching ridge. I must have forgotten that I did not have two such engines at my disposal. As I entered the Kitchen on its open side, high enough to pass over the sharp rim ahead, I noticed that my air speed was inexplicably falling towards stalling speed. My engines sounded all right. Then I realized that we must be in the grip of a deadly down draught, the wind ahead flowing up the far side of the rim and abruptly down towards us into the Kitchen's depth. Nature abhors a vacuum. Instinctively I had been progressively easing the control column back to maintain height, thus bleeding away the aircraft's speed. While applying maximum engine power, making little difference, I pushed the nose down towards the precipice, now with its rim well above us, and very, very gingerly turned the aircraft about, through a hundred and eighty degrees, at as low a speed as I dared. I spared a thought for the department's curator, sitting behind me and no doubt horrified. When the turn was complete, the ground sloped downwards and away so I could follow it while regaining vital speed. Oddly, what had saved us was the down-draught wind itself, a headwind, of course, which, as soon as I began to turn, helped blow us away from the cliff face. Does one ever learn? Relief was exceeded only by shame at my disregard of basic principles, and the polite, controlled silence of the curator-photographer.

With Michael I swooped over Meteor Crater in Arizona at a safe height, explored for two days the sixteenth-century Spanish town of Santa Fe, and gasped, on foot, in the thin air of Pike's Peak (14,000 feet) near Colorado Springs. It was a wonderful six days for both of us. Of course we argued – I was right at least half of the time – but we parted on good terms.

I should also mention his offer on the first day after my arrival of a trip in a hired helicopter. I knew he had recently got his private helicopter pilot's licence, and I was intrigued to accept, not being qualified to fly one myself, although I have flown them as second pilot.

On arriving at the heliport I was nonplussed to see that the hired helicopter was not a sleek Alouette or other smart new ship but an old, almost bicycle-chain model, straight out of the earlier episodes of *MASH*, circa 1953. I was silent and thoughtful as we strapped in. The engine start was a shock, and the whole machine shook like a pneumatic drill as Michael increased power and took off. As soon as we left the ground I became much more conscious of the lack of doors, open space all around and the grinding, not very reassuring noise of the engine, which seemed long overdue for a decoke.

It was probably safe enough, and Michael flew it gracefully and landed gently. When I got out I found that I was still wearing the fixed grin that had stamped itself on me at engine start.

In 1986, a year before Michael was selected for astronaut training, the space shuttle Challenger blew up just after launch, killing all its crew. The aircraft-shaped shuttle is not just powered by its own internal rocket engines but is assisted on launch by two solid rocket boosters. It also carries a large external fuel tank to feed the main engines, and this and the boosters are jettisoned at a late stage of the journey to orbit. A faulty seal on one of Challenger's two solid booster rockets had allowed hot flame to escape and reach the enormous external tank, full of volatile liquid rocket fuel. The massive explosion threw the craft into an uncontrollable dive to the ocean.

Mary and I happened to be spending a few nights with Michael at Clear Lake at the time, and remember the horror and dismay in the voice of the radio announcer, who interrupted a classical music programme. Michael later came home for lunch, and the most memorable thing about him was not his sadness at the loss of fine colleagues, all of whom he knew, which brought him to the edge of tears. It was his already deep and analytical thinking about how it might have happened and how it could be avoided in future.

The next time Michael was brought close to tears, by his own admission, was an entirely different event. He and his shuttle crew had been living in quarantine for a week, and his first launch was two days away. The shuttle was lit up at night by giant floodlights so that observers and relatives could make a night visit to see the awesome sight. Michael and a fellow astronaut drove quietly, and privately, from their beach accommodation also to view it, and he found the sight almost overwhelmingly beautiful.

From the moment Michael had arrived in Houston, he had carefully prepared an application for astronaut training every time they were invited, which, due to the small size of the corps, was not often. He and I had found ourselves talking on the phone during these attempts, each of which failed. In 1986, Michael arranged to see George Abbey, then a senior member of NASA and now director of the Johnson Space Center, to ask why he was consistently being denied a place.

....

George Abbey said, 'I do not normally answer that kind of question because the answer is so rarely welcome. But in your case, Michael, I am prepared to make an exception. The reason is that you have been too young.'

In the event, Michael had to wait for acceptance until he was thirty, in 1987.

At thirty he was the youngest in his class of sixteen. They were to include friends like Bill Readdy and Ken Bowersox, who, with their families, have remained close ever since. The same year, he and a beautiful young woman from Kentucky called Rhonda Butler got married. She had already come to visit us in Cambridge in 1986, first alone, and then at Christmas with Michael. The wedding, attended by parents and special friends, was on the windsurfing island of Aruba in the Caribbean. All year round it seems to have a twenty-knot trade wind. The couple paid all their own wedding expenses. All we guests had to do was get there. We learned that one way to guarantee a small, select wedding is to choose the right faraway location.

We worried when Michael and Rhonda disappeared for hours on end on their sailboards, and as sunset approached, I strained my eyes looking for them from the hotel roof. It was always so good eventually to see them, a pair of far-off figures on the water, returning with the sunset behind them. Rhonda was not just an expert windsurfer but also a trained geologist. She soon had herself newly qualified in space sciences to take up a post on the ground in NASA, which she held until their second child was expected.

Michael's first three space shuttle missions are themselves worthy of separate accounts. His first mission was in 1992, his second a year later and his third in early 1995. But we are concerned here only with the drama of his fourth, his mission to Mir.

By 1995, he was considered to be a sound, middle-range NASA astronaut with three successful shuttle missions in four years. The last one had included a lengthy spacewalk on the cold end of the shuttle arm, to test the insulating effectiveness (or otherwise, as it turned out) of the latest spacesuit modification. Michael was forced to call for the abandonment of the experiment after four hours, because of freezing fingertips. On that same mission, the shuttle also made the first close rendezvous with Mir, a kind of dress rehearsal for a later mission which made a real docking for the exchange of articles and astronauts. For both these reasons, and as he had operated successfully as flight engineer for the Mir close-manoeuvring phase, he became more widely known both in the USA and here in Britain. He was also amiably disposed to speak his mind publicly while in space; when asked by the British media how he felt about the then British government's attitude to space, he said frankly that they were not doing enough to satisfy the British people's interest in manned space exploration.

Neither NASA nor America appeared to have any objection to these forthright statements (which they probably agreed with) criticizing the British government. And their American astronaut Michael Foale was, after all, British-born. In truth, he is still British as well as American. Since 1974 the US government has allowed continued dual nationality for Anglo-American offspring, if they wish it, who inherit dual nationality at birth. Michael's comments may have prompted the first official British recognition of his space exploits, because he received a somewhat terse invitation to make himself available for an interview with the British ambassador, were he to pass through Washington. This turned out to be a reminder of the important part played in space matters by British industry, particularly in communications – a fair comment. But nobody tried to deny the lack of enthusiasm shown by the then British government towards space matters – in 1999 things now appear to be changing.

It is worth reminding ourselves that Michael is still the only British professional astronaut, and he is so simply by virtue of the chance that I married an American lady, which enabled him to go for it from Britain under his own steam. In recent years both America and Russia have accepted, trained and used as crew selected nationals sponsored from many other countries, for example, France, Germany, Japan, Canada, Belgium and Saudi Arabia among others. It is true that many of these crewmen make only one or two missions, but they are fielded by their countries expressly to gain experience for their governments' further interest. But not so here – even British astronaut Helen Sharman with her one privately sponsored week on Mir in 1991 appears to have had little or no government interest since her courageous 'first'.

Present US–Russian cooperation in space can be seen as a direct outcome of the end of the Cold War. Russia was soon desperate for hard currency as their people were released from the bondage of an enclosed,

....

directed economy, a release welcomed in the long term but chaotic in the short term. This chaos, and a general perception that it might spread to a lack of supervision of nuclear hardware, suggested that real danger could spring from a neglected stockpile of nuclear weapons, which, even if not criminally sold from the back of a lorry, would become dangerous and unstable if not disarmed. US interest in Russia's accepting assistance in this respect must have been a contributory factor to the beginning of the Phase One shuttle/Mir cooperation programme. Soon, Mir was sporting on its Kristall module a brand-new docking ring to fit a similarly brand-new docking ring in the cargo bay on the shuttle orbiter Atlantis.

4

Destination Russia

After Michael's STS-63 rendezvous with Mir rehearsal mission, a string of four US astronauts were selected, trained, and, in turn, delivered to conduct American experiments on Mir. Then, in October 1995, only six months after his STS-63 mission, Michael became slowly but surely aware that his friend Jim Wetherbee (STS-63's commander), a senior astronaut with more power and influence than Michael could then claim, was becoming increasingly and inexplicably distant in their personal relations. Mike did not feel that this had been caused by something he had said – rather it was something that was *not* being said by Wetherbee. Wetherbee's reserve was soon to become clear. Mary and I were on holiday in New Mexico at the time, and during one of our regular phone calls to the family in Houston Mike said, 'Dad, I now know what has been on Jim Wetherbee's mind. I think you and Mum should know that he has asked me if I will go to Moscow for eighteen months to train for a four-month stint on Mir, launch in May 1997.'

Rhonda and the children, aged four and one, would accompany him, and he would have to learn Russian, for eight hours a day at first and then two hours a day throughout his training. He would return to the US only to be delivered by shuttle to Mir for the four months. Rhonda and the family would stay in Star City, outside Moscow, throughout his tour on Mir until he was picked up, again by shuttle, in September, when they would be reunited in Texas. What did I think?

I suppose that, like most frugal people, I was as brief as I could be on the phone when it was an expensive call on my motel bill, and I remember saying what I must have said time and again to so many people in the RAF, including myself, on receiving news of a new and unexpected posting.

'Well, Mike, NASA knows that you're a good, steady professional, and they must think you would be an asset representing them with the Russians. You say that you're in the space game for keeps, not just for a few missions to enhance your reputation. So, like the good soldier you are, I think you will want to accept.'

Carefully phrased, I know. He seemed to agree that this would be the right path to take, and would say so to his bosses.

That night and the following day I pondered what he and I had said, and reviewed the implications of the proposed Russian venture. It would obviously enhance his experience in so many ways, and he could soon become the most experienced international astronaut in the world. Little did I know. But then I remembered the old adage we had in the RAF – don't allow yourself ever to be too specialized unless you are happy to stay with it, if events dictate, for ever. Pilots in the RAF are in the officially named General Duties Branch, as are all aircrew, a strong implication being that without further specialization, they can do anything. In the context of Russian collaboration, such specialization could indeed go on for ever – Michael would become NASA's Russian expert, the man for the job. Our grandchildren would spend so much time in Russia, Russian would become almost a first language. They would be happiest in furry hats and boots, and Mike would lose control of his general-purpose (General Duties equivalent) astronaut career.

I called Michael again in the evening and warned him of the dangers of overspecialization.

'Now you tell me,' he said. We laughed, a touch hollowly.

By the time Mary and I visited them in Russia in October 1996, Michael and his family had been in Zvyezdy Gorodok (Star City, near Moscow) nearly a year. They had been visited earlier by his sister Susan, who spent two weeks with them in May, and who had told us all about it on her return. She had been accommodated in Michael and Rhonda's specially built house,

....

provided for them by the Russians to American standards. She was impressed by the relative isolation of the handful of Americans in Star City, and the dedication of both Michael and Rhonda to the task of learning Russian. She was particularly admiring of Michael's already well-developed conversational skills in this difficult language, and the number of Russian friends he had made.

Susan's admiration, if not awe, of Michael had persisted undimmed over the years. She also probably showed more faith in his judgement than was always wise. As the smallest and lightest family member, Michael tended to think of her as experimental material. When she was ten he asked her to test a novel way of launching more efficiently, less cumbersomely, an unstable kayak canoe, by sliding it lengthwise down a muddy slope straight into the river. She sat in the single seat, and Michael and Christopher provided the vigorous propulsion forward. The scene was Houghton Mill on the River Ouse. Mary and I did not know of this experiment until they returned at least an hour late for supper. The boys looked sheepish. Susan looked, and smelled, awful: she was covered in mud and slime and soaked in river water but had a proud, tentative smile on her face, no doubt for her faith and courage. A further experiment, when she was to test a hang-glider from the roof of the house, was fortunately not pursued to its conclusion, but again I knew nothing of it until later.

Her relationship with Michael did undergo some strain when she almost dropped out of college, or so it seemed, and joined a London squat, too far off the conventional track for Michael to approve, and he had not been slow to criticize. We were all of us still missing Christopher, and it showed in practical ways. But she got her degree and later a Masters, acquired a flat in Southwark and a good South Bank University management post. She and Michael continued to need each other and occasionally resorted to long telephone conversations. Always attractive, she is now a very self-possessed young woman, elegantly fashion-conscious, and an excellent first mate on my yacht. She is now in the final year of a PhD in philosophy, which she hopes to teach. She has a light and loving touch, but cannot suffer fools gladly, and to some lesser mortals could, I suppose, seem formidable as well as exciting.

The visit to Star City for three weeks in October was memorable for us because of the gradual onset of a golden Russian autumn, with the birch trees around the lakes near Michael and Rhonda's house shimmering with an ever-increasing depth of colour. Every day the sky was a clear blue, but the days were shortening and a winter weather break was expected at any time.

In the depths of the previous winter, Michael had completed his winter survival course, based on an emergency Soyuz descent and landing somewhere in the Siberian wastes, where he and his crew would have to survive and assist their being found by rescue forces for several freezing days. His colleagues included Commander Korzun, the gentleman who began this story fighting a fire on Mir. Michael actually enjoyed the experience, gathering wood for the constant fire necessary for warmth and helping to devise and make a shelter from the parachutes' silk. Parachutes were provided on the assumption that they had descended by parachute. There was a gun to deter wolves. He took it very seriously, knowing that learning to do the right thing now, although they were actually close to civilization, could save their lives in future. He admired Korzun, and noted that he too took the whole exercise as seriously as Michael did. At the time, the plan was for Michael to launch with Korzun, but the latter was also in reserve for an earlier crew, the commander of which had had to cancel, so Korzun was moved forward.

NASA had installed a direct telephone link to give Michael and the family unlimited access to NASA and to close relatives in the USA. Four other American astronauts were also in Star City: Michael's forerunner Jerry Linenger, due to launch in January; Mike's back-up astronaut Jim Voss, who would cover for him if he suddenly became unfit for his mission; the astronaut due to follow him on Mir (Wendy Lawrence, later changed to a male astronaut because of spacesuit size problems), and her back-up. The American group in Star City itself was therefore very small, and included two doctors and other staff, although there were more NASA employees based in central Moscow and at Russian Ground Control (TSUP). In Moscow the staffs handled the administrative detail of the US–Russian cooperation programme from a room at the US embassy.

Domestic shopping was very limited for Western tastes in Star City, and Rhonda made twice-monthly visits to the embassy commissariat to stock up on familiar items, particularly for the children. A NASA-contracted vehicle and driver were available virtually twenty-four hours a day, so they never needed to purchase a car. While this may have been a subconscious Russian

....

continuation of the habit of constant supervision and observation of a foreign resident, Michael and Rhonda welcomed it as an easing of the unfamiliar and sometimes trying conditions of their life in Russia.

For example, Michael was not only still spending two hours a day learning the Russian language, but he was also completing a detailed course on Soyuz and Mir systems which, in his typically conscientious way, he took extremely seriously. During our stay he faced all-day examinations, both written and oral, set for the completion of the stage of training he had reached, all, of course, in Russian, and in each of which he achieved one hundred per cent. I have always been proud and deeply satisfied with his achievements at every stage, but in Russia he took us all by surprise. He had never as a boy shown more than a passing interest in foreign languages – if there were exceptions, they concerned his scientific studies. Yet here he was, talking easily with all levels of Star City society, not just being understood, but making jokes and giving toasts. The Russian language is not easy, with its ragbag alphabet of Cyrillic, Greek and Roman symbols. Mary and I knew this only too well, because we had tried to show family solidarity by learning a little Russian ourselves, if only to impress his Russian colleagues with verbal hit-and-run raids if the opportunity presented itself.

One night, at a local restaurant for dinner, we found that one side of the room was taken up entirely by a seventy-strong wedding party. We were to be seated alone on the other side. One of the guests knew Rhonda from their aerobics class, and immediately invited us to take part in a toast to the bride and groom. Glasses were produced, filled and handed to us, a very pleasant gesture. But the event had farther to go. Following a pause, Michael stepped forward and delivered an off-the-cuff speech of congratulations, the graceful contents of which were obviously widely appreciated. As he finished, music started and two strapping Russian ladies swam into view, one saying to me, '*Menya zovut Olga* [my name is Olga] – and now we dance.'

Knowing better than to argue I was swept away, remembering to say '*Menya zovut Colin.*' I noticed that Michael had been similarly captured. Later, as we watched the dancing from our table, it was clear that in the West we have no monopoly in overtly sexual dancing: the ladies rhythmically thrust their hips provocatively to music similar to Western rock, yet wildly Russian. It was determinedly joyful in expression, which seemed defiantly appropriate in this confused, exotic land. Michael's dedication to his Russian language studies was to be of incalculable value during his time on Mir.

Walking through the woods with Michael one day, he suddenly stopped to examine a torn piece of parachute silk on a bush. He said, 'Look, this is where we were dumped for our survival exercise. Here's where we made our shelter, and that's the stump of a tree I cut down for fuel.'

He was obviously glad to have found the spot where they had spent frozen nights and days, an area which in winter had looked so different under snow and seemed so formidable, as it probably was so long as they did not cheat. I think he was surprised by its closeness to civilization. He was not sure whether they had ever really heard the howling of wolves, but with the wind and the blizzards, they could have imagined it.

In the summer before our arrival Michael had taken part in a different survival practice, this time based on their Soyuz escape capsule landing, after an emergency, in the sea. Once the hatch was opened, they would be in great danger of the capsule capsizing – the flooding in of water would be sudden and final and they would all quickly sink. The training was to practise avoiding such a disaster when hastility leaving the capsule for the waiting boat or helicopter. Michael felt strongly that a little more ship's architect's influence on the Soyuz design would not have gone amiss. He joked with his Russian colleagues who took it in good part. They knew that Michael meant well in everything, and that he wanted, needed, to be able to get on with them all. He had a normal degree of Western-style reservation towards the Russians, and probably still has, but he never allowed it to show.

Russia has been such an enclosed society, perceived for so long to be an unfathomable threat to our liberal and open Western way of doing things. It is easy to continue with the assumption that nothing has really changed, perestroika and glasnost notwithstanding. However, we were able to assemble some basic facts and impressions about the Russian organization now in charge of Michael's comfort and safety, on earth and in space, for the next twelve months.

There are four elements. The most visible is Star City near Moscow, where cosmonaut and astronaut pre-launch training is done. It tends to be militarily slanted in style, and is run by a relatively lowly two-star general. Entrance to Star City is restricted to people who have an involvement and

....

need to be there, but the area is not secret and is not dominated by watchtowers as it might once have been. Military fighter pilots who are favourites to become cosmonaut commanders feel at home there.

The second element is the gigantic Russian industrial complex known as Energiya, which traditionally has designed and manufactured Russian rockets, Mir components and other space hardware such as the discontinued shuttle, Buran. It is directed by a single powerful person, presently Yuri Semeonov. One of his four deputies, Valery Ryumin, an older retired cosmonaut, directs the Mir programme part of it.

A third element is a substantial military space defence organization, significant enough to be run by a four-star general. Like any truly military organization, its purpose and activities remain shrouded in secrecy which, anyway, it has seemed to me, is second nature for Russians.

Finally, there has emerged the Russian Space Agency, which is the developing child of Russia's response to international commercial interest in Russian space activities, particularly Mir. For example, Germany, France and the United States have all bought time and facilities for experiments on Mir, or other space involvement such as guest cosmonauts, or satellite launches. It would have been politically unacceptable in Russia for the governments of these foreign countries to deal directly with a Russian company like Energiya. Hence the creation of the Russian Space Agency, essentially a bureaucratic fund collector and sender of bills, a quango in fact, but, as go-between on matters involving hundreds of millions of dollars, growing in power and influence.

Where then does Moscow Ground Control (TSUP) fit in? It is manned and controlled by Energiya, the hardware manufacturers. While cosmonaut commanders come from military fighter squadrons, their crews, known as flight engineers, invariably come from personnel at Energiya. Thus the hardware designers and manufacturers have enormous influence on space operations. As well as dominating Ground Control, they are able to impose their policies on all aspects of life on Mir. Members of the crew, including the commander, have one overriding duty which is made very plain before launch, and that is to do precisely what Ground Control tells them. If there are no instructions, they expect to wait for them. As it will be seen, this modus operandi, so different from American requirements and practices on shuttle

....

operations, presented Michael with unexpected difficulties.

A very pleasant but unforeseen consequence of Michael's final months in Russia before launch was that Cambridge was palpably much closer for a Christmas visit in 1996 than Texas. In any case, the family had decided to move back to Texas permanently in April 1997, when Michael would complete his final shuttle refresher training before his launch to Mir in May. So the decision was made, and all the Foales gathered for Christmas in the traditional style. Everybody enjoyed it, and everybody enjoyed everybody else. Mary and I were very pleased that all was so harmonious and convivial for the little children too – as England-based grandparents, we have a natural vested interest in keeping England firmly as a factor in everybody's mind.

As a child, Michael had loved the sight of the last steam trains, and, like so many others, had a toy train set. A holiday highlight was Michael's fulfilling a promise to his little son Ian to take him for a ride on a real steam train. Ian had developed a fascination for toy trains, just like his father (and *his* father) had, and Michael felt that Ian should see the real thing. Privately I thought that it was to be primarily Michael's treat; but then, I was not averse to the idea myself. So we all went on the Nene Valley Steam Train Railway, pulled by a convincing replica of Thomas the Tank Engine: 'Five and two halves return, please, Wansford to Peterborough.'

The many months in Star City had been pleasant enough and the Russian staff helpful, but, unlike a British or American army or air force overseas tour, which would have been supported by a well-founded and experienced organization, the handful of NASA folk had to be largely self-supportive and some sense of isolation was inevitable. This time, on their return to Russia after Christmas, they all knew it was only a little over three months before they would be returning permanently to their beautiful home on Galveston Bay, to blue water and a handy selection of sailboards.

In April 1997 they packed up their belongings in Star City and returned to Houston. Michael was keen to get some leave away from it all and had already booked accommodation for the family on the coast in southern Texas where they could play, relax, windsurf and dream a little. This was a wise move, as he well knew how all of an astronaut's spare time can be picked away before a launch by professional and well-meaning people, who seem to

....

need him just because he is there. He took care not to be. We received the following e-mail from him on holiday on 22 April.

Dear Mum, Dad and Susie,

We had a good time in Corpus Christi, staying in nice beachfront condos, with some friends joining us for the last three days. The weather was fairly cool, and we only spent one full day out in the sun, at Bird Island basin, but that day was perfect, with good wind for Rhonda and I to sail, in turn, and the children loved splashing around in the shallow water. I took Jenna on a board to a little island, where we explored its beachy shore and collected shells. Time flew by for the two of us, and Jenna keeps talking about going back to Jenna Island, some day. The children did not get burned at all, but I ended up really scorching the backs of my legs – I do know better, but just forgot that I had been in Russia a while.

We visited an aquarium there, twice, and played a lot with the Bowersox boys, and Terry and Rene's son, Charles, so when we got back to Houston on Friday, I really felt very relaxed. On the weekend I did some major woodwork and house repair, replacing rotten, rain-soaked door jambs. With luck I have improved the rainproofing as well. So when I got to train with my shuttle crew on Monday, in the simulator, I felt refreshed. I did notice a mass of out-of-date messages demanding my attention from last week, while I was far away. So I am feeling very smug that we pulled off the vacation, and were not tempted to spend time in Houston, where I could be reached! The family is nicely settled back in our house. I am even driving the Vanogan again – after it travelled to Moscow and back without me ever seeing it.

The launch date is still 15 May, but a number of factors have used up all the reserve time in the schedule, so a slip of two or three days is definitely possible but not yet decided on.

The press is starting to get very hyperbolic about the risks of further American (my) presence on Mir, in the light of the generally misunderstood reports about the health of the station given out by the Russians, who did not intend to create such an effect. The real issues

....

are being addressed very seriously, here in Houston and in Washington DC. Without doubt I will launch, but the rhetoric is whether I will be left to remain on Mir until the next shuttle. I would bet very high odds that I will get to stay.

I have four guest slots at the beach house, the day before launch, for a barbecue with my crew and their spouses. You three came to it for my first launch. If you can think of an additional single guest who would not distract us from our own Foale family farewells, and who might especially be a pleasure for Susie to have with us, let me know. For now I am just planning to have the three of you, and of course Rhonda.

Time to get Ian to bed.

Love, Mike

It was very useful to get this update from Michael on official American thinking. The dangerous fire which had added to Jerry Linenger's troubles in February continued to bother Americans concerned with the safety of their astronauts on Mir, as more details of the incident unfolded. Up to his delivery by the shuttle Atlantis, it was conceivable that Michael would not be left on Mir, but brought back with Jerry Linenger in a specially placed extra seat in the shuttle. Linenger was palpably relieved at the prospect of soon being taken back home, and he said nothing to encourage a continued NASA presence on Mir. He had in any event seemed reluctant to identify closely with his Russian crew as a team member – not that his brief required him to – and had chosen to remain aloof, attending to his own scientific duties. He spoke little Russian, and had contented himself with seeing his colleagues and the Mir station as a service to support his scientific space research. This was true in terms of strict international agreement, but not an attitude which Michael would wish to uphold. Both Vasily Tsibliyev and Sasha Lazutkin, from their time with him in Star City and in Baikonur, knew already that Michael would be very different.

As the day approached for Linenger to be collected by Atlantis and brought back to earth, so the political and public debate gained momentum. That Linenger would be collected there was no doubt, but whether Michael would be left behind on Mir was. Michael's letter was the last we received in

....

England before our own departure for Clear Lake, Houston, where we had booked an apartment not far from Michael's home. We were thus able in the interim to see a lot of him and the family up to the beginning of his quarantine period. We met Susan, newly arrived in Houston from London, and went on together to Orlando in Florida.

Susan's late evening arrival in Florida, and the fact that she had had no recent contact with Michael, led him to make special arrangements for a beach picnic with her that night, for each to catch up with the other before the launch. His sleep patterns had already been adjusted in preparation for his departure, so that for him it would have been the middle of the day. As he was now in quarantine, Susan first had to have a formal medical to be conducted by Michael's doctor, Terry Taddeo, after her arrival at Cocoa Beach at about eleven pm. A family support person called Trudy, an amazing lady with a lion's eyes and the most amiable personality, picked Susan up and drove her to the crew quarters. Here Michael met Susan with a gleaming white convertible, owned by NASA, to take her to the beach. It was all pure glamour for Susan, and just as well, as she had had no real sleep for thirty-six hours. Michael too had put himself to a lot of trouble to make the evening happen. It was a measure of their appreciation for each other. She rejoined us, tired but happy, at four am, without waking us. She then slept for twelve hours.

Astronauts live a normal life until eight days before launch, when they go into quarantine in special 'isolated' crew quarters – three or four days are spent at the Johnson Space Center near Houston, and the remainder at the Kennedy Space Center at Cape Canaveral in Florida. This is to isolate them from normal community germs and also to establish new sleep patterns, ready for those imposed by the mission. Only very close relatives (but excluding children) – wives, sisters, mothers, fathers – are allowed to see them during this period, and then only after medical examinations and blood tests. Even so, visits are restricted to two or three per astronaut until the evening before the launch which Michael had referred to. This is when all medically cleared relatives are invited to the so-called beach hut for a barbecue supper with wine and beer. One needs to banish the unsuitable connotations of last suppers and to concentrate on what it is, a quite joyful, laughing gathering of loved ones, before the rigours, real or imagined, of the mission begin.

The beach hut is exactly what it sounds like, a wooden structure built on stilts on the dunes with one main room, twenty feet by twenty, a twelve-foot veranda on the beach side and the white rollers of the blue Atlantic murmuring softly only yards away beyond the sands. People tend to congregate on the deck outside until the sun goes down, its great red disc adding brushes of silver and gold to the darkening breakers. The Americans have got this absolutely right, and the beauty of the position and the warmth of feeling among the select company are exactly what a pre-mission astronaut would want.

As the light fades, people drift into the lighted interior to pick up food from the buffet tables, another can of beer or glass of wine. On this occasion, as people finished their meal, Charlie Precourt, the mission commander, called for attention and made a short speech, gave a few facts about the mission's aims and then introduced his crew, who stood with him. They in turn said a few words too. It is all quite unselfconsciously American, but it seems to suit any nationality present. On this Atlantis mission the Russian director of the Mir programme, Valery Ryumin, was present with a small Russian party (his young wife Elena Kondakova was a crew member, very striking with her long legs and high cut-off jeans to show them). Everybody also felt honoured by the presence of Valentina Tereshkova, who was the first woman anywhere in space, and who was Kondakova's guest. At one stage the Russians sang a heroic space song which Michael joined in. During the introductions, I remembered to say *Ochen priatna* (a pleasure to meet you), watching their expressions as I did so.

The glamour of Kondakova's legs and mischievous, challenging eyes was complemented by the pilot of the shuttle, Eileen Collins. I sought her out to praise her multicoloured patterned shirt, even more dramatic than the one I was sporting, and we had a photograph taken together. She is a very attractive version of the American female achiever, beautiful and charming, a superb pilot and dedicated, at least for now, to being an astronaut. There is obviously a great deal of steel beneath her smile.

I said, 'I understand that you are a happily married lady. What does the lucky man do?'

'He's an airline pilot,' she said.

'Does that ever give you time to be together?'

....

She smiled. 'Well, enough for us to have had a child,' she said. 'We have to rely on a lot of paid childminder help, but apart from shuttle missions and quarantine, we at least manage to live a normal airline pilot's married life in Houston.'

A remarkable lady. She was soon to command a shuttle mission of her own, in 1999, when she and her crew were to deliver an X-ray telescope observatory into orbit. Inevitably, the time came for us all to part and quiet farewells were said.

The next day, before noon, we and the other invited guests were taken on a tour of the launch site and the whole astronaut crew lined up in their blue overalls and caps, with their enormous orbiter on its launch pad in the background, to be photographed together and called to by the observers, who were separated from them by a twelve-foot ha-ha ditch, the kind English country houses have to keep cattle away from the house and garden. For the astronauts, the time is just before supper and bed, where they would have a full 'night's' rest before beginning their eight-hour countdown. At the barbecue the previous night, it had been breakfast time for them.

There was Michael, lithe and fit, in the company of his Atlantis crew colleagues but this time with an unmistakable aura of distinction not shared by the others. One does what one wants to do – I did in the RAF for so many years, loved the risks, the uncertainty and travel, and, yes, the sheer glamour of it, as much an inner private thing as looking for approbation. But I remembered those rare occasions when I and my squadron were on show to the public and the pride and excitement which the event generated, producing in me a calm, confident, almost serene pleasure. Michael looked just like that: on show, responsible, ready for the stars.

A party of friends of ours from New York who were with us as guests were fascinated by the idea that Michael would not be returning with the shuttle ten days later, but would remain in space for four months. The eldest member whispered to me urgently, 'What psychological preparation has he had for this venture?'

I hadn't the first idea, so I shouted, 'Michael, Herb here wants to know what psychological preparation have you had?'

He called back, almost proudly in his British way, with a broad smile, 'None whatsoever,' thus dismissing the question as irrelevant.

....

The fact, to my mind and his, is that no psychological preparation is likely to be effective if you don't want to go – and he did.

I felt deeply, personally proud of him and his show of bravado, strong echoes of some of my own. I was well aware of the occasional bout of butterflies he would feel as the thought of the launch swam into his mind, but he would show no sign of it. He would be glad when the mission was truly under way, but then, unlike the others, he would remain on Mir for an extended stay in space, away from his loved ones, weightless, possibly lonely, for a hard to imagine four months. One hundred and twenty days, equivalent to ten continuous twelve-day shuttle missions, a whole earth season.

At quiet moments he would review his training, both in respect to Mir itself and the experiments that would be in his charge. He would concentrate on the practicalities of the mission – the routine planned tasks followed by the regular sleep periods – and he felt more aware of the reality of his immediate future on Mir. He found this to be reassuring, and he slept well in the hours allocated for this, before rising and joining the Atlantis countdown.

Launch to Mir

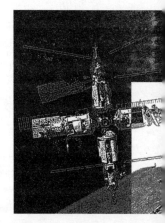

The launch of STS-84 was to take place on 16 May, just after midnight. The shadow of the Challenger accident is always present, unremarked but there, in the minds of all spectators and the crew. The noise, vibration and terrifying power of the solid rocket boosters and main engines is always a shock to a new astronaut, and something to be reluctantly anticipated and endured even by the experienced ones. Of course, their minds have been concentrated and busy for the eight-hour preparation and two-hour countdown in launch position, but thoughts will stray from time to time. In everybody's minds, the prayers and hopes are for safety, yes, above all else, but also that all systems, the weather and the emergency landing areas are going to be fit to clear the orbiter for ignition. A pre-launch abort or delay is tiring for all concerned, and ultimately, for the crew, brings new dangers.

There were six of us in the Foale party from England and fourteen from the United States, an assortment of relatives and friends, assembled at Cocoa Beach in readiness for the event. I had made it clear that I was in no way the team leader. All guests had been independently invited, and independently had to get to the right bus at the right time to get to the right place for the launch viewing stands. A complex proposition in the middle of the night, and worse when the launch timing needed virtually the whole of the evening in preparation, and much of the rest of the night until dawn for the action.

Susan, Mary and I had thought to put our heads down during the previous afternoon for a little sleep, but this did not happen. We had found a two-bedroom motel apartment with cooking and cooling facilities, essential both for economy and for tasting real American life. Many of our friends were also booked in at the same motel, and imperceptibly I found myself taking the lead, in spite of my intentions, simply because I was asked how *we* were going to prepare and act. In the early evening, Michael's close friend and fellow astronaut, Captain Bill Readdy, came to spend some hours with us for a tension-reducing session of a glass or two of red wine and a chat. It was a generous and thoughtful thing for him to do, and more valuable than attempts to sleep.

At 9 pm we drove in darkness to the designated car park where we were to find our buses. Over a hundred people were assembling; conversation was friendly but subdued. If they were like us, they had been awakened just a short time before – and they had not had the revitalizing effect of large mugs of British tea in their rooms, which we had specially imported. On our arrival at the site, the NASA representative told our bus companions where to go to find refreshment or memorabilia stalls and the viewing stands themselves. One and a half miles across the flat, swampy ground of Cape Canaveral Nature Reserve, all lit up like a great white bird, was the shuttle Atlantis on its launch pad, in the final hours of the countdown. The voice of the NASA commentator occasionally intruded over the loudspeakers, telling us of the successful completion of each stage of the pre-launch sequence, reminding us of how much time there was to go until lift-off. Weather reports of local cloud cover, conditions at the abort-landing grounds in Spain and Morocco, and any comments from the crew concerning their flight checks were calmly relayed. The voice, however, was never cold – it seemed warmly and humanly aware that what it had to say would be gratefully received and understood by all present.

The guests' conversations became even more muted or, occasionally, self-consciously jolly. A launch is above all a serious business.

About a minute before launch time all the lights around the launch pad were switched off, and those at the observation site one and a half miles

....

away were dimmed, as the loudspeaker voice announced: 'FIVE, FOUR, THREE, TWO, ONE, LIFT-OFF OF THE SPACE SHUTTLE ATLANTIS.' During these last words, there was the sudden appearance of a flame, beneath the shuttle, of unbelievable incandescence, the craft began to move upwards, booster rockets and main engines together giving maximum power, but so far in silence. The craft cleared the gantry and at that moment, the sound wave hit the observation party for the first time, like a thunderous earthquake, eight seconds after the first flame. The loudspeaker voice continued, 'God speed, Atlantis!'

Everybody clapped, cheered or cried in a release of tension – but the tension persisted for two minutes until the two solid rocket boosters burned out and were jettisoned at about twenty miles high. The two little fiery snakes could just be seen from the ground as they parted from the main diminishing flaming centre of the assembly, and everybody clapped and cheered again with more obvious relief.

The main engines of the shuttle continued to burn until all the fuel in the great orange external tank was used up, and then that too was jettisoned. The commentator's voice continued to inform us as each command decision abort point was reached and passed. The shuttle, now 170 miles from the earth and travelling at 17,500 mph, shut off its engines and, at last, entered silent, vibrationless, weightless orbit. It is a moment of profound satisfaction and relief for the crew.

Michael's five-and-a-half-year-old daughter, Jenna, watching with her mother the far, receding point of light which was Atlantis, suddenly cried, 'Daddy is turning into a star!' and burst into tears.

But tears in the crowd are common. I suppose the tension gets to all of us, and I remember feeling unreasonably angry that one of my oldest friends was not in our close party in the viewing stands but watching elsewhere during the actual launch. I had searched for him. When we were reunited on the bus I said rudely, 'Where were *you*?'

And how had it been for Michael? Two hours before lift-off, the crew were driven out to the launch pad in their silver-coloured van. Once again, Michael found the approaching view of Atlantis, so brightly lit up in the surrounding darkness, very special, and he remembered when he had first seen it, three missions ago, and how its beauty had moved him so profoundly.

....

Their police escort was flashing its lights in the lead, but everybody else, it seemed, was driving away. He remembered ruefully that normal people consider proximity to a fuelled rocket, ready for launch, something they want to be well away from, and he was being driven right up to it.

High up on the two-hundred-foot level of the access tower, the electric hum of bright lights was mixed with the hissing of cryogenic fuel boiling off from the enormous orange-coloured external tank. While Charlie Precourt, the commander, and Eileen Collins were being strapped in, he walked around the tower and could just see the white, translucent waves of the ocean rolling silently on the deserted beach a mile away. He reflected how that would soon be far behind them, assuming that the two imposing white booster rockets, with LOADED written on them, did their job. Then he found his place and strapped in.

Eventually the countdown picked up five minutes before launch. He wriggled in his suit and tightened his restrainer straps as far as they would go. Looking around the flight deck, he was again struck by how similar it appeared to any other large aircraft cockpit. But this was a rocket-driven launch, at the sharp end of technology, with all the danger that so much explosive delivery of energy over such a short period of time implies. The slight bumping of the main engines, far below him, could be felt as the hydraulic actuators responded to pilot control checks. None of the crew were saying much as they concentrated on what was about to happen.

Elena Kondakova's place happened to be close to Michael's. Looking at her face, he saw that lines of nervousness at her first US shuttle launch were etched deeply on it, so he stretched out a hand to her. She knew it was there without looking, and grasped it firmly and thankfully and held it throughout the launch. Far away, a roar began as the main engines came up to full thrust, followed by a sharp jolt in the back as the two boosters fired. Very quickly they rose smoothly and the launch tower passed out of view as they rapidly rolled counter-clockwise to line up with the required ascent path. Ninety seconds later, the continuous shake of the two solid booster rockets came to a successful end and they were jettisoned, followed shortly afterwards by the main fuel tank.

It took Atlantis a couple of days to reach its docking position with Mir. Its speed of orbit would have been calculated to bring it near to the same

....

position in space as the space station. Then, at a predetermined point and with clearance from the station's commander, the shuttle's path would be adjusted to bring it closer and into the correct attitude for its docking port to be slowly nudged towards the receiving port on the station.

Michael meanwhile felt happy and relaxed as his craft entered orbit. Launch tensions (terrors, if the astronauts allowed themselves that much unwise introspection) were over. No stranger to weightlessness, his mind settled back to enjoy the journey. Although an accredited crew member, his monitoring duties were not onerous, and he contemplated again what he had let himself in for. Of his shuttle crew, he knew the commander, Charlie Precourt, best, and also the pilot, Eileen Collins, and enjoyed their company – they could joke and chat together without inhibition. Elena Kondakova was a personality in her own right, and Michael's readiness with the Russian language often led her to find his company. Once or twice, as the craft continued to get closer to Mir, he found himself beginning his sleep period, and hoped that he had not, this time, bitten off more than he could chew. Jerry Linenger, the American astronaut on Mir whose place he was taking, had never replied to his earlier e-mail asking about conditions. This could have been because of Linenger's own behaviour pattern, or conditions on Mir, or a bit of both. He would soon see.

He knew that, along with his parents and sister, there had been many friends on earth who had done him the honour, as he saw it, of attending his launch. Like all crew members, he felt relief and satisfaction that the launch had happened on time and on a clean first attempt, so that all the friends back at the Cape could now really begin to enjoy their holiday. Invariably he spared a thought during the countdown for the well-being of his people on the ground, knowing the anxieties they would feel.

Our family's self-catering motel apartment was on Cocoa Beach. It lay within sight and sound of the Atlantic rollers and was always well used by many who would come to watch a launch. After mentally echoing the launch commentator's fervent 'God speed, Atlantis', we all climbed wearily but happily into our buses, with dawn in the sky, everybody intent on getting a few morning hours in bed before properly celebrating our undoubted post-launch relief and happiness. We woke at midday, and I immediately rang everybody we knew who was still at Cocoa Beach, to give them celebration

....

information. This was simply: 'At six pm this evening, an hour or two before sundown, we will be on the Wakulla Motel terrace above the beach with our champagne and our glasses. If you would like to join us, with your champagne and glasses, we would be so very glad to share with you our delight and satisfaction.'

Having accomplished that task and found that everyone wanted to come, we switched on the NASA channel on the TV to get an update on developments and the likely docking time. This cable channel is available throughout America and runs almost continuous news and features on NASA events.

A little before six, we went to the terrace overlooking the ocean with picnic wine glasses and two bottles of well-chilled Moët et Chandon at the ready. Gradually we were joined by all our friends, bearing varying types of champagne from Californian to Spanish to French, and we drank and spoke softly to each other with the surf murmuring on the beach and the sinking sun adding gold to the tanned skins and happy laughing faces of us all.

I thought, 'Michael almost certainly knows what we are doing at this moment, knowing us as well as he does,' and I said so out loud. People involuntarily looked upward to the darkening but still translucent sky. Appropriately a V-shaped flock of pelicans flew low overhead in a northerly direction, towards the launch site at Cape Canaveral.

It is gratifying to discover again how easy it is to organize beautiful parties of lovely friends when we all have something to unite us. Everybody took pictures of everybody else. It was quite soon that I remembered that we had said nothing about dinner arrangements, and nobody was showing any sign of wanting to leave as they got to know each other better, although most of the champagne had been consumed. Their previous meetings with each other had, for most of them, been in the pre-dawn darkness of the launch observation gathering. I had, however, taken the precaution of making a provisional booking of a table for thirty at a well-known seafood restaurant in Port Canaveral and after the inner bounce and lift of champagne, nobody queried my now familiar lead. The restaurant provided a long table for us all, and between courses we moved positions, took photographs and laughed a lot. Susan had made many friends during a six-month stay in New York, before university, in 1980. Some of these were present, knew of her recent

....

birthday and got the restaurant to give her a cake. Its arrival provoked a unifying round of applause from our disparate group. Susan blushed prettily.

Meanwhile, 240 miles above the earth, the space shuttle Atlantis was already in synchronous orbit with Mir and steadily overtaking the station preparatory to docking. Late that night we all somehow crammed into the Foale motel rooms to watch the 'live' docking pictures on the NASA channel. As I was serving drinks, I glanced at the sea of faces, all smiling, soft and emotional and all avidly focused on the TV screen.

Bringing a 120-ton mass of space shuttle into proximity with 130 tons of space station requires a process of exemplary precision. Watching from a window on Mir, Jerry Linenger thought that, after four months, Atlantis was the most beautiful sight he had ever seen, or was ever likely to see. The aim is slowly to bring the docking port of each vessel together, inch by inch, until they interlock, and clamps are deployed to hold the two vessels fast. The shuttle's port is in the centre of the wide open cargo bay; Mir's special port to accommodate a shuttle is on the end of the Kristall module. The station and its inmates are in a stable attitude situation to make the shuttle commander's and his pilot's task of creeping up for this delicate manoeuvre as trouble-free as possible; they operate the shuttle's manoeuvring jets so as to have the great bird-like structure in exactly the right position, only feet away from its goal, at a closing speed of only a few inches per second, before the decision is made to proceed with a 'hard dock', the term used to describe the final clamping together of shuttle with station.

Before docking and while in orbit together around the earth, both vessels and their contents are weightless. However, the force of momentum, mass multiplied by velocity, is always potentially and dangerously present. Thus 120 tons of shuttle moving at only a few feet per second would still give a potentially damaging jolt to the Mir station, so the final closure to dock is executed with the greatest controlled gentleness. Once clamped and hard-docked, pressure is gradually equalized between the two vessels' interiors. The procedures to remove the respective hatch seals separating the two vessels' interiors are than begun, resulting after two hours in the possibility of free movement, in a balanced atmosphere, between the two units.

At this stage, local pressure in our motel room was also palpably reduced, and there were many stretches and sighs of relief. We managed to

....

stay up and awake for the ceremonious meeting of the two commanders with their handshakes and an exchange of gifts. Everybody we could see on board had good reason to smile, it being an enjoyable occasion for all – a successful meeting, still relatively uncommon, of souls in space. The authorities, both in Russia and America, made an effort to down-link clear TV pictures of the event. Sasha Lazutkin, Mir's flight engineer, was especially moved to be warmly greeted by his Energiya colleague, Elena Kondakova.

During the period of four to five days while docked, much activity took place between the crews, moving recently requested supplies or spares on to Mir which had not been available for inclusion in previous Progress deliveries, and the removal to shuttle of experiments or other items due for return to earth. Michael technically remained a member of the STS-84 crew, while being shown around the station's modules and his Spektr living and science quarters by Jerry Linenger. But he spent as much time as possible with his Russian colleagues from the start, taking all his meals with them and getting used to the station's facilities. Linenger technically remained a Mir crew member until the process known as 'seat transfer' was completed.

Seat transfer is a necessity for the Soyuz. Russian cosmonauts are launched into space by a rocket carrying a Soyuz spacecraft which, after arrival and initial aft docking at Mir's Kvant capsule, is subsequently undocked and flown to a forward position on the station's central Node where it is redocked and retained. In this position the Soyuz manned delivery and earth return craft naturally doubles as an escape vehicle for instant use by the Mir crew, including, of course, the guest American, in the event of a disastrous, life-threatening event demanding immediate evacuation. The ergonomics of this craft require each crew position and seat to be custom-made for the individual expecting to use it, and when one member of the crew is relieved by another, so the appropriate seats and safety harness must be changed. Atlantis had not only brought Michael to Mir, but also his personalized Soyuz seat and suit.

Once the familiarization and experiment handover procedures had been completed, seat transfer took place, Linenger's Soyuz seat being removed to the shuttle and Michael's being fitted to the Soyuz. Immediately, Linenger left Mir for good, becoming now an accredited member of STS-84 on Atlantis. Similarly, Michael said farewell to his crewmates and position on Atlantis, and transferred to Mir.

....

Michael's first communication with us from Mir while we were still in the USA was typically upbeat, happy and businesslike; it was perhaps too easy a life for him compared with what he had expected. He had sometimes wondered if this mission would be more stretching. Back in February he had gone out of his way to be present at his first crew's original launch from Baikonur in Kazakhstan. He had temporarily left his training and studies in Star City to be with them in the tense days before launch, to meet their families, drink a little vodka and make a video record of the Soyuz ascent for the families.

This made good sense psychologically, and was his first move towards the goodwill which he felt should be fostered among any crew. I had told him often enough how, during our lives in the RAF, an absence of ready goodwill can ruin an otherwise good squadron or station. He had spent every holiday of his youth at home with us, in close contact with whatever flying unit I was in charge of at the time. He was abundantly aware of the infectious good humour and mutual respect of everybody concerned within a succesful flying unit.

On one occasion, Michael arrived 'home' from school to our palatial official house in Malta, where I had just taken over as station commander. The morning after the farewell dinner held in the officers' mess for my departing predecessor (at which it was inappropriate that I be present), the latter was despondent. He had had difficulty delivering his farewell speech due to bad behaviour from some of the officers on the lower tables, who should have known better. The room was too long for easy control from top table to bottom. Apart from the indiscipline, it was unacceptable to me as a discourtesy within the station's brotherhood, and I would have none of it. The day I took over command, I had all one hundred and fifty officers assemble. I expressed my disgust, told them why and what I would expect in future. I must have told Michael of the incident because during the following summer holiday, when he was taking advantage of the station's deep-sea diving club, he remarked that my little lesson must have had an effect: what a happy station it was! What a perceptive boy, I felt.

However, no effort of mine to foster and maintain affection and comradeship could have succeeded without the wholehearted agreement and participation of the 'station commander's wife', Mary. Her warmly direct manner and unexpected humility in the way she saw her position charmed the station's wives of all ranks, spreading confidence and goodwill among the families. At the end of the final Wives' Club meeting, before our departure from Malta at the end of our two years in command, there were many unashamedly moist eyes saying goodbye to her.

Unlike all his NASA predecessors, in Russian eyes Michael was far more European than American, with fewer perceived Cold War associations. He was perhaps more naturally sympathetic and, above all, he was far more adept at the Russian language. Also, he was no stranger to his new companions, who took him to their hearts in a way that they had found difficult with his predecessor.

Vasily Tsibliyev, the commander, already felt that somehow on this mission fate had plotted bad luck for him. He was in any case prone, when tired, to periods of pessimism, and his mission so far had had more than its normal share of mishaps. To begin with, there had been the fire. Although ostensibly it had been successfully dealt with, he too suspected that the fire extinguishers had had no real effect in operation, and the fire had continued to burn determinedly beyond control until it literally burned itself out. Then there had been the nerve-racking attempt to dock a Progress vessel manually, a technique he had no faith in, and he felt that he had been saved by the bell only when the Progress TV camera, on which control depended, failed. Then he could formally cancel the exercise. The poisonous ethylene glycol leak had been detected but not its location, requiring continuous and laborious searching. But he was ready to welcome politely the new astronaut who had taken the trouble to see him launch.

It was Vasily who, as commander, was responsible for seeing Michael make a trial of positioning himself in the new personal seat designed for him in the Soyuz escape craft.

'You need to think yourself small when fitting yourself in,' said Vasily as Michael looked disbelievingly at the cramped, inadequate space provided for his body.

'I'm trying to,' said Michael as he struggled, impossibly he felt, to get himself in position.

'Now hold that,' said Vasily, 'while I attach and tighten your straps.' Michael saw that Vasily was himself having difficulty and tried again, very

....

hard, to be small. Vasily immediately tightened the straps, forcing Michael into an even smaller shape.

'Again please,' Vasily said. And again he further tightened the straps.

'All right. That is good. Now we could escape and not leave you behind.' Vasily said this seriously and Michael knew that he was not joking.

Sasha Lazutkin with his lighter personal style had also looked forward to working with Michael, whose facility with the Russian language was widely known and who could therefore be expected to be helpful with Sasha's English. He had found Michael very approachable in Baikonur. Sasha was a sociable person, quite different from Vasily's reserve, but in an odd way Michael and the Russians officers made a good, natural team of differents, respectful but curious about each other, slowly and imperceptibly bonding due to their situation and willing for it to happen. It is as well they did.

On Monday, 19 May 1997, we received this communication from Michael.

Darling Rhonda, Jenna and Ian, Mum, Dad and Susie,

I am finally moved into my new house in space, Mir. It smells fairly musty – not an allergy threat, but a noticeable old smell, rather like old books in an attic. Seeing Mir was spectacular, before we docked, and more so than on STS-63 [when he had previously only visited] because there are more modules now. After docking yesterday, I moved over to Spektr and set up my Russian sleeping bag, and am now wearing only Russian clothing. I have given all my US laundry to the shuttle and am eating all my meals with Sasha and Vasily in the Base Block. But of course the shuttle crew join us for evening meals, when it gets very merry. Yes, there is stuff to drink, using straws, sucking up a strawful by capillary action, each swig. The Mir is much more homey, especially in the older modules, and not sterile-looking like the shuttle.

Vasily, Sasha and I get on pretty good, and they are making an effort, I can tell. I had a very frank first-night conversation with them, as we were alone together, which ranged widely over recent events. So that I adapt to Mir as quickly as possible, I am purposely avoiding using anything on the shuttle, like toiletries, etc. It is initially harder

....

for me to get things done, but necessary if I am to be comfortable here.

Vassy and Sasha really did a good job cleaning up the passage-ways and gathering up innumerable useless, but still preserved, pieces of equipment. The old Progress supply rocket is jammed with trash, but there is still a similar volume waiting to be thrown away. The shuttle really could help by hauling away a lot of the foreign equip-ment, to make more room, but even now we are fighting a battle to get MCC [Houston Mission Control] to let us even send back Jerry's seat liner, which is light, and which no one else can use. The shuttle has masses of spare volume in Spacehab, and we have almost none!

We have completed the Soyuz seat-liner fit with me in it, and the pressure check. It is so cramped and jammed with equipment, more even than I remember in the trainers. I was actually quite alarmed [that he was not going to fit], but then as Vassy and I methodically tightened up my seat straps, etc., I started getting scrunched down more and more and ended up fitting more or less comfortably – good enough for an emergency landing. A continuing problem for the Americans has been to find astronauts lithe enough to fit safely into the cramped Soyuz vehicle.

The view of the shuttle out the windows is reminiscent of the views I had on my EVA on STS-63, [when he was perched on the cold end of the extended shuttle arm], but I have almost no time at all to look, because I am putting priority now on just how to be comfortable living and working here.

Tell Jenna I love her, and I cried when I read that she thought I had turned into a star. Of course I will come back from them, in the shuttle, and she will see me get bigger and bigger, up to landing. Ask Steve Vander Ark for Mir viewing times in Houston. It would be really neat for you to go out on the deck in the evening one day, and see us fly overhead.

Better get back to work. I hope Mum and Dad and Susie are back in Houston safely, after a nice time in Florida. They can write to me too, via Trudy while in Houston, if they want to.
Love, Mike

....

PS Show Jenna the Mir model on my desk, and point out the module with two pairs of V-like solar arrays. I am sleeping in the very end of it, Spektr.

Michael found that his new colleagues were not without humour. When the irrevocable moves for the departure of Atlantis had been made, the final hatch had closed and the familiar world and shape of the American shuttle was undocking and falling away, Tsibliyev said quietly, after a pause, 'And now we beat you!' He waited for Michael's startled look, before breaking into his rare but wide smile.

Michael quickly developed a practical common-sense daily routine. The station's physical nights and days change every ninety minutes, the time it takes to orbit the earth from the light to the dark side, and obviously this is no good for the human metabolic rate. So Moscow Mission Control sensibly keeps Mir on Moscow time, about two hours later than in the UK, eight hours later than in Houston. The crew wake up at eight am and retire at eleven or eleven-thirty pm. All had scientific duties, but especially Michael, who was officially there to engage in delicate biological experiments. He felt somewhat guilty that his colleagues Tsibliyev and Lazutkin seemed to be working very much harder than he – in fact they were almost continuously involved in repair work, attending to the temperamental Elektron oxygen generators, the CO_2 extractor and the stability gyrodynes, and attempting to trace the potentially dangerous ethylene glycol leak.

But Michael's own routine was straightforward. His day was punctuated by three mealtimes, when he encouraged his overworked colleagues to have their meals too, all together, on time and all anchored the same way up so that they could talk together, watch a video, plan ahead and so on. He had also been instructed to do two one-hour sessions of exercise each day which, as a fitness-conscious person, he was more than happy to do. He told us that in Kristall, his science base and later living module, he had discovered an alcove with two windows where he could sit and watch the world go by for twenty minutes' relaxation after each exercise session – it also happened to have a cooling air duct where a camera had been fitted, which he found pleasant when mopping down after his exertions. He never had any trouble sleeping – he had some of the best nights ever, he said, and it

....

seems that during those first four weeks he probably had a surplus of energy.

While settling daily more completely into his Mir routine, Michael did not forget to pass on useful comments and advice to his colleagues still in Star City, as his letter to Jim Voss, his original back-up, shows, which he reproduced for Rhonda back home in Clear Lake, Houston. She had just received the first batch of boxes and baggage from their eighteen-month stay in Russia, so was even busier than usual. She passed this letter on.

3 June 1997

Hi everybody,

Things are going pretty well here. We've had lots to do. I got rid of all the boxes over a week ago, and was able to do a birthday dinner for Marcy [a local friend], but the workers have been back in the kitchen since then ... I've heard only good things from and about Mike, and I've heard a lot. He is splendid. I'm passing on one of his more informative notes.

Cheers, Rhonda

28 May 1997 From Michael to astronaut colleagues in Star City

Jim, it's good to hear from you. I am sorry you're having the same old trouble with management, etc. Just enjoy the weather, and the company in Star City. Please give Mike, Daria, Dave, Andy, Rick, Ann, John and Wendy my very best wishes. I think of them fondly, and look forward to seeing everybody, when this is all over.

The same old time-line pressure [daily detailed work pro-gramme] in the shuttle world comes to bear here. Vasily and I have been trying to convince Sasha that he doesn't have to try and do the micro-sampling stuff which I don't have time for today, just because it's in the time line! Vasily, and Sasha especially, are terribly over-worked, and had their first real day off last Sunday, after three months. I set up the miniature video and we watched movies together – *Total Recall* and *Crocodile Dundee*. They like my little movie theatre which I have set up at the end of Spektr, where I have my sleeping bag. It is quite private, because a huge camera is between it and the rest of the module. In general, for background, we play loud contemporary

....

Russian rock music on the stereo in the Base Block.

Pass on to Wendy (Michael's planned successor) that her privacy will certainly be respected, after she announces goodnight, and that the Spektr end cone is a good place for her also. There are about two lockers' worth of stowage which I have set aside, behind a panel, for clothing, hygiene kits, etc.

Exercise takes more time than given in the time line – at least one and a half hours even with just a simple wipedown with a towel in place of a wash and rinse with the bodybath. Doing it twice a day, first on a treadmill, then on the ergometer, and doing the expanders per plan, is a full programme, but you do feel good afterwards. After two weeks off, the first three days I could not get through the sequences, my muscles hurt so much, and felt too tired. So obviously it is essential to keep up.

Because Sasha and Vassy are so busy responding to every communication pass, four more a day now, and are also always at work, tearing down, setting up hoses, tanks, etc., troubleshooting the cooling system, they don't seem to do their full exercise programmes per the sheets. Being part of the crew, and going to the Base Block for the comm passes also takes time for me, but I consider it essential. I am then ready to tell the consultant group where we are at, as well as understand the problems the crew are working on. As a result, the guys listen to my ideas about cooling problems and want to discuss it with me over meals.

We do try and sit down to each meal together, if only for half an hour, and this is really our only time of relaxation, other than sleep, because everybody always has something to do, right up to bedtime, which so far has never been earlier than eleven-thirty. We get up at eight am. I have only looked at the earth through Sasha's cabin window, for a few seconds at a time, while eating a meal with the guys. And I promise, Jim, I am not going to overwork all the experiments, and make the ground think that normal people will always do all the stuff they send us – they know even less than I do, how much time it might take to find stuff, then set it up, and do all the other things you have to do living in space.

....

Yes, the toilet is pretty good. It is easier to do number twos than the shuttle's, but still takes me a good fifteen to twenty minutes from start to finish. I ration myself to once a day, because it is so time-costly.

I had better go and do something the ground thinks I should be doing, instead of writing to my friends. Best regards to everybody. Pass this on if you like.

Back to you, Rhonda: as you can tell, I am a little frazzled, but the Greenhouse experiment, though taking more time than planned, is really coming along. I start planting seeds tomorrow. I am quite excited, actually. With luck, I will get the time to draw the plants for Jenna to colour. Tell Jenna she is my Princess, and Ian is my Prince, and you are my Queen. I love you.
Mike

After an initial feeling that he could be underemployed, Michael was beginning to sense the size of the inexorable housekeeping needs of his new home, and the preoccupation it inevitably had for his more experienced colleagues. At our home in Cambridge, it was summer and the growing season. We were tickled that our son, who had never to our knowledge shown any interest in turning the earth with a spade, was now embarking on a series of agricultural firsts in space.

chapter

A Tour of the Station

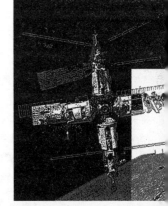

After the days in the shuttle, Michael was relieved by the sheer size of Mir, although it was so cluttered. The large Base Block with its formalized 'floor', 'walls' and 'ceiling' was the most attractive area to be in, except for the rather high noise level (seventy decibels) from central fans, and sometimes uncomfortably high temperatures, due to the many batteries in the block, receiving charge from the block's own solar arrays.

The dining table in the Base Block was thoughtfully designed, and had beneath its centre a fan that sucked air down through its open-mesh surface. The purpose of this downward flow of air was simply to keep food, implements or utensils from floating away unheeded. It worked, and was much valued. The overall build-up of dirt was everywhere, often originally caused by careless eating or drinking when globules of food or drink escaped en route to the eater's mouth and fetched up unpleasantly elsewhere. The dirt bothered Michael. The fan's suction helped to reduce this tendency, but did not prevent the build-up.

The fitted stereo system seemed very important throughout the waking hours, with extension speakers to most parts of the station. The music played as background was almost invariably Russian rock, which Michael found that he liked. There appeared to be no video. There had been one, but it had broken down. Michael was glad he had brought his own miniature equipment.

Beyond and aft towards Kvant were four large fans, with felt filters over them, to move and clean the air constantly, in this case towards the aft end. Movement also helped to prevent local carbon dioxide build-up from expelled breath. The fans were suction-oriented to pull air through the filters, and Michael soon discovered that if any object was temporarily mislaid – you cannot ever put something 'down' in weightlessness, there is no down, it has to be secured – it would often have drifted on the slow-moving air currents to land on the felt filters, where it could be retrieved. He was pleased with his discovery.

A large cupboard on the 'wall' contained food boxes, each of which had enough food for one person for one week. Half were of Russian origin, often canned food, and the other half were American, usually pre-processed and dried food. Both kinds were shared by the crew. Further aft, travelling along one of the two parallel traverse bungees, the entrance to the oldest additional module, Kvant, was reached. Whether by accident or design, Kvant was known and used as a cellar for junk. The accumulation of surplus equipment on a long-term space station is a hazard that has so far apparently never been fully grasped by Ground Control. No one will decide that something will not, one day, be useful again. Experiments, tools, spares, specialized space equipment all accumulate. Their original use, dimly remembered, prevents them from being discarded. So much junk was floating about in this dark, oily, smelly area that Vasily had stretched nets of the coarse fishing variety, specially requested and delivered, over much of it, simply to hold so many impeding objects closer to the module's skin and out of the way.

Kvant led directly to the aft docking port and airlock, at which the Soyuz crew and Progress supply vessels would arrive. Before the crew could properly unload supplies from a newly arrived Progress, they often had first to move much of the stored junk all through the Base Block and Node away to the shuttle's docking area on Kristall, which would temporarily be clear. Then, when a shuttle was expected, the whole miserable chore was reversed.

An unexpected design feature was that the Base Block and Kvant would often get overheated by the sun if they were not insulated by a docked Progress vessel or a Soyuz. The Progress supply vessel would therefore be retained in its dock after unloading, and reloaded with cans of waste, human and otherwise, until the time when it had to depart to make room for a new arrival, Progress or Soyuz. It was then undocked and controlled for re-entry

....

into the atmosphere to burn up over the Pacific Ocean.

Within a concentric wall surrounding Kvant were the station's own thrusters, used remotely by Ground Control to alter the station's attitude or orientation in space. Only Ground Control could operate them, but the station's Base Block battery power was invariably needed to have the command received and executed.

Turning with his back towards Kvant and oriented to 'floor' and 'ceiling', Michael saw the thirteen-foot-wide Base Block stretching ahead, the two traverse bungees, the food cupboard and galley, the water-condensing equipment, the dining table and, at the far end, the commander's control desk and panel. Everywhere there were removable panels hiding electrical leads, cooling pipes or even more junk. If he propelled himself forward, hand over hand on one of the bungees, he could pass over the control desk and through the hole (hatch) in the end wall above the desk, and over the commander's head – taking care with his feet. This led straight into the large spherical Node. The Node's forward hatch was directly in front of him, the entrance to the Soyuz escape vehicle. Everyone knew exactly where the escape route to Soyuz was: there was never any doubt or confusion about where to go in a hurry. It was simply forward.

The Node's other four hatches led into the four modules fixed in cruciform at right angles to each other and to the Base Block. They could be confusing. Perhaps they should have been colour-coded. Michael nearly always had to think which way to dive for what, except to Kvant 2, which contained the toilet. Like the Soyuz escape craft, everybody knew where the toilet was, without another thought. All Michael had to do to get there from the Base Block was to float forward over the control desk, enter the twelve-foot-diameter Node sphere, roll through a hundred and eighty degrees on to his back and follow his eyes into the hatch of Kvant 2. (To remind the reader, had he wanted to go to Spektr, whose entrance is directly opposite that of Kvant 2, he would not have rolled but simply bowed at the waist, again following his eyes, and floated into Spektr. Had he wanted to enter Priroda, he would have rolled ninety degrees to face left; if Kristall, ninety degrees to face right. In each case, after reaching the centre of the Node he would roll (or not) appropriately and then bend his trunk to float in the direction his eyes were looking.)

....

Unlike the Base Block, which was deliberately fitted and coloured to look as though it had a floor and ceiling, none of the other modules was as completely delineated, except perhaps Kvant 2. Common sense says that this must be because it had the toilet, and a toilet *has* to be on the floor. The 'floor' of Kvant 2 faced forward towards the Soyuz end; if you sat on the toilet, your head would be pointing 'forwards'. Michael found that there was a protruding valve handle above him against which he could push his head, allowing his body to fit more firmly with the toilet arrangement and to retain necessary suction, a bonus whether designed or not.

Like every module attached to the Node, Kvant 2 had a small command post on entering from the Node, where, for example, a headset could be plugged in. Because of the virtually continuous hum of fans and working equipment, a normal voice did not carry from module to module. But often, unfortunately, such command posts were partly hidden by bags of trash or junk.

Kvant 2 is where the crew conducted most of their water, and other liquid, processing. There were many twenty-two-litre cans stored in Kvant 2 containing all kinds of water – drinking water, distilled urine, unusable urine water – and solid human waste. They were all anchored under the 'floor' boards or up behind panels in the 'ceiling'. Eventually, the waste containers would be moved on to the Progress.

There was an Elektron oxygen generator, which by electrolysis produced breathable oxygen from water, which in turn may have been distilled from urine by a distillation machine. Recycled urine water was not used for drinking – psychologists had recommended against it. Instead, the humidity in the air had its water extracted as condensation, and this was used as recycled drinking water. Michael always felt that this was illogical in view of the still untraced ethylene glycol leak. The recycled water was quite likely to be dangerous, if the condensate contained significant amounts of the poison dissolved in it.

Alongside the toilet were two gyrodynes. Four more were situated deeper within Kvant 2. These are substantial gyros spinning, friction-free, in a vacuum. Their speed and direction were powered electrically and controlled by the main computer in the Base Block. There were a total of twelve gyrodynes fitted on the station, which stabilized the station's attitude in

....

relation to the earth, to allow the solar arrays to pick up maximum power from the sun during the daylight passes. The central computer commands the gyrodynes to move in such a way as to turn or shift the station to be in the best attitude for the solar arrays. It evaluates information from a variety of sources, from thermal imaging of earth surface temperatures, sun and star tracking, and radar positioning data transmitted from monitoring stations on earth. As long as there is power, the system works well.

Floating deeper into Kvant 2, Michael passed into a secondary airlock area with closable hatches, and beyond that into a main airlock from which EVAs are undertaken through a hatch which opens into space. There is a large storage position for two external-use spacesuits, an oxygen filling facility, more stowage space where two large earth observation cameras were once fitted and a very large window. Beyond the main airlock was the best observation window on the station and there, to his annoyance, Michael found that his predecessor had left a tether during an external spacewalk, obscuring and completely spoiling the window's function. The poor man's ears must have burned many times as the crew daily expressed their irritation. Removal of the tether had to wait until the next EVA. Kvant 2 also had two solar arrays of its own, charging batteries separate from the Base Block.

He next examined the older module, Kristall, pushing off to float back into the Node, looking into the Base Block, then rolled to face ninety degrees right, and followed his eyes into Kristall (or if floating from the Base Block into the Node, he would roll to face ninety degrees right, bow and again follow his eyes). Kristall had been used for many earlier Russian experiments in astrophysics. It was rather power-hungry, and although solar arrays had been fitted, they were folded throughout the flight. Without power fed from the Base Block, or from Spektr's solar arrays, it would be dark and cold. It was quite long, and its outer end was originally intended for use as the docking module for the Russian version of a space shuttle, called Buran, but this project was discontinued at an early stage. So another extension was fitted to it to match up with the American shuttle's docking stack in the craft's cargo bay. As already mentioned, a dreary fact of life was that Kristall was often full of junk, removed from Kvant to make room for unloading a Progress supply vessel. But the actual entrance to Kristall near the Node had to be kept clear for one of the two exercise treadmills located there. The

....

other treadmill was in the Base Block, not popular with Michael because of the greater heat there.

In Kristall Michael delighted in the four-windowed docking sphere, a marvellous place for earth observation. It still had the cooling jet fitted for a camera which had since been removed. His predecessor did not know that the windows could be uncovered, and had not learned the command to do this because he so rarely talked to his Russian crew. Michael would do his exercises twice a day on the secondary treadmill in Kristall's entrance, then, when perspiring at such a rate that he was literally, as he puts it, in water and could steam up a window in seconds, he would float to his jet-cooled window and happily watch the world go by as he cooled off and mopped down. On such occasions he felt that life was not at all bad.

It was also in Kristall that, seven years earlier, the so-called Greenhouse had been positioned. Some of Michael's experiments were to examine seed propagation and cultivation in zero gravity, so he 'communed' here with his plants every day. He loved these experiments and found that they could absorb his attention and provide a calming effect on his spirits. Michael knows that generally he is a well-controlled and equable sort of person; but living in space and especially on Mir, as it turned out, generated a succession of irritations which he had consciously to deal with. He says that his Greenhouse experiments reduced his irritability.

Opposite the module Kristall was Priroda. He could therefore float to the Node and proceed directly across from Kristall to Priroda's hatch (or if from the Base Block, float face to 'floor' into the Node sphere, roll to face ninety degrees left, bow at the waist and follow his eyes into Priroda). This is the newest module, and certainly the best suited for scientific experiments. It has the stamp of up-to-date labour-saving technology, for example, all panels and covers can be removed without the aid of a screwdriver, unlike anywhere else, and it houses expensive modular experiments funded by France, Germany and America. It has no power of its own, and takes all its needs from the Base Block. Although not normally a living area, it was a pleasant place to be in. Fifty per cent of Michael's physiological experiments were set up in Priroda and Kristall, and the rest in Spektr, which we will turn to next.

The Spektr module was fairly new, second only to Priroda. It had four solar arrays and contributed a significant forty per cent of the station's total

....

power generation. It was filled with American hardware: a fast-freezer for blood samples and another for long-term freezing, a blood centrifuge and much of Michael's life science experiments. The work here was largely medical in nature, and produced a lot of waste – wrappers, papers – great for sterility and quick action in a hospital emergency room, which is regularly cleaned, but agonizingly and ceaselessly productive of trash in space, for Michael a real pain. However, a major US–Russian programme was under way, and the work had to be done.

From Michael's point of view, the most valuable part of Spektr was the far end of it, often referred to as the 'duck's beak' for reasons of its shape. He had set up his sleeping bag there, and his laptop computer. He was able to play taped American movies on his small personal VCR, and then display them on the screen of his laptop. He had been sent a number of films, and had also found others left behind by John Blaha and Shannon Lucid, two of the US astronauts previously attached to Mir. His Russian crewmates had long since given up trying to view films because the screens which had been provided for their use were simple, commercial products which had over-heated themselves to destruction in zero gravity, zero convection conditions. Thus, at an early stage Michael was able to show hospitality to his commander and flight engineer by welcoming them to his quarters to watch a late-night film, after supper together in the Base Block. They were glad of this entertainment and crammed amiably close to each other to watch Michael's tiny movie theatre. All the films were in English, without subtitles, but Michael's Russian was good enough for him to maintain an adequate con-tinuous translation of the kinds of action film which were most popular. He carefully avoided Shakespeare, he says.

In this way, and almost by accident, he set up an early bond with his crewmates which presaged friendship and trust beyond anything normally required in the contracts or international agreements, or in previous bi-national crews' experience.

This warmth of feeling led to Michael's first public support of his crewmates against their seemingly rather hard Ground Control taskmasters in Moscow. The Russian Space Agency had been able to bring in hard currency income from the continuing succession of guest astronauts. This led them to publicize the facility whenever they could. They sometimes called, without due notice, for a television down-link. Their call in early June coincided with the Russian crewmen having removed dozens of panels in the main operational area where the TV link would be made, as they were still trying to find the ethylene glycol leak. Ground Control's request that they 'tidy up' for the TV link, even before the leak had been located, was very dispiriting for the Russian crew and was perhaps too typical of the unsympathetic and unimaginative attitude of Ground Control at that time. Up to then, Ground Control were unused to intrusion or criticism from the world's media and were, by Western standards, arrogant and perfunctory. This was to change. But the change was started by Michael, who made a point in his CNN interview of saying how splendid and self-sacrificing his Russian colleagues were, working every minute of the day, like heroes, he said.

Rhonda wrote to us to wish me a very happy birthday on 10 June, with big kisses from Jenna, Ian and herself. She had attended a reunion party for the returned crew of STS-84, the crew that had taken Michael to Mir. With perfect timing, and research, she got everybody to go outside the house at the end of the evening to watch Mir fly over. This impressed everyone – including Michael. She copied to us a letter from him.

Thursday, 5 June 1997

Rhonda,

I am just loving your drawings. Tell Jenna she is a real honey to spend time doing them. I discovered two notes you sent me, only last night, with drawings around Memorial Day (30 May), lost on the packet computer because the TSUP [Ground Control] guys have been using a computer with an old date stamp (1994), and Sasha and I sort the mail that's new, based on the most recent date! I suspected I had missed a note or two from you and decided to scan for them, and found them. I just told Keith and his boys to get their computers in shape – friendly-like.

I am thrilled you go outside to watch us. The STS-84 party sounded great. Ed Lu sent me a note as well. Even the TSUP passed on a message from Frank Culbertson, that they all saw us fly over. No one mentioned it was you who agitated them into doing it. Well done.

Every time I get mail from you, it is like getting a present, or

....

chocolate, for which I have a major craving. We have chocolate here, but we are getting through it fast. And the Progress is not due for another month. Oh, well. Anyway, I want to warn you that sometimes you may get the same note from me twice. This is because I use whatever method is available, packet (which is frequent but not as reliable), or telemetry, which is reliable, I think, but only every three days or so. Today I send by telemetry, but may try packet if there is a comm pass that lets us. All you need to know is that your notes always come to me by packet, and it seems to be a two-day delay. My notes to you, I guess, are a little longer, maybe three days, by packet. By telemetry, even longer. But the good thing is that they seem to get through.

Sorry I haven't done a drawing for a while. But I started to have less free time, as we got the Greenhouse going. My plants (turnip) are a centimetre high now, after four days. A little stunted, I think, compared to earthbound growth, and only twenty-five per cent of the seeds seem to have shown shoots. But I am hopeful. I have noticed that though some are sensing the light, and growing up towards it, others seem totally lost, and grow sideways along the seed bed. Weird.

I did a CNN interview today, not very good because the comm was so bad, but you will probably see a clip. The Russians wanted Vassy to make a pretty scene, in the Base Block, where we eat, etc., but as usual the panels were pulled off, cooling system repairs spread out everywhere, and Vassy and Sasha were deep in repair work when they asked for the TV. Understandably, Vassy was very fed up that he had to rearrange yet again the panels and equipment, to paint a fairly unrealistic picture of orderly life on Mir. I made a statement that Vassy and Sasha are working incredibly hard, heroically I think, while I am just doing our science and being pretty relaxed, so that I wish I could help more with their burden. We will see if I really can help out or not. I do not want to burden Vassy with my initial ignorance, if they ask me to help him.

Hugs to the kids.

Love, Mike

We had e-mailed him from England via his Moscow-based server, as had Susan, and we were rewarded by a direct reply to his English family support, dated 3 June.

Dear Mum, Dad and Susie,

Thank you very much for your two nice notes. I am really pleased everything went off on time, and that you did not have to suffer through all the uncertainty that a launch delay entails. I am interested to know the level of newspaper interest in Britain, and the flavour – i.e., is it just another human interest story, or a little more substantial?

This will be my third week in space on Thursday, and I must say it feels like I have been here a lot longer already. This is probably because I have got myself pretty well settled in and a good routine going. The most significant part of the routine is eight hours of sleep, which is always full of vivid earthbound dreams, as well as visible flashes in the eyes/cerebral cortex when radiation passes. After that comes the three meals a day that Vasily, Sasha and I sit down to, making a point not to work during them, and just conversing sociably. The conversation is always pretty interesting, mostly initiated by myself or Sasha. Obviously we discuss the differences of our languages frequently – Sasha clearly wants to improve his knowledge of English, now that I am here, so I am doing a lot of instruction.

The other major routine is two planned one-hour periods of exercise, one on the treadmill with bungees to hold you down, and extra ones to work against with legs, arms, neck, in between running. The other exercise period is on a bicycle ergometer – though planned for an hour each, they take at least half an hour extra, what with cool-down and wet bodybath. Surprisingly, I feel overall that I am keeping my body pretty clean and have not developed a severe acne problem, as I initially feared.

The only relaxation we have done as a crew is to watch an English film or to do our own thing, but we always have some tasks planned as well.

Currently the Mir is in a solar orbit, in perpetual sunshine, so it is a little warm, eighty-three degrees but starting to cool off again.

....

The author as a young fighter pilot, with his Vampire Mark 9, Egypt, 1953.

Colin and Mary with Michael (standing) and Christopher, 1958.

Michael in an early test of weightlessness, 1960, a photo since used widely by the Press.

Brothers ahoy! (Christopher left,
Michael right) 1964.

...And again in 1975 (Michael left,
Christopher right).

left to right) Mary, Christopher, Susan
and Michael, 1977.

Training on the zero-gravity-simulating aircraft (familiarly known as the 'vomit comet') with his first crew in 1991. Michael floats at the top.

Emergency bailout training, Houston, Texas, 1992, in preparation for the Atlas 2 mission in spring 1993.

Michael, back to camera, floats freely by the securely tethered colleague on the end of the space shuttle Discovery's cargo arm during his third mission, before his fingers began to freeze, 1995.

Michael is instructed in the use of a cosmonaut's space suit at the Yuri Gagarin Cosmonaut Training Centre in Star City, Russia, in 1996.

Michael's children, Jenna and Ian, with Susan, on the visit to Houston for Michael's launch to Mir.

The beach hut party with the Atlanti crew who delivered Michael to Mir, on the day before their launch on 16 May 1997. Michael is second from left. The Commander, Charlie Precourt, and pilot, Eileen Collins, are at far right.

Michael and Russian cosmonaut Elena Kondakova at the Kennedy Space Centre, before their launch. Michael was to remain on Mir for four and a half months.

s docking onto Mir in May 1997 in order to deliver Michael for
ograph was taken from Mir.

Combined crew portrait, Atlantis and Mir, after Michael's delivery. Michael, bottom right, has already dressed as a 'Russian cosmonaut'. Front row, left to right, are Jerry Linenger, whom Michael was relieving, then Commanders Tsibliyev and Precourt, and Aleksandr Lazutkin.

Mir, the Soyuz seat handover and fitting, supervised by Commander Tsibliyev. Michael's smile belies the seriousness of the operation.

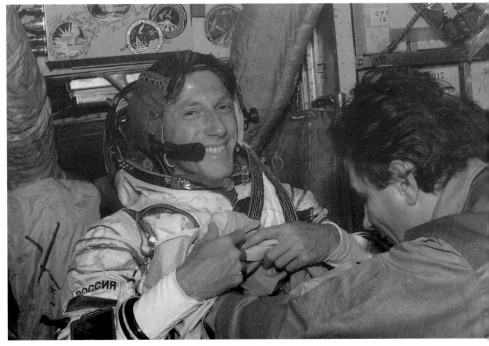

We are flying continually over the boundary between the lighted and night sides of earth in perpetual sunset or sunrise. Very pretty, with rosy-pink tinges to the clouds against the brightest blue earth rim of the atmosphere.

As for experiments, they are going as planned, so far, and rape seeds, which I planted three days ago, after a lot of checkout in the Greenhouse, are showing some little sprouts with leaves. Very encouraging. Soon I will be a busy bee – literally.

Love, Mike

I soon replied to this, Michael's first personal letter to us after establishing himself on Mir. I wanted to tell him that, seen from the ground, he was tackling the whole business of being a spaceman with exactly the right attitudes of thoughtfulness and cheerful endurance, which must have been of direct benefit to his Russian colleagues. At least it should have been, unless they had moved to the stolid 'looking forward to the end' stage, which might be expected after the halfway point, though not necessarily desirable. He was going to experience it all himself, and would need to keep an objective memory of it for the guidance of others.

I was glad that he was finding time for his exercise sessions, which I knew were so important for his mental as well as physical well-being. His practice of windsurfing daily had shown that his mind needed it. Some rueful colleague had made the point that if he achieved everything in space that he was asked to do, there was a danger that requirements would be raised yet again, to an impossible level, for his successors.

Until his third, high-profile mission and EVA in 1995, neither the UK media nor Michael had shown much interest in coverage. This time, I told him, the coverage in England had been extensive, leading up to the launch and later, the docking. We had begun to collect a reasonable selection of clippings from tabloids and broadsheets and were promised a copy of the ITN footage that was actually broadcast. I thought that all the items were serious and measured in their view of the importance of Michael's mission, particularly for US–Russian relations and the future of international efforts in space. A main article in the *Daily Telegraph* ended with Michael's plea that Britain stop sitting on the sidelines and sponsor more young people in astronaut training.

We had begun to think of him constantly, as I knew Rhonda and his own little family did too. I could not resist telling him that we might make a gardener of him yet.

Michael's next letter was to his sister Susan, who had e-mailed him from her London office.

Sunday, 8 June 1997

Dear Susie,

Thanks for your nice note. I got it a few days ago, but have not had a chance to down-link a reply until today. I am generally limited to about one file a day, if it is to go fast.

I thought a lot about you all in Florida, and I was as much pleased that we got off on time, because you would be pleased. But it's good to be off and running on this mission, and so far it feels like a long-term camping expedition. There are still a number of experiment bags I have not yet opened up, and other things that I am only now getting a good routine set up for. Bathing and toilet were the first priorities, of course.

I just finished my second mandatory exercise period of the day, which is good, on the ergometer. In the mornings I do the treadmill. Because I am covered in sweat afterwards, I like to find a good vent and cool off in the cold air, and a wonderful place to do this is where two windows are close together, with a special vent next to them to demist them. It used to be the site of some monster camera. And from there I listen to my Walkman (New Order today) and watch the earth. We were approaching the terminator, the boundary between light and dark, and were moving north-east over Africa, then Malta, then between Greece and Cyprus. It was beautiful, and I thought of our family times in the Mediterranean with the RAF. It was incredible that we passed over all those places in just a few minutes. The Mediterranean is really quite small, in comparative world terms.

I always try and imagine the activities people are doing at the time of day we are over them, and today it was Sunday evening for them. You, in England, were far off on the horizon, probably having

....

tea, as the sun was still quite high for you, but by Cyprus, the few high thunderclouds were subsiding and the tall, dark blue shadows of the dark side of the earth were starting to envelop the eastern Mediterranean and Turkey. The wonderful thing is I get to see a scene like this every time I cool down from exercise, maybe two hours a day. It is very important to have a routine to look out of the window, or you forget to, and just float about the station, staring at boring, technical, cluttered spaces.

Life, as you have probably heard from Rhonda, and seen in my other note to Mum and Dad, is not at all bad here, and I am basically enjoying it a lot, even though I am away from the children and Rhonda.

I am glad you got to go sailing in Aeolus [our little family yacht]. It is a unique thing to do, and is quite similar, I think, to going around the world in the station. The solar arrays, in my field of view out the window, look like fixed sails against the blue of the ocean, I like to think.

Enough. If I write too much, it won't get down successfully. Love, Mike

A space station and a yacht? He would also remember the never-ending things to do on a yacht, its constant call on the attention of its crew.

We all much enjoyed his thinking of us and our past family times together. It brought everybody closer and rekindled memories. After many tours of duty in the Mediterranean area, my own detailed recall of the shapes of islands and coastlines is good. But over the years an odd thing has happened to the scale. I know that at high-flying cruising altitude my aeroplane would take about fifteen minutes to fly east from one end of Crete or Cyprus to the other, during which one sees the western end's shape, then the centre, finally the eastern extremity, then, in the case of Cyprus, the panhandle. Yet my memory puts me at least twenty times higher, and I see these places much as I know Michael saw them, as complete as on the pages of an atlas, entire, in the surrounding blue of the sea.

Malta would remind him of two separate school holiday sequences, first from the age of twelve to fourteen, and a few years later, from seventeen to nineteen. Although they attended the same schools in England, Michael and Christopher saw much more of each other when they were at home with Mary, Susan and me, wherever that was. This was partly due to the age gap between them and their class levels, but also because Christopher's humanities bent in his studies contrasted with Michael's scientific emphasis. Each was an intellectual spur to the other, and having them both at home together was a great delight.

But on holiday, it was daily swimming or dinghy sailing, and for Michael diving in the clear waters of the Blue Grotto in Malta. We were all given a taste of sailing a large boat by the senior engineer officer, Peter Hann, who owned and sailed a beautiful old Hillyard ketch. He and his wife sailed it all over the Mediterranean after he retired from the RAF.

During our later sojourn on Malta, when I was station commander, Michael, Christopher and I, with an experienced RAF Marine Branch skipper and mate, sailed the station's modern thirty-five-foot Arpège yacht from Malta to southern Sicily, making our landfall at the ancient port of Syracuse. Susan had so much wanted to come too, but there was just no room. Winds were light and our progress slow, needing occasional use of the engine to move at all. The day following our arrival, we were interrupted in our desire to catch up on sleep by discovering that we were moored next to Peter and Moya Hann – what a small world. Our skipper did not like the forecast of fast deteriorating weather, and would have preferred to delay in Syracuse a second or third day until the weather had blown out. But I needed to get back and my wishes prevailed, but it proved to be a very rough two-day and -night passage.

We motored out of the ancient harbour soon after midday, and as we cleared the ancient sea walls, the near gale-force wind hit us and we were all suddenly in action.

'Can we cope with this?' I asked our taciturn skipper, who had expressed the preference for a delay.

'The boat can if you can, sir,' he replied. I was on the spot, and knew it.

We both looked across the heaving deck at the bronzed figures of Michael and Christopher, their long hair, fashionable at the time, flying in the wind, determinedly struggling to get the mainsail further reefed. They were focused, working hard and in control. The skipper nodded in satisfaction. At least they would be able, his expression said.

....

It was dark for the time of day, and as the rolling, bouncing hours passed, sunset appeared to have been cancelled. In the west there was just a vestige of pale ominous yellow. Our course was set, navigation and steaming lights switched on and we settled on a very much reefed beam wind for Malta. At least there was nothing much to wreck us en route, except, of course, other ships, and the height of the seas made an efficient all-round lookout difficult. Rather unbelievably, as it got very dark, the winds actually increased, and we had to shout to be heard.

The skipper decided that either he or his experienced mate would always be on watch, and that we three should provide two men per four-hour watch, allowing the other one of us and skipper or mate to sleep. It was a long and terrible night, and the wild motion of the ship made it dangerous to move about at all. As station commander, and because it was my fault that we were at sea at all that night, I volunteered for the messy job of keeping a flow of hot drinks and food coming from the galley, but eventually had to settle for unspillable sandwiches. Seasickness hit us all in brief waves. Christopher was only susceptible when in his bunk, which denied him much rest. I on the other hand felt better lying down – most convenient. We didn't say much, but I was aware of a mutual Foale feeling that we must not let the skipper down, let alone each other.

The hours passed, the vessel continued at the behest of wind and wave and a firm hand on the tiller; we were automatons in its service. Then, shortly before dawn, the wind began to subside and we suddenly found that there was no longer a need to shout. We were moving to the lee of Malta, as yet unseen. We were all very tired and very crumpled, but dared inwardly to imagine that soon, in a few more hours, the voyage would be over. We looked at each other and each seemed satisfied by what he saw.

We all survived, and I felt so blessed to have two such excellent sons. They rose uncomplainingly to the demands of the occasion and could laugh about it, even while it was happening. An abiding memory is that of being in the lee of the island while still twelve miles out from Marsaxlokk harbour. The wind had dropped now to a brisk breeze but was suddenly laden with the scent of wild thyme and a strongly nostalgic smell, which, though indescribable, was just the welcoming land, after two days of being away from it. It was lovely.

A year or so after their marriage, Michael and Rhonda visited us in Cambridge and we all went for a brisk day sail in my twenty-nine-foot yacht Aeolus, kept on a romantic deep-water, swinging mooring on the River Stour, upriver from Harwich. In our party were Mary and her friend Ann, Susan and Rhonda, Michael and Joff (a friend in the SAS), and me. When we got back to the mooring the romantic quality was impaired by a rapidly rising wind, and the unavoidable prospect of a very rough and wet row to shore in the little inflatable dinghy. It was only safe with a maximum of three on board – the oarsman (me) and two passengers. I ferried them ashore in the same order as I have named them above: the two older ladies first, the younger ladies next and then the two strapping young men. Afterwards Michael said approvingly, 'I liked the way you did that, Dad.' It was no big deal, but it pleased me that he had noticed.

chapter 7

Halcyon Days

I n the second week of June, after Mike's first letter, I experienced my first impact of NASA's 'psychological balance' programme aimed at astronauts' relatives. One morning our telephone rang and on answering I heard a male voice say, 'Good morning, this is Houston.'

Impressed, I said, 'Good morning, Houston,' in reply. A female voice belonging to a lady called Kelly then said that, as it was known that I, the father of Michael Foale, had a birthday on 10 June, they were making preparations to patch me in to Mir, so that Michael could dutifully telephone me many happy returns at eleven am BST. Would I be at home?

Of course I would, I said, privately reflecting that Michael's filial love and respect for me had in the past often needed a friendly nudge from Christopher or the female side to get a birthday card from him on time. On this occasion, NASA had taken on the responsibility. On the day, the phone duly rang on time and I had a very pleasant chat with Michael, who sounded very contented and relaxed. He said that his crew, Vasily and Sasha, also wished me a happy birthday. Clearly they were all getting on very well. Mary listened and joined in on the extension phone, and NASA had thoughtfully tied in Susan in her London office, so the event made our day for each of us. Both Mary and Susan stayed gallantly quiet on the phone, allowing birthday boy his head.

Mike: 'Hello, Dad. Happy birthday. How are you?'

Me: 'Hello. I'm fine. What a treat to have you call. How long have we got?'

Mike: 'Oh, five or six minutes, I think. What have you been doing?'

Me: 'I have had e-mail good wishes from Rhonda and the children, and some nice cards.'

Mike: 'Vassy and Sasha want to wish you happy birthday too.'

Me: 'I'm overwhelmed. Please tell them that we admire them so much for all the work they're doing to maintain Mir, and we know that you will all look after each other well.'

Mike: 'Yes, they are overworked, and I'm trying to find ways to help them.'

Me: 'Mary took me out to dinner for a birthday treat last Saturday, to a high-class restaurant called Stocks, opposite the old pillory in a nearby village. And on Thursday I dined at Selwyn with Professor Owen Chadwick [Master of the college during Christopher's time]. And I will dine at St Catharine's this week and tell them all about you.'

We chattered on like this until our time was up. He sounded fresh, relaxed and happy. His voice had come from space as if he was in the next room. Mary, Susan and I re-established contact afterwards so that we could revel together in our orbital conversation. We all agreed that he was truly concerned about trying to reduce his colleagues' demanding time lines.

This experience tended to make us slightly blasé over Michael being in space, and this was further encouraged a few days later by another unexpected psychological balance performance, beginning again with the majestic telephone introduction, 'Good morning, this is Houston.' I returned the greeting, this time perhaps a bit more briskly, and Kelly's voice politely followed, saying that NASA would be pleased to arrange for Michael to telephone me with, unbelievably, Father's Day good wishes. Now I knew that Michael had been working in America for some years, and was indeed a father twice over himself, but this occasion was to be a first for this father, from any source. I gracefully accepted, already catching the whiff of power felt by somebody only getting his due. Again we were patched in in three

....

ways and we had another, this time more practised, family forum, again with father entitled to priority.

Later in the month, I received a call from Michael's Cambridge college, Queens', from the President, Lord Eatwell, who asked if I could forward a message via our e-mail to Mir. He said that at a recent meeting of the governing body discussing their forthcoming reunion dinner, it had been unanimously decided to send a good wishes message to Michael. Of course, I agreed to do this with pleasure. The president added that I might know that he was married to a Russian lady. When he had proposed to the governing body that Michael be sent a message, he had brought the house down by saying that he hoped Michael was enjoying sleeping with the Russians as much as he was. The exchange of messages follows.

Dear Michael,

Greetings and very best wishes from the President and Fellows of Queens' College. Your College is thinking of you, and hoping you are enjoying life with the Russians. We do hope that next time you make a long-distance trip it will be to Queens', and that you come to stay in the Lodge. Saturday, 21 June is the date for the annual reunion dinner, and I know that members of the College would be delighted to receive a message from Mir.

Very best wishes, John Eatwell, President

Michael was very pleased to be so honoured and replied:

20 June 1997, Space Station Mir
Dear Fellow Queens' Alumni,

I received this morning news of the imminent reunion banquet to be held at the College this 21 June, and good wishes from the President of the College, in a letter read up to me by our people at the Russian control centre in Moscow. At the moment I heard those words I was struggling to make what substitutes for a cup of tea in space. It involves placing a teabag in a flexible mylar packet with a straw and an orifice to inject hot water. One of a number of things I miss here during my five-month stay is milk in my tea.

....

Here on Mir, my Russian crewmates Vasily Tsibliyev and Sasha Lazutkin and I spend our days in a state of constant unpacking and packing, trying to execute the day's experiments, and in the case of the Russians, necessary repairs to the station's life-support systems. Although the station is quite massive for the three of us, its liveable volume is substantially reduced by the presence of ten years of mostly no longer used, outdated experiment and system hardware. So it's like being in a garage full of old junk, and the thing you need to use today is somewhere at the very back of the garage.

Unlike a garage, however, the view from the windows into space or towards the earth is astounding. I never tire of spending half an orbit, after each exercise period, cooling off and admiring either the constellations and the Milky Way or the incredible vistas of the earth. England, even Cambridge, we see occasionally, when not covered by cloud. It goes by underneath us in a matter of a minute or so.

I have spent many hours discussing all kinds of topics with Vasily and Sasha, and one which truly interested them was my recounting of life and study at Queens' College. I think of the students, supervisors and dons with great appreciation, and would like to convey very best wishes to all members of Queens', from my crew Sirius, as we are known by our call sign.

Michael Foale, 1978 [his graduation year]

As mentioned before, Michael had already anticipated occasional difficulties with TSUP in getting his personal mail down to earth and up to him. From his childhood he had had an interest in those worldwide international enthusiasts known as 'radio hams', whose pleasure it is to find and talk to each other on the internationally agreed frequency bands available to them. Originally they were part of the so-called short-wave network, which, under the right conditions, gave clear voice communication over vast distances due to the properties of short waves, bouncing the signals from the surface of the earth to the top of the atmosphere and back, around the world. But since the advent of satellites in orbit, radio hams increasingly use very high or ultra-high frequencies, whose properties are signals of great clarity along, as it

....

were, an uninterrupted line-of-sight distance. By using the transmission relay system of a convenient satellite, the signals can be sent and received beyond the earth's horizon. Michael had wasted no time in establishing contact with some of these strategically placed enthusiasts, who could allow him access to the world's telephone system, or, at the very least, to receive e-mail or voice messages for their onward transmission.

Michael very much valued his excellent relations with these radio enthusiasts, who were delighted to be contacted by Mir. This relationship with the 'hams' was to have unexpected significance in later emergencies, as the communication used so little Mir power. He talked to Dr David Larsen in California, Miles Mann in Massachusetts, Dr Graham Tilbury in South Africa and others in Dublin and in Harrogate. One enthusiast in Holland concentrated on listening to the open frequencies of Mir's official communications when he could tune in at the time of the station's overhead pass, and was thus often aware of events before the world's media had picked them up from Ground Control at Korolyov.

It was against this background that, on 22 June, I found the following e-mail message waiting for me.

Hello, my name is Dr Dave Larsen,
I send messages to Mike every day – he sent this message to me and asked that I send this to you – you can do a reply to my message and I will upload it – my last pass today is at nine pm California time.

Dear Dave,
Could you send this e-mail to my parents at their Compuserve number. In case they need to send timely message. The TSUP went down for a week! I warned them.
Mike, KB5UAC

We had had some difficulty in getting the Queens' College messages up within the necessary time scale, and I had mentioned this to Michael during the Father's Day phone call. He responded with the following illuminating message.

Monday, 23 June 1997

Dear Mum, Dad and Susan,

Sorry you had such a frustrating time trying to send the letter from Queens', which under normal circumstances would have been timely. When a mail server, such as the one all the NASA people use at the control centre in Moscow, goes down, all mail sent to it is returned as undelivered. I hope you did not fret that you yourselves, or Compuserve (our e-mail server), were doing something incorrectly.

Personally, I find these hiatuses in e-mail communication the most bothering and frustrating aspect of this long-duration flight. What is happening is that NASA has installed high-technology systems that normally work fine in a Western industrial environment, but in Moscow, at the control centre, where they [NASA] have no control of the environment in which the equipment and wires are located, the fine thread of high-tech comm can be brought crashing down with a simple hammer blow of an unknowing workman, or similar. I think I can name six events in the last year when this has happened. Once, the server in Houston, JSC [Johnson Space Center], was simply removed, said to have been stolen!

The lesson from all this, which I have tried with little success to explain to the data service people at NASA, is to have back-up means of comm, which use the existing Russian infrastructure, like Compuserve over the local phone. It too goes down regularly, but an arsenal of tricks provides much more reliability.

Actually, as you may have guessed, I have found other ways to communicate, using in particular radio ham contacts to send e-mails to Rhonda. We have been using this method for the last week, during the hiatus, exchanging notes every day. However, the system is completely open to other hams reading our messages (by law, ciphers are not allowed), so it lacks the better privacy of sending via Terry [his monitoring physician in Moscow]. Also, it is even more limited in the volume of text that can be sent. My ham contact, Dave Larsen at Berkeley, has a good antenna and talks to me, mostly by e-mail, every day. The passes last three to ten minutes, about six times in twenty-four hours. But he has a life on earth too, and can't be waiting up for me all the time. I am also cultivating a contact in South Africa, Graham Tilbury in Durban, who is working with me to automate his sending and receiving of text messages from Mir by ham radio. Graham was very excited when I gave him a report of the southern aurora australis over Antarctica, as he is a physicist at the university there, and passed the info to their base in Antarctica.

I will have Dave Larsen, my main contact, send you his e-mail address, so in the event that another hiatus develops in Moscow, you can send a short note through him. As well as e-mail, Rhonda and I have spent four days last week talking on the ham radio, with the ham shack at JSC. There has always been a party of people there to join in, with Russians too, so Rhonda and I only exchange a sentence or two. But Ian and Jenna got to talk a little, and then the rest of the visitors had a go. Bob Cabana, my boss, talked, Ken Bowersox twice, Kevin Chilton, Ellen Baker and other good friends. It's like dropping in on a party, for ten minutes only. Rhonda and the kids will soon be in Kentucky to visit her parents, and very happy to go, it seems. Ian has some additional Thomas and Clarabel trains for his collection, and Jenna has a rubber snake she loves. I got to hear both children talk yesterday, via TSUP, and Ian tried to tell me about his trains.

I received two letters from Dad, and a paragraph from Mum since I last wrote. I am very glad Dad enjoyed the phone calls. It was fun to do them.

(Very interesting news about Bill Gates. Is it a Microsoft initiative, or a private one of Bill Gates's? What is it aimed towards?)

Next week we undock the Progress, and receive a new one on 29 June. So we will be busy. My plants are flowering, and I am being a busy bee. Some are producing seed pods.

Take care.

Love, Mike

Michael had now been on Mir for six weeks. It was a halcyon, almost pastoral period. We should take a brief look at how a typical day on Mir went for him during this time. I do not think he had been aware before just how completely Russian Ground Control dominated every minute of life on the station, at least the lives of the Russian cosmonauts. Towards the end of each day Ground Control would tell the commander what was expected, in detail, from the crew for the following day. The process was called 'time-lining', and was supposed to account for everything, including personal hygiene, meals, exercise, work, recreation (if any) and sleep. Nothing so precise works very easily where most Western human beings are concerned, and Michael made it clear at the outset that he was not going to drive himself into the ground voluntarily for anybody – unless he was directly ordered to. He spoke with the confidence and experience of an enthusiastic three-mission astronaut. He knew he was energetic, that he would be unlikely to let anybody down, but 'Do not hassle me, thank you' was his watchword.

His firm attitude was not something Russian Ground Control were used to in the Mir environment, but as he was a NASA astronaut, they were circumspect in trying to influence him except, if they found it necessary, through lengthy discussions with NASA. There were always NASA representatives at Ground Control who were available to talk directly, albeit openly, to Michael for ten minutes every day, which was scientifically important because all of Michael's experiments were American in origin. So the daily time line sent up by Ground Control was somewhat tentative for Michael, but utterly rigorous for the Russians.

It is worth taking a closer look at this situation, because subsequent emergencies drove astronaut and cosmonaut together away from time lines in order to survive, a factor eventually admitted, even encouraged at a later stage by Ground Control. But for now, while Ground Control had no whip of influence over Michael, they wielded a heavy hammer over the cosmonauts – the threat of pay withdrawal. Under the communist regime, there had been no need for threats of this kind: if a cosmonaut disgraced himself in space, he would be consigned to professional oblivion one way or another, every alternative unpleasant. But in their democratic new world, the authorities (i.e. Energiya) contracted with the cosmonauts personally on each flight and paid them a single agreed amount, after a successful mission, which could be reduced by fines for each and every failure of achievement. It is quite different from the NASA system of salaried, career astronauts, and could become a problem if there are in future more complex mixes of Russian and Western crews on the International Space Station.

....

On a typical working day Michael would be awakened by the alarm set by the commander, Vasily, for eight am Moscow time, which was relayed to Michael in his sleeping position in Spektr. Vasily slept in an alcove with a window on the wall of the Base Block. Sasha was supposed to sleep in another alcove opposite, but such was the success of the ceiling/wall/floor configuration on Sasha's psychology he was unable to sleep 'vertically' on the wall, so instead he anchored his sleeping bag in Kristall, which had no such orientation. Michael found little or no competition for the toilet in the morning as Vasily had already been up for some time at the command post, checking pressure, temperature, power levels and the composition of the atmosphere. Ground Control expected Vasily to communicate with them as soon as possible each morning. Because of the speed of orbit (90 minutes, half light, half dark side, 45 minutes of which was on the wrong side of the world for direct communication with Moscow), and because even when on the good side, little more than half of that time was within Moscow's communication horizon, only about 20 minutes were available for two-way communication per 90-minute orbit. Such a period was referred to as a comm pass. Having risen and got ready for communication, the commander and crew might have to wait an orbit before contact could be made.

Meanwhile they drank fruit juice out of tubes and got hot water from the galley for tea. When Moscow was available, they did not spend much time talking except to discuss any change to the time line or the data uplink plan. The data uplink was the means by which the ground staff actually controlled the functions of the station itself. They then had breakfast together and shaved before the next comm pass 90 minutes later. Moscow now wanted to know how the first 90-minute period of their time line had gone. Usually Vasily and Sasha would be ordered to continue to search for the unlocated, dangerous ethylene glycol leak, which involved taking down panels and checking pipe pressures, so far to no avail. This onerous but necessary chore had dominated the lives of the two cosmonauts since their arrival three months ago.

Michael would get on with his experiments. Each day he went to Spektr and his desk and laptop computer and collected his thoughts. He had two experiments to do each day. It always took time to gather the necessary bits together, so at first he only managed one experiment per day. On repeating

....

the experiments, he found no difficulty in doing two, or even more. He tried to influence Ground Control during the comm passes to show that the time lines were rather inflexible, and that familiarity with his tasks had brought more speed. He felt that he was being honest and up-front about how things were in reality. He found that what he said was apparently accepted with no rancour and no problems.

Then it would be time for the first of his two daily exercise sessions on the treadmill or exercise machine. His almost daily windsurfing session from his home near NASA's headquarters in Texas, had over the years made him very fit and hardy. Indeed, it had been found by NASA's medical staff, before his departure, that he had the densest bone structure of the entire astronaut corps. He needed little reminding to follow this part of his time line. He would change into his exercise underwear and go to the machine in Kristall or the Base Block, pitting his muscular movements against the springs in lieu of weight. After forty-five minutes, he would get water from the galley and retire to clean up, and then go to Kristall to cool down under his valuable air jet, and watch the earth roll by. Thirty more minutes, and he would go back to Spektr to dress.

It was now time for lunch, usually lasting about half an hour and often taken during a comm pass. He noticed that it was Sasha who displayed most of the social graces and would remind him to join them for a meal, or simply to take a break. Sasha and Vasily were still spending their working time in the Base Block, the evidence of the untraced ethylene glycol leak being strongest there. Michael could not always respond to these calls if he was in the middle of a tricky experiment, but he did his best to be there. Then it was back to work.

At seven pm he began his second daily exercise session on the other machine, as designated in his time line, followed again by cooling down, cleaning up, watching the earth and listening to music. Usually he returned to his experiments until about ten pm, when the crew got together for their last meal of the day. This would be finished by about ten-thirty pm when their final task was to print out all the messages received on the computer relevant to the following day. These included a NASA portion for Michael, which now simply listed priorities that were for him to decide on. If anything needed the help of another person, Sasha would be time-lined for it.

....

Michael had been a little concerned in his first weeks to find that there was no formal procedure for handling the daily arrival of the communication packet. Such a packet would not just have instructions for the next day's time line but also his personal mail from family and friends. His own knowledge of how computerized messages work was very wide, and he found himself getting involved with the reception and transmission of communications quite early on in his stay, sorting out their subject matter and priority. His commander and crew seemed not to object, sensing his equal or superior knowledge.

At 11 pm all windows would be 'closed' (by operating external shutters) so that the regular orbit periods of daylight would not disturb their 'night's' slumber. The internal lights, always on for their work period, would be switched off. Vasily would set the wake-up alarm for the next work morning.

Michael was surprised at his commander Vasily's remoteness from him. Michael is used to the Anglo-American style of command, where the commander tries to establish a rapport with his unit, to foster knowledge and trust. Vasily made no such attempt, although he was pleasant enough. There were a number of possible reasons why, beyond Vasily's natural reserve. There was Michael's NASA position, with the US paying good hard currency for his presence on Mir. Vasily's experience of Michael's immediate predecessor was, by all reports, that he had kept very much to himself. And there was the overwhelming thought in Vasily's mind that he, he and Sasha, had to get everything right or lose substantial sums of money – sums which they and their families were probably already counting on.

One day Vasily surprised Michael by actually asking him how his experiments were going. Michael was very glad to be asked, and told Vasily how he had organized the tasks from his time line into high priority and low priority, and then planned his work contours around these, as he thought fit. His work and achievement levels were now fairly predictable for him, and he told Vasily so. Vasily was not entirely happy with this mild show of independence, and would have preferred Michael to stick to the letter of the time line, even though it might be illogical and possibly counter-productive. Michael could see that if Vasily was typical of the style of Russian colonel commanders, they were primarily executives, proudly carrying out implicitly the orders they had been given from above. They expected their superiors to show imagination and to give sound further orders in a changing situation. Their superiors expected nothing less than total obedience, and clearly seemed to get it. It was gloomily reminiscent of the Western Front trench mentality of generals and their staffs during the First World War, and the tragically loyal, fatal obedience of company-level officers on all sides, for so many years and so many battles and bringing so many deaths. Trench warfare left little room for initiative, except the willingness to die *pro patria*.

Every ninety minutes during the working day another comm pass was possible, and communication was mandatory. Apart from his once-a-day talk with the NASA representatives, there was no apparent need for Michael to be present at the command post. He sensed, however, that Vasily was actually encouraging him to be present in case a fast ball came up concerning 'the foreigner', and, above all, Vasily wanted to avoid being caught napping. So every one and a half hours Michael attended the comm passes, meticulously watching Vasily, and he felt that gradually Vasily became more comfortable with his presence and grateful for it. Michael too began to enjoy these periods. He was not overly busy with his experiments and he retained an enquiring mind, and his Russian, both spoken and understood, was adequate enough for him to know in detail what was going on. It also allowed him to see Vasily and Sasha in action with Ground Control, separately and together, and he found himself getting to know them. While listening in, he was tickled to find that on some of Mir's technical systems matters he knew as much, and once or twice more, than his colleagues. He had after all passed his Star City training, all in Russian, with very high marks.

At weekends, in theory, there was relaxation time. For Michael there was a half-day of science, although of course he still had to monitor his experiments, particularly in the Greenhouse. He was supposed to have time off for his letters (e-mail) to family on earth, but he usually found himself at work until nine pm. He noticed with concern that Sunday was the only time that Vasily spared himself time to exercise, still spending most of his working hours removing panel after panel, tracking the elusive ethylene glycol leak. Lack of regular exercise was unwise, because of its deleterious effect on his morale, or spirit. He was, perhaps, anxious by nature, but by any standards he had already been through a hard and unnerving series of events. But

....

after his exercise on Sundays, Vasily could be seen to relax.

After dinner, he was willingly persuaded to accompany Sasha and Michael to Spektr's 'duck's bill' to watch a miniature film with Michael's basic translation. Although Vasily clearly enjoyed most films, he occasionally fell asleep halfway through.

Before retiring, Sasha liked a social drink of tea or other beverage. Friends or relatives would occasionally send them luxury items as gifts on the Progress supply vessels (Michael's favourites were chocolate and good British tea bags). Gifts were often heavily disguised to avoid tempting potential pilferers among the Progress packing staff. Gift contents were usually shared. Before the film began, Sasha would clear a point of English language with Michael that might have been bothering him. On one occasion he was quite firmly interrupted by Vasily who said, 'Misha, what was it really like to be a student at Cambridge for six years? And how did you feel being in such a small and privileged society? In fact, how did you get there at all? Was it your family's influence and money, and did you think that it was fair?'

Michael realized that the question was sincere and well meant, and that for Vassy's generation of Russians, all education would have been according to strict communist principles and interpretation. So he answered slowly and carefully.

'Vassy, you are right that, having got to Queens' College, Cambridge, I was indeed privileged. But my father or money had nothing to do with my selection for the university. It was due entirely to my own performance at school, and then at the Cambridge interviews. And we certainly did not have any spare money with which to bribe the system, even if they would have accepted it.' Michael was rather uncomfortable about this part, knowing of the high fees charged to foreign students, but did not want to complicate matters.

'But how was it that you went to a school good enough to bring out, on time, all the talents that earned you a place at Cambridge? Surely your family had something to do with that?' Vassy had heard of the English public school system but did not understand its high fees, privileges and links with the older universities.

'A good question, Vassy. There is, I suppose, a privilege in attending these schools at all, and for most, it does depend on parental money. But in

....

my case I had to board at school because of my father's RAF job. Our government recognized the difficulties for children in this position, and offered assistance to parents for half of the fees.'

Vasily was for the time satisfied with this answer, but Michael knew that, whichever way you looked at it, his background had been a privileged one, even the parental wisdom of paying a share of the cost of a splendid education. He saved his answers on what it was actually like at Cambridge for another night. He would have to think through how he would present the scenario in a way his friends would understand.

Michael was settling comfortably into the Mir routine, but still felt left out of general station matters concerning upkeep, and the search for the leak, and felt he ought to be of more help. German and French guest astronauts attached during cosmonaut crew handovers had felt the same frustration. After detailed courses on the Mir systems, they were never to be time-lined for tasks on them. There are, from the Russian point of view, good reasons for this, apart from a national habit of secrecy and exclusion. Energiya is in full control; it designs and builds all the hardware, trains both pilots and engineers, and runs Ground Control itself. They are aware of how difficult their language is for foreigners, who may be less than dedicated to the study of it. But in any case, their advisory engineers at Ground Control do not always match their technical strengths with good voice communication skills, and are therefore more effective dealing directly with their own people. But the reluctance to include foreigners in the running of Mir is probably also due to the fact that they have no pay 'hammer' influence over them, as they have over their own people.

The situation, in which Vasily and Sasha were so preoccupied with repairs and station maintenance that other important items were being neglected, eventually pushed Michael to try to do something about it. Apart from anything else, he had grown to like them. The Elektron oxygen generating system needed checking and turning on and off at regular intervals, and other attentions. It involved only simple commands, which Michael fully understood, and he therefore offered theories when something went wrong. This surprised both Vasily and Sasha who asked, 'How did you know that?'

They even suggested, humorously, that he must be a member of the CIA – echoes of the Cold War are not felt exclusively by the Americans.

....

Michael insisted that he was competent and willing to take over system work, and to help with the regular cleaning and maintenance tasks. His persistence led to an argument on the subject between Vasily and Sasha. Sasha, less indoctrinated with Vasily's command principles, said, 'Look, we have got to let him do it. I don't have any time for it, you certainly don't have any time for it.' Vasily's response was to worry openly about Ground Control's reaction.

'What will they do to us, how will they react if they know we are letting Michael do it?'

Michael found it extraordinary but also rewarding to have them argue openly in front of him like that. They could have argued privately – he had previously left them alone to do that – but this time he had not had the chance. The two cosmonauts had often discussed their contracts together, and at such times Michael had felt it was right for him to retire to another part of the station.

Soon after the day of the open discussion between Vasily and Sasha, Michael took his chance to influence Ground Control directly concerning their time lines. Vasily had complained that the amount of maintenance work they had been doing had meant that they had not had a free weekend in three months. The maintenance work continued to include cleaning up water condensate and ethylene glycol residues thought still to remain in Kvant, a task that seemed endless and now urgently needed doing just before they were time-lined to try a manual docking with a Progress vessel. When would they ever have time to do it? Michael, who was present as usual during a comm pass, said, in Russian, deliberately loudly, 'Look, I aim to spend Sunday doing the clean-up. I said that I am going to do the clean-up on Sundays.'

There was a long pause for a comm pass. The Ground Control personnel then laughed and said, 'OK, you do it.' There was no real agreement, just laughter.

The NASA liaison controller, Keith Zimmerman, came up on a comm pass half a day later and said, 'Mike, we hear that you have offered to clean up the ethylene glycol spills, is that right?'

Michael firmly replied, 'Yes, it is.' So neither Russian Ground Control nor NASA were left in any doubt that he was willing to do 'Russian' work.

Michael told me later that he had been driven to interfere as a

....

'foreigner' because every time in the past when he had offered to help, Sasha had said softly, 'No, you are here for research, not Russian work.' Michael felt that Sasha's attitude was also gently patronizing: 'We are Russians and can do heavy work; you are a soft American poodle and are not of the same kind.'

This thought was like a red rag to a bull for Michael, and had provoked his loud intervention. Perhaps Sasha had more wisdom than he would admit, because as a result of this incident, Vasily immediately began trusting Michael to do general station work, which helped all of them. The ground staff, too, after a month's delay, came round to time-lining him formally for Russian station tasks when one of the Russian crew could be time-lined with him. He felt he had made distinct progress, a first in the development of Mir international relations.

Another event that happened every normal day was data uplink. This was an interaction between Ground Control and the station which could be done independently of the crew. Each comm pass of the station over Russian territory allowed the ground a glimpse, through telemetry, of the station's state of health – temperature, attitude, pressure, and so on – and as a result Ground Control would command appropriate changes to be made, through the data link, on a later pass. Unlike an aircraft or even an American shuttle, Mir is not a ship responding appropriately to the commands of the captain through his crew. It is a complex system in orbit which can respond to the controlling of ground staff as if it were unmanned, as indeed it was at first. In this respect, it is not unlike much smaller robotic systems which have been sent to investigate distant planets. So each day, after considering the station's automatic telemetric transmission in response to a ground interrogation signal, Ground Control would transmit coded computer instructions to be received by the crew, read back to the ground for correctness, then entered as a command to the on-board computer.

Events were soon to prove that it was as well that the Russian crew members and Ground Control had already accepted Michael as a fully capable executive, if only reluctantly. Two days after Michael's last letter to us, everything changed. His 'honeymoon' period on Mir was over, and with a vengeance. He was to discover within himself new strengths previously unexercised, along with an unexpected sense of personal responsibility both for the station and its crew.

....

Collision

Back on earth, I had been looking forward to 25 June for a long time. From eleven o'clock that morning I was to be in Wolverton, Milton Keynes, attending a second grammar-school class reunion, which I had arranged. Our first reunion in 1996, 'fifty years on' since we took our School Certificates at age sixteen in 1946, had been a roaring success, and I had been unashamedly proud of how it had gone. Now, following popular request, we were to have a second go.

The hall where we were assembling had been part of an old Church Institute, used by the grammar school in our time for some overspill in classes, following the influx of evacuees from London and the wartime bombing. I had driven over from Cambridge and arrived outside the building, before parking, to deliver wine and other goodies. The traffic had been heavy from Cambridge, and it was now a little past eleven. I was met by the first arrivals.

We walked to the hall and up the stairs to our assembly room, where morning coffee, fruit juice and wines, and later our buffet lunch, were laid out. About forty of us were expected, and we had the room to ourselves until four pm, to allow people to arrive and depart in their own time. A steady number were arriving.

Suddenly I saw Aileen Button appear in the doorway, one of my favourite teachers at school, perhaps because she was a most attractive young woman. Still slender, she was as elegant as she had always been. Most of our excellent teachers have long since passed on, but Aileen's arrival was followed by John Thomas, ninety-three, our French teacher, and Anton Cadman, eighty-seven, who taught us mathematics. We pupils had all been in the school during the earlier years of their careers, and perhaps that is why they remembered us so well. Wine was sipped, lunch plates picked up, and all of us basked in the warm glow of friendship, memories and wonder.

As lunch was completed, I called for silence to ask the assembly if they wanted this second occasion to become a regular event, to be held, say, every three years. Some looked appraisingly at each other, and then seemed doubtful. So I asked if they wanted it annually. To a resounding *yes*, I went on to finish my own lunch, happy, uplifted, almost euphoric in the atmosphere of so much goodwill. Then I found myself being approached by a stranger. I searched his face, which I noticed wore a very serious expression. I found that I didn't recognize the man.

He said, 'Air Commodore Foale?' I nodded. 'Have you heard about the collision with Mir?'

Each word struck deeply into my head and repeated themselves like echoes.

'No,' I said, conscious of my own control, 'have the crew been hurt?'

'There are no reports of injuries. Mir is still in orbit. I am from the BBC. The accident took place about three hours ago. Would you, as one of the crew's relatives, agree to an interview?'

Here he indicated a microphone and tape recorder.

I said yes, but I wanted to read whatever news transcript he had from the wire services (the news agencies) first. He handed me two crumpled pages from an inside pocket. Whatever he had told me, my professional experience of the finality and fatality of aerial collisions clouded my vision as I read.

The Mir crew had been ordered by TSUP to undock the current Progress supply vessel and position it some distance away above them. They were then to redock it with Mir using a new manual method. Something had gone very wrong as the Progress was brought close to the station again, and control of it had been lost. The Progress had collided with Mir at the Spektr

....

module (Michael's living quarters), causing damage and loss of air pressure. The crew had managed to isolate the leaking module, thus overcoming the danger of immediate pressure collapse throughout the rest of the station and their resultant deaths. There were no injuries, but the station was critically short of power. There were no plans to evacuate the station at this stage.

After a short interview, conducted in a corner of the reunion room but unnoticed by my colleagues, I rejoined my friends and told a few what had happened, noticing that I had some difficulty with my throat, which I think I managed to overcome.

My wife Mary and I are both basically unflappable, to use an old RAF term. Many years of life on RAF airfields with occasional danger and disasters, not to mention watching in more recent years Michael's four spectacular shuttle launches, have taught us not to waste time or energy wringing our hands and worrying before the event. Sufficient unto the day, as they say. Perhaps it was this ingrained habit that allowed us both to talk to the media in the weeks that followed in a measured, controlled way. Indeed, I usually found it easier to talk to the media than to sympathetic friends, whose real concern could trigger my emotions. For the same reason, Mary and I were always careful not to allow our individual concerns and worries to spill over to the other.

I had kept the BBC radio reporter's wire transcript and quickly reread it. A collision with anything as fragile and vulnerable as a pressurized hull is very dangerous, and usually results in a catastrophic failure, whether of a jumbo jet full of passengers or a submarine. How much more likely that disaster would follow an impact such as the one Mir had apparently suffered. There was no information on this, only that the crew 'were out of immediate danger'. All the euphoria of the reunion had now vanished as if it had never been. I left the room to telephone Mary at home in Cambridge and, maybe, share some information.

Our phone was busy, and I remembered that the BBC correspondent had said that it was Mary who had told him where I was, hence his quick arrival in Wolverton. Mary was meanwhile undoubtedly being besieged by the press. I finally got through to her and she said that yes, she was besieged, knew no more than I did, and what time would I be home? I said I was leaving right away. The reunion had come to an end anyway, and I was able to say fond but hurried farewells to many on the way to my car. Here I was intercepted again by the BBC, this time with a TV camera. I agreed to be interviewed for a few minutes, to show personal optimism for Michael and his colleagues, then began the drive home. It was beginning to rain. I drove automatically towards Bedford then Cambridge through the June green fields, my thoughts following unbidden lines of their own.

The loss of a child often does two opposite things to parents. It makes them more protective and concerned for the remaining children but, oddly, makes them more fatalistic towards further loss. The shock and devastation of the first loss, so absolutely irrevocable, has to be dulled and salved, comforted and healed. The regular onsets of destructive pain and grief do gradually get less frequent, but the memory of events never fades. The process does not make the grieving hard or callous. It simply convinces one, for ever, of the futility of anything but acceptance.

When Christopher was killed and Catherine received fatal injuries on 10 July 1979, at about four-thirty pm, UK time, in Yugoslavia, I was just leaving my London rooms in Victoria Street, kept handy for my job at the Ministry of Defence in Whitehall. Also at four-thirty pm, as I was leaving the building, I experienced a psychic shock that stopped me in my tracks, and I imagined Michael and his companions driving south to Greece. I said a brief, silent prayer for their safety. That night, for some reason, I drank too much beer, not in itself an unknown occurrence, and I felt a bit fragile the next day leaving London on the train to Huntingdon for the village of Wyton which was where we then lived. Mary was still at her library job at the University in Cambridge when I got home. The phone was ringing.

It was Catherine's mother in London. Had I heard of the accident? I had not. Catherine was critical. Michael, she thought, was all right. Christopher? She couldn't say, but Catherine was *critical*. I said I would call the Foreign and Commonwealth Office for information. I got a well-spoken young lady, after a number of blind alleys, who said that, yes, there had been an accident, and yes, injuries, but she could tell me no more. I pressed her but she had been briefed, I suppose, to leave it to a police call at the home with what is known as an 'agony' message. I seemed to know the worst already and said, 'Please, is Christopher dead?'

She said, 'Yes,' and burst into tears on the phone. I comforted her and

....

apologized for pressing her so hard. There was a knock at the door almost immediately. Two large policemen were there, with a piece of paper in hand. I looked at them.

I said, 'It's all right, I know.'

They said, 'Are you alone? And are you sure you're all right?'

I said, 'Yes, thank you.'

When I tried to call Mary, I found she had already left work to drive home, and I told her the devastating news on the doorstep when she arrived. We telephoned King's School in Canterbury, to tell Susan. I then spent hours on the phone booking flights to Yugoslavia for the next day for all three of us, having arranged financing from my bank as only first-class seats were available at such short notice. Catherine died a few days later, never regaining consciousness. Michael was discharged from hospital. Enveloped by loss and grief, we flew back to England for Christopher's funeral at our village church and burial in the nearby graveyard, alongside a spot occupied by RAF crash casualties, all young men.

The journey, from Wolverton back to Cambridge, took a little over an hour, but I hardly noticed it, so much were my thoughts occupied by the foregoing memories. Were we going to lose another?

No, said an inner voice, you are not. I felt better, and when I got home soon after, my mood infected Mary.

Mary had heard the news about Mir and Michael just as she got home from a morning t'ai chi session, finding media representatives on our doorstep. She had immediately telephoned Susan to warn her of what she might hear on the news. Susan later said that she was both impressed and worried by her mother's kindness and calmness. Their conversation was interrupted by the arrival of the press at the door. She had been busy with the media ever since, without knowing what exactly had happened. When I arrived home, it was nearly five pm and an Anglia TV team were already in place to have my comments, if I would please. I agreed, which meant that interested friends saw me on the five-forty news on ITV in Cambridge and at six pm on the BBC TV news in Wolverton. The wanders of instant transference. But we badly wanted an update beyond the BBC man's initial report.

On Mir itself, Wednesday, 25 June, had begun like any other day. The station was in normal orbit, stable, with a flavour of permanence to its path

....

around the earth. However, this day had been planned to be different because Ground Control at Korolyov had earlier sent instructions to Commander Tsibliyev that he was to practise a *manual* docking with the old Progress supply vessel (M34). This vessel had been laden with waste and would soon be sent to its destruction over the Pacific, to be succeeded later by the arrival of a fresh supply vessel. It had been undocked ready for this exercise the previous day from its normal long-term docking port on the Base Block extension, Kvant. The purpose of this practice was to introduce an economy. The automatic docking system (KURS) normally used was expensive and to an extent wasteful, because the part of it installed on the Progress had to be expendable; it was destroyed along with the vessel. The elements of KURS were manufactured in the newly independent state of Ukraine, a country as badly strapped for cash as Russia, and they wanted to raise prices. The Russians decided they should try to use a cheaper system.

A manual docking, by definition, would dispense with this sophis-ticated automated sensor control in bringing the Progress to its dock. In its place, a relatively inexpensive TV camera on the docking mechanism of the Progress, pointing at Mir (and, eventually, hopefully at the Kvant docking port), would display images of Mir on-screen for the commander in the Base Block operation area on Mir. He would see an image like the view he would expect to see if he were actually in a pilot's seat on the Progress, looking towards Mir. He would then assess what thruster power and direction would be necessary to bring the vessel safely in. He would apply this assessment using a system of levers to signal manually to the Progress thrusters. In theory, he could steer and brake the Progress and bring it all the way towards Mir, slowing it down as it approached its docking position. Such a procedure had been shown to be possible, and had also been demonstrated in the simulator at Star City, but it had not been done recently nor under all possible positions of the Progress relative to the station.

A few months earlier, before Michael's arrival, a previous attempt at this exercise had been abandoned by Tsibliyev, when he found that he was not receiving a clear television image of the view of Mir from the camera mounted on the approaching Progress. In terms of the theoretical pilot on Progress, it was as if he had gone blind. He had therefore immediately fired the remotely controlled deflector thrusters on the Progress, sending the

....

vehicle well clear of Mir to avoid what he felt from his last view had been a too fast and thus dangerous approach.

Tsibliyev spent several days setting up and completing tests of the manual system, known as TORU. He was not happy with having to try an exercise similar to one which had previously gone wrong. It had been a frequent subject for conversation during the past few weeks.

'I tell you, Sasha, you just do not know the problems faced by a pilot in this procedure.' Sasha, as an Energiya employee, was naturally prone to support his employers.

'They would not ask you to practise this if they thought it could go badly wrong. They will have thought everything through and matched it with your known ability as a fighter pilot.' Sasha felt that his commander's confidence needed boosting, and did not hesitate to try. But Tsibliyev only shook his head slowly.

'It will be dangerous,' he said flatly, and the worry showed on his face.

Michael may have had a view, but he felt that the procedure must have been fully worked out by Ground Control. Although the operation was a purely Russian affair, he was a little surprised that he had not had a full briefing. It was clearly to be a significant event, but this omission was typical of many of his Russian dealings. You were told what you needed to know, as judged by somebody else, and not much more. It was not malicious or neglectful, just a Russian habit.

On the Wednesday, as midday approached, Mir was in an inertial attitude, gently monitored by its gyrodynes. Tsibliyev methodically set up the manual docking equipment and the TV viewing screen on which he would see Mir as seen from Progress. He made himself comfortable before it. A video camera was set up behind him to record the viewing screen's images throughout the exercise. As the camera on Progress would not give precise ranges, he had decided to equip Michael with a laser range-finder to be at the Kvant window when the Progress came closer to the docking port. He placed Sasha Lazutkin similarly to observe from a window nearer to him in the Base Block. Unfortunately, both windows had only very limited cover of the sky, and neither observer could see the Progress in formation with them at the start of the practice. Tsibliyev concentrated his whole attention on the TV screen. The Progress camera was working correctly, at present on a wide

....

field of view. Beyond the image of Mir lay the great shape of the earth, and the speckled blue and white of far-distant clouds and seas.

No advice had been available as to the best start and finish positions of the Mir and Progress duo relative to the earth. Hindsight has shown that the scenario chosen for the exercise was as bad and difficult as it could be, with the image of Mir received by the Progress liable to be confused with those of earth's features, moving slowly in the background.

Tsibliyev called to check that Sasha and Michael were in position at their windows. Both replied in turn that they could see nothing as yet.

At the moment when Tsibliyev activated the Progress thrusters to begin the docking exercise, a series of events began that appeared to take all three crew and Ground Control by surprise, although the latter more so because it coincided with Mir being temporarily outside the radio visibility zones of Russian Ground Control relay stations. Hindsight again shows that the surprise of the crew was largely due to the very small angles of view available from the windows, making the Progress unseen by them until it was too late to take a measurement.

The existing night pass turned into a day pass soon after eleven forty-five am. The commander could already see the lights of Mir on his TV screen as seen from the Progress over a kilometre away. He kept the cross-hairs of his Progress docking camera steadily lined up on the centre of the station. He continued to apply control inputs that brought the field of view on to the Kvant docking adapter. For a time the size of Mir on the screen seemed to remain constant, although the distance was steadily decreasing. At last, as Mir began to show signs of increasing in size, Tsibliyev brought in a narrow field of view. The port of Kvant was now visible, but was unaccountably sinking towards the bottom of the screen, allowing the Spektr module to appear in Progress's line of velocity.

When he considered the range to be three hundred metres, he asked Sasha to begin range-finding from the Base Block windows. He began a series of pre-planned braking manoeuvres, as the growing size, and therefore nearness, of Mir on the display called for them. As the station grew to occupy a quarter of the display, it was apparent that Progress's motion was more towards the Node than towards Kvant. He had kept a continuous braking input on Progress from about two hundred and fifty metres.

....

When Tsibliyev called fifty metres, Sasha had still not had an initial sighting. Suddenly Sasha saw something that was clearly very wrong. The Progress supply vehicle had appeared much closer, larger and moving at a higher speed than he had expected, and worse, it was on a direct course to impact with the central Node. Total disaster seemed imminent.

He shouted, 'Michael, go to the Soyuz, *now*! *Vasily, stop!*'

Tsibliyev was desperately working his thruster deflector control handles to avoid what he too now saw would be an immediate, possibly annihilating, collision. Michael, who at that moment was on his way back through the Base Block from Kvant, was stopped by Lazutkin's voice which continued to shout that he should go to the escape capsule immediately, as they were about to be hit.

He rapidly dived into the central Node and across it to the escape craft hatch.

As he got there, there was a loud and deeply disturbing thud.

Michael thought that the station might have lurched violently as the collision took place, but he was floating and was only lightly touching the hatch (the others who had their feet in restrainers had no doubt of its severity). He paused as he felt the sensation in his ears that one feels in a climbing aircraft. But Mir was in space, not in the atmosphere, and in orbit, not climbing. *The station had to be losing air pressure.* His conclusion was underlined by a loud hissing noise. These considerations probably took no longer than one second. As if he needed further confirmation, the pressure warning klaxons began to sound. And within the same moment, Michael knew that the collision had perforated Mir's hull somewhere, allowing air and pressure to escape and that if the escaping air enlarged the hole to bring rapid decompression, he would in the next few seconds feel agony in his ears before loss of consciousness and death.

He looked at the open Soyuz hatch. A large vent hose and power cable led into the Soyuz, part of a system for keeping the craft dry and in shape, but these would now have to be removed if the Soyuz hatch was to be closeable and the vehicle used to escape. He began on the hose and was joined and helped by Sasha. The row of the klaxons made communication difficult, but Sasha conveyed to Michael that he had seen the Progress through his window actually hit the module Spektr. Michael was soon able to report the Soyuz ready for evacuation – it had taken only seconds – and together they dived back into the Node towards the Spektr hatch, which they intended to close in the hope that it would isolate the leak – if they had time.

Both astronauts were immediately busy disconnecting all the power cables which ran from Spektr's interior through the hatch to the rest of the station. Sasha went inside Spektr to find the junction block from which to disconnect the impeding cables. He said he could hear that the loud hissing of escaping air was indeed within Spektr itself, and this made both men work harder and faster. Precious moments were lost trying to find the origin of two cables not plugged like the others into the quick-disconnect box. Speech was still difficult over the noise of the klaxon. The two cables had to go, and there was no recourse but to cut them. Easier said than done. One was quickly cut by Sasha with a knife which he had grabbed from the Base Block table. But as soon as he attacked the second cable, showers of electrical sparks streamed out with every cut. Sasha was very worried, and Michael remembered why. Sasha was understandably frightened of starting a fire, having experienced a bad one three months previously. But pressure was falling and he urged Sasha to continue. Sasha refused, and abruptly disappeared into the darkness of Spektr.

After a long twenty seconds, he returned triumphant with the cable unplugged from its interior junction. At the same time Michael was aware that the dropping of pressure, though continuous, had not noticeably increased in rate, so they still had a chance. Sasha Lazutkin had made it clear that he had actually seen the Progress strike the Spektr module and its solar arrays, so he had known that Spektr had to be one source of the leak. If Spektr could be sealed off, then the remainder of the station might still be safe from further depressurization. With the last cable disconnected, Michael and Sasha reached inside the entrance to Spektr to pick up and then close the interior hatch cover. However, as they pulled it towards them, the pressure difference sucked it back into Spektr, and they could not hold it firmly enough to close and lock it.

They looked around helplessly, until they both saw a spare hatch cover lashed to the Node wall. Working even faster, they got it free and Michael and Sasha offered it towards the now unimpeded hatch opening. As they moved the cover nearer the opening, an invisible force eagerly grabbed

....

it hard from their hands, the air pressure difference working on it. A most gratifying experience, Michael felt, as the cover clunked home and he turned the air seals tight. He looked at Sasha with admiration and gratitude. Sasha had been magnificent.

At the same time, while examining the rate of loss of pressure, Tsibliyev had calculated that at the moment of impact they had had only twenty minutes left before they would *have* to evacuate to Soyuz and abandon ship. Michael and Lazutkin had taken twelve minutes to the point of hatch closure. One source of air leakage had been closed. Their inner sighs of relief were accompanied by a cessation of the drop in pressure, so that they knew there had been only one source. Now they could take stock of the new situation. Tsibliyev had regained contact with Ground Control and kept them dramatically informed of events, in particular pressure level readings. With the pressure stabilized, they were ordered to open a tank of spare oxygen to repressurize the station to an acceptable level (in fact, equivalent to about eight thousand feet above sea level on earth). The new pressure remained stable.

At the moment of collision, Tsibliyev's screen had gone blank, then an image of Mir had reappeared, showing the Base Block moving very slowly out of the camera's field of view. This was an indication that most of the Progress's collision momentum had been absorbed by the station. The impact had delivered a glancing blow to the Spektr module and its arrays, some distance from the station's centre of mass, the central Node. Had the Progress hit the Node itself, it was possible that its momentum would have been of such magnitude as to rupture the station conclusively and the crew would have quickly died. Their satisfaction with having for the present stayed alive was marred by a worrying awareness that all was not well with the station's life blood, electrical power. The necessary disconnection of Spektr's cables had robbed them of forty per cent of total available power generation. The impact had also transmitted a torque (turning) force to the station, which, while absorbing some of the momentum and probably saving their lives, had put the whole structure into a rotating tumble far beyond the station's inbuilt gyrodyne stabilizing influence, thereby taking its usable solar panels out of their steady alignment with the sun. But again there was reason to be thankful. Had the impact been further out on Spektr's extremity, the increased momentum might have caused a torque rupture at the Node junction.

Russian Ground Control had been properly careful to get the facts straight before talking to the world's media. They had been unable to think of any advice or instruction to offer the crew, even if they had been in continuous contact, which, due to the orbit, they were not. The collision took place at 12.09 pm Moscow time, and all staff at Ground Control remained focused on the crew's initiatives in recovering the crippled station before making time for a press release. Apparently the first official reports were made about two hours after the start of the incident. Because of time zone differences, Michael's loved ones in England and the USA received their first intimations of something being wrong at different local times. In England, the wire services picked up the first official report at about one-thirty pm. On Mir, the fight to save the station had been continuous.

Rhonda, Michael's wife, and their two children were staying for a few days with her parents in Kentucky. She was in a time zone six hours ahead of England, so she had been awakened early in the morning, her time, to be told the news. She found herself calm and not deeply worried, although she later realized that she should have been. NASA are extremely good and very careful in looking after the relatives of their astronauts, so Rhonda had been given accurate and timely information and valid assurances that yes, there had been danger, but now the crew's lives, though perhaps uncomfortable and occasionally desperate, were no longer directly threatened. The call was made to her from Moscow by Michael's medical adviser, Dr Terry Taddeo, whom she knew well and trusted. She thus managed to miss the body blow of shock and waves of worry that I had felt at my school reunion, which stayed with me for some hours.

We received an e-mail from Rhonda that evening repeating for our benefit what NASA had told her. The ruptured Spektr had been isolated. Michael was all right but had lost all of his personal belongings. She expected no e-mail from him because he was probably very busy (!). The chief astronaut had just telephoned and big meetings were in progress.

The Mir crew had also been too busy in their urgent survival measures with Spektr's hatch to switch off many non-essential systems, and Tsibliyev had been ordered to stay at his communication post. All batteries were now found to have been drained to dangerously low levels, caused by the

....

fundamental power loss of Spektr's forty per cent share, and poor alignment of the remaining arrays. They now switched off whatever they could that used power, except for vital life-support systems, and addressed the problem of regaining station altitude control. Without the restoration of a stable attitude and the generation of life-giving, life-sustaining solar power, the station would die.

The loss of attitude control had left the station tumbling in a confused fashion around two axes which had mixed moments of inertia, impossible for Ground Control to assess. Ground Control said, 'We can order your station thrusters to begin a counter-motion to your tumbling rotation, but first we will need you to tell us your rate and main plane of rotation. We will need to move quickly to activate the thrusters while you still have enough electrical power to respond to the signal.'

No on-board instrument was capable of carrying out the required measurement and for a moment the crew were nonplussed. Michael found himself rising to the occasion. He improvised an instrument by putting his thumb out at arm's length to the stars and timing the apparent passage of stars that passed it, coming quickly to the conclusion of about one degree per second in the main plane of rotation. He told Ground Control his findings and they acted on them without delay, starting the station's thrusters remotely. Slowly the station's rotation came to a virtual stop, but, by chance and, annoyingly, left its solar panels a long way off the line of sunlight during the day passes. Stabilization had been achieved, but little else. Without a better re-alignment of the station's remaining arrays when the sun was present, it would remain powerless and would eventually become lifeless.

The station was now totally silent, a silence described by Sasha Lazutkin as deafening. They had never experienced Mir without noise, and it affected them in different ways. The way forward was not yet clear. Michael found the new silence exhilarating, and saw the dawns of the day passes full of new beauty and peace. He said, 'Vasily, cheer up, it's not all bad. Without the problem, we wouldn't be here enjoying this unique experience of beauty and peace.'

Vasily would not be moved from his dark depths, which Michael was concerned could lead to inertia if his spirit weakened. They had to think. Vasily simply shook his head and murmured, 'It is a terrible day.'

During the next night pass, the crew managed to twist the Base Block arrays manually from their internal mountings to a better initial angle to greet the sun on the next day pass. Kvant 2's arrays were too far in shadow to allow for a similar treatment. The Base Block arrays now showed themselves able to give just enough power in the daylight, but not enough surplus to sustain battery power during the night passes.

On a normal Moscow-time working 'day' on Mir, the night pass part of each ninety-minute orbit would hardly be noticed by the crew. Power was plentiful and the fully charged batteries would maintain constant light and atmospheric control. Now, during the night passes without power, life was unpleasant. It would have been unwise to sneak a bit of power from the batteries which were already at a low charge and barely being replenished during the day passes. If a battery was used to the point of exhaustion, it would take months of normal charging to restore it. So during night passes, everything had to be switched off. If the toilet was to work, as it had to, those batteries which had received a significant charge in the Base Block had to be manhandled to Kvant 2, whose batteries had received no power.

Night-pass energy conservation had to include the air ventilation system, which kept the air in motion to prevent the build-up of carbon dioxide pockets of expelled air around the crew's faces. Without such ventilation, the crew had a new danger of loss of consciousness, even suffocation, due to local displacement of oxygen. They kept a close eye on each other, fanned their faces with maps and papers to disperse the CO_2 and moved from one module to another. They spent the night passes in total darkness and used flashlights sparingly. They dared not sleep.

During a later day pass, Ground Control requested Vasily to attempt to move the station into a better solar attitude by using the only thrusters he could directly control, those on the docked Soyuz, protruding from its forward position on the Node. It was, after all, at an extremity of the station, and even small amounts of thrust would give a substantial moment of force. It sounded simple enough, but was to need long, arduous hours of experimental work from the crew. Clear, imaginative thinking was needed, while their minds and bodies were beginning to cry out for sleep.

The station had stopped its rotation in a somewhat arbitrary position, and the crew now had to figure out in which direction to nudge it for the

....

arrays to catch the sun better during the day passes. If that could be achieved, they would still need to try to stabilize the new position. It might even be necessary to introduce a spin to the station to stabilize it, like a big gyro (no gyrodynes being available because of lack of power), so that the arrays would stay in sunlight as long as possible throughout the day pass. How to find the sun was not something that Michael knew how to do really well – the computers normally did it using Mir's thermal sensors, which took the earth's surface temperature and provided an earth surface position and time. He was not very happy either about the theory of spin stabilization. Mir was not a regular, symmetrical toyshop top. A spin, induced to keep the arrays in sunlight during a day pass, would almost certainly involve turning the station about more than one axis, or cause an in-built precession because of the non-uniform position and nature of the station's mass. After considerable thought, Michael concluded that the most efficient use of the solar arrays still operable would be first, to nudge the station until the module Spektr was pointing towards the sun. This would be their reference position. And second, to begin a stabilizing spin around the Spektr–Kvant 2 centre line, actually the station's Y axis.

It was difficult to convince the others, particularly Vasily, for whom the theory and calculations were puzzling. Sasha came around to Michael's view first, but even when Vasily agreed, there was still a problem. To move the station's attitude using the Soyuz thrusters, fuel would be used up, which, as commander, he thought they still might need for evacuation and escape. There was indeed spare fuel, but to use it made Vasily very nervous, and he had had a bad day. But only he was trained to 'fly' the Soyuz. Michael needed all his patience and powers of persuasion. There were more complex difficulties. For the station to begin to rotate in the right direction to bring Spektr to face the sun would need an accurately directed push of power, not too much and not too little, to start the station on its slow path. Its gradual rotation towards its celestial goal could only be measured (and therefore modified if necessary) by watching the apparent movement of identifiable stars during a night pass.

But at night, where was the sun? There is no easy north, south, east and west in space, and so Michael had to use his astronomical knowledge to know which stars to turn the station towards to get Spektr to point at the sun

....

during the following day pass. Once the station reached the angle which would permit this, the re-alignment movement had to be stopped, precisely, and held.

Michael understood that to reach this re-alignment would be the most difficult thing of all. To do the rotation would need the stars, but to find the sun would require daylight. Vasily went to the Soyuz in its docked position forward of the Node and prepared to operate the thrusters in accordance with Michael's instructions to rotate the station. He could not see the same parts of the sky on which Michael would base his instructions, and would need to follow him blindly – left, right, up, down. He was not happy.

Just after an orbital sunset, at the beginning of a night pass, Michael noted where the sun had been in relation to the stars he now could identify and decided the direction that Vasily should thrust from Soyuz to begin a required rotation direction. He had no idea, nor did Vasily, how many seconds of thrust power, which he called pulses, would be needed. It was vital that Vasily be constant and accurate in his response, so that if the instruction turned out to be wrong, Michael could ask him to apply a directly opposite equal force. He would say, 'Vasily, I need ten pulses left.'

Vasily would reply, 'No, I am not going to give you ten pulses, we must conserve fuel.'

So Michael would try, 'OK, give me three.' They were not getting near their goal, and he had to make a great effort to control his frustration. In fact, Vasily never applied pulses, only rather brief and reluctant bursts of thrust.

Then Michael discovered another reason why his instructions were apparently never precisely followed by Vasily. It was because of a difference in their orientations. When choosing a window through which to measure the apparent movement of the stars, Michael had to think carefully which way he was facing in relation to the station, and then to imagine Vasily's position in Soyuz in relation to that. Only then could he give a sensible instruction, say, two pulses to Vasily's left and two pulses down. In his imagination he had seen Vasily sitting in the Soyuz lined up with the rest of the station. But in fact it turned out that Vasily was not lined up in the same way, and it was by no means his fault. The Soyuz docked position on the Node happened to put the craft in a forty-five-degree rolled left position, compared to the rest of the station, so that whatever simple directions Michael gave were out of correct

....

line by at least this amount. Finding this out was a big step forward, but how to compensate? Nothing was going to be easy.

He tried a number of ways to allow for this: for example, if he wanted a pulse left, he asked Vasily to give one pulse left, one pulse up. Vasily did not like this – it meant using twice as much fuel – so Michael, on finding a suitable window, stared at the stars, leaning forty-five degrees left, to harmonize with Vasily's perspective. As it turned out later, there was plenty of spare fuel available, and Vasily need not have worried, but he did not realize this at the time.

It was very tiring. First Michael had to find a window which faced the stars at the beginning of a night pass. Then he had to imagine himself as part of the station and decide which way the stars should move, to start the station on its desired turn. Then he needed to decide which way the Soyuz thrust should be applied, remembering that Vasily was rolled forty-five degrees left of the normal station axis. Vasily now knew this well enough, after Michael had convinced him by demonstration. But away out there in his cockpit he could see nothing of the station, but still felt instinctively that he was in control and that he probably knew better than Michael. Pilots are always thus, knowing that they are right, and, as it happens, they often are. But in truth, the calculations and decisions being made by Michael were probably beyond Vasily's comprehension, sitting in the Soyuz, and he could show this only in his reluctance to follow instructions. And there were echoes too of his training and brief – he was the Russian commander, and Michael the foreign paying guest.

It was a hard thing too for Michael, who, while appreciating the sensibilities of command, found himself presently to be in command of his commander. But he knew that his conclusions were based on clearer and more informed thought than his commander could muster. He *had* to get Vasily to do as instructed, or they could never begin a proper resuscitation of Mir. Soon they would have to evacuate, and Mir would be part of history. He eventually found an ally in Sasha, who added his weight of opinion to convince the pilot, in his unfortunate and unenviable position, that Michael was probably right. (I remember that some RAF aircraft used to carry two navigators, no doubt to gang up on the pilot when he was being disagreeably obstinate – and wrong.)

....

Some five hours went by as they got the station to move, checked its rate of rotation while the night pass gave them the stars, and then saw how far it still had to go in relation to the sun, during the next day pass. They did this many times, Michael usually asking Vasily to give him ten pulses of thrust and Vasily saying firmly, no, only three. Eventually, after one twenty-minute night transition to get Spektr pointed to where he hoped the sun would be, he decided to stop the rotation, and prayed that when they stopped and the day pass began, Spektr would be pointing at the sun. He used his watch to assess the angle they had moved through on the last pulse and, more confidently than he felt, instructed Vasily to do exactly the opposite thrust impulse, so as to bring the rotation to a halt. As the station slowed and stopped, he was aware of a glow on the horizon which presaged an orbital sunrise. Spektr was pointing straight at it and he knew that, finally, they had done the right thing.

He checked the rate of rotation and found that there was still some left. He chastised the commander, 'Vasily, I asked you for the exact opposite and you did not do it fully. More.'

He controlled his annoyance. He checked the rotation again and found, wonderfully, that it *had* stopped, and that they were hanging in space. Then the sun rose. Even Kvant 2's solar arrays were being drenched in God-given sunlight, and they could hear the arrays' automatic responses, as they came slowly alive, turning the blades to an optimum angle. Most of the arrays could get a good perpendicular dose of sunlight and, with the fresh and substantial charge, they could hear many fans coming on and the rest of the station waking as from a long, deep sleep.

Michael said, 'Now we must stay pointing at the sun. If we do nothing we will lose it, and it will be all over. Vasily, you must spin the station around the Kvant 2–Spektr axis as fast as you can. A bullet that spins fastest goes straightest, so we need ten pulses in that direction to get going.'

But Vasily only did three pulses. Michael steadied himself and said in a low voice, 'All right, see what happens.'

After two more orbits the arrays were totally out of orientation. They had actually done an alarming gyroscopic flip. But in those three hours the batteries had recharged enough for them to talk to Ground Control again and to sustain full Base Block power, even during the night passes. Vasily felt that

....

at last he had won something, and Michael was delighted to agree with him. Playfully the station then flipped back, but it did not matter. Although alarming, the tendency to flip out of the spin and back again was thought not to be too worrisome, when they found that the times with Spektr pointing at the sun, though random, were always greater in duration than the transition away from the sun. Psychologically it was only worrying if you happened to be looking out of a window when it happened, and saw the universe apparently turning over. In their weightlessness, the motion was too slow to be felt by the crew.

After twenty-four hours of intense activity, Michael was allowed by his commander to sleep. He took five hours. Vasily and Sasha much valued what he had got them to achieve together, and let him sleep first.

They had enough power, over a total of thirty hours after the collision, for the ground staff to take over attitude control again. By using station thrusters, Ground Control ordered rotations which restored the station's thermal sensing of the earth's surface, which in turn told the central computer the station's attitude, so that the gyrodynes could be restarted. For the time being at least, Mir would not be evacuated.

Michael had stuck to his intellectual guns while under great personal strain, and in the face of considerable scepticism. The parallel between a dedicated and clever navigator and his disbelieving pilot, in an RAF aircraft, is close enough for me to remember a story. If Michael had any inclination to dream during his five hours of sleep, I like to think he may have dreamed of one of the RAF's navigator jokes about pilots:

The pilots and navigators of a well-known squadron were always arguing about which was the cleverest group, the pilots or the navigators. One day the CO said, 'Enough,' and ordered a football match for that afternoon between the pilots and the navigators, the result to be the final verdict. The match took place, and at four pm a nearby factory whistle blew. Immediately, every navigator left the pitch and went home.

At four-thirty pm the pilots scored the first goal.

I began my operational career in the RAF flying single-seat fighters. When, on promotion to squadron leader, I was posted to command No. 73 light bomber squadron in Cyprus, where the aircraft were Canberras, crewed by one pilot and two navigators I used to say, unkindly but typically for a pilot, that until I reached this squadron I did not even know how to spell the word. A time came when one of my navigators probably saved our lives. His name was Gerry Foster. We were on a dark night approach to an island runway, most of the descent being over the unlit sea. Had I monitored the descent properly, we should have crossed the coast at a height of about five hundred feet. When we were still a mile out over the sea, Gerry said, 'Navigator to pilot, do you know that we are down to four hundred feet already?'

The fact is I did not. I had been fascinated by the lights on the coast, had ignored the low-angle appearance of the flare-path, and had visually slipped through several hundred feet towards the unseen water below for too many seconds, without a glance at my altimeter. I might have noticed in time to avoid plunging into the sea. But I cannot be sure.

Thoughtful Aftermath

Following their triumphant recovery, Michael had found time to write to Rhonda from Mir on 26 June, the day following the accident, but postponed sending it by a day because it had to be transmitted by ham radio due to the overall power loss. With such a wide potential audience, he thought it might be premature for general consumption. The letter follows and is a model of brevity and modesty, much appreciated by us all at the time, but gives only a hint of what had really been happening. He knew that NASA would have been in touch with Rhonda, and she with us.

26 June 1997

I hope you've not been fretting. I had the same feeling I had in my stomach when I was with Ken, over Galveston Bay [Michael had had a complete engine failure in his light plane, forcing him to ditch into the sea and be rescued by the airport launch]. Sasha was with me in the Node, disconnecting cables so that we could put a hatch on Spektr, to isolate the leak. We could feel the pressure falling in our ears, and the hiss of air rushing out. Of course we were worried that the rate would accelerate. It was impressive how fast we got it all done, when the common understanding was that it would take too long to try.

It was Sasha who first saw that the Progress would hit us, and told me to go to the Soyuz. I felt the impact while I was going through the Node. It was a dull thud. Since then, after using our spare air supply to repressurize the rest of the station, we have been in total darkness each night pass, until this morning [Moscow time – when Base Block power had been restored for both night and day passes]. Totally quiet, just waving books to keep CO_2 off our faces and looking at the aurora and stars. Now we have power on the Base Block constantly, and our big task is to get power on to the module which has the toilet! [Kvant 2.] It is now thirty hours since the impact, and we're all tired, but basically in good spirits.

We are very thankful to God that the impact was not further away from our centre of mass and the Node, causing a much bigger torque on the Node with very different consequences [total rupture]. The resulting tumble of the station, and loss of constant sunlight, caused the power-down of the station. Vassy used the Soyuz jets to spin the station, so at least the Base Block arrays were pointed at the sun.

I have much more to say about the impossible situation Vassy was in to do the docking. There was no way, in my opinion, that the docking could be achieved from the original set-up of the Progress in relation to Mir. But that is all hindsight now. I think NASA had a similar experience in the Gemini programme, with Jim McDivitt. The position (quadrant) he was in, in relation to the target, was above and behind, if I remember right. The same as Vasily was put in. But all this will be worked out properly, in future simulations. I feel guilty that I did not pay attention to the rendezvous planning, but that was not my job. I was to measure the range with a laser, from a small window in the Progress docking port. I didn't get to do that before the Progress hit us.

I have lost all my personal stuff, Messager files, programs, books, pictures of you and the kids, etc., and the STS-84 charms, I am afraid. But I am still happy with the outcome, nevertheless.
Love, Mike

....

We received a Mir status report from NASA, also dated the twenty-sixth, giving bare details of events and the immediate situation. Because of the new (and apparently ever-changing) situation on Mir, we continued to receive these reports until Michael's eventual return to earth. They were sent to us by his friend, astronaut and test pilot Bill Readdy.

The NASA reports were models of restrained exactitude. If they did not know, they did not speculate. After the collision, they knew that the pressure leak had been isolated and some minimal power restored and that the crew, so far, were surviving. They summarized the known facts.

The chemical removal of carbon dioxide was being handled by US-supplied lithium hydroxide canisters. The normal carbon-dioxide scrubber had been shut off to conserve electricity, but could be reactivated, once and if on-board batteries had been recharged. The atmosphere in Spektr was probably not yet at complete vacuum, but was very close to it. The exact location of the leak was not known.

Mir's orientation was not providing the best electricity-generating capability for the station through the five solar arrays still available (a NASA-style considerable understatement), but power generation through the arrays was expected to improve once Mir regained full attitude control capability (if ever). Once the batteries were recharged, the gyrodynes on the station would be activated to restore automatic attitude control.

Russian flight controllers continued to develop tools and procedures which might be used by Tsibliyev and Lazutkin to recover the use of Spektr's solar power. The options included a possible procedure to hook cables from the Spektr arrays to Mir's Base Block, to route power from the disabled module to the operational batteries. Tsibliyev and Lazutkin would wear spacesuits to perform any such procedure, which would not occur earlier than mid-July, following the arrival of hardware and new cables on the next Progress ship. The launch of the new Progress was planned for early July.

I attempted to send a brief e-mail to Michael on 26 June via Terry Taddeo. We wanted Michael to know that we were being kept informed from various sources and that he should not waste time worrying about us. It took a long time to reach him, and I would have been better sending it via his ham friend, Dave Larsen. I told him that we had been continuing to champion space exploration to the media, and Mir's part in it, and that Mary had said, after one TV interview, that I sounded just like him, which made me proud in a different way. We did not underestimate the seriousness of the incident, but knew that the three of them could and would overcome it. It seemed that they had the benefit of lots of advice, perhaps too much, but they would know what to take on board.

Michael and his friends had not only survived the unimaginable danger of a space collision; he was obviously continuing to think coolly and carefully about the next moves. The criticality of the power levels had to be addressed, and meanwhile they were to be tested by the caprices of this criticality. He could hardly be called 'safe', but we had not lost him yet and our feeling that he would survive strengthened. However, our fears had sharply reminded us of a similar ordeal some years ago.

That tortured question, are we going to lose another child, was one that I had asked before in very different circumstances, as I recalled while we waited for more news of Michael and Mir. We were all briefly in New York in the summer of 1982. Michael had joined us there from Houston and we forged lasting idyllic memories of this extraordinary place, including a family game of softball in Brooklyn's Prospect Park and dinner at an Italian restaurant, openly redolent of the Mafia, under the Brooklyn Bridge. It was here that we bade tearful goodbyes to Michael, who had to return to Houston.

Two days before Mary, Susan and I were due to fly back to England, Susan became ill with a painful stomach complaint. It seemed important to get medical advice on her fitness to travel. Her humour and liveliness were gone, and we were worried. We took her to the local hospital where, in Emergency, four hours passed before anyone could see her. She was continually being bounced further back down the queue by another stabbing, or a gunshot wound. It was nightmarish, and like a medical *Hill Street Blues*, the TV New York police series popular at the time. She is a brave lady and did not complain, but the pain increased.

Eventually, she was seen, tested and pronounced as having enteritis, painful and unpleasant to endure during an eight-hour night flight, but they said she could safely travel.

She had a truly miserable flight, and became so unusually subdued in spirit that I asked the crew to warn Heathrow airport emergency staff that we wanted a doctor to see her immediately on arrival. They responded, and at

....

Heathrow, after he had examined Susan, the doctor said that she must go immediately to the nearest isolation hospital, which was at Harrow. She was in real danger, he said, having difficulty breathing, and he suspected a virulent form of salmonella. She was rushed away in an ambulance with Mary beside her, while I collected our luggage and followed in our car, tired out after the flight and racked with worry. At the hospital she was put into an isolation unit behind glass where we could see her and talk to her, but not touch her. Salmonella poisoning was confirmed. Salmonella can be fatal if not treated. It took several days of repeated faecal testing to find out which strain of organism was attacking Susan before they could prescribe specific treatment. She was monitored constantly, and had intravenous drips inserted into her arm to keep up her fluid levels. It was all a question of whether she could survive until they identified the strain.

Leaving our lovely Susan there behind the isolation glass was very difficult. It felt wrong, yet there was nothing we could do to help – indeed, we were in the way, and Susan herself was almost past noticing or caring if we were there or not. She told us later that it had been all she could do to hang on. In silence we drove to Cambridge, exhausted.

The following day, we returned to Harrow. No change. And again the following day. Again no change, but that at least meant no further deterioration. But she could eat nothing, and seemed so helpless, and we were equally helpless and desperately worried.

On the fourth day we were told that the organism had been identified. Susan was very, very weak but treatment had begun. We could only watch and pray.

The days passed. Slowly her eyes returned to being large and brown, she could smile and she began to look like herself again. We were allowed to bring her home where, gradually, she recovered completely. Never before had we felt so helpless. The familiar funeral words – in the midst of life we are in death – seemed daily to ring in our ears. We could not bear the thought of losing her. But, thank God, we still have her – and Michael.

Our strengthening feeling that events on Mir had at least stabilized was dramatically undermined by news on 27 June. The men on Mir might have expected Fate to be kinder, after their unremitting efforts to get the station back on an even keel had eventually been rewarded with success.

....

During the sleep period of 26–7 June, which they needed so much, the station playfully lost attitude control again, without the aid of a collision to start it this time, beginning another frightening power-draining tumble. They were wakened by the alarms, and there was no alternative but to rouse themselves immediately and deal with the matter before the station slid into the almost irretrievable situation they had just experienced. From Michael's next letter to Rhonda, still calm and understated, it is clear that the hard-won stability was on a knife-edge and victim to random and unpredictable internal stimuli. Neither Ground Control nor NASA had said much to them about plans for future remedial action. Michael first learned about what was being discussed through his ham radio friends and the media!

Friday, 27 June 1997
Dear Rhonda,
I wrote the 26 June letter yesterday, but thought twice about sending it as it would have been the first item in our postbox after it had been powered off and reset, and very visible. I slept pretty good last night, but Vassy and Sasha are very tired. We were woken up by an alarm, when the station attitude-control system failed. We spend a lot of time looking out at the sun, and the solar arrays, to figure out how manually to orient the station, and hence the arrays, back towards the sun. A bit like sailing on a large yacht!

Dave Larsen has been forwarding me news, and I spoke to hams in Australia and New Zealand who told me what they have heard. Now the talk is that Vassy and Sasha will do an EVA, but inside, to open up the hatch to Spektr that Sasha and I closed in such a hurry! But they will be in Orlan spacesuits, and I will be closeted away in the tiny space of the descent module of the Soyuz. At least it has two windows. But I won't see the guys working, they will be in almost total darkness trying to cut a hole in the hatch of Spektr, connecting up the cables we disconnected, and then sealing the hatch again. Not a 'dream' spacewalk by any means, but Sasha still seems pretty excited by it. Maybe they will retrieve the ice cream that is still in the freezer there! We're just kidding. Sergei Krikalev talks to us every day from TSUP, very businesslike, and is the leader

....

I think of the EVA project. It is good to hear his voice.

We have spent all day checking wires and batteries [to conserve as much power as possible], and now it is time to eat supper. Please pass on this news to my parents. My lost words to you were, I don't have a close-up picture of your face, without sunglasses! Now I don't have pictures of any of you, except the one of Jenna on Vasily's knee, which is on Vassy's wall.

Ken Bowersox is going to get the key to our house to get some files off the hard drive, to send me on the Progress. I spoke to him and Bill Readdy in Houston. I am glad the press wasn't too hard.

Love you. Hug the kids.

Mike

By 28 June, with a slight temporary surplus of power, the crew re-established a link with Ground Control and NASA representatives, voice only, and Michael was asked how he was, post-accident, and what he needed after the loss of the contents of Spektr. Michael responded with a list of essentials which he wanted to be sent on the next Progress vehicle. It was a model of restrained, pragmatic demands and tickled the fancy of the world's media in a number of ways, and they reported it as being so typically British.

A medical kit, NBX

Exercise shoes [he had none, and none on board fitted him]

Treadmill harness

Hard drives from my home computer

A shaver

A toothbrush

A tube, no three tubes, of toothpaste

Yes, the Greenhouse experiments have been saved, but leaf bags are needed

Bio experiments were lost in Spektr, but have been properly turned off

I'm worried about the beetles [an experiment involving insects in zero gravity], they are existing on batteries at the moment

On 29 June, Moscow NTV's *Segodnya* programme broadcast in Russian the following interview with the Mir crew:

> Today, during the first video communication session since the accident, it became clear that the two Russian cosmonauts and the US astronaut acted professionally and fended off a real threat to themselves and the Mir station, a threat which specialists have rated as 'without precedent and posing a real danger to the survival of the crew'. Until now such communication sessions were not possible because of the need to conserve electricity. Only today are we able to see the cosmonauts' faces. Aleksandr Lazutkin described how they acted in the emergency situation.
>
> 'Individual actions in the event of depressurization had been rehearsed. When I started working, I felt that my brain would function automatically, that I was able to carry out all the actions automatically, without thinking, without reflecting, without asking questions. Just do it, just do it. The brain was ready.'
>
> (Interviewer): 'The American Michael Foale kept a great presence of mind during the accident, and amazingly fitted in with the team which he had joined only recently.'
>
> (Foale, speaking in Russian): 'There is a great deal of experience here, very great. Even when everything went according to plan it was great working with these men.'
>
> (Tsibliyev): 'Our friend Michael Foale here, he can rightly be described as that, has become a true number-two on-board engineer. He is helping us with literally everything that needs to be done here at the station. In my opinion, he is more knowledgeable than many other US astronauts.'

On earth, we loving relatives were being well taken care of by NASA and Michael's other friends. The real and ugly danger of the accident and our awareness of it had long since penetrated and no doubt left its mark. Oddly, it left us calmer and more resigned to the difficulties of maintaining an uneventful life in space. Collisions are rare, and usually an enormous effort is made to avoid the slightest chance of one. This one had been rated by a

....

Russian official, using a 'dangerous accident rating' of 0 to 7, as deserving 5. How serious a hit would have been deserving of 6? we wondered. Immediate evacuation? We assumed that 7 was unquestionably fatal.

We drew comfort from our knowledge and experience that once an accident happens, in almost any context, it is usually rare for another to happen very soon afterwards, simply because people have been shocked into taking greater care. We were also aware of the Russians' willingness, perhaps, to take more risks than their Western counterparts. In a society as closed as the Soviet one had been, managers and executives rarely, if ever, had had to face scrutiny by anybody, let alone the media. Now events were beginning to bring the world's attention to TSUP and Star City, and it was interesting to watch the gradual change in the style of Russian spokesmen from defensive bravado to a careful, more constructive and informative approach. Meanwhile I often found myself on the media, a lone champion of Mir's achievements.

We knew that the Russians needed to retain Mir as a money-making vehicle for American and European cooperation at a time when space research was not the only activity that needed cash. Even the Russian armed services were frequently left unpaid for months. So it was little wonder that the Russians should be aggressively defensive of their undoubted technical marvel Mir, and that they concentrated on the restoration of power from Spektr's arrays, on which future crew handovers and the accommodation of paying guests would depend. A French astronaut, Leopold Eyharts, was due for a twenty-one-day attachment during the next crew change in August.

At first the accident seemed to shake NASA's confidence in their programme of cooperation with the Russians and also, perhaps, their wish to continue working within the Mir complex. Certainly it gave new fuel to Washington congressional committees, whose hostility to US–Russian co-operation was already established. For a time I had to rely on Michael's media statements and Rhonda's letters to help formulate a view which, since I was frequently questioned about it by the media, I felt ought not to be in conflict with Michael's.

I sensed that, as a professional astronaut who had always dreamed of man conquering space, Michael was unlikely to want to agree to a curtailment of his Mir duties, even if it were possible (it wasn't) to send a rescue shuttle to bring him down. It seemed to me – and in our first direct communication

....

with Michael I was shown to be right – that far from wanting to leave Mir at the first sign of trouble, he regarded every incident as another challenge to be overcome, to be recorded as experience in space and of enormous help to the success and survival of the future International Space Station (ISS) that would supersede Mir in 1999.

And of course, he and I said to ourselves, he always had the Soyuz earth-return vehicle handy, like a fighter pilot's ejection seat, in which he, Tsibliyev and Lazutkin could, *in extremis*, return safely to earth.

Rhonda and the children were still in Kentucky, but keeping in close contact with NASA and with us, as the following letter dated 29 June shows. It also reflects her never failing objectivity and concern, which we knew was of such help and comfort to Michael.

Dear Colin, Mary and Susan,

We talked to Mike this morning and he sounded very well. He joked about Sasha and Vasily having to scrounge supplies for him. They tease him, calling him a vagrant, a street person. He puts his sleeping bag in one of the disused modules which is cold and damp. His head sticks out into the Node. Sasha scrounged some long johns and a sweater for him. He is using an old Russian toiletry kit of Jerry's and has already worn out the toothbrush. The plans for the EVA have gelled. An extra hatch door will be modified ahead of time with electrical connectors. Sasha and Vasily will don the Orlan suits, vent the air in the Node to space, replace the hatch including reaching into Spektr to connect cables, seal the hatch and repressurize the Node with a can of air. It may take six to eight hours. Mike will have to wait it out inside the Soyuz in the Sokol suit. Otherwise he would be cut off from emergency escape. It will require equipment from the Progress and is planned for mid-July. Repairing Spektr is beyond capability at this point. Also, they don't want to enter Spektr for safety reasons – there may be toxins as a result of the contents of experiments reacting with the vacuum. I learned the details from Frank Culbertson [NASA head of Mir cooperation]. Mike also said they are very busy, and TSUP isn't letting them have a whole lot of rest time. I have been working with Steve Vander Ark on the phone collecting items to send on the Progress.

....

Daria called from Switzerland after passing through London. She said Mike is pretty famous there. As you know, he is shown on CNN and other news programs several times each day. Best wishes for all of your adventures with the press.

I told Mike that gillions of people here are praying for him. Even people I met in eastern Kentucky from Tennessee are getting their churches to pray for him. People from my parents' Sunday school class have been calling. I am hoping that Mike will return normally on the shuttle in early October, *but a whole lot of things will have to go right* [my italics].

Lots of love, Rhonda

Our own church in Cambridge, Great St Mary's, had also begun to include Michael and his Mir crew regularly in their intercessions, which I knew would please him.

Dr Dave Larsen, Michael's faithful radio ham friend in California, sent Rhonda's letters up and Michael's down whenever he could, in spite of his being due for some surgery. In turn, Rhonda passed many on to us. The following crossed with her e-mail above of the same date.

29 June 1997
Dave, sorry about the mix-up with call sign. Were you on seventy cm at all today?
Mike.

Dear Rhonda,
We have had a long Sunday, and it is time for bed. I just read your note you wrote after we spoke. Tell Denise and John 'Hi' from me. I still daydream about flying up to see them. Maybe when we go to Benham. We just finished up a long meal together. Vassy found a container of mystery red liquid, we think Manakov may have sent it up in anticipation of his flight last summer. It was in the back of the fridge, which got powered down in our blackouts, and showed up while he was trying to figure out what had spoiled. A very nice surprise when we tasted it, and we told each other stories. I mentioned that there was a

....

rumour in the US that cosmonauts had seen strange apparitions, angels in space. (We were listening to Litzei, a good Russian girl group, singing 'Angelli'.)

Vassy said that during his last flight, he saw a strange glowing object, not far from the station, descend to the clouds and vanish. He took pictures with three different cameras, but none came out. His flight engineer was busy in the toilet, and did not see it. They were near the south magnetic pole, so I am guessing it was probably some kind of plasma – but in bright sunlight, it is an incredible phenomenon.

I will always remember being in total darkness, no power, no fans, and all of us in front of the big window, looking at incredibly complex, swirling auroras with the galaxy showering down on them, with nothing else for us to do.

I know, you are thinking the red liquid has got to us.

I look forward to your next note. I hugged Sasha for you, and he hugged back.

Love, Mike

Michael wrote again the next day.

30 June 1997
Dave, thanks. Just talked to Graham Tilbury [a South African scientist and radio ham]. Could you send him the info, and he has promised to send it only as a file to me while I experiment with winpack. Do you have winpack, or more pertinent, Yapp upload/download capability? Mike.

Dear Rhonda,
That was a lovely message about Ian not eating chocolate, so he wouldn't take his eyes off the trains. It makes me want to whisk him to England to ride a steam train again [as we had all ridden at the Nene Valley Railway the previous Christmas]. We have had a better day today, normal exercise again, and looked out the window after-wards, listening to music. The passes over the US are incredible.

....

Western US is totally clear and Yellowstone, Jackson Hole, etc. very visible. I am learning lots of geography.

Semeonov, the boss of Energiya, Progresses, Soyuzes, etc., wants to talk to us. Vassy is obviously concerned. We are steadily improving things on board, and Vassy is working hard to move all the EVA gear from the Kvant 2 airlock to the Node [for the IVA]. I moved the beetles out of Priroda, where there is no power, and it is very cold. I put them near the Greenhouse, in Kristall, where there is also no power, but I have run an extension cable to get light to the Greenhouse lights. The modules present a different aspect, having moved so much around, when trying to move essential equipment like solar power batteries from one place to another, so putting some light into the cold damp space where the Greenhouse is makes it seem a lot cheerier. The plants show pod development, and are not yellowing yet, to be ready for harvest. Maybe with light, after four days of darkness, they will pick up again.

We are having a good time together, especially in the evening, and are determined to stay relaxed, even having good laughs about the collision and its implications for the programme. I try to cheer up Sasha and Vassy. By the way, all the French gear was out of Spektr, ready for Leopold to use, so we don't figure he will be delayed. But what do we know! Ken Bowersox got to talk to me from the ham shack today, which was fun. You will be in Houston on Wednesday. Travel safe, if I don't send before then.
Love, Mike

So far, we at home were being kept well informed, not only of events, but, of greater importance, the feelings of Mir's severely tested custodians. For days this had been possible only through the goodwill of the many ham radio contacts Michael had made at the start. He did not forget to thank them in early July, with a general note to Dave Larsen for the ham net.

8 July
Dave, here is a ham net piece:
The Mir crew are very grateful for all the good wishes and interest

....

across the world in our troubles and tribulations. In particular, the few hams who work tirelessly on our behalf to pass us information of current events in the world, and in particular how the world press is reacting to our situation, are very valuable to us. We do not get this sort of opinion from our controllers. During the extended power-down of Mir after the collision, our contact with the TSUP in Moscow was predictable, but totally congested with essential technical conversation. It was impossible to get any personal news of our well-being to our families, in a private way, by means of the official comm, for about a week. However, ham radio has allowed us to fill the gap, and I and my wife are extremely grateful to those hams who pass on our messages for us.

We are particularly interested in contacts longer than simple technical exchanges. We are interested to know about normal life in different places. It is good to tell people about our life here on Mir, and our problems, but the lives of hams on earth are also interesting to us, and I hope more hams will take the time to tell us about themselves and their surroundings.

Mike Foale, KB5UAC

Michael, like everybody else, was interested in maintaining an even keel and objectivity on board. Visions of earth, their earth, would be helpful. To keep their heads would be vital if the station was not to be abandoned but truly set on the path to recovery. It was perhaps fortunate that he did not know that for many more weeks there would be a succession of dangerous events and accidents.

Make Do and Mend

A s June came to an end, I found my imagination frequently reaching out to Mir to feel more clearly what Michael had told us in his letters. It is a habit of thought of all pilots to imagine themselves in whatever hot seat a colleague has recently been in, to enter and share his learning curve, however steep or final. Focusing my thoughts on Mir was natural enough. Michael is basically a cheerful sort of person, and that is how he sounded, during radio communication or on the telephone to us in Cambridge. He also did numerous voice and video interviews for the American media, some of which reached the UK. Always he was upbeat, he could smile and even joke. But it had been a close call, and it was still dangerous – indeed, going into space is *always* dangerous. Things there need all your attention.

On earth we had so many friends feeling agonies for us during the suspense of the dramas on Mir, so many letters and phone calls, we sometimes felt overwhelmed. Reporters would resolutely attempt at every given chance to get Mary or myself to shed a tear during an interview, the cameras inanely focused on what they hoped would be knuckles white with tension. We appreciated our friends' concern and valued their love. But we were never even tempted to cry or to wring our hands, or fall about in disarray. As the perceptive reader will know, this had nothing to do with lack of love or concern for Michael – quite the opposite. Nor as a family are we unemotional – none of us ever hesitates to let a tear come for Christopher when our memories of him occasion it.

We have concluded that people who live with risk are different from those who don't. It is an entirely practical difference, and involves a conscious decision always to think in terms of controlling the risk, and never letting the risk take control of your thoughts. Being a pilot helps. It soon becomes a habit of mind of both risk-takers and their dependants and loved ones, usually leaving no time or room for fear or worry, which you quickly learn are themselves dangerous and destructive. So yes, we are cool, but not cold; clear-thinking, but not unaware of the dangers. The effect on Michael of hearing, while he was at a very risky workface, of parental collapse over worry for him, would have been dangerously unsettling. Knowing him, he would still have coped. Knowing that he knew us, he would know that would be very unlikely to happen. But it was a risk worth avoiding. All it needs to be able to do this, by the way, is to have lots of practice. Even my dear old parents learned it, then Mary too, and the children knew nothing else.

Michael had likened the first shock of knowing that the Progress had hit them with his similar shock when flying over Galveston Bay. The single engine of his light aircraft suddenly stopped over the Bay, when on an approach to Galveston airport. He was only a few hundred feet above the sea at the time, so had only seconds to glide until the plane hit the water, not much time to decide whether to splash down with the aircraft absolutely level, or to aim for as little speed as possible with the nose held high before hitting the water. Whichever he did was apparently right, as neither he nor his good friend Ken Bowersox was hurt. Both had time to climb out of the aircraft and on to the wings before the plane sank below the surface. The controller at the airport had acted promptly in response to Michael's hurried 'mayday' call and the rescue launch was already on its way. His insurance policies covered the loss of the aircraft. His main concern had been to keep the incident out of the papers – 'Two Astronauts have to Ditch' would not necessarily be good for their image.

But the incident had provoked an alarm bell somewhere in the upper stomach, a knot of butterflies which had had to be held and controlled so that he could think.

....

I could identify with that experience at least, as I have had a fair share of engine vagaries, as Michael would have known from my stories. Over the Egyptian Canal Zone, I was one of four silver Vampire jet fighters of No. 32 Squadron flying at twenty thousand feet (about four miles high) in that country's so frequently perfect blue sky. Below was the long straight channel of the Suez Canal stretching south from Port Said through little Lake Tewfic, then entering the Great Bitter Lake, on the shore of which was my airfield, Deversoir.

During a vigorous manoeuvre, I whipped into a steep turn and 'poured on the coals', as the phrase was, to increase power. There was a loud *plop* noise from my engine, then silence and a rapidly decreasing air speed. Behind me I could see a stream of white vapour pouring from the jet pipe – unburned fuel, as the engine had stopped, or 'flamed out', to use another popular phrase. I straightened out, closed the throttle and fuel cocks and felt just like Michael was to describe forty-three years later, but I had more time. In fact, I had lots of time. To maintain speed and controllability I had to lose height in a descent. Sooner or later the aircraft would hit the ground or water, and either would mean certain death if I was still in the aircraft. On the other hand, there was no ejection seat in these early jets, and to leave by parachute involved the hazard of striking the tail on the way out, just as fatal, after climbing into the 180 mph air flow. The engine, a De Havilland Goblin, could not be restarted in the air. I made a decision. I would continue to descend – not that I had any choice – but I would do so over the lumpy desert towards my airfield which, at my gliding descent rate, I calculated I could reach with a few thousand feet to spare. Then all I had to do was judge everything nicely so that the inevitable contact with the ground took place into wind, at the beginning of the main runway, at landing speed. There could be two problems. If I misjudged the approach and undershot too low, I would hit the lake, and, unlike Michael's light aircraft, the Vampire was known *not* to ditch satisfactorily, but to dive to the bottom. If I misjudged the approach too high and overshot, I would hit a thick plantation of palm trees beyond the runway, which would bring an end to any further problems I might have had.

Throughout the descent I was aware of unpleasantness in my stomach, but knew that if I let it dominate, I could not think clearly. I arrived over the airfield at 3,000 feet, reached a position for the final 180-degree turn at 2,000

....

feet, which was 500 feet higher than normal, put the undercarriage down, flaps down and airbrakes out, even a touch of top rudder for a slight descent-increasing side-slip, then straightened out at the threshold and sank gently on to the tarmac with an enormous grin on my face under my oxygen mask. The air traffic controller had been silent after clearing away all other air traffic to allow me to concentrate. As I began to brake the aircraft and was obviously under control, the Wing Commander Flying, Bertie Wooten (of Battle of Britain fame), who had gone to the control tower to watch, broadcast a terse 'Good show.' My day was made.

So much for an experience of having to control an emotion like fear in order to continue to function properly, as Michael was doing so superbly on Mir. It is only right to recount another occurrence from that period which was utterly stupid, much more frightening and which I survived only by the grace of God. While serving with the same squadron, we were asked to give army units which were exercising in the Eastern Desert some experience of tactical fighter air attack. No weapons would be fired, of course, but we would have the practice of finding vehicles and tanks in the sand and making dummy attacks, and they would have the practice of swivelling their guns at us.

I must have flown four packed sorties that day, and it was enjoyable and interesting, but also tiring. We would dive in a stream on our selected targets from about 2,000 feet, breaking off and roaring over their heads at 200 feet or less. On the last sortie and the last attack, as I levelled out low over the troops, I had an uncontrollable urge to show off – a barrel roll over their heads, just to show them. I pulled the aircraft up into a slight climb and rolled. I had not climbed steeply enough: I had rolled too early, and as I came out of the roll, the ground was hurrying up to meet me. At that moment there was nothing I could do to alter anything. The moving finger writes with a vengeance. My stomach was in knots. I kept backward pressure on the stick to a maximum without incurring a high-speed stall, and the desert sand beneath me and ahead came close enough to blur. There was not even time to pray. A second later I was climbing away, feeling oddly chilled in the 120-degree (Fahrenheit) sweaty cockpit, very thoughtful and very thankful. Fortunately for my reputation I had been the last in the stream, and nobody but the troops had noticed. They may have admired it,

....

but they would not have known how close to disaster it had been.

The great difference between the fright that Michael had got in space and ones I had experienced was that with mine, they were brief and finite, followed soon after by a cool shower, a change of clothes and at least one ice-cold beer, to stimulate clear reflection and perhaps a story while sitting safely on a bar stool. The traditional line-shoot is just an RAF way of off-loading the tensions. For Michael the fear must have been just as real, the danger just as great or greater, but he never had much opportunity for the same kind of clear-cut relief that the danger was now past, such as following a dangerous flight incident. As he must have said to himself many times, he was stuck there with a fundamental loss of usable electrical power that made everything more precarious and often unpleasant and uncomfortable. He soon knew that people at Energiya and Ground Control were doing everything to enable an early restoration of Spektr's power by means of an internal spacewalk, and he sensed the resulting heavy pressure that would fall on Vasily and Sasha. They would be expected to prepare and position the suits, tools and repair equipment, and also to remove the pervasive array of impeding cables in all the hatches that would have to be closed, so that the unprecedented 'internal EVA' (IVA) could take place.

These last few days of June had moved him for ever from 'guest' to 'crew', from foreigner to brother. He felt profound satisfaction with this development, not just because it gave him responsibilities of greater interest to him, but because of the new, trusting relationship he now had with Vasily and Sasha. After that twenty-four-hour period of intense activity following the collision, and then when the station's attitude and regained power maintenance stabilized, it was Michael who was ordered to rest. Vasily was going through an agony of self-reproach over the collision. Although dead on his feet with fatigue, he decided properly as commander not to be the first to begin a sleep shift. There was another reason. Michael had saved the station with his bright initiatives, forced through in spite of his colleagues' initial reluctance. He not only deserved a prize; it would be prudent to continue nurturing his clarity of thought. And, they had to admit, they had grown very fond of him too.

Following the unexpected and unexplained loss of attitude on 26–7 June, sleep shifts were necessary for a few more days until enough surplus

....

power was built up in the batteries to justify bringing all ten working gyrodynes on line, and attitude control could be left to them. When Spektr had had to be isolated, and the station had lost the benefit of Spektr's solar arrays, an overall forty per cent of normal electrical power was lost. The amount of power generated surplus to normal consumption, particularly that consumed during the alternate night passes, was very small. However, once all available batteries had been fully charged, it was safe for Ground Control to command the station's thrusters to put it into the best attitude to receive the sun's rays, and then to order all the steadying gyrodynes to spin up. The gyrodynes were never intended to be able to right a toppling station, only to nudge the station gently to help it keep the attitude it had been placed in by other means. At the time of the collision, the tumble force imparted by the impact far exceeded anything that the gyrodynes could have coped with, and in any case they had then spun down, as their batteries were exhausted though lack of solar-charged power.

Until the lost power from Spektr's solar arrays could be regained, the amount delivered by the other arrays remained critical and not sufficient to deal with unforeseen occurrences. Everything on Mir depends on solar power in one way or another, far more immediately than life on earth, and this post-collision criticality had a continuing impact on the crew. It meant that risks of upsetting attitude control had to be taken during night passes so that selected gyrodynes could be turned off to conserve battery power. Power to Kristall had also been lost with the loss of Spektr's arrays, and the Greenhouse experiment was at risk. Kvant 2 also was not always powered, especially inconvenient because it contained the toilet. Nobody wanted to risk yet another chaotic tumble, which would again drain the batteries so quickly that even Ground Control might be unable to help if the station's thrusters were powerless.

In order to understand Mir's ongoing situation over many weeks, it is worth taking another look at Mir's electrical power, attitude-control and life-support systems. For power, the station has batteries, charged by solar arrays; for attitude, it has thrusters and gyrodynes; for human responses it has a crew on board, and, for consideration on the ground, a committee of minds at Ground Control. With fully charged batteries on Mir and a stable situation, Ground Control commands the station thrusters to swing the station into a

....

good position relative to the sun's rays. The solar arrays then keep the batteries fully charged. The gyrodynes are started to increase the stability of the station in its best attitude. As more power is absorbed and stored in the batteries, some is permitted to flow to every life-support or experiment system. The cooling system works, oxygen is produced electrolytically from recycled water, carbon dioxide is removed from the air, air circulates in motion to prevent CO_2 build-up, there is abundant light and power for regular comm and night passes. In this stabilized situation, the gyrodyne spins are gently modified by computer to maintain the best station attitude according to a number of stimuli: the earth's magnetic field, the horizon and the relative position of the sun. A final factor, the station's position in relation to earth, is determined by radar stations on earth which measure and transmit to Mir its latitude and longitude. It is a three-dimensional process which, if the components did not wear out and there were no collisions, could go on for ever.

On 1 July I had thanked Dr David Larsen for getting Michael's e-mail to us. He replied:

2 July

Mr Foale: this is a message Mike sent to me – and thought you might like to read. There is a little more to this message; I will try and get it down this next pass.

I uploaded your message to Mike – I knew he would like to hear from you. I saw you on CNN – way to give them heck – some of these news people *really* make me mad.

I was a warrant officer in the Navy – flew choppers in 'Nam for 6 months, 29 days – got shot down two times – the second time they had to ship me back to the States to get 'wired' back together.

You a retired colonel? Message to follow – please confirm you got this.

Dr Larsen [PhD]

The reference to CNN was a live interview I had given through their London office. I had also done others for Australia, Saudi Arabia and South Africa. When Michael was the main news story in Port Elizabeth, South Africa, the

....

studio broadcast began with a rendering of 'God Save the Queen'! How nice, I thought.

What I did not know when reading this amiable, kindly message was that Mir had suffered yet again. The station had remained in stable attitude since the crew's interrupted night on 26–7 June. They had enjoyed four stable days, but with low power availability, and were soon to turn in after a full working day. Michael had recently ended a short phone conversation with Rhonda, when attitude was suddenly lost again.

To have a second failure, never fully explained, so soon after the first, was deeply worrying for the crew, who could soon expect the arrival and docking of a heavy Progress supply vessel. For this manoeuvre to be safe, let alone possible, the station's attitude had to be steady all the way in for the vessel until it docked successfully. Without this, the situation could deteriorate quickly into an emergency, like the one that had preceded the collision.

Extracts from the letter from Mike, referred to by Dave Larsen, follow.

2 July

Dear Rhonda,

We lost attitude control again, after we spoke, and once again were rushing from one dark module to another, trying to look out windows and point the solar arrays. The station dies very quickly if we don't do this. It happened just after our last pass of the day with TSUP [Ground Control] when they had telemetry. So the next pass over America, through Dryden, was very frantic. It is very much like being on a yacht at sea, with the wind changing all the time, and having to rush around pulling sails down, or putting them up, before a storm comes. You can tell Ellis [a Texas friend with a boat] or my dad this! Not knowing why the attitude control keeps failing leaves us a little wary of the next Progress supply vessel docking, on the seventh. Vasily will be watching through its TV eye, and if the automatic system acts up, or Mir is out of attitude, he is ready to command the Progress to break off. If we lose all comm with it, we will just make an emergency run to the Soyuz. Life on Mir is characterized by long periods of monotonous, serene calm and short interludes of extreme frenzy, I am learning.

I have been helping Sasha and Vasily in their different tasks,

....

moving airlock, spacesuit equipment to the Node, and checking pin connections in cables, to get things in shape for the IVA.

I think Semeonov's talk to us yesterday, saying we should only look forward and not think about what happened, was pretty uplifting for Vasily especially, and Semeonov also seemed keen to know my reaction as well to the plans being laid. He talked about it being a great lesson for cooperation with France and America, so I presume Leopold is still on schedule. His stay will be interesting, and not per plan, I expect.

Hug the kids. Record Ian's voice if you can. Pay the bills.

I love you, Mike

On this occasion, attitude control had been lost by the failure of a database component in the computer system, losing half the gyrodynes. The station quickly lost solar power again. The action required was becoming a drill – the crew would switch off all non-vital power usage, then Ground Control would apply thruster control to restore what attitude it could to begin power generation, the crew would locate the failed component and fit a replacement; then Ground Control would hold a steady attitude until batteries were recharged, restarting the gyrodynes, and switching on the sacrificed facilities again. When considered prudent, the crew would swap a fully charged battery, say from Kvant 2 if Kvant 2's arrays were charging, for a low battery in the Base Block if the Base Block's were not, and vice versa. Batteries have substantial mass, and it was an arduous process. It was very wearing indeed for the crew, as each attitude failure could take over a day to overcome, leaving them with diminished time and energy for other duties and adding to their fatigue.

While in this state, which did not make for an orderly daily life, the crew were abundantly aware of Energiya's anxiety to get the lost Spektr power restored as soon as possible. The Frenchman Leopold Eyharts, who had been fully trained for a crew handover period with French-sponsored experiments, was awaiting the blast-off date of the relief Russian crew. However, it was clear, but not yet admitted openly, that without the restoration of power, Mir was hardly in a position to support a three-week crew overlap, let alone the involvement of a sixth man undertaking power-hungry

....

experiments. Understandably enough, the Russian authorities must have been reluctant to give up the substantial hard-currency income which would be due to them after Leopold's successful attachment on Mir was completed, at least not without a struggle. Great efforts were ordered, both on the ground and in orbit. On the ground, this effort centred on designing a system for picking up the lost power cables languishing uselessly in isolated Spektr, while still keeping Spektr's vacuum condition sealed off from the rest of the station.

The crew also had to concentrate on preparations and training for the proposed internal spacewalk, to try to reconnect these lost power cables. This would involve a new hatch, which was currently being designed and made at Baikonur. A mock-up would be tested in Star City. Much consultation between American and Russian space experts had taken place, and in record time the Russians produced the new hatch and the mock-up for testing. From conception to drawing to production to test took only six days, a remarkable achievement by any organization, bringing awed but heartfelt congratulations from NASA's Washington-based boss, Dan Goldin. It was no doubt also a measure of Russian financial urgency to get back in business. The testing was done in the gigantic water tank at Star City, which contained a mock-up of the Node and Base Block, so that cosmonauts could practise the techniques which Tsibliyev and Lazutkin would be expected to use. The hatch, special tools, supplies and replacements for Michael's kit lost in Spektr were due to be launched in Progress M35 on 5 July.

Michael talked at length with his crewmates in order to be helpful and supportive during this step into the relative unknown. In Star City, one of the most celebrated, youthful cosmonauts, Sergei Krikalev – the widely experienced 'last Soviet citizen' (having been alone on Mir when the Soviet Union collapsed, and in danger of being stranded) who was for us at least the Russian Michael – was in the forefront of the internal EVA studies. Sergei and another great cosmonaut, Nicholas Budarin, thought deeply, talked to the Mir crew, helped design the required new hatch and began a series of personal tank tests. In one conversation with Michael on Mir (they knew each other well and Michael had flown with him in his aerobatic aircraft), Michael said, 'Sergei, you sound as if you are inventing something!'

'Yes,' Sergei answered, 'I am.' They did. There is still a lot of priceless

....

dedication to the Russian space programme from many of its people.

On 3 July, the factual, unemotional NASA/Mir status report included a note that the station continued to rely on its reaction-control thruster jets commanded by Ground Control, but that Soyuz jets were not at this time required as a supplement. The 'interface problem', i.e., the data control unit in the computer, was not expected to be overcome for a day or two. The report continued:

> Otherwise, the crew spent the day continuing to prepare for a possible internal spacewalk to route solar array cables housed in the sealed-off Spektr module to the Base Block. Preparations today included continuing checkouts of the spacesuits, which will be worn by Tsibliyev and Lazutkin during the procedure. Foale will be housed in the Soyuz capsule during the internal spacewalk. The spacewalk is currently planned for around mid-July, following the arrival of the next Progress supply ship. That Progress, which is carrying the needed repair equipment to Mir, is scheduled for launch at 05:11 BST July 5, with a docking to Mir planned at 06:58 BST on Monday, July 7.
>
> Tsibliyev, Lazutkin and Foale successfully reactivated the Elektron oxygen generation unit in Kvant 1 today after reconfiguring cooling loops associated with the device. The Elektron's oxygen production and performance is being monitored by the cosmonauts, who are continuing to burn occasional oxygen candles to augment the Elektron's output of O_2.
>
> Today is the 144th day aboard Mir for Tsibliyev and Lazutkin. Foale is nearing the completion of his seventh week aboard the outpost.

As Michael had said before, and would say again and again with resignation there is never a dull day on Mir, as his letter to Rhonda of 3 July, copied to us, testifies.

> Rhonda,
> We had a long night last night, with the guys getting their suits ready in the Node, where I sleep. The suits checked out OK, airtight. We are all tired now, after getting up at six am. Tomorrow Goldin wants

to talk to me, so we have to get up early again.

How are *you* feeling? I feel we should think about how the time is passing, and whether you ever feel a little lonely, next time we talk. I love talking to Jenna and Ian and friends, but we must not forget each other.

Another power supply burned up, powering the laptop for our TSUP messages as well, so I have spent the last hours cobbling tape and wire together. The smell of burning insulation was a big shock to me when I came to the Base Block. Sasha and Vassy had fallen asleep they were so tired, until I shouted out 'Fire!' They rushed to where we do the O_2 candles, but I sniffed around and found the smouldering wires. A strange failure – I think the power converter failed and put higher current through the power leads, 28V instead of 12V!

The TSUP just asked if I had everything fixed and I said yes. I got to do real on-board engineer stuff today, turning on Mir equipment while the guys were in their suits. The flight feels totally different for me now after the collision, since I am now just being an astronaut – not much science. I am even busier than before, like it is a different flight. Maybe because I am sleeping in a different place, and don't have any belongings now!

Please send what you think is appropriate to my mum and dad, they not having such good contact with me, with all the questions they are being asked.

Love, Mike

Then came a welcome personal note about an impending phone call.

3 July 1997

Dear Sir,

I just downloaded this message from Mike. It is *no* problem for me to upload a message back for Mike's family – any way I can help out, please let me know.

Dr D Larsen

Dave, could you pass on the following to my Dad. Thanks.

....

Mum and Dad, and Susie,

We are hoping to do a phone call to you on Saturday about 21:12 BST, I think. Steve Vander Ark at NASA will call you. If you have any specific questions I will try to answer. But we are tired. We got the EVA suit checkouts done today, and an additional electrolysis machine making oxygen I myself started. I am doing ninety per cent station maintenance work with Sasha, filling in at the command post, when Sasha and Vassy are in the spacesuits. Keep in touch with Rhonda, I am giving her the bulk of my daily news ration. I got two letters from you today, I don't know when you sent them. We have been having trouble with TSUP e-mail, and even ham: nothing today, because our laptop/modem power supply burned up (literally). Sasha and Vasily were asleep after lunch, they were so tired, and I noticed the smell while going to get a camera to take a picture of my somnolent crewmates! Up early again – so Mr Goldin can do a TV call to me. I have to get some rest.

Love, Mike

I sent our heartfelt thanks to Dr Larsen, but also took the opportunity to write to Michael. I was anxious that he should know that we continued to be well informed. I said that we had been kept in very close touch with events through his ham radio friends, especially Dave Larsen and the mail he had been able to copy to us. NASA through Steve Vander Ark and Terry Taddeo in Moscow had called us, and Bill Readdy telephoned regularly as well as sending us official updates. I told Michael that everybody was deeply impressed with his determined handling of events, but that he should not allow himself to get too tired. His clarity of thought would continue to be of premium value to everyone. We had tried not to worry too much, as it had a corrosive and unhelpful effect, but we were with him in thought and prayer all the time, as it seemed all his friends, and our friends, were. I told him how we got letters, cards and phone calls every day.

On a lighter note, I told him that we had been at the Royal Regatta at Henley the previous day, guests of Professor Alastair and Ginny Cameron, and that Mary was delighted to see her Minnesota University win its race. That night we were going to St Catharine's College dining members' guest

....

night, but wherever we would be, the conversation would be about him. We were beginning to see him become one of the most experienced international astronauts ever.

4 July

Dave, thanks for the contact. Hope your pain is decreasing. Mike.

Dear Rhonda,

Today, 4 July, is quiet. We go to bed early because we are up at three am to do attitude-control tests. Mir has continued spontaneously to lose attitude control with resultant power criticality, so Vassy changed out a block (computer component) today, and bit tests are scheduled with telemetry coverage – hence an early rise. My job was highly technical, to clear out all the trash boxes that were stacked in front of the panel, behind which the block lay.

I feel a little down right now, because I got distracted by my work and missed the Houston pass. I called the next orbit, and got Dave on the radio who told me that four astronauts had been there to say 'Hi' to me. If you come across them, please apologize for me. They had to have gotten up early too, on a public holiday. I don't know who they were, although I expect Ellen does. Also, I don't know the contact times for Sun., Mon., etc. If you could get those from Ellen, you can tell me when we talk tomorrow, Saturday, at 7:07 am your time. After that, I talk to my parents via Miles [another ham] in Massachusetts.

I think I am going to go and watch the sunrise out the big window, to make myself feel better. Look forward to talking to you tomorrow. I expect you to be sleepy.

Love, Mike

Our phone call took place right on time. I cannot remember much of what was said. We were interested mainly, I suppose, in Michael's tone and demeanour. We knew that they were under great strain, if no longer fearing directly for their lives. There was frequent lack of sleep and an apparently continual succession of attitude-control and therefore power problems. If he sounded pressed and ragged, we would indeed be worried. God bless him, he

....

did not. When his buoyant, cheerful voice came on the phone, Mary and I both smiled broadly and a considerable weight was lifted from us. He had had some really good discussions with Vasily, both about the collision and the forthcoming IVA. Vasily still felt under a heavy burden and increasingly asked for and welcomed Michael's opinions and support. The friendship tentatively begun by Michael was now solid. Here in Cambridge, I think we loved all three of them.

The difficulties in maintaining attitude and thus power on Mir were correctly perceived by Ground Control to be a threat to the internal spacewalk, planned to be done by Tsibliyev and Lazutkin soon after the arrival of the Progress, expected on 7 July. The crew were still attempting to rectify the faulty interface processor, so Ground Control decided to postpone the internal repair attempt for over a week, following the arrival of the Progress, until 17 or 18 July. This would give the crew more time to unpack the supply vessel, a lengthy and strenuous operation in itself, and then rehearse preparation of the Node for the Spektr repair work. The forthcoming repair operation was described by Sergei Krikalev as 'risky', after he had practised several times in the tank, straining through the thirty-one-inch Spektr hatch mock-up while wearing a complete pressurized spacesuit. The dark, damaged interior of Spektr remained an unknown factor. Many cables would have to be found, identified and reconnected to the new hatch.

The Progress 35 launched, and thankfully it docked successfully on 7 July, using the well-tried automatic system while the crew were still controlling the station's attitude manually. The previous Progress 34, the one involved in the docking accident, had been sent into a self-destruct descent into the Pacific Ocean, and the Kvant docking port was free for the new loaded supply vessel. Ground Control ordered the crew to relax and begin off-loading the next day.

7 July

Dear Rhonda,

You were sweet this morning with your sleepy voice. I was a little frantic as I thought the radio was going to die on me – but luckily, because we could not unload the Progress today, I had free time and was able to rewire completely the power set-up for all this gear. And

....

now it works much better, and I know the radio is not burning up, as I first thought. It was a low-voltage problem.

By the time you read this you will have had your first day at school. I really get a kick out of knowing about the everyday things people are doing on earth, now that I am in space. Hams are quite thrown off when all I want to talk about is what is it like where they live! They always wait for me to talk about space stuff.

I am really looking forward to seeing what you sent me in the Progress. I think there will be enough power on Mir to let us go free drift and do the leak pressurization checks of the hatch, so we can open it tomorrow.

Love, Mike

Michael continued to value his close contacts with ham radio operators all around the world. They were deeply interested in him and his feelings, and very generous in the time and phone line costs on his and our behalf. Michael loved talking about ordinary earth things, but many hams only really wanted to talk about radio equipment performance and availability. One day, a ham promised him a picture which would interest him and Michael spent a lot of time preparing and setting up to receive it. The day came and the picture was electronically received, to be eagerly examined by Michael. It was a picture of a radio antenna.

On the day following the docking of the Progress and opening of its hatches, Michael wrote to Rhonda again.

8 July

Dear Rhonda,

We are just now unpacking the Progress – the smell was heavenly, of apples. I have opened two work packages so far, for me, and found my hygiene stuff. Also, all the computer stuff Ken did, and a new video tuner for a laptop so we can make a cinema again, for Vasily. They sent a bunch of videos too, so I am looking forward to getting that together.

The guys received some magazines and letters, one of which smelled of perfume. The smell was intoxicating! Listening to a Russian

....

actor telling a fairy tale, on tape, this morning, written for adults, I realized how sensitive we had become to no female contact – we all noticed how enchanting it was to hear female laughter in the audience. But we aren't getting rowdy in a stereotypical male group attitude, I should add. I found some nice music cassettes, which is great, since I lost the CDs and player in Spektr. I am praying that the stuff from you and my family in UK are in another packet, behind the huge garage full of stuff still in the Progress. Oops, scratch that – Sasha just brought me an unmarked bag with lots of pics, Bible, *chocolate* and other so far unseen goodies. I will post this and go and indulge.

Love, Mike

PS Goldin wants to talk to me on Thursday, I heard, and I will try to show some Greenhouse video.

To know that he could enjoy and revel in a hamper from home, just like when he was at school, we found to be very satisfying, and helpful.

Preparations for the IVA

W hen the off-loading of Progress's supplies began in earnest, Michael's patience was severely tested when he found that many of the bagged items had no labels, or other means of determining the contents, before the labour of opening the bag. The crew were especially interested in the new Spektr hatch and tools, which would be the subject of their combined efforts in the repair venture on 17 July. That date was important in all their minds as marking the first step to get them off the power supply knife-edge. Michael was somewhat mollified

when he found some more goodies which Mary and Susan had sent him, including chocolate and tea. The space shuttle Columbia, on a separate and independent mission, happened to pass within communication range at the time. During an interchange of compliments, Michael jocularly invited them to come over to tea. Reluctantly, Columbia had to decline. In view of the tribulations with which Mir was beset, the commander, James Halsall, said later:

> We all agreed that judging from his attitude – his voice, the inflections in his voice – they were not stressed, they were very cheerful. Mike is a cheerful kind of guy to begin with, and you can see that character trait has been carried with him throughout the problems they've experienced on Mir.

NASA's chief executive, Daniel Goldin, in Washington DC, had been deeply impressed by Michael's cool efficiency, and managed to contact him by phone on 10 July. We first heard of this from Michael's friend and ours, astronaut Bill Readdy, who continued to ensure that we received most of the official NASA–Mir status reports.

10 July 1997

Mary and Colin,

I was at an awards social function last night, and Administrator Goldin as well as George Abbey spoke very highly of Mike. Goldin also commended Frank Culbertson and his team for their spectacular support during this especially challenging mission. Goldin then got up around 01:00 CDT to chat personally with Mike on the radio, and commended him on his professionalism and accomplishments to date. Everyone is very proud of the job he's done, of course, but few people can know or appreciate the leadership and enthusiasm as well as team spirit he's demonstrated to our Russian colleagues – both aboard the Mir and to the Ground Control centre.

This afternoon Ken Bowersox and I chatted to Mike. He and the crew are indeed doing well, but are very, very busy coping with the unloading of Progress and configuring the Node for the internal spacewalk which is currently planned for 17 July. They also sounded a bit fagged out. He said to pass along his best.

Steve Vander Ark will be trying to arrange a phone patch for you all this weekend – Saturday, I think.

All the best, Sean and Peter's Daddy (Bill Readdy)

Michael sent a brief note, after an exhausting day manhandling heavy experiment equipment. It is a model of restraint, but for us who knew him, he had found the hauling imposed by the ill-thought-out contents of the Progress very depressing indeed, as had his colleagues.

10 July

Dear Rhonda,

I liked the description of the children with lunchboxes. It is great that

....

you have some time on your own, to think a little. Also that Ian isn't showing his pugnacious side at school.

I had a breakfast session with Mr Goldin. He was quite personable with me, and seemed genuinely interested in my conditions. I said all was fine, and thanked everybody for their efforts on my behalf. I showed the huge umbilical hatch cap we got on Progress – he was impressed. Then we talked about Mars and Pathfinder, and he said I was young enough to go to Mars. I said I was glad to hear that. Then he said that the Prime Minister of Great Britain wants to talk to me! I said it would be a privilege and maybe, getting a trip to England won't be so hard, after all! [A meeting with Prime Minister Tony Blair was arranged to take place at a White House dinner in January 1998.]

We are all pretty worn out getting a huge piece of equipment out of Progress and Kvant, all the way through the station and the Node to the 'ceiling' in Kristall, taking all of us three hours, and then searching through all the different bags for things the ground just thought of at the last minute, all unloaded from Progress. Of course, those things will have to be stored in modules that have no power, are +5 degrees Celsius and covered in water condensation. A hard day. No chance to exercise properly, I think, for any of us until it is all over. But it is never dull here!

Kiss Jenna and Ian for me.

I love you. Mike

Another note was written two days later.

12 July

Dear Rhonda,

I hope all is calm at home. It feels a little better here, now that most of the work of going through all the supplies and EVA items on Progress is complete. Sasha is building up the hatch umbilical adapter in the Node, and is attaching thick cables to each of its thirty-six connectors. It looks like a huge jellyfish, with Medusa-like cables.

Vassy and I have been clearing out the Soyuz of non-essential

....

items, so that the living module part can be used as an airlock for them in the event the Spektr hatch can't be reclosed airtight, for some reason, and therefore in turn they cannot repressurize the Node and enter the station [the Soyuz living module would then provide an otherwise unavailable escape route for them]. I feel pleased that it was I who came up with this contingency plan first, a week ago. We have been talking with Sergei Krikalev every day, discussing the IVA. He is in charge, I think. He is listening to our questions and ideas carefully. I think it is all going to work out OK, but the danger here is in not thinking out the little details, so we are doing our best to go over every little thing. There will be a training run on Tuesday. I will be in the Soyuz, playing out my role as the IVA monitoring crew member reading out the IVA checklist and time line. I will be on comm with them the whole time, as they will be using electrical umbilicals for power and comm with me and the TSUP.

I have decided not to try to wipe down Kristall today – I need a break from that cold, dark and wet place, which I call 'podval' [cellar in Russian].

I just had a good phone patch, courtesy of Dave Larsen and Miles, with my parents. They ask very good questions, so as to be ready if questioned by the press. I have asked Dave if he could do the same for Larissa Tsibliyev, and that he should use our phone number to bill the calls. It is very important for Vassy, I think.

Enough. I love you. Mike

The phone call Michael referred to had this time been different. NASA warned us about it, and we found that we would be away staying with friends Ross and Kate Lambert at their old farmhouse, Pomfrets, in Norfolk. Ross and Kate too were retired RAF folk, he with his distinctive deep voice, no doubt nurtured by Hertford College, Oxford, and she with her clear expressive style, often in use at the local amateur dramatic society. Their home was being battered by violent summer storms, and sitting in their glass conservatory it was hard to hear oneself speak. But during a lull in the thunder, and right on time, we took the call there and our friends were deeply impressed that their phone had received a call from space. In spite of the

....

continuous local storms, we all planned the next day to attend an open-air concert in the evening in the grounds of the Queen's Norfolk home, Sandringham. The event would be attended by thousands, for a picnic, music and fireworks. The weather magically cleared in time. The whole splendid affair seemed to us and our party of ten friends to be an emotional celebration of Michael's continued survival and endurance.

The huge piece of equipment referred to by Michael was a tank of liquid the size of a double bed, one of the items shunted into Kristall for storage, then back to Kvant when a shuttle needed to dock there. Moving the tank was a soul-destroying experience for the crew, very difficult to shift without risking damage to walls and piping (indeed the possible cause of ethylene glycol leaks in the past), or damaging their fingers, in my view reflecting no credit on the ground for blandly sending it up without proper measurement control.

Hard work had become the norm on Mir. Due to the general power shortage, it had been necessary to isolate the Priroda and Kristall modules from heat or ventilation and large amounts of condensed water were accumulating, threatening equipment and experiments. There was no alternative but to turn to with towels in a continuous mopping-up exercise. The day's status report referred to the crew spending most of their day 'conducting housekeeping chores' aboard the station, a phrase that conjures up a scene of relaxed domestic labour, but which was only too necessary and actually very demanding. If the crew were becoming bored with the repetitive nature, hard labour and discomfort of their responsibilities, a new twist was about to change their internal spacewalk plans fundamentally.

On 13 July Tsibliyev was found to have a heartbeat anomaly which might be an early sign of a threatened heart attack. The crew were regularly checked by Ground Control's medical staff, and Tsibliyev was asked one day to provide oscilloscope readings prior to and during his morning exercise on the ergometer. The doctor at Ground Control asked him first to relax, to form a base line. The oscilloscope showed an abnormality even at this stage, and provoked a string of medical questions, the most important of which was how long had he been conscious of it? 'A few days,' Tsibliyev answered.

Michael had his back to Tsibliyev at the time, handling the comms packet. He overheard and turned around. As soon as he saw the oscilloscope,

....

he says, he sensed that this was going to put him in the IVA hot seat.

Although the worst symptoms appeared to diminish over the next few days, it was enough to tip Ground Control towards a closer look at Michael as an immediate replacement for Tsibliyev on the spacewalk. The crew were ordered meanwhile to rest, and on 15 July NASA was formally approached by Ground Control, who asked for agreement that Michael should participate in the internal spacewalk.

At first Michael was happy enough with the idea – he had already conducted a four-and-a-half-hour external spacewalk from the shuttle on his previous mission in 1995, and appeared to have no fears about leaving the station to go into space. During his time in Russia he had trained in the use of the Russian spacesuit and he was the right size, and, like his crew, he longed for the restoration of power which the IVA would hopefully bring. NASA unhesitatingly agreed his suitability in principle, but postponed a final decision while American and Russian discussions about the conducting of the work continued in Korolyov.

It is amazing how quickly the world's media pounce on such events, or rumours of them, and by 15 July we were beginning to be besieged by enquiries about Michael's IVA participation. We sent a request for advice or confirmation to Terry Taddeo, Michael's doctor in Moscow. I felt that he was bound to know the facts. This provoked a welcome phone call from him, which allowed us to deal more informatively with the press.

Communications from Mir to Ground Control had improved due to the installation of equipment brought by the Progress, allowing for transmissions via the newly placed geostationary satellite, Altair 2. This was a Russian satellite which had recently been moved to a more useful orbit. But communication also depended on the new, if only temporary, stability of the power tightrope-walk on Mir. Michael was able to send more thoughtful advice to his nominated successor, Wendy Lawrence, via TSUP, knowing how the prospect of her launch to Mir might at the least be sobering.

Wednesday, 16 July
Wendy,

Priroda is a good module, with good equipment, well organized. No problem doing work there. The Greenhouse is in Kristall, and is also

....

working well, getting power from Base Block (only source of light in that module, no source of light in Priroda). The bulk of my experiments were associated with these modules. I simply lived in Spektr and kept biology-type experiments there. If the IVA goes OK, and power is restored, then Priroda and Kristall can be powered [again]. Independent of what your crew can do, you can do good worthwhile stuff there. And earth observation is potentially good from Kristall or Kvant 2. I am enjoying myself, as I did before the collision. I just have different duties now, because there is little science but lots of maintenance. But it's fun. Even wiping wet walls in dark, cold modules, if you get to drink hot chocolate afterwards with your crewmates. I am now camped out in the PNO of Kvant 2, very comfy, potentially private.

If power is not restored, Priroda can't be powered for long, Kristall can't be powered for long, and dockings, etc., are very power-critical – so in this case I think the whole issue of Phase 1 [i.e., the continued attachment of NASA astronauts] will be rediscussed. But as I say above, I am still enjoying the flight, even in a power-critical condition, because I have things to do with the crew. So watch the results of the IVA closely. If you think of being a helper to your crew, and your goal is just to be here, then that will help you also. It is never dull on station Mir.

All the best, Mike

At this time David Larsen suggested to Michael in his e-mail an experiment in computer file retrieval, a subject which had great interest for them both. But for one of the first times ever, Michael was unenthusiastic because he was so busy. He was tied up with station maintenance and preparations for the IVA. He realized that the success of the latter was critical for the future life of the station, and much still remained to be worked out. Without more power, the other modules could not function properly. Being cold, they collected more and more water condensation. He was therefore much occupied trying to keep pace with the water on the walls, at a temperature of ten degrees Celsius or lower, in the dark, with a flashlight in his mouth. Michael's efforts freed Sasha to make pre-IVA installations and Vasily to install the Antares

....

transmitter, which would allow two-way video conferences and forty-five-minute comm periods. Ground Control was eager to have the system working before the IVA took place.

Always during the night passes it was prudent to check the charge levels of all the batteries and to accept the chore of swapping a strong one for a weak. Michael was once again reminded of how weightlessness does not stop the momentum of a high-mass object, like a battery, maliciously pinching your fingers as one tries to manoeuvre the thing to its new position. This whole process, he once said to me quietly, was *awful*. For Michael, this was strong language indeed. It was cold, wet and dreary. It was physically tiring and spiritually diminishing. A pinched finger could produce tears.

The crew were often very tired, and needed to take full advantage of their sleep shifts. The residue of the Russian crew's basic brief, to look after the foreigner, as well as their new relationship, made sure that Michael was offered a good share. But he was increasingly worried about Vasily, who just would not take enough time to sleep. Sasha too was concerned, and sometimes did the comm passes without reminding Vasily. Michael and Sasha did a deal for one of them always to be awake, no matter what. But Vasily heard.

'Michael, I must be awake for this pass; don't let Sasha do it. Wake me up!' said the exhausted Vasily.

Michael had no option but to carry out Vasily's instructions, but there came a time when Vasily was so tired that he left him alone, as Sasha would have wished. Ground Control noticed Vasily's absence from the comm pass.

'He is sleeping,' Sasha said.

'Good,' they said, 'let him sleep.'

Preparations for the IVA to take place in the vacuum of Spektr and a depressurized Node required an overall rearrangement of sleeping and storage positions. This was because the central Node would have to be used as the decompression start point, all five hatches closed and sealed with the cosmonauts fully dressed and checked out in their spacesuits, after which the Node's atmosphere would be vented to create a vacuum. This would permit removal of the hatch to Spektr, whose interior was already in a vacuum. Much preparation was needed before all other hatches into the Node could be fully closeable, including the one to Soyuz where the third crew member would be positioned in case they all had to escape.

....

Immediately following the collision there had been nowhere for Michael to sleep, because there was no power or ventilation except in the Base Block and the Node. He had therefore arranged himself for sleep with his lower half in Priroda, where the air was stagnant and very cold, and his top, breathing, half in the Node where it was warm, and, because of air movement, he would not risk suffocation from CO_2 build-up. Even this inconvenient arrangement now had to cease.

All the EVA items normally stored in Kvant 2, such as the spacesuits which would be needed and the TORU control box, had to be moved to other places. The suits went to the Node, which prevented Michael's top half from sleeping there, but now Kvant 2 had a little free space and had regained a little power since attitude stabilization. Thankfully, Michael accepted Vasily and Sasha's conclusion that there really was no place left now for him to move to except Kvant 2. With a cleared space, warmth and ventilation, Michael continued to sleep there until almost the end of his stay on Mir. As far as sleep was concerned, it was his first taste of a sense of permanence since the collision, and raised his spirits enormously.

Now, whatever the primary activity happened to be on the station, he was an active helper to either or both colleagues, but he was still not being formally time-lined by Ground Control. Perhaps they feared they might have to pay him. He watched his colleagues, measuring their natural resistance to interference, and made tactical sallies, to let Vasily sleep, or to go away and think about something else. With his influence, they remembered to take breaks. They began to avoid working for more than three hours straight, if the work involved normal routines. They stopped and had tea. I proudly see him as imposing a kind of British influence, beneficial and heartening.

Michael's Greenhouse in Kristall had been in danger from lack of light and heat after the loss of Spektr's power. For some reason, the equipment had never been powered directly from Kristall's batteries, but from a lead to the solar arrays of Spektr, which were no longer available. He discovered that one of the cables that had been recklessly, but necessarily, cut was the one that led from Spektr's interior to the Greenhouse, now lying dormant in the Node. All he had to do was repair the hacked end, plug it into an extension lead from the Base Block (now often fully powered) into the Node, and at a stroke he could save his crop. He was jubilant. Of course, whenever there

....

was a power crisis in the future, he had to remember to switch it off again. He did this several times, but everything survived, probably from residual heat when there was no power, or perhaps his crop acquired a new, tough resilience in its first season in space. He also kept his Gobi desert beetles in the same area.

Those areas which were not regularly powered and heated, such as Kristall and especially Priroda, continued to collect condensed water steadily in enormous and, for Michael, alarming quantities. The water sat in giant globules held together by surface tension. He spent two hours every day trying to mop them up. He carried a twenty-two-litre metal can with a pump and hose, and, the flashlight in his mouth, sucked up each ball of water he could find adhering to the skin of the module. He got very wet and developed a skin rash from dissolved chemicals in the water. He took a break after two hours to examine his catch, which, because of nil gravity, was always a uniformly mixed fluid of air and water. He found that trying to separate the air and water in the can was very hard to do in weightless space, and resolved that this deficiency would be a major item for research in his debrief when he returned to earth. He tried everything, even swinging a flexible container around his head to force water centrifugally to one end, then squeezing it quickly into a can before it diffused again with the air.

Working in the dark areas, he had become very conscious of the consequences of the cold. But the opposite effect in the Base Block was increasingly trying. Because of the fundamental lack of power available for Kristall and Priroda, neither module had fans working to help the overall effort to move air through the station. So while each of the inert modules was full of very cold air (and increasing amounts of water), the Node and particularly the Base Block got correspondingly hot. Sasha decided that something had to be done about this, and Michael wholly agreed. A plan was made.

There were a number of cloth-like ducts snaking through the station which were redundant, since inadequate power prevented all the station's large fans from working together. They found they had some smaller, low-power fans whose 'bore' would fit inside the ducts. With suitable extension cables leading to remotely positioned fans, and some realignment of the ducts, the system gradually gathered up hot air from the Base Block, passed

....

it through the Node and then deep into the cold, wet hearts of Kristall and Priroda, a hundred feet away. Slowly but surely, the cool, damp air was displaced and floated back towards and into the Base Block. The effect was only slight, but so welcome. They conferred and drew complex schematic diagrams of air flow and used lots of grey tape – probably a major contribution to keeping the station viable for full resuscitation after long periods of limited power. Michael praises Sasha as the expert on this, and found himself quietly displaying this expertise later to the relief crew.

He continued to feel spoiled by the way both Vasily and Sasha made time for him to do the twice-daily physical fitness exercises, which they rarely did for themselves. It made him feel a bit like Sasha's American poodle, but he had to comply or they would have lost some of their contract money. Sasha did exercise, but Vasily almost never did, and he was still suffering from post-collision malaise exacerbated by his awareness of a heart problem.

Gradually Michael's meticulous, punctual presence during comm passes began to be recognized by Ground Control, and they finally began, without ceremony, to use him formally. He was entirely reliable in receiving instructions in Russian during comm passes, and equally reliable in passing them on to the relevant crew member. He also found himself checking that the instructions had been implemented, tricky ground for an outsider, but by this time neither Vasily nor Sasha minded. He also took it upon himself to remind them of the comm passes and get them in position on time, for which, because they were so pressed, they were grateful. They had indeed begun to see Michael as an essential, equal part of the team.

Often, as a mass of messages came in, he found it helpful to sort them for the commander and the flight engineer. There were many pages of messages directly concerning the upcoming IVA repair work. Michael managed to organize and collate the mass of individual messages into coherent sections, and then print out the results with appropriate priority designation for Vasily or Sasha. Knowing how labour-saving clear organization is when you are overwrought and not thinking clearly, they were very lucky indeed to have him. Michael ruefully remembered that excellent character Radar, a worth-his-weight-in-gold corporal in the old TV series *MASH*. Like Radar, Michael had no actual title, and the Russians never accepted that he should do *real* system work. But now they allowed

....

him to fulfil this essential function as the comm officer, who could track all the things that had to be done and see that they happened. Nobody had a job description for this, so nobody was accountable. To myself as an air force officer, it seems close to exercising command. Whatever it was, Michael was heaven's gift to the Mir crew. In his landing interview, Mike said that the software program he wrote for this purpose was his most permanent gift to the Russians.

Knowing everything that was being thought and said, Michael even found himself deciding whether a message needed to be seen by Vasily or not. Vasily was not sure at first whether this would work, but within three or four days he went out of his way to help Michael in the making of such decisions. He had learned to trust and welcome his judgement.

I asked Michael during our Mir talks whether he had ever considered where his ability to rise to the occasion so often on Mir had come from. Was it his school, King's, Canterbury, or Cambridge University, or was it simply genetic? Wisely, he avoided the genetic possibility in his considered answer – few sons can see themselves as anything if not a radical improvement on their fathers, most of the time. But neither did he offer his school or college. He said it was all to do with being the son of an RAF officer. I of course beamed, but he said that he was not unique, and that the trait was common in service children, wherever or whatever their parents were. He thought that it was to do with travel, constantly meeting and adjusting to new people and making new friends. Well, yes, that much was obvious, I felt. But in addition, almost all of his parents' friends had been active, efficient officers, with command responsibilities, so a lot of RAF adventure, good judgement, humour and wisdom would have rubbed off, whether he liked to admit it or not. In fact, he has long since accepted that it did. On the genetic point, not every son of an air force officer wants to become a pilot, let alone an astronaut, but I have observed that his closest astronaut friends are ex-service pilots themselves, and the sons and daughters of similar. Later I asked him what qualities were most important. He said, somewhat grimly, dogged endurance. And clear thinking, he added.

He felt that his major contribution seemed always to be to help his colleagues think clearly. But his thinking also brought practical improvements in the technical area, devising the software printing program, moving and

....

improving power supplies, working out complex orientation problems – all things which the Russians had not been able to do, so he saved them a lot of time.

One day as they sat together for a meal, Vasily said, 'Do you know, Misha, of all the things that we have lost since the collision, the one thing I miss most?'

'No, what is it?' asked Michael, thinking of heat, cooling, lack of oxygen generation, lack of the CO_2 scrubber, loss of experiments, less use of the toilet.

'It is your video cinema, when we huddled together in the duck's bill, and your vivid translations.'

Michael was moved off-balance by this unexpected reply. He had been too busy to reinstate his little picture show complete with video tuner, which had arrived over a week ago on the Progress. He quickly rearranged his priorities.

He found that Vasily as well as Sasha was becoming ever more companionable and forthcoming, as the pressure to start the IVA to restore Spektr's power increased. He was already very aware of the international commercial and scientific pressures on the Mir station, of which they, the crew, were on the receiving end. Vasily and Sasha's tenure had featured a series of rare set-backs, some very frightening, and all causing discomfort. They had already endured as much as it was reasonable to expect of them, but now the pressure was on them to undertake a unique and unrehearsed internal repair activity into the vacuum of Spektr.

The planned twenty-one-day attachment of the French astronaut, Leopold Eyharts, would be in question until Spektr's power was restored. If power was not restored by the time the relief crew launched from Baikonur, Leopold would not go. The Russians could ill afford the loss of the many millions of hard currency such a withdrawal would entail, and they would do everything they could to keep up French hopes that the possibility of a timely repair was real. From the Russian point of view, and given their financial situation, their attitude was reasonable and at least still worth a try. The strength of their determination and the wide understanding of it within Energiya had, in a matter of days, led to the design and production of the unique new Spektr hatch cover.

....

An obvious corollary of this zeal, and the will to pull things together quickly in order to restore Mir, was that the Russian crew felt more pressure, especially Vasily, whose morale needed a boost, but also Sasha, who gave him so much support. Both continued to feel, rightly or wrongly, that they were the objects of a wave of Russian anger for causing the interruption of the planned succession of lucrative and prestigious commercial attachments.

Michael too was conscious of the anger being directed at his colleagues, and the possibility of an expensive delay for Russia to French participation. No doubt urged by the Russians, the French remained silent, awaiting events. They would of course be happiest if the repairs were carried out successfully and on time by the existing crew. It would be surprising if, meanwhile, NASA was not also looking carefully at events as they unfolded. They were impressed by Russian inventiveness and resolve on the ground, but it must have crossed their minds to wonder if the Russians were not pushing a little too hard, perhaps even inviting a worse mishap than the collision. Two ground-to-air discussions involving Energiya's chief, Semeonov, had already occurred, and in both the main aim was clear: to attempt the IVA as soon as possible.

The pressure's first victim had been Vasily's heart. Michael knew that this could put him in the hot seat. But as the spotlight of pressure moved inexorably towards him, he too found that, thus illuminated, he was not very comfortable. The source of the pressure now was not science, but money. NASA rightly saw this as a Russian problem, and for the time being did not interfere, but they carefully withheld final agreement for Michael to participate in the IVA. In the general spirit of international accord and cooperation, they obviously would prefer to see the repairs completed, the French keep their Mir appointment and the NASA–Mir astronaut attachments continue. But they could see too that money considerations were becoming dominant. One must imagine that the American and French space agencies were having interesting discussions too, the Americans perhaps pointing out that the possibly unwise pressure on the Russians was entirely due to their, the French, programme. In America, meanwhile, some congressmen were again expressing anti-Mir sentiments, doubting the benefits of American–Russian cooperation, and demanding that it cease.

Nobody at this stage said openly that the French should pull out and

....

relieve the pressure on the crew. Ironically, this was brought about inadvertently by the crew itself.

Pulling the Plug

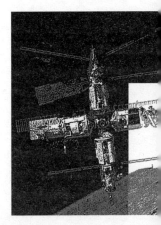

The plan for the internal vehicular activity in vacuum (IVA) to restore Spektr's power was necessarily complex. To be able to open the closed hatch to Spektr and enter its interior, presently in vacuum due to the collision rupture, the cosmonauts in their spacesuits would first have to be in an 'airlock' where pressure could be reduced to zero, like Spektr. The only access point was from the Node, so it would be necessary to depressurize the Node itself. The Node had five other hatches, to the Base Block and to the other modules, all of which would have to be closed and sealed. During the development of the station, more and more ducts and cables had been passed through these hatch openings, of varying sizes. The possible need to depressurize the Node, turning it into an airlock, had never been thought likely.

Before the Node's atmosphere could be depressurized, each of these openings would have to have the ducts and cables removed or unplugged or connected temporarily to the module's own internal batteries, so that each hatch could be closed and sealed off. This process would be complicated and time-consuming and needed rehearsing, getting as much done before the IVA day as possible. The crew would need to conserve their energy before beginning the internal spacewalk, which promised to be arduous.

It was a new process, so Vasily and Sasha would be starting from scratch. The one hundred and forty cables involved were not colour-coded, all were a uniform yellow, so it was important to use a descriptive manual to ensure that the disconnection and reconnection were done in the right sequence. An ill-timed disconnection might have unknown repercussions on a station entirely dependent on the complexity, and present paucity, of electrical power.

Two days before the start of the IVA, Sasha positioned himself in the Node to begin the work as he had been instructed. He was to disconnect 100 of the 140 cables running through the Node, in advance of the last 40 which would not be disconnected until just before the IVA itself.

Book in hand, he set about identifying the cables and establishing the sequence of action. When he had gone through the process notionally, it was time to begin the actual movement of ducts and disconnection of cables. He began the planned sequence, frequently having to take his eyes off the cables to refer to the manual and vice versa. All went well: he knew which were the dangerous cables, those that had to be done only during the IVA. His cross-referencing action with the book became more frequent. Once, he nearly pulled the wrong plug, and in a tense moment thought that he had. Thankfully, it was all right.

Sasha continued happily enough, and then, after further consulting his book, he pulled a plug and froze.

He looked at the manual again and whitened. At first he was relieved to notice that nothing seemed to have happened. He floated to the Base Block and put his face through the entrance.

'I have pulled a wrong plug. Has anything happened?'

Almost immediately a sombre-toned alarm boomed and he knew that it had.

He had inadvertently disconnected the vital inter-gyrodyne communicator, the system that, with computer back-up, allowed the stabilizing gyrodynes to influence each other's speed and precession effect, so that the combination of forces kept the station steady in space.

He could hardly have done worse. He knew that the disconnection would be like a lobotomy to the balance of the cells of the brain. He did not know, nobody knew, what precise effect it would now have. It was no good putting the disconnected piece back – the injured system would need time to

....

recover. With a sinking heart he nevertheless re-established the connection, but with no real hope. Already, he could sense the gyrodynes' spinning notes changing, and it was not long before the station began a slow tumble that, to the crew, felt like an animal's death throes.

He tried to speak and failed. He tried again and said hoarsely, 'Vasily, I have disconnected the wrong plug, the one that affects the gyrodynes. I would rather have shot myself.'

Vasily took the news calmly, almost with fatalistic resignation. He talked briefly and urgently to TSUP as, with the station's tumble, their solar power dwindled with frightening speed. Michael was on his sleep shift.

The cable was part of the Base Block's attitude-control computer, which enabled the gyrodynes to communicate with each other and to work in harmony. Suddenly this had stopped, and the effect on the station was immediate. From being the station's intelligent, helpful and cooperative attitude monitors and correctors, they became random vandals signalling wrong and contradictory information about station attitude control. It was as though the system had gone mad. To lose this degree of control in space is close to losing everything. It is possible that Ground Control should immediately have seen the implications for power loss, and advised them to switch off all non-essential functions. But they did not. As the station tumbled chaotically, Vasily and Sasha exchanged helpless glances. The batteries had almost fully discharged. Michael was now wakened from what had been a poor sleep shift, and told of the mistake and its aftermath.

He began to assess what was happening by mentally going through each of the system's components in turn. The gyrodynes are large, heavy masses positioned around the station. They spin in the opposite direction from that in which they want the station to turn. Their speed and therefore the strength of their influence is ordered by the main computer depending on thermal sensing of the earth's surface and also Mir's rough geographic position. The computer's instructions are themselves affected by feedback from the gyrodynes, so that an unreasonable demand on an individual gyrodyne cannot be made.

The plug disconnection, even only for seconds, had left every gyrodyne to sense the break differently and respond differently, no longer in touch with the next gyrodyne along. They continued this chaotic ramble into unreason

....

until they all individually gave up and spun down, at varying rates, into power-saving mode. One moment the station had been steady and stable, oriented to the sun, the next all gyrodynes were spinning down at different rates in different directions, each giving a different signal to the station's orientation to spin in the opposite direction. The station tried desperately but forlornly to comply, resulting in a multi-axis spin.

Freed from all restraint of control or possible braking, the gyrodynes took three hours to complete their spin-down, continuing to impart random signals for another two orbits as battery power bled away and was not replaced.

The crew were again in total darkness during the night passes, life-support systems were again threatened and they were all back, with a vengeance, to the conditions of near helplessness which had followed the collision of 25 June. Electrically it was worse. There was now power only for the simplest of communications to Ground Control, and that had to be undertaken from the Soyuz escape craft. It was a demoralizing blow, but at least they thought they knew what they had to do, having had the practice. Indeed, the greatest danger would be from the collapse of their own morale and clear thinking, in this game of snakes and ladders. First, they went to Soyuz to reopen communications with Ground Control to tell them what was happening.

On earth, we knew nothing of this latest space drama. We were looking forward to an annual treat. Our family enjoyment of Shakespeare takes us each year to a celebrated amateur company's productions near Stamford – *Macbeth* was being played in July, and this was the drama that occupied our minds. The Stamford Shakespeare Company is dedicated to excellence, performing in a tented garden arena at Tolethorpe Hall just north of the ancient town. Dinner can be bought in the Hall before the play, but if the weather forecast is good, it seems right to take one's own special summer champagne picnic to eat in the extensive grounds. For the past few years, my retired English schoolteacher, Aileen Button, has been our house guest for the occasion. After all, she led me to Shakespeare over fifty years ago, and it seems most appropriate now to return the favour, and it was she who shared the first news I had of Mir's collision at the class reunion on 25 June.

On Wednesday, 16 July, Aileen had barely had time to put her case in

....

her room after her afternoon arrival at our house in Cambridge, when the phone rang. It was a TV network news desk, and would I be prepared to comment on the latest happenings on Mir? I did not know that there had been any 'latest happenings', so I found myself once again asking the media to tell me all they knew. The news desk person said, 'We don't know much. Somebody on Mir has accidentally disconnected a plug which has caused the station to spin chaotically. It has lost altitude.'

'What?' I said. '*Altitude?*'

'That is what Moscow has said.'

I got a grip of myself and thought carefully before my next question. If Mir was indeed losing altitude, something had happened to slow down its orbital speed; it would eventually reach the atmosphere where it would begin to burn up. If evacuation by Soyuz was still practicable, it would have to be done without delay to give the crew half a chance. But I was wary as well as actively hoping that it was not true. Altitude is not a term much used in space; orbital distance or orbital height is the normal way of referring to distance from earth. The station was spinning, so that meant it would automatically have lost its best *attitude*, serious enough because of the consequent loss of solar power. But I much preferred a loss of attitude to a loss of altitude.

'Are you sure that Moscow said "altitude"? I asked. 'Could it not have been "attitude"?'

'Stand by,' said the news desk, obviously impressed by the possibility. A little later he confirmed that no current reference was being made to altitude, only attitude. I was very much relieved. Attitude had been lost – and regained – before. No doubt the crew could do it again. Its loss was not an immediate killer.

We tuned in to the next scheduled TV news programme. Our phone had been ringing almost continuously with local and national reporters and news agencies seeking us out for comment, which we have always been ready to give, provided we thought that we knew the facts. I was actually talking to one reporter when the early evening newscast started. They showed Moscow Ground Control's chief controller, Vladimir Solovyov, and he was speaking in English, but looking as if he was under pressure. He said that a plug on board Mir had been pulled out in error, and that this had destabilized

....

the station to an unprecedented degree, with the result that the station was now spinning chaotically out of control. Ground Control were unable to help, and he did not know what efforts were being made by the crew, if any were possible. After a sentence or two directed, as it were, off-stage in Russian, he seemed to say in English, in a low voice, 'What am I supposed to be dealing with, a kindergarten?' It was not clear to whom he was referring, controllers, crew or the media.

Although not as catastrophic as I had feared, it was severe enough to have left this normally cool controller without any reassuring answers whatsoever.

Mary, Aileen and I had a thoughtful supper that night. The phone continued to bring requests for media interviews, ideally to be held in London, but if we were going to take our anxiety anywhere the next day, it was going to be to *Macbeth* at Tolethorpe Hall. The last news I picked up before going to bed was on teletext. It said that the crew had begun to reduce the chaos of the tumbling, and expected to regain some stability by tomorrow. We tried to sleep, knowing that once again the harrowed crew, and our Michael, would be sleepless for hours trying to find a way to restore the station, before facing a final decision to abandon it for good.

I could not forget how Ground Control had been so clearly shaken by Tsibliyev's brief report. The words used by them to the world's media were that attitude control had been totally lost and that the station was spinning *chaotically* out of control. In their minds it was a very serious situation. No immediate action had yet been decided upon. All talk of an internal IVA was postponed. 'Human error' was mentioned, but they declined to say who was in error. Ground Control was disturbed to hear the crew having what might have been a laugh over the incident, perhaps leading the Head Controller, Vladimir Solovyov, to mutter the phrase we had heard, 'Is this a kindergarten?'

The crew were in fact more alone than ever before. The chaotic tumble was far greater than a ground-originated signal to the thrusters could possibly have coped with, and in any case, power to receive instructions on the station was dwindling fast. Ground Control said, 'Vasily, we cannot help you, and nothing the station thrusters will produce can have any effect. The situation is entirely new to us. We think that you should try again the Michael Solution.'

The Michael Solution was the procedure invented by Michael on the

....

View of Mir from docked shuttle.

View of departing Atlantis - too late to change his mind now.

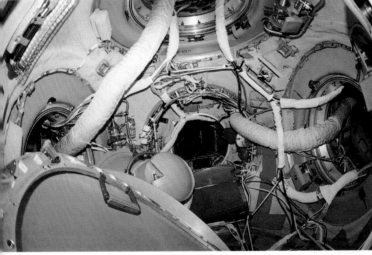

Aleksandr (Sasha) Lazutkin, Michael's first crew engineer on Mir, with typical Mir clutter.

Inside Mir's node. It is relatively uncluttered except for the tangle of cables and ducts which had multiplied over the years. All would have to be removed for the node to become an air lock for the IVA to Spektr.

New Spektr hatch cover with reconnection cables for those so hurriedly cut for crew survival on 25 June.

Soyuz with new crew approaching Mir on 7 August.

Mir from the Soyuz fly around with Spektr's damaged solar arrays against the dark sky. Kristall and Priroda modules are just visible left and right of Spektr. Kvant 2 module is hidden by the Base Block and its aft dock which faces the camera.

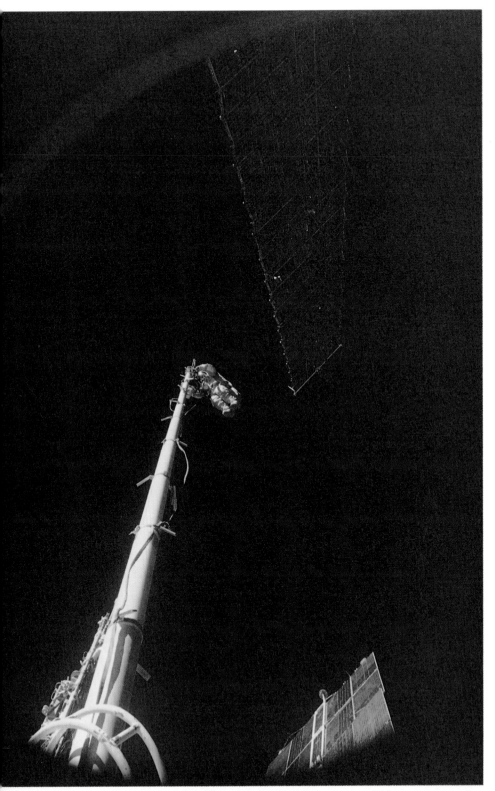

EVA from Mir on 6 September, Anatoli on the end of the crane arm. This was operated with great care by Michael, who was also outside the spacecraft.

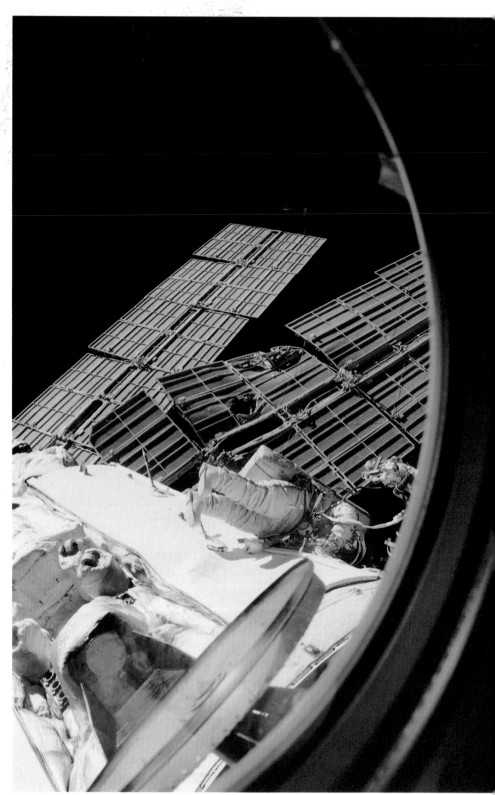

EVA, Mir's hatch in airlock open to space. Some of the collision damage to Spektr's solar arrays can be seen.

TS86 Atlantis launch to retrieve Michael and deliver his replacement. Michael heard
f the successful launch from ham radio enthusiasts at an English girls' school.

1ichael's second Russian crew on Mir, Pavel Vinogradov on left, Commander Anatoli
olovyev on right. Centre is Michael's relief, Dave Wolf.

Michael shortly before coming down, unquestionably happy!

A delighted but weak Michael greets Ian and Jenna back on earth on 6 October – note Jenna's grown-up restraint.

Mike and Rhonda, celebrating Hogmanay in Scotland with the family following Michael's safe return.

occasion of the first, collision-induced tumble, using the Soyuz thrusters, but at that time it had at least been preceded by Ground Control managing to stop the wildest part of the station's rotation.

Vasily readily agreed, and went to the Soyuz cockpit during a night pass while Michael went to a window to assess the apparent movement of the stars. He gave Vasily a trial correction, which Vasily this time willingly imparted to the Soyuz thrusters.

BANG! BANG! BANG! BANG! Oh, no! All three crew shrank within themselves. There had been an immediate staccato noise like machine-gun fire from Soyuz. It was a frightening shock, and Vasily rapidly turned everything off and evacuated the Soyuz craft with its dramatic malfunction to rejoin the others in the Node. An urgent conference began, interrupted by Vasily returning to the Soyuz to report the unexpected phenomenon to Ground Control. The noise and reaction of the Soyuz thrusters was something else not experienced before. It was very worrying, not just because of the startling effect on the crew, who briefly wondered if they were going to be blown up, but also because of the nagging background worry that something was wrong with their escape craft, at a time when the station in its sinister tumble might soon be powerless and escape the only remaining option.

Ground Control were baffled and then very worried. This showed in Controller Vladimir Solovyov's voice; he was no expert on Soyuz operation, a distinct preserve of pilots. Vasily, too, was baffled and unwilling to try again. There followed a period of desperate thinking.

It was Michael who postulated the idea that the trouble could be associated with the random nature of the gyrodyne spin-down and the station's erratic responses about numerous axes. Through the Soyuz link he called down to Ground Control, 'I think it could be an interaction between the random gyrodyne effect on the station and an automatic Soyuz thruster system trying forlornly to compensate. If this is so, then the Soyuz is attempting the impossible, because its thrusters are too close together for them to make any difference to the behaviour of the station. They will tend to overcompensate every second.'

The ground pondered this, then entered into a detailed review with Vasily on the Soyuz automatic attitude and control system which, under normal steady flight conditions, would be switched 'on' to smooth out and correct any slight non-pilot-induced influences. As a trial, it was decided to isolate the thrusters from the usual automatic sensing system, converting them into dumb rockets responding solely to the pilot's demands, a purely manual set-up. All agreed that this must be a step in the right direction, but that it would also be prudent to wait another orbit to see if the gyrodynes had spun down sufficiently to reduce their mischievous influence on the station.

The crew meanwhile floated about the station switching off anything that had been missed and feeling each gyrodyne as they passed it to sense whether it was still spinning. Some still were, so they waited another orbit and the next night pass. All then agreed that it was time to try again. With a look of some solemnity and continued resignation, Vasily nodded to Michael and went once more to the Soyuz cockpit. Michael went to Kvant 2 to observe the motion of the stars. Michael gave an instruction to Vasily. Vasily responded tentatively on the thrusters, all of them fearful of the result. It worked! There was no machine-gun effect.

The relief was so heartfelt that for a moment they forgot what they were trying to achieve. Where was the sun? Gone, during hours of tumbling orbit. Michael applied himself again, giving instructions to Vasily, who readily complied. After fifteen or twenty minutes Michael asked for the exact opposite input, and again Vasily accurately complied. In RAF terms, a perfect harmony in the union of pilot and navigator had been achieved. The crew thought that they heard the sound of triumphant celestial music as the sun rose with the beginning of the next day pass, in an effective position for the solar arrays once again to stimulate the station into life.

This time, Michael was able to persuade Vasily to impart a faster spin rate to stabilize the station. When power was sufficiently regained, the gyrodynes would be restarted. The faster spin rate did not remove the tendency of this imperfect top to flip, but it did reduce the flip frequency. Psychologically this was good for the crew, not because they physically felt the flip – being weightless they would not – but they had found it disturbingly confusing suddenly to notice the sun in the wrong place. They steeled themselves, waited another orbit and lo, the flip was reversed. Good.

On earth in Cambridge the next day, it too was bright and sunny and the news was good. The station was stable in space and the batteries were

....

slowly recharging. The crew were very tired indeed but safe. Michael's e-mail to Rhonda, copied to us, was calm, tired, understated as ever.

17 July

Dear Rhonda,

We never seem to avoid having something unusual happen here. Sasha, by accident, while disconnecting maybe a hundred cables in the Node, which pass through the hatchways, pulled one out that was to be done right before the IVA. It controlled our attitude control, so we lost it. I had gone to bed, slept poorly, while the guys and TSUP tried to regain a nav base, but not in time before we lost all power. Again in the dark in total silence, again 'running' from window to window seeing where the sun is, and again trying to figure out with Sasha how to orient the station, with a cock-eyed Soyuz, yelling commands to Vassy. We are tired but happy, now we have got power on through the night passes, but not yet in Kvant 2 where I sleep, so I will sleep in the Base Block tonight. I love you. More to follow, I will send Messager messages via Terry.

Love, Mike

We went happily enough to Stamford, finding release from our and Mir's troubles in the machinations and tribulations of the family Macbeth. Much later, Michael told me the whole story, which is so briefly summarized in the above stark letter. I do not think that I could have concentrated on the play at all had I known then the details of this extraordinary mishap, and the additional fatigue it had to have caused them. I am glad that he was not aware at the time of our apparent nonchalance. But then, neither would we ever wish him to be aware of the depth of our concern at the times we were really worried.

Although he had not sounded despondent, Michael had cause to be. He had known immediately that this serious accident would cause a postponement of the IVA planned for 17 July, whether it were he or Tsibliyev accompanying Lazutkin. The dreary weeks of surviving on this power-capricious station would be extended, for how long would not be known until the shaken Ground Control had made new considerations. He was aware

....

of the probability of better living conditions receding, perhaps, for weeks.

The phrase 'pulled the wrong plug' was much enjoyed by the media, and its implications of human frailty aboard Mir, on top of its other troubles, were an unexpected bonus. To give the members of the media their due, they did not once ask me if I thought it might have been Michael who had pulled it. I doubted that it had been, and we were soon assured by NASA that he had not, although we had never asked them, either.

Poor Sasha. I thought of my own frailties, and of an event years ago when not pulling the *right* lever had put me in a hazardous position. I was practising night landings in a Meteor jet. After landing, I opened up the engines and rolled on for another take-off, circuit and landing and so on until final landing. My hands and eyes moved with practised speed: air brakes in – one-third flap down – undercarriage lever down – three green lights, therefore wheels are down and locked – turn finals – full flap down – at the runway threshold, look at the flattened flare-path V, ease gently back on the control column and let the slowing aircraft sink to kiss the ground with its tyres. Perfect. Open throttles, feel the increasing speed pushing my back, flaps up, ease the aircraft up off the ground into a steep climbing turn towards the beginning of the downwind leg again. Things were going very well, each landing was perfect, the Meteor and I were as one, the whole night sky was ours alone. I repeated this four times and decided that the fifth should be my last. Air brakes in, one third flap, final turn, full flap, crossing the runway threshold at exactly the right speed, bringing up the nose gently to reduce the speed and to sink on to the . . . ! What happened next happened in all its detail over a long period of about half a second. My tyres should have kissed the tarmac. They hadn't. Yet I was exactly right with the flare-path angle for a landing with just the right amount of sink. I checked the instrument panel. *No green lights!* My undercarriage was *not down*. I went to full power to avoid the disaster of a wheels-up landing and felt a slight bump on the ground as the thrust took me up and away. I had been a lot luckier than Sasha. I landed very carefully, with only a small dent in the aircraft's ventral tank and a very large one in my pride.

The Mir loss and subsequent regain of attitude control was the second time that Vasily, Sasha and Michael had retrieved the situation from a position in which it was impossible for Ground Control to make any contribution. The

....

first time it had taken twenty-four hours to achieve restoration of power generation. This time it took twelve hours. But it was always painful for them: no toilet, no hot food, no light, and for hours the crew could do nothing but wait, so that everything, all tasks, was set back. It would be another twenty-four hours before all the batteries were restored to a full charge, ready for the next unknown (and who knew?) event.

These adventures not only interrupted Michael and Lazutkin's space-walk rehearsals, but also postponed the medical assessment which had been scheduled for Michael in preparation for his acceptance by Ground Control (and NASA) for the spacewalk. Michael was still taking a leading part because of the doubts concerning Tsibliyev's health. However, the latter had not had a recurrence of his heart problem, and indeed expressed a wish to be allowed to do the spacewalk himself as 'it was his duty'. So he and Michael amicably trained in tandem, each helping the other.

Meanwhile, the scheduled replacement Russian crew, Anatoli Solovyev and Pavel Vinogradov, were continuing to train at Star City for their launch on 5 August from Baikonur. Because of the carefully managed spacewalk investigations by Sergei Krikalev in the Mir mock-up in the giant tank, the two new crew were asked to do an experimental repair run in the tank. It was about this time that Ground Control and NASA together began to see an advantage in further postponing the actual internal spacewalk repair until the fresh crew had arrived on Mir, expected to be on 7 August. After all, the present crew had shown themselves, no doubt reluctantly, to be past masters at regaining attitude control and power no matter what the mishap, and they could probably be expected, poor souls, to continue to do so. It was of course hard on them at once to deny them the honour of the risky repair – a first in space history – while asking them to extend their vulnerability, living on the edge of power sufficiency for even longer, tiring and worrying as it would be. However, the use of the specially ground-trained replacement crew must always have been a reasonable alternative, so long as the money-making element of including the French paying-guest cosmonaut was formally postponed, not cancelled. It was only following the plug-pulling incident that the French broke their silence and asked for a postponement of Leopold Eyharts's attachment.

The overwhelming argument in favour of postponing the work for a new crew was that the latter could continue to rehearse in the tank until they launched, removing at a stroke the former disadvantage facing the existing crew of going into the unknown without any previous training on earth. Only in the extreme case of no alternative would such unrehearsed activity have been contemplated under normal conditions. Postponement had now to be the answer.

From this point, the Russians logically and sensibly moved their focus to the preservation of their agreement with the Americans, that of maintaining the permanent, continuous presence of a NASA astronaut. It is possible that in focusing so hard on a payment for Leopold, they had neglected safeguarding the much bigger prize from America. All that had changed now, and efforts were concentrated on keeping the Americans both interested in and confident of Mir's survival. There was a sense that money from America could well have been lost in the headlong rush to keep the French sweet. The attempt to lash up an early, unrehearsed IVA was now enthusiastically abandoned. Anatoli Solovyev and Pavel Vinogradov were formally designated and further trained for the task. The Russians were prepared to do anything to ensure that the shuttle flight STS-86, to bring Michael back home, would not be the last shuttle flight to Mir. The doubts thought to have been felt in NASA, even if not expressed out loud, needed Russian recognition and handling.

From Michael's point of view, the sooner the better. Even with a stable attitude restored, there was much equipment that did not work. The Elektron generator, for oxygen, continued to fail, leaving no recourse but to strike and burn oxygen 'candles'.

Perhaps events had turned the crew to new anxieties, but one day Vasily saw sparking, flashing lights deep in the heart of Kvant, aft of the Base Block, through the open hatch. They were all worried about this, Vasily so much so that he wanted somebody to sleep down there to monitor the danger. Michael's firm view was that sleeping there was not possible due to the excessive ethylene glycol levels in the area. Instead he arranged a shaving mirror in the Base Block angled so that Vasily could see deep down into the module from where he was. The flashes had almost certainly been the result of electric current short-circuiting, caused by a bit of metal debris floating across some contacts. It was a terrible situation, with its threat of an electrically induced fire, and the possibility of a thing like that happening on

....

an American vehicle would have driven NASA technicians nuts, Michael thought privately.

He was a little disappointed with the decision to put the IVA repair in the hands of the new crew, as he had prepared himself mentally and physically for the challenge. It is frustrating to build yourself up for something and then have it cancelled. I thought I knew how he would feel, so I sent him another message.

I told him that, as far as we knew, a final decision had not been made yet, but I could see that it would be a balanced one in which I hoped political pressures were not allowed to influence operational realities. On the one hand, he and Sasha were there right from the start and had closed the hatch and disconnected the power cables, and must have rehearsed in their minds, when events allowed, what they would do. I assumed that Vasily's physical condition would not affect his efficiency while monitoring them both from the Soyuz. And there was much to be said for getting power restored before the arrival of yet more life forms to support.

On the other hand, the replacement crew had had the benefit of water-tank training specific to the task. They would also have the additional advantage of having Michael, with all his recent experience, monitoring and directing them from Soyuz. It is possible that they would also be fresher physically, but he would know best about that. Against that, using them added more than two weeks' delay before this vital work could begin, the effect of which, once more, he would be in the best position to judge.

I had been saying all this too on the phone to Bill Readdy, Michael's friend at NASA, the previous night. I think Bill Readdy thought I was trying to run NASA from Cambridge.

The decision that the new crew would undertake the IVA was eventually made on 21 July, to everybody's satisfaction including, I think, Michael's, and almost certainly that of the foreign guest cosmonaut, Leopold Eyharts, who might otherwise have gone to Mir for the handover period of the two crews before power was restored to Spektr, leaving him with no power for his experiments. The decision meant that Michael could spend more time back with his own science experiments, although still with limited power conditions. He began harvesting space-grown seeds from his Green-house, which he would later replant so that a complete plant cycle could be observed in microgravity conditions. He also had time by 22 July to resume his ham radio contacts on 145.985 mc. Chris Vandenberg in Holland received the following from Michael:

Subject: Status: I am having frequent power problems with tnc, and losing all messages. Sorry. No supply store is near at hand. I would do anything for a nine-pin serial adapter. Getting ready for the next crew, 7 August.

NASA managed to arrange a TV link between Michael and Rhonda on her birthday, 21 July. He sent the following letter afterwards.

Dear Rhonda,

Thanks very much for sending Walter's prayer. [Walter is the minister of their local episcopalian church.] Please could you tell him that we, Vasily, Sasha and myself, thank him and all the congregation for their kind thoughts and prayers. We feel their effects here in orbit, and know that people are caring for us. It has helped all of us to handle the recent events with additional resilience.

I am so glad you had a good birthday. I just wanted to stare at you all on the TV. I was a little sad afterwards, but it was definitely worth doing. I am sorry that you did not get to see my 'Special Forces' Russian haircut. Terry says maybe in another week they will have the US equipment in TSUP repaired and we can do a real two-way video conference. Since we can't be private anyway, and they go a lot longer than a phone call, I would enjoy seeing other friends of ours, if you would like to invite them. But watching the kids at the same time must be difficult. I loved seeing Jenna and Ian hug each other.

It is wonderful that you are getting a lot out of your classes. I will be very interested to hear all the new ideas people have about teaching, and what you make of them, especially in relation to how we can help Jenna and Ian throughout their school years. It is all totally new to me. I am not surprised you are doing really well in the class.

I think the right decision was made about delaying the IVA.

The crew might now be a little accident prone, just in the way their characters are. Vasily is actually quite religious, and superstitious, and seems to have decided in his own mind that he will always have the worst things happen on his watch. Partly because his last flight had a number of mishaps too. Sasha is such a good engineer, but he works so hard, could be more careful, and doesn't take care to sleep well, so occasionally he makes mistakes. With Vasily's health so closely tied to stress and how he perceives things are going, moving the IVA to the next crew took a lot of that stress away, and he has shown a big improvement, gaining appetite, sleeping much better. Partly because of the medications. I am trying to be as disciplined as possible so I will be up to speed and have the same attitude as I think Anatoli will have and expect, even though Vassy and Sasha are now tending to kick back, knowing they will be home in three weeks.

Would you mind giving Chuck Miller [now the only other co-owner of the Tiger Cub aeroplane] a call, to see if he has been able to fly the plane, and what its current status is? Maybe Jenna could see their horses again!

TSUP is asking if I need anything brought up on Soyuz, with Mir 24 crew. Could Kelly do another video in time? Or send more edible goodies?

Love, Mike

Then we were delighted to receive a direct letter from Mike, dated 22 July.

Dear Mum and Dad, and Susie,

I got your note consoling me about the IVA, or the lack of it. Thanks. Terry is sending just as fast as Dave Larsen, and some of the text dropped out, via Dave, so send via Terry now if at all possible. Dave has to be up at the small hours of the morning to get our mail right now, the way our orbit is. It will be better in a couple of weeks or so, for him.

I was a little depressed after all the excitement had calmed down. Vassy and Sasha are looking forward to the end, in three weeks. I am looking forward to more activity when Anatoli Solovyev and

....

Pasha Vinogradov come on the seventh. Until then, I am settling down to getting the seeds I produced last planting, planted and producing the very first space generation. And Ken Bowersox sent me software to help me program, and do earth observation photo work, so that will be another thing for me to do. Our biggest problem here is lack of power to run the two modules (Kristall and Priroda), and hence my chore is to wipe up maybe four litres a day of water condensate, off the walls, in the cold and dark modules. Not very pleasant, and mould and corrosion are setting in remarkably quickly.

Rhonda's birthday TV event was a big landmark for me – first time to see how they all look since the shuttle left. I just wanted to stare at them, and not say a thing. Sasha recorded the scene for me, so I can replay the flickery black and white images, and get all soppy.

Susie, I have been listening to the cassettes you sent. A great relief, and change from my taste, which came up on the Progress. Other than your music, my favourites are contemporary Russian female soloists, which teach me good romantic Russian language. I have had no time at all to read yet. Most likely won't get to do that, unless the shuttle is delayed a lot.

Send more.

Love, Mike

Among the regular attentions of the media, thirsty for our personal news of Michael, we agreed to a visit on 23 July by ITV's *Good Morning* team at our home, live. We needed the alarm clock set for five-forty-five am to be ready for the team at seven am. It was a struggle, but not as hard as for Jim Lovell, on video link from Chicago, who had been asked to make comparisons with his own epic mission on Apollo 13 in 1970. Back then an explosion on the way to the moon had caused a critical loss of power and oxygen, making a landing on the moon impossible, and even making an immediate return to earth doubtful of success. For him, now, it must have been the middle of the night. The GMTV team quickly made themselves at home with us, using my TV set as our monitor with Chicago. I was interviewed first, and this was helpful. I knew all about Apollo 13, and knew how immediately life-threatening its acute emergency had been and continued to be until they splashed down. Mir

....

had started out with a similar dangerous event, the collision, but since then, four weeks on, things had moved from an acute to a chronic condition, in medical terms, with ongoing threats and recoveries.

Jim Lovell agreed with me – he said that with Apollo 13 they just had to get down, there was no alternative, and that the Mir crew must have shared the same degree of terror until they got the Spektr hatch closed. He knew how frustrated Michael must be, as a scientist, to be on such a knife-edge of power availability, his experiments having to take second place to station survival. He was also asked what he thought about that other older astronaut, John Glenn, who had been quoted as saying that he would go into space again to do research into ageing. Would Lovell like to go as well? Lovell immediately quipped, 'If John Glenn at seventy-five can go into space again, then so can I. Move over, Mike.'

I told Michael of this when I replied to his letter. The consolation I had offered him, about not now doing the Spektr repair which he had prepared for, had also been because I wanted him to know how the rest of the world seemed to feel. In another way we were uplifted at home by our exchanges with Jim Lovell, and we were also joined by Susan that weekend for a pleasant sail.

On Mir, by this time, most of the planned gyrodyne repairs had been done, and, in the absence of any further attitude component failure, the station had remained on an even keel since 19 July. Once the decision was clear that Tsibliyev and Lazutkin were not to attempt the IVA, they began to tidy up their belongings and prepare for the arrival of the fresh cosmonaut pair on 7 August. Michael was able to devote time to his experiments and all of them could work with less interruption on the problems of the new Elektron oxygen-generating unit, which tended to turn itself off. The older, usually serviceable one in Kvant was still switched off because of the narrow margin of power available.

On the ground, another decision was made, arising out of experience and the perception of future needs. The IVA was now planned for 20 August at the earliest, but it was also perceived that a number of external spacewalk occasions would arise, if the punctured Spektr hull and damaged solar panels were eventually to be repaired. Michael's nominated successor, Wendy Lawrence, was too small to fit snugly into the Russian on-board Orlan spacesuit, so it was decided to substitute her back-up, David Wolf, to undertake her period on Mir, expected to start in late September when Michael would be relieved. This decision required Wolf himself to complete more EVA training in Star City, and consequently a week was added to Michael's time on Mir, deferring his return to early October.

Michael wrote again to Rhonda on 28 July, copied to us.

Dear Rhonda,

I have had some really interesting celebrations with the crew. Vasily is relaxing more now, and we talk easily and openly. He and I both value our families in the same way, as opposed to Sasha who is more independent emotionally. Turns out that Sasha was persuaded to be baptized two days before launch. At Baikonur! Sasha's wife and kids have been baptized for a long time, but Sasha is not sure he believes in God yet, as far as I can tell. Vassy told me that ever since Alexei Leonov became the chief, since Gagarin died, he would insist that all cosmonauts be baptized before they went to Baikonur. This right in the midst of heavy communist repression.

On Saturday night we had a bedtime drink together after we had watched the video film of Apollo 13. Vassy had tears of emotion in his eyes at the end of the film. I think he feels a certain identity with Jim Lovell, and he already likes Tom Hanks as an actor. When we watch the movie, we are in the airlock, with five spacesuits behind us, three windows around the sphere and the screen fixed to the opposite hatch lid. We lie side by side with our legs sort of floating towards the hatch, and backs against the opposite wall. It felt a little like the Apollo command module looked, with the three crew side by side also. (Our Soyuz is so cramped, it did not come to mind.) It was neat watching the re-entry scenes of the movie, and the moon, while I could see the real earth through the windows behind our heads, and later the rust-brown moon, setting as a half-moon, through the atmosphere. The moon looks crisp, fully coloured with brown, and yellows, when viewed above a normal daylit earth. I am not sure why we see it so hazily white, in a blue sky, on earth – my understanding of atmospheric absorption doesn't account for this.

....

I do feel that the halfway point has been reached. It is really nice to have a good science routine going, earth observations, and the Greenhouse, and my gels. Not as demanding as before the collision, but keeps me busy, and the time goes quickly without me feeling rushed. I also hope the rest of the time will be event-free, but I fully expect problems to crop up when Anatoli and Pavel start preparations for the IVA. Sasha unsticking a cable was just the tip of an iceberg of possible problems, I am afraid.

The Mir is starting to be more and more in a solar orbit again, so there is less moisture on the walls, which is good. I use our old underwear, T-shirts and pants, and towels, to soak up the water, if it is a film on the walls. We get new underwear every three days, and use the last set for exercise for another three days – ends up being used six days, and then we would normally throw it away in the Progress. But now I put the soaking clothes into a rubber bag, and seal it before disposing of it. For great big water balls that cling with surface tension, rather like full-bodied spider's webs, in very cold corners, I use a sealed twenty-two-litre can with a rubber bladder inside it, out of which I have pumped some air to create lower pressure and some suction inside. Then with a tube and valve attached to the port of the bladder, I suck up water from the walls. It makes a good gurgling sound, like bathwater running out.

We are currently loading the Progress with trash, including eight rubber bags of water, with four hundred litres which we have collected and are throwing away (probably contains a lot of ethylene glycol). The bags are like big, floppy, wobbly balloons, a metre in diameter each. It is important that they are stowed carefully in the Progress, or their wobbles may affect the flight control of the Progress when it undocks to free up the docking port for Anatoli and Pasha. There have been some accusations from TSUP that Vasily did not load the last Progress properly, which hit us, in their attempt to explain why the Progress did not slow down as it should have, but I don't consider that reasonable – there was no water on that Progress, and Vassy says he loaded all the masses per the procedures.

I will stop now, and write more in a day or so. The kids would

....

starve if you read this all in one sitting!

I love you, and think about you, Mike

In this letter, Michael had begun to take stock. He had been on Mir for over two months, half his allotted time period. However, half of that time, a whole month, had begun and continued with dangerous contingencies and unexpected frights, from technical failure to dramatic human error. I felt that I had understood these happenings well enough because of direct parallels with my own experience of fearful incidents – I have recounted some of them. Now I could see that he was exploring new ground beyond a simple ability to respond to emergencies. It was the need for determined endurance, to make light of personal discomfort and frustration, to carry on in a well-balanced way until the job was done. And in this he was suddenly more lonely, because those with whom he had shared so much were soon to depart, to leave him with a new crew.

Nothing else had changed. There had been a ten-day mishap-free period, but the station remained on its uncomfortable knife-edge of power, which was not to be improved now until the replacement crew had completed their takeover. But he had made a conscious and successful effort to raise his eyes to the hills and look ahead to the second two months on Mir, whatever they would bring his way. He helped to preserve this attitude by attending more closely to his experiments than recent circumstances had allowed, and preparing his mind positively for the new crew.

2 August

Rhonda,

Got your nice note, after anniversary. I am glad you are doing so well in school. It seems incredible you are almost over with the first period. Afterwards, you should just try and enjoy time with the kids before everything gets busy again, and I come back.

It looks like STS-86 won't be launched before 28 Sept and therefore return won't be until about 8 Oct at the earliest. If weather or something delays STS-86 beyond 5 Oct, then there may be an additional delay of three weeks, to about end of October, because 5–20 Oct is the Cassini launch window, and the range will be dedicated

....

to getting Cassini off (I won't be too insulted – Saturn and Titan need to be studied!). So if 86 does not get off on time, and is delayed by more than a week, I may not end up back on earth until early November. Bill Readdy will know all the nuances of this.

Meanwhile, there is again serious talk of me doing EVA, but outside, to do an examination of Spektr, with Anatoli, on 3 September. Frank says many concerns remain, because of Jerry's debrief. I would love to know what he said – as would Vasily!

Love, Mike

One evening, Vasily was feeling conversational as his time on Mir drew to a close. He reviewed the past long months. He said, 'We have had fire, Elektron oxygen failure, gyrodyne spin-down, a very dangerous collision, an almost catastrophic plug-pull (although inadvertent), and I may have had a heart attack. What else is there left for us to have?'

Michael probably shares my own unwillingness to tempt fate in dealing with such a question, particularly as he had at least two more months to go on Mir. He ducked the answer. He said, 'Well, we still haven't been invaded by aliens.'

Vasily rolled his eyes upwards.

An Arrival and a Departure

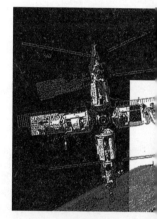

I n late July Vasily Tsibliyev and Sasha Lazutkin began their last three weeks on Mir. The end of their personal trials was in sight. The replacement crew, Anatoli Solovyev and Pavel Vinogradov, launched successfully from Baikonur on 5 August. In place of the postponed French astronaut Leopold Eyharts they carried 96.5 kilos of extra, specialized repair equipment and some unexpected 'goodies' for Michael. Our faithful and vigilant psychological support group in Houston, hearing of the decision to postpone Eyharts, had immediately telephoned us (actually Susan in London – Mary and I were out), to say that if we were quick there was an opportunity to get a few unexpected pounds' weight to Michael. Susan and Mary moved heaven and earth, that day's commitments notwithstanding, to buy items to send by FedEx to Baikonur via NASA: anything to alleviate the grimness of wiping down those dark, wet and smelly walls. Susan included new music tapes for his Walkman and Mary sent some chocolate, always popular.

Michael had met his new commander-to-be, Solovyev, and had a deep respect for his fame and experience drawn from his many and varied missions and EVAs. He felt that if the Russians had a doyen of cosmonauts, Solovyev would be it, just as John Young is to the American corps. He was looking forward to working with him and meeting Vinogradov, the engineer, who was on his first mission. Anatoli Solovyev had taken the trouble to seek Michael out before Michael left Russia for his shuttle launch from Cape Canaveral. He had introduced Michael to his wife, and they had shared a bottle of Russian champagne together. It had been a formal initiation of Solovyev's command, Michael felt, and he was grateful for it.

The first few days of August were fairly quiet for Michael, and gave him time for personal reflection. Vasily was busy at some of his last chores on Mir, packing the Progress with all available waste before undocking it from its position on Kvant on 6 August, to leave the port clear for the arrival of the new crew's Soyuz. Michael watched Vasily and Sasha, knowing how they must be feeling, so soon to go home to earth. They had already discarded some of their well-trained, habitual commitment to the hassles of daily life on Mir, so that when they spotted Michael working hard, scrubbing old food particles off the Base Block walls, it brought them up short and they were abashed, although it was not the first time Michael had done this cleaning chore. He was becoming increasingly aware of the arrival, soon, of the new crew, and he felt embarrassed over the dirty state of the walls and panels. True, much of it was the result of the continuing extreme conditions in which they had been forced to live. But he couldn't help looking back and remembering how it was when he had first arrived in June, and how it now looked, as if it had all gone downhill. He shrank from imagining what Pavel Vinogradov, the new flight engineer, would think, particularly as Michael's own first impression of the station's cleanliness had also been pretty bad, even back in June.

His sleeping place in the Kvant 2 airlock was neat and tidy, a place to retreat to when he felt the need. The window there allowed him to watch the continuous orbital sunrise and sunset which their present path had been following for the previous few days. For some time he had been taking photographs of an extraordinary phenomenon of what to him were unique cloud structures in the ionosphere. He wrote to us all on 3 August:

I have spent some time taking video of unique cloud structures in the ionosphere. They look like silver pancakes, high up above the airglow layer. Because the moon is so close to the sun right now, almost new, I have got some great scenes of the moon rising through the

....

atmosphere, while the sun is just below the horizon, illuminating the 'pancakes'. Scientists have only seen this once before, as far as I know, from the shuttle, and saw only single layers. I have videoed multiple layers, which seem to be almost braided. The air force meteorological guys who are coming out to the ham shack with Ken Bowersox are very excited about it. As is Graham Tilbury, the ham physicist professor I talk with in Durban, South Africa. They are asking me a lot of technical questions about sizes, heights and correlations of lightning strikes across large distances, linked by upward discharges from the tops of thunderclouds into the ionosphere [known as 'sprites']. All very new stuff, and quite unexpected. By the way, Graham wants me and the family to visit them there. They have a house overlooking the Indian Ocean and the harbour, and two young sons, one of whom has been in surfing competitions the last few weekends!

With all the interest in Mars recently, I have daydreamed a little about how they might send married couples to the planet. I wonder if you, Rhonda, would be willing to go, after the kids are in college? When I was being interviewed by ABC on Wednesday last week, in the middle of the interviewer's difficult questions, I said, 'Today is my wife's and my tenth anniversary, and I would like to wish her a very happy anniversary, and that I have loved spending those years with her, and that I am sorry I cannot be with her today. Let's spend our thirtieth anniversary together on the surface of Mars!' The interviewer didn't say a word, and went right into the next question, about who unplugged the cables, then caught up with himself about thirty seconds later when he suddenly said, '. . . And congratulations to you and your wife.' It took him a little while, or somebody told him what I had said, with a big grin on my face.

For his more immediate future plans Michael was still focused strongly on doing the next Hubble telescope repair mission in late 1999. This mission had been earmarked for him, partly at his request, because he knew that after spending so long in the Russian sphere of activities – two years, including his time in Star City – he would want a strong dose of NASA 'rehabilitation'. After that, he foresaw that he would be happy to be part of the lunar–Mars programmes, or the International Space Station. His experiences on Mir and insights into human behaviour, including his own, under conditions of extended stress, had shown him how important it is to make the right decisions and judgements while on the station, and his imagination was reasonably tempted towards aspirations of command.

On 6 August we in England saw something unforgettable. The NASA family contact man, Steve Vander Ark, had earlier supplied Rhonda with timings of when Mir would pass over Houston and be visible in the night sky. I have already recounted how she had been able to call the STS-84 reunion party outside on time to see Mir and her Michael pass overhead. She had been equally successful in bringing friends at her house out on to the deck at a time when she could say, 'Look, there's Mir with Michael and his crew.' Little Ian, two-and-a-half years old, also saw the large white star as it passed swiftly but silently through the dark heavens. Too young to perceive the difference, he later excitedly called, 'Daddy, Daddy,' whenever he saw a lighted aeroplane pass overhead.

Michael had been especially pleased that she had been able to do this, and we asked for the times when Mir would pass over Cambridge or London so that we too could keep our eyes open for him. The orbit paths and times are mathematically pre-set and extremely precise. The times can be given for any point on the earth which lies below or near to the orbit path, first as a rising time above the western horizon, followed ten minutes later by a setting time in the east. Directional bearings were given for all events, including variations to the vertical overhead, if the path was oblique.

In early August, armed with these figures and enjoying a succession of clear night skies, we all had enormous pleasure in going outside, Mary and I looking and waiting in our secluded Cambridge back garden, Susan on her balcony in London. Susan was the first to be able to take up her post and rang us to describe what she had seen. Exactly on time, a large glowing starlike object had appeared, climbing in the western sky, silently moving nearly overhead and continuing on to its fall to the east. It seemed to move quite fast, like a plane at medium height, but with no engine noise. The following night Mary and I were watching too, in the softness of the dark. We found it profoundly satisfying and it provoked emotional responses in us. Again, we all talked to each other triumphantly on the phone afterwards.

....

The sixth of August was once more a clear night, and Mary and I went into our garden in anticipation of an appearance at 9.58 pm on a bearing of 260 degrees and altitude of 88 degrees, virtually overhead at its highest position. Like a faithful friend, Mir rose again in shining splendour, our Michael and his now close friends on board, and we revelled in the clarity of the sky and the swift yet unhurried passage of the great light in the arc of its passage. It was impossible not to wave and give a cheer and allow a silent sob to escape. Then suddenly we both exclaimed in amazement: Mir was not alone. Another, smaller bright light, about a thumb's-length distance (arm outstretched), was in line astern behind it, in hot pursuit. We were witnessing the arrival of the new Soyuz with its fresh crew, Anatoli Solovyev and Pavel Vinogradov, on board, with spares and tools, steadily reducing the gap between themselves and Mir, ready for the docking the next day. The experience was unforgettable.

The automatic approach on 7 August was so perfect in its alignment that a central guidance crosswire was obscured from Commander Anatoli Solovyev's vision, so as a precautionary measure he reverted to manual control for the final, equally perfect, docking. The Progress vessel had of course been moved to allow the Soyuz to dock, and was station-keeping out to one side. That night we saw that pinpoint of light too. Mary wrote to Mike to tell him.

8 August 1997
Dear Mike,
On Tuesday night we saw Mir bright and clear almost directly over our garden, and on Wednesday we saw you again, with Soyuz in hot pursuit not far behind. Then last night we saw Mir again, this time with a fainter companion, further behind – no doubt the undocked Progress following obediently. Tonight, if it's clear, we are going to show Christine [a neighbour] where to look – Steve Vander Ark sent us a list of times and altitudes for UK, and we have been delighted to be able to see you, if not communicate directly.

We're sorry you're having problems with the Elektron generator, but are reassured by spokesmen for both Russia and NASA on the ground saying there is no urgent concern. You will be getting acquainted with your new crewmates, but also feeling very sad I'm

....

sure to have to say farewell to Vasily and Sasha soon. You have been such a great team, and I'm sure they too will miss you. Is there any sort of souvenir we could get here, that we could send to them in Russia, on your behalf? Would you like us to do that?

We'll be watching out for you, take care.

All our love, Mum

Anatoli Solovyev was forty-nine years old with a strong Russian face which could look composed, even forbidding, but could also light up with a provocative and challenging smile. His eyes were arresting and steady. In a crowded room, he would be the one you first noticed. Pavel Vinogradov, like Lazutkin, was a quiet, dedicated engineer from Energiya, anxious to do well on his first mission. Their arrival was dominated by their feeling that, yes, things had gone wrong in the past, but now they were here to make things go right. After they had transferred to Mir, the long and detailed handover process began, bringing Solovyev fully up to date on all the working and non-working systems on Mir. In particular he was familiarized with the knife-edge, low-tolerance power situation on the station, either getting just enough power from the solar arrays or tumbling helplessly with rapidly discharging batteries. In fact, the various component parts involved in Mir, including a very careful crew, had now permitted three weeks of a relatively alarm-free existence. Michael took something of a back seat during the handover, seeing it as primarily a Russian affair, at least in the eyes of the new commander. However, for two months he had been so much an involved and participating crew member in every respect that he found he could not easily stop now. Neither would Tsibliyev and Lazutkin have wished him to, as he had given such tangible and innovative help to them. There were few discussions in which Michael did not make an uninhibited contribution. He did feel a little wary of Anatoli Solovyev at first, out of respect for his professional stature and reputation. Michael wrote in reply to Mary on 11 August, soon after the new crew's arrival.

Dear Mum and Dad and Susie,

Sorry I have been so long writing directly to you. It must be strange for you to see us flying overhead at twilight, knowing I am here, but

....

not hearing from me. It's great that you were able to see the Soyuz as well.

As you probably know, things are fairly calm here, and Vasily and Sasha will soon be saying goodbye, on Thursday. Sasha has been spending most of his time trying to explain all the different configurations to Pavel, which are not understood, or taught, by instructors on the ground. I have been playing the busy bee, pollinating my broccoli for the third day in a row. I have also been doing a lot of the odd jobs that need to be done, but aren't. Like getting all the orders from Ground Control, by packet. I spent a day with Anatoli, with whom I am getting along just great, going over and assembling an EVA TV system, which he at least thinks I will be doing with him on 3 September, to create a handhold route to the collision site on Spektr and then to conduct a survey of the exterior damage. If I get to do the EVA, it will be a very interesting one for me, since it involves using the Mir cranes – sixty-foot telescoping poles to get from the airlock, in Kvant 2 where I sleep, all the way to the opposite module, Spektr. On the way back, if there is time, we will install a vacuum valve on the Base Block, so that a critical system in the old Kvant module that scrubs CO_2 can be moved to the Base Block. The Elektron oxygen generation system is currently inoperative and has a very awkward failure – the tubing that vents the unwanted hydrogen to space. We can't close the valve that isolates the vacuum from the tube, so we can't unattach the equipment to replace it, without creating a leak!

Other than on the actual day of arrival, we have all been fairly subdued, getting our tasks done, as there is little time. I was very pleased to receive a care package from the hands of Anatoli, that included the presents from you. Thank you very much [Mary and Susan's efforts had not been in vain].

I need to get on the ergometer now, to increase my strength for the EVA, as it is my turn, so will finish.

Lots of love, Mike

Eventually, on 14 August, the time came for Vasily Tsibliyev and Sasha Lazutkin to leave. Michael's help and concern for them during their many dark hours together had made him feel personally protective and they had warmly responded. Now, as they packed themselves tightly into the Soyuz, he found it hard to turn away. He remained with them, fussing over their straps and harnesses, saying, 'Have a safe trip' and 'See you on earth', until hatches had to be closed. He moved back, still wanting to say something more, which he hadn't had time for. The Soyuz undocked and Michael watched it through a small window, falling towards earth. Unexpectedly, he found that he had an enormous lump in his throat and needed to be by himself. He wrote to us as follows.

I am about to go to bed, exhausted. We sent Vasily and Sasha off today, closing the hatch at 8.40 am; we got up at 06.00. We went to bed last night at 02.00 am. They were doing first-day covers! Anatoli and I were the ones that forced them to go to bed, but I think Sasha still crept about in a daze, sorting things. We hugged, and I was amazed how choked-up and tearful I got, especially watching them fade away in the moonlight, with the earth below. The departure was rather like that of the shuttle – slow and cheerful, because we were still in comm with each other, but very final, because they became such a small speck so quickly. The next orbit, when they did their de-orbit burn (braking thrusters so as to enter the atmosphere), I videoed them as a bright star rapidly dimming above a lighted earth. And soon after that they passed below us, over Kazakhstan, and we didn't hear them any more (we were the relay for TSUP), and then we heard that their Soyuz was on its parachutes, and a little later as we passed in darkness over Kamchatka, that they had landed. It was a very strange feeling, having them go so swiftly.

We feel so remote here, I more so now that Vassy and Sasha have gone.

But Anatoli and Pasha have quietly got on with starting Elektron up again, successfully, and I spent four hours fixating plants in a glovebox. Very pleasant company. Tomorrow we will all three fly around the station in the Soyuz. I will climb into the living module of the Soyuz, with Anatoli and Pavel in their seats still, to take pictures of Spektr from fifty metres, for twenty minutes, before we dock the

....

Soyuz at the Node, free now since Vasily and Sasha have vacated in their Soyuz. The next day the Progress is going to redock with us, the one we have loaded with trash. As you know, it is used simply to shade the back end of the station, Kvant, from the sun, until the next one arrives.

We would not have felt so comfortable, nor would he, if we had known what would happen when Michael's old colleagues did return to earth on 14 August. The downward thrusting engine which should help to guarantee a soft landing in the Kazakhstan desert failed at the crucial moment, and both crew members were subjected to a very severe jolt. It is reported that Commander Tsibliyev considered that, had the third crew position been occupied (i.e., by Michael), he would have been severely injured by the impact. It is as well that Michael had not had to continue to keep in step with Tsibliyev's apparent run of bad luck, and we found ourselves once again breathing thanks.

The day after the old Soyuz and crew had left for earth, the planned redocking of the new Soyuz referred to by Michael was undertaken, from the aft Kvant port to the now vacated forward port, where it would remain for emergency or eventual earth return of the current crew. The vacated Kvant port would the next day be filled by the presently undocked, but station-keeping, Progress 35, in order to protect the area from undue solar heating as well as be in position to receive more waste material.

Ground Control had decided that the crew should all enter the Soyuz for the redeployment as a reconnaissance flight, and that they should inspect and photograph as closely as possible the damaged areas of Spektr's exterior. They flew around the station for forty-four minutes, achieving the best lighting positions possible for Michael to video the whole area, reorienting the station to illuminate the most important parts. Like a thrilled small boy, he took much pleasure in the trip, another flying sortie in space, and he was able to direct Solovyev so as to examine Spektr's exterior as closely as possible for his camera to record. It would be where they would both later be working in their spacesuits on the EVA. The video taken was transmitted down to TSUP three days later, where it was used to plan the external spacewalk to examine Spektr, close up, in September.

When the Soyuz was finally docked, forward, the crew returned to the station via the Node and prepared to have Progress 35 redocked aft by well-tried automatic means. The supply vessel responded and began its passage towards Mir.

Suddenly, Ground Control intervened.

'We must stop the docking. *Stop* the docking. Progress is ordered to pass you by.'

An error had been transmitted by Ground Control to the Mir computer, fortunately noticed at an early stage.

'Go to Soyuz, all of you go to Soyuz *now*. We do not know how close Progress will pass to Mir.'

The crew needed no encouragement and had already been seated in Soyuz when the Progress was still approaching.

While sitting together in the Soyuz, Anatoli said to Michael, 'Look out of the window for the approach of the Progress, in case you can see it go by.'

Michael said, with a mild twinkle, 'No thank you, it would really be too frightening. It would be much better if, like ostriches, we all closed our eyes and at least *felt* safe!'

This remark made the Russians crack up – they had momentarily forgotten Michael's earlier vivid experience of a colliding Progress approach. This time the wayward vessel passed them six hundred metres away, close enough for the precaution of going to Soyuz to be justified.

Their temporary evacuation to Soyuz led Michael to point out to Anatoli that in a real, rapid escape move such as he had earlier experienced, there was a critical tube running through the Soyuz hatchway that had to be undone quickly. There should always be a wrench tied there handily, he thought, for immediate use. Anatoli had not himself considered pre-positioning the wrench. After the Progress had flown by and he and Anatoli were later studying systems relating to the forthcoming IVA, Michael noticed that indeed there was now a wrench taped in place and ready. Anatoli had acted quickly, and had not been fussed about taking advice from the foreigner, Michael was pleased to note. Michael asked Anatoli, 'Surely these sorts of problems with Progress must have been solved long ago, as the programme is so mature.'

'No,' Anatoli replied, 'undocking a Progress, flying it around for a

....

while and then bringing it back to Mir is something that has not been done very often at all.'

So it looked as if Vasily was even less to blame for the original collision than some had thought, and that he had been put into a situation that was virtually new to everybody.

The BBC1 news staff were quick to ask me if I would comment on the Progress docking cancellation, this 'new difficulty', as they put it, on their morning news programme. I did this with pleasure, to try to reduce the continuing tendency of reporters to 'bash' Mir.

Fortunately, we had been treated to a NASA radio ham phone call from Michael, about ten minutes, on 17 August, so we had already asked him about the media report of an unsuccessful attempt to redock the Progress 35 vessel to the Kvant port, its abort and perhaps a near collision. The media commentators did not know why the Progress docking had been aborted, and Michael was able to tell us the full story, that it had been because of the timely recognition of wrong computer data transmitted to Mir by Ground Control, and immediate safety action.

I did not blame the media generally, and on this occasion the BBC in particular, for taking a pessimistic view of almost anything to do with Mir. It had and was likely to continue to have dangerous and exciting moments. So will any human activity in space. The trick is to have eternal vigilance, anticipating the worst, indeed planning for it. A problem foreseen is a problem which can be solved and the danger deflected.

I got up early to be at the Cambridge studio by eight-fifteen. The questions were predictable and concerned with this, 'yet another' dangerous incident on Mir. I decided to say nothing about the crew's precautionary move to Soyuz, which, for a space station, could be as routine a procedure as a fighter pilot tightening up his ejection-seat straps. I said, 'The whole emphasis of a space station has to be on safety. This should and does affect everything that is done. It is of particular concern when any other object, like a heavy Progress vessel, needs to be brought close to Mir for redocking. If at any stage of the procedure there are doubts, a safety cancellation is made, not unlike an aircraft being waved off from an aircraft carrier. So, unlike the collision in June, there was nothing very remarkable about the incident.'

I parried other expressions of gloom by restating what a marvel Mir was, and how important it was to have it manned in preparation for the forthcoming International Space Station.

I was happy enough with all this, and drove home. A few minutes later the phone rang and it was the BBC saying that the Russian ambassador in London had asked them for my telephone number. Did I mind if they told him? I said no, I didn't. But I wondered what he could want.

Not long afterwards the ambassador, Yuri Fokin, telephoned. I remembered to say *zdrabstbyte* (hello), and *ochen priatno* (pleased to meet you), which amused and impressed him, if this were needed.

He said, 'Air Commodore, I listened with interest to your broadcast this morning. You may know that people in this country treat Mir in two different layers, one professional and the other pessimistic and critical. I watched your statement and the way that the interviewer tried constantly to push you into the latter layer. You always successfully resisted this. Indeed, had I seen your script (I had not had one!) before the programme, I would have been happy to countersign every paragraph.'

I was pleased to have this gesture of friendship and approval from the Court of St James, and his complimentary remarks about Michael. I ruefully reflected that, until 1979, I had spent over thirty years constantly in preparation to fight him and his country, if necessary.

Progress 35 was again ordered towards its permanent docking port on Kvant on 18 August. Michael was wakened from his sleep shift at three am to video the approach. Docking this time also presented problems. It was successful but only just. Just before the Progress vessel completed its automatic approach, the Mir central computer suddenly and unaccountably shut down, forcing Ground Control and Anatoli to switch to manual control for the last seconds of the actual docking. The takeover fortunately was thus at a much later stage in the procedure than that which the unfortunate Tsibliyev had been ordered to attempt in June, which had resulted in the collision. This time manual control was called for and exercised only when the Progress was already very close and well braked. None the less, the commander executed a perfect docking just in time, as the station, without computer control, fell into a tumble.

It was an impressive display of Anatoli's coolness and skill, but it had been a somewhat harrowing experience for Michael. He had sleepily watched

....

the Progress coming at them from below, against the earth, but moving very fast, growing visibly larger, and he found himself becoming very alarmed. He says that it looked like a fighter or a missile coming up at them, threatening, with its bright searchlight on. He was videoing the approach and got a distinct déjà vu sinking feeling in his stomach. At the last moment, or so it seemed to him, it did an effective automatic braking. Ground Control then broke in.

'Go manual, your computer has failed, go manual.'

Anatoli, already at his desk with the Progress camera's image of Mir on screen, took over with a quick and sure touch. Everybody felt relief and satisfaction at this success, but it was followed by anxiety, as the station fell quickly into its familiar tumble (familiar to Michael, that is). It was something of a baptism of fire for the new crew. Michael, by this time the world's greatest *in situ* expert on Mir attitude recovery, was ready to give immediate advice from the benefit of his experience.

It had not been long after three am when the computer had failed. Michael, recently risen from his sleep shift to record the docking, found that Anatoli was looking very tired indeed. He had been up all night. The station, in its tumble, had already reached a very low power position. They still had enough power for communication to Ground Control to be possible, briefly, except that they were presently out of range, over the Pacific Ocean. Anatoli looked straight at him and said, 'We have lost our computer.'

Michael said, 'I know. You know what this means. We are going to lose all our power unless we quickly start a rotation.'

Anatoli was not to be pushed. He was tired, he had achieved a brilliant last-minute manual docking and he was in command. He said, 'Maybe.'

Michael said, 'I have seen this happen three times already: we are going to *have* to do it.'

'Well, we are going to do nothing without talking to the ground.'

Michael said, 'Anatoli, we could lose all power so that we cannot talk to the ground at all if we don't spin the station now.'

Anatoli dug in. He said, 'That may be, but we are going to talk to the ground first.'

Michael gave a weightless shrug.

'OK, if that's the position. I think we *might* make it to the next comm pass, but it will be very close.'

They did make it, with enough power left to talk to TSUP, to whom Anatoli reported events. The leading controller, Solovyov, replied and said, rather carefully for him, 'Well, Anatoli, Michael has had a lot of experience with this problem and knows the technique. Will you please follow what he suggests.'

Michael sighed inwardly with relief but kept a very straight face. He need not have worried. Anatoli was not just the commander of the station. He was also fully in command of himself. He showed no annoyance or hubris whatsoever, and Michael continued to be careful not to give him any cause. Anatoli had just followed normal procedures, and now, after clear instructions from the ground, followed Michael's advice willingly. As Michael explained to him as quickly as possible how they should move, Anatoli listened with evident pleasure to learn this technique, new to him, that apparently worked. He took up his position in the Soyuz and followed Michael's instructions to the letter, resulting in the quickest, quite flawless attitude resumption and stabilizing spin-up that Michael had yet experienced. This time they never lost total power in the Base Block, but TSUP themselves turned off power in Kvant 2 as a power-saving precaution to help the remaining batteries recharge. Coincidentally, this forced Michael to move his bed to endure a very cold sleeping period in Kristall, which, though without heat, now at least had a single air-moving fan powered from the Base Block. While he thought he might freeze to death there, he would not suffocate.

In turning off Kvant 2 power, Ground Control had shown that they too had learned some new tricks. As soon as they were aware of the tumble, they turned off all power in the modules with the lowest battery levels, to prevent them from discharging to the point where recharging time would be much increased. If they had done this at the time of the collision, the station would not have been in such bad shape afterwards, requiring so much effort to restore it. But, as Michael says philosophically, everybody learns some lessons. On future power-downs, the ground would quickly specify which services had to be turned off, and not always to the crew's liking, such as when it involved the toilet in Kvant 2, but it was always a case of 'hurt now to save you later'. TSUP was exercising the essence of good ground control.

The shutdown forced TSUP to delay the internal spacewalk again

....

until 22 August, in order to give the crew a chance to restore fully the station's attitude-keeping and power.

The latest failure, brought about by a faulty computer component, caused much concern at Ground Control, where the hope had been new crew, new deal. The failure was to repeat itself again and again until a Russian replacement computer was delivered by space shuttle Atlantis (and even, post-Michael, after that). Recovery of attitude had been relatively quick, and the station began to absorb solar power efficiently again within three hours of the event. Restoration of a serviceable computer by component change, and then its rebooting, took longer, until the following day. At the height of the station's tumbling, Pavel Vinogradov, the new crew member on his first mission, was heard to exclaim, 'They did not tell me that this could happen.'

The media reported this verbatim, and until the station's recovery was complete, made us feel that the situation this time had been more than usually serious, which it wasn't. It was just the same.

Michael, Anatoli and Pavel gradually but steadily got used to each other. Pavel, like Sasha, was an intelligent and thoughtful systems expert, and not difficult to talk to or get to know. His manner was relaxed and friendly. Anatoli Solovyev, however, was someone Michael instinctively continued to treat rather carefully. He had had four long space missions and was the most experienced active commander cosmonaut. He had a reputation for being successful, no matter what, and for being as tough on himself as he would be on his crew. He seemed to be a convinced believer in the Russian system of almost total, detailed ground control of the station. This showed in his unwillingness to be flexible unless directly instructed to be so. He was a conservative in his cosmonaut outlook, and probably also found it outlandish that the American space shuttle now regularly called on Mir and, worse, that Americans were even included in the crew. It was not what he had been brought up to expect, and, while it would never affect his performance or dedication to success, he did not really approve of how things had changed.

While thinking of Michael and his new superman commander, I reflected again on my own past. An incident came to mind quickly. If I had had the iron temperament (which I cannot help but admire) and training of Solovyev, I would probably have lost a Hunter day fighter in 1957, the year of Michael's birth. I was flying at ten thousand feet, practising an aerobatic

....

sequence over the Lincolnshire coast, within sight of my airfield RAF Strubby, when the engine fire warning light came on. This was a large red light set just below eye level under the port cockpit coaming, in a position to get immediate unfailing attention from the pilot, should it come on. This was because it came on only if the single engine was on fire.

A fire of this kind is obviously highly dangerous near to fuel lines and tanks. There was little or no expectation, in a single-engine aircraft like the Hunter, of being able to switch off, get the fire out and glide down successfully to a convenient airfield (even if one was available) with heavy, imprecise manual control, with all power assistance lost. Not only would the procedure be dangerous, with far less chance of success than in a lightly controlled Vampire, but one could not know if the aircraft would blow up catastrophically on the way down. The engine filled most of the fuselage space, and the rest was guns and me. So instructions advised the use of the ejection seat to escape, abandoning the aircraft to its fate on a heading to open country or the sea, and parachuting to earth.

I made a quick call to the control tower intending to 'mayday' my position before ejection, and, at the same time, I put out my left hand to tentatively touch the beaming red light. It went out! I checked all the engine instruments, varied the throttle setting, and everything responded normally. I touched the light again and it came on. I touched it a third time and it went off again. My trouble was that I did not know if it was a real fire warning *and* faulty wiring, or simply faulty wiring. I decided two things: that I would not touch the light again, and that I would firmly assume that it was a wiring fault. I told air traffic control that I had a fire-warning-light problem (which made the controller very thoughtful), and that I was descending for an immediate, engine-powered landing. Would they give me priority and keep their eyes open, watching for me to confirm that no smoke was issuing from my jet pipe before I got too low to eject? Nobody tried to question my decision, and I approached and landed in silence. There was no smoke; there *was* a wiring fault. I had saved an expensive Hunter.

But I will never know whether it was fear or courage or simply a balanced decision that made me stay with the aircraft, engine running. I had also put my superiors into a slightly difficult position. I had ignored the recommended instructions for the situation, but I had brought the aircraft

....

back for examination, and perhaps modification of the whole fleet of aircraft. Apart from the technical follow-up, the incident and my part in it was quickly and conveniently forgotten. But I think Anatoli would have ejected, or bravely courted disaster with a manually controlled dead-stick landing, as perhaps, strictly speaking, so should I.

14

The New Commander, IVA and EVA

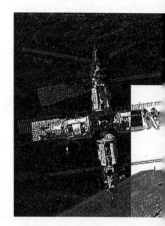

Michael soon forgot his disappointment at being relieved from IVA duty when the decision to postpone it for the new crew was made. The process, however, would have been tiring. When you are called unexpectedly to meet a set of new demands, even hazards, a lot of energy gets used up in becoming accustomed to the idea and conducting mental rehearsals. You try to rise to the occasion. If before the event the requirement is cancelled, it is accompanied by relief, or a sense of let-down, depending on when the cancellation takes place, but the energy has been used.

As an experienced commander, I find it interesting to speculate how Anatoli Solovyev himself had mentally prepared for dealing with Michael, this astronaut with a growing reputation in Russia. He had gone out of his way, while Michael was still in Russia, to meet him convivially, so he already knew that Michael was a fluent Russian-speaker and, in a variety of ways, a different kind of NASA astronaut. He was well aware of the troubles that had beset his predecessors and Michael on Mir, and I suspect that TSUP's tacit, if not then open agreement to Michael's participation in the recovery operation was known to him. A crew of three is an uncomfortable number, and it could normally mean that one member would often be left out of the activities of the stronger pair, as is the case in most walks of life, professional or social.

With Mir, the third man would comfortably be the foreigner. But this foreigner was different, had behaved differently, and actually seemed, for a short time, to have been the primary executive when events and the previous crew had demanded it. He, Anatoli Solovyev, would almost certainly have none of that in any situation normal to him, and he would know exactly how to stop it, from the outset.

I too have been in situations where I have formally taken command, while knowing that one or two senior subordinates were not only fundamentally better prepared and trained for certain tasks than I was, but would not hesitate, for the sake of the unit, to take the initiative for themselves if they thought it necessary. 'Twas ever thus, and if a commander is to survive as commander, having been selected by his seniors and betters, he must deal with potential, often well-intentioned but disruptive influences the moment they threaten. Most intelligent and imaginative subordinates can learn a short, sharp lesson very quickly indeed if it is applied early, clearly and unambiguously. Their innate loyalty and professionalism demands no less, and usually, at one stroke, the new commander applying the lesson gains their immediate respect. Their greater knowledge and experience is henceforth exercised only in very close step with the commander, who, in turn, will see that their initiatives are recognized and properly rewarded. It really is as easy as that.

Oddly, it was Michael who made the first move, towards the end of their first week. He said, as a tentative question, in front of Pavel, 'Anatoli, a lot of things have happened during my part of this flight, and twice we almost abandoned the station. Do you feel that you still could have so much to lose on this, your fifth flight, that you would always, unquestioningly, carry out every instruction from TSUP?'

Anatoli replied with surprising vigour.

'No, no, no! I don't need all this rubbish, all this rubbish I am getting from TSUP, all this rubbish I am getting from the programme. I don't need all this, I am fed up with all the decisions that have been made. This is my last flight and then I am out of here. I can and will make decisions that are right to protect our lives on this station, in spite of what TSUP wants.'

This was something of an outburst, and Michael felt that perhaps he had unwisely sailed a bit too close to the wind with his question. But he was

....

generally pleased with the response. He had been deliberately provocative to see if Anatoli was, in Michael's terms, simply another disciplined follower. Anatoli's reply suggested that he would be more 'flexible', again to use Michael's term, as was a NASA shuttle astronaut. But at first, to Michael's disappointment, Anatoli showed himself to be, if anything, more determined than ever to remain an executive carrying out orders.

The dreary succession of unpredictable computer failures, with immediate loss of attitude control, was beginning to exercise Michael's mind in relation to the problem of Atlantis's being able to make a successful docking with Mir in October – *his* Atlantis. He wondered if, before Atlantis approached, they should revert to Ground Control operating their attitude-control thrusters only, keeping the unreliable computer/gyrodyne system out of the loop. He was disturbed at the thought of missing the Atlantis bus home.

When Michael later suggested that the idea be transmitted to TSUP, Anatoli reacted and was unequivocal in his refusal.

'No, I will not have a member of this crew giving any ideas to TSUP; we are executives, we carry out orders. If no orders, we wait.'

Michael believed that this attitude was wrong but was unsurprised. He knew also, in the American cavalry idiom, that this time he had come across a 'real hardass'. He could not help but like him, however. Anatoli was true, honest, consistent and reliable, with a formidable presence. He was great in the old-fashioned Soviet sense, Michael said, a dedicated and brave commander who would do exactly what his bosses wanted and expected of him. By the end of Michael's term on Mir, it had become clear to Michael that Anatoli had become very fond of him.

I think that it is too easy to draw the conclusion that the apparent wide difference in attitude between the two men was simply a symptom of the difference between a Western liberal society as opposed to a Russian enclosed society. There is a much simpler, practical reason, which, as far as I know, neither man saw clearly enough at the time to be able to express it to the other. Recent American experience in space had taken place almost entirely in the shuttle, in flights that were not only short (a couple of weeks) but geared to *travelling* in a spaceship. The shuttle is a travelling spaceship from earth to orbit, or earth to satellite, or now, earth to Mir, and back to earth again. Each shuttle mission is well defined but frequently involves new

....

situations and therefore new problems. The unexpected must be included in what the shuttle commander and his crew expect and are ready for. Judgement and initiative and freedom to act accordingly are as much a responsibility for a shuttle commander as for the captain of any ship at sea or great transport aircraft in the air. All these commanders have to be flexible in exercising their judgements and responsibilities, ready to listen to their experts but making their own decisions.

A space station, on the other hand, is not, strictly speaking, a travelling spacecraft. It is a semi-permanent, human-inhabited satellite with stable life-support conditions and is constructed in such a way that it can be monitored and controlled from the ground. The crew are occupants, estate managers, of a complex whose human input was largely in its design, construction and launch to orbit, with data-link control by its numerous ground staff. The station could exist without human tenants at all, under the right circumstances. In this situation, it might be more reasonable to have in place a commander whose first duty link is to those at Ground Control, who are completely familiar and in step with all the systems, for long periods before his tenure begins and for some time afterwards. Michael's space-shuttle experience and different attitude to the station was further shaped, if not warped, by his highly colourful time earlier on Mir, having been faced with a series of unexpected emergencies perhaps more to be anticipated in a volatile spaceship than in the theoretical stability of a space station.

Michael had the following remarks to make to us in a letter of 17 August.

I am rapidly warming up to Anatoli and Pavel, but of course they have very different characters and strengths from the Sirius [earlier] crew. Their call sign is Rodnik, which means 'spring', as in a spring of water.

Anatoli has a character a little like our own best commanders, only he has a lot more operational experience than ours, at least in space. This is his fifth long flight. When I talked earlier about their coming being like in *Outland*, you may not have understood that Anatoli is the John Young of the cosmonauts, and his very professional arrival, manually flown because of another KURS failure, felt a little like the cavalry had ridden in to sort out the station. That impression

....

is only getting stronger, as I watch him work. I help him a lot, in surprisingly simple ways, like reminding him to be on the comm, or making sure he has paid attention to the time-line messages, which I think he appreciates, but when it comes to manoeuvring the Soyuz in a fly-around, or instructing me on how to get in and out of my seat in a spacesuit, without bumping him, while he is locked on to flying around the station, he is totally self-sufficient and gives orders very clearly. We have been discussing our EVA, and it is actually fairly complex, but I have no worries since I know he is going to be a good leader.

Anatoli, like many fighter pilots, had lived a life that made him feel almost infallible, that he must always be right, and if he survived, he probably had been. It is partly the influence of single-seat flying. The pilot is on his own. The buck stops – and starts – with him, and he is always conscious of that. But a trait that Michael found particularly attractive and valuable was Anatoli's refusal to be shaken or hurried when coming to a decision. His pulse rate went up, he would tell everybody to stop when he was deep in thought, he thought hard and never quit, kept at it, always pressed ahead. As Michael said, he was quite unlike the idea of a popular adventure character like James Bond facing murderous human adversaries. In space the action, even a threat to life, is usually much slower.

'These are just ordinary people who know their own failings, but will concentrate on steady thinking and persevering, doggedly, to the end.'

He could just as easily have been describing himself.

A letter from Michael copied to us on 21 August just before the IVA said:

Dear Rhonda,

We should be in bed, as we get up at 1.30 am. It is now 18.52, and we have just closed Priroda and Kristall. I think we are ready for the IVA. I am kind of looking forward to being all alone in the Soyuz. Anatoli trusted me to do most of the emergency Soyuz preparation, with suits, etc., on my own. The three suits are strapped into the couches, like three little people. I will float above them, with just enough room

....

to stretch diagonally from window to window. Not bad. I have packed a night bag of food, toiletries, etc., plus some very warm clothing. It is going to be no more than ten degrees C in there. There are now two ready spacesuits in the Node [which would become the airlock] for the IVA.

There are also two spacesuits with us in the Base Block, one of which will be mine for the later EVA, so I am getting excited and already planning and thinking ahead to it. The airlock in Kvant 2 is almost empty of articles in preparation, and the exterior hatch is accessible, and looks just like the trainer in the hydrolab in Star City, so I can review my future actions with it. I am the one who will open and close the hatch, going out first and coming in last.

Better get this off.

Love, Mike

On 22 August Michael helped Anatoli and Pavel into their spacesuits, and then installed himself in the Soyuz, in position should Anatoli and Pavel need instant evacuation.

In the Node, Anatoli and Pavel were now ready and spacesuited. All hatches to the other modules were closed and depressurization of the Node began. Depressurizing the Node was easy. All Anatoli had to do was open a valve on the Spektr hatch, the one fitted with such determination by Sasha and Michael after the collision, and depressurization was quick. Hatch seals were checked as the pressure in the Node dropped.

A problem was discovered. Anatoli found that the seal in the Base Block hatch was not perfect, and that Base Block air was leaking from it into the Node. This was a vexing beginning. There was no alternative but to repressurize the Node and reopen the Base Block hatch to check its seal. Anatoli laboriously got out of his spacesuit, and, on opening the hatch, found a very small piece of tape lodged against the seal which was causing the leak. Once he had removed it, the seal became airtight. Anatoli got back into his spacesuit and depressurization began again.

This time all the hatch seals held. Michael in his position in the Soyuz was in continuous contact with the Node occupants but he could not see them. He could hear every breath and word as decompression proceeded.

....

The Node was almost in a vacuum when Pavel, who was wiggling his fingers in his glove, said that he could feel air flowing past his hand. Michael was thoroughly alarmed at this sure sign of suit depressurization and malfunction. If Pavel's suit failed to pressurize in the vacuum, Pavel would be unable to breathe, his blood would begin to boil and he would die. He interrupted Pavel to shout, 'Pavel, stop moving your hand!'

Pavel had not appreciated the danger he was in and continued to move his hand while experiencing the unexpected and not unpleasant phenomenon. Anatoli quickly picked up the urgency in Michael's voice. Michael surely felt that they were about to see Pavel killed by decompression. Anatoli, now thoroughly alerted to this possibility too, shouted, 'Pavel, *stop!*'

Michael thought, *Oh, God, this is it, we are going to lose Pavel.*

He felt sick, and certain that Pavel would go in that moment. Michael and Anatoli were now both shouting at Pavel to shut up and stop moving before it was too late. A combination of first flight, first spacewalk, courage and complacency had combined to make Pavel initially unreceptive to his comrades' warnings, as the rapid flow of air seductively tickled his wrist. TSUP, who had also been listening, jumped in too to shout warnings. Pavel froze obediently.

Anatoli's greatness is in his patience and unshakeability. He re-pressurized the Node for the second time, as quickly as he dared, saving Pavel's life. Another spacesuit gauntlet was found which Pavel put on, and, for the third time, depressurization of the Node was started. This time all was well. Finally vacuum conditions were reached. With a warning to Michael, Pavel and Anatoli opened the hatch to Spektr for the first time since 25 June. It was now one pm.

The real job had only just started, but the preceding twenty minutes had demonstrated the Russians' amazing patience and resilience, not to mention capability, in being able to furnish a replacement glove and to continue doggedly with the mission. The pair worked steadily and well, Pavel in the Spektr interior locating the disconnected cables which transmitted power from Spektr's solar arrays, then feeding them through the hatch for connection to the inner side of the new hatch cover. The interior was very dark, but with the aid of flashlights, Pavel was able to retrieve a few objects belonging to Michael, that he had left behind in June in such a tearing hurry.

It was during this vital IVA that our willing cooperation with media interest was particularly well returned by Sky Television. I had already used their twenty-four-hour news desk by phone to ask for the latest Mir news available on the wire services, which, knowing us well now, they never hesitated to pass on. On this occasion this generous organization phoned me back and put one of their telephone receivers against the speaker which was receiving live Mir–Moscow transmissions, including the dialogue, in Russian, between Anatoli, Pavel and Michael. We were thus able to listen in to the whole process, counting off each of the reconnected cables until the work was nearly completed, also hearing Michael's voice from time to time, recognizable even in Russian, especially when he laughed.

The work was completed, with the new hatch and its new cable connections fitted in place, the hatch sealed and the Node repressurized, at about four pm Moscow time. Michael was then able to rejoin his colleagues and help them carefully to remove their spacesuits. Michael said a number of things to Ground Control, among them, in English for the benefit of reporters, 'We did everything that we set out to do and more.' He sincerely complimented the internal spacewalkers for succeeding at a difficult and potentially dangerous job, a thoughtful contribution to the upbeat side of Mir without, I trust, stealing any of the commander's thunder.

After it was over, Mary felt impelled to congratulate them all, and Rhonda felt the same.

22 August 1997

Dear Bill and co-workers at NASA,

We have spent today, Friday, playing host (polite and cooperative) to the media and I am feeling rather jaundiced. However, I want to express my feelings about the fantastic achievement of the crew of Mir, Anatoli, Pavel and our dear Mike, an incredible first, of accomplishing the repair of a *major* malfunction of a space vehicle, in space, in a completely untried, unimagined exercise, and with complete success. This day has been a triumph for manned space enterprise, against all the nay-sayers. I wish more people could appreciate what has been achieved. Please express, if appropriate, our appreciation of what they have *all* accomplished.

....

Best regards, and love to you all,

Mary Foale

This message was also copied to Mike.

All three men retired to their next sleep period deeply satisfied with their achievement. In their minds' eye, they saw the brand-new, beautifully fitting Spektr hatch with its array of power-laden cables leading from its face into the Node. The promise of an early restoration of full power for the whole station was in their grasp at last.

On the ground, too, the designers and craftsmen sighed with heartfelt relief that their urgent teamwork had borne such fruit with this Mir crew. Soon the cables would be checked and connected. For the crew it would be like returning to another world. Even an exterior repair to the punctured Spektr module could perhaps be contemplated.

Rhonda felt the same relief and satisfaction as Mary had.

22 August 1997

Dear Colin, Mary and Susan,

I hope this finds you all together having a nice weekend. We are all feeling a bit of elation after the spacewalk today. I listened to it on NASA Select this morning and it was great hearing Mike talking and laughing. The translator told him the press and ground controller wanted him to say something in English, and then she translated his Russian as 'I've forgotten English.' Of course what he said has been used all over the media about it being a super day.

I went to the ham shack today at one pm and talked to Mike for a minute with ten other people. I'd heard from him so little this week, and wanted to tell him and the crew 'Congratulations' right away. We'll be getting up early in the morning for his phone call, so I'll get off to bed now.

Lots of love, Rhonda

A day later, the newly retrieved cables from Spektr had been connected to the main battery systems of the station. The modules, which for two months had been without power, were one after another brought fully back to life. Kristall

....

(100 amps) and Kvant 2 (47 amps) were the first to be provided with temperature-control and fans and lighting. This permitted more flexibility in the science experiments for which Michael had originally been primarily responsible, particularly his Greenhouse and gel experiments. But as has been seen from Michael's earlier letter, Anatoli already considered that Michael was the right choice as his companion on an EVA outside the station complex, to inspect the exterior of Spektr for damage, and to locate the likely area of pressure leakage. The planned date for this EVA, if NASA approved Michael's participation, would be 3 September. Michael already had approval for on-orbit training for an EVA, but as is their custom and wisdom, NASA withheld final approval until nearer the proposed date, when a review of risks and readiness would take place.

On 24 August Michael was having a brief conversation with his daughter Jenna on a phone link, and because the speakers were interconnected at the time on Mir, Anatoli was able to listen in. He rather surprised Michael by saying what a nice clear voice Jenna had, he could understand every word. Encouraged by this, when Michael was having a ham pass conversation with the NASA director of the Johnson Space Center, George Abbey, he called Anatoli over to join in. Anatoli was engaged in talking to TSUP, but he came and spoke some sentences in excellent English, and his understanding of the language was further underlined.

Michael had recently asked Keith Zimmerman, a NASA representative at TSUP, to give him a rough outline of the EVA which it was planned that he and Anatoli should do. Zimmerman promptly responded with a full plan, in English. Anatoli at that stage had not seen anything in Russian, and was also wondering what the plan would be, so he asked Michael if he might see the English version. He seemed to have no problem understanding it. The next day he told the Russian specialists on the ground that it was high time they got the Russian-language plan out. He then proceeded to streamline the plan, based on what he had read in English. Michael was very impressed, and amused at how the Russian EVA specialists were taken aback by Anatoli's justified sally. A major part that Anatoli deleted was the personal instructions that he was to give Michael concerning the operation of the EVA 'crane'. Anatoli was sure that Michael would have no difficulties, having been thoroughly trained on the ground. It looked as if Anatoli, in turn, was finding

....

himself impressed by Michael. Michael admits to a glow of unexpected pleasure at this show of confidence. In the past he had gone out of his way to show his independence of spirit to TSUP. He now felt it necessary to make it very clear to TSUP that of course he would do anything the commander wanted. The ground was glad to hear this, although some echoes of guest-astronaut separateness remained. Anatoli had also been including Michael in all planning discussions and decisions, which brought the two men closer in their mutual confidence, understanding and regard.

Back on earth, we continued to have very hot weather, at least in Cambridge. We enjoyed another great weekend sailing with Sue, and later, sitting out in the garden eating good food, talking about Michael and looking forward to his return – not so long now. The heat had brought on our beans very well in the garden but we had to water them at least twice a day. I had harvested the first bean crop and we were being inundated with plums as well, so we had to eat them quickly. Apples were yet to come. Mary told 'farmer Foale' of this by e-mail to Mir.

We went to a performance of *The Tempest* in the gardens of Girton College and also to one of *As You Like It* in Newnham College gardens, both delightful evenings. On Mir, things continued stable with the welcome restoration of power and life was much more bearable.

The preparations for Michael and Anatoli's EVA were then said to be influenced by an unforeseen US domestic problem. The American Labor Day national holiday was on Monday, 1 September, and NASA was said to have expressed reluctance to guarantee the presence, after the holiday, of all their necessary staff on 2 September. This would have been the day when Russian and NASA decision-makers would review the whole EVA plan and refine the instructions to the crew. No problem, said the Russians, Foale could probably use more time to familiarize himself with the Russian spacesuit, as it was many months ago, in Star City, that he had last donned one. There may well have been some basis for these reasons, but from Michael's viewpoint it was Mir that was not ready. For one thing, Anatoli had been kept so busy with station maintenance matters as to have had no time for personal preparation, which included putting together the scaffolding which would be taken outside later on the EVA. He had once again been diverted to servicing the Elektron generator. A necessary postponement of a few days was agreed. However, the

....

broad parameters of the EVA were decided: that a close examination of Spektr's exterior would be made to identify areas of major damage, and perhaps the likely location of air leakage. The solar-array linkages would also be manually rotated, as they had failed to respond to fine-tuning signals designed to turn them to optimum angles with the sun after the IVA. The scaffolding and handholds were also to be fitted to aid future EVA participants in repair work.

On 31 August, media reporting of Mir, as of everything else, stopped with the news of the tragic death of Princess Diana. I e-mailed Michael, in case he had not heard, but of course he had, as his radio ham friends around the world talked of nothing else. He later said that his cosmonaut friends had also expressed their deep personal sadness.

On 2 September we were disturbed to hear that some so-called 'space officials' in Russia were openly blaming Michael's previous crew, Tsibliyev and Lazutkin, for the collision accident of 25 June, after a 'thorough examination', and that they would be fined. Tsibliyev immediately went public in disagreement, asking, what thorough examination had taken place? He had not yet been asked any questions! Further enquiry disclosed that the 'space official' responsible was Valery Ryumin, the Russian side of Mir–NASA Phase I coordination, who had been present (and whom I had met) at the beach hut during the pre-launch party. We wondered where or in what way his 'thorough examination' had been conducted. Ryumin had not said. However, other Russian views were reported, for example, those of the deputy director of the Russian Space Agency, Boris Ostroumov, who said he was preparing recommendations for the cosmonauts to receive honour and decorations. Other space officials and most of the media openly distanced themselves from Ryumin, who, they pointed out, was also a deputy director of the company, Energiya, that designed and built Mir, and suggested that of course people will always support their own firm's technology, whether at the expense of cosmonauts or not.

On 4 September the NASA–Mir review committee approved the EVA for 6 September with Michael to accompany Anatoli. On the same day, we received an e-mail from Michael dated 1 September, which brought us once more up to date.

....

1 September

Dear Mum, Dad and Susan,

Thanks for your letters, which I received today, and Mum's about a week ago. We are very busy here getting the airlock and suits ready. The EVA is currently scheduled for opening of hatch at 04.00 am our time, or 02.00 am UK time on Saturday sixth. The EVA will probably take the full six hours available in the suits. There is a slight possibility that it will be postponed beyond the weekend, because the 850th year Moscow celebrations are on the same day. I doubt it, however. The EVA is too important to delay much.

Tomorrow Anatoli and I will be in suits, in the airlock, and the secondary airlock (where I normally sleep) in Kvant 2. It is for my benefit, to familiarize me again with the suit and airlock operations. Anatoli completed his tenth EVA when they went into Spektr, so he doesn't need the experience, but will do it anyway. He is a strong, calm commander, with possibly the most experience of all the active cosmonauts. I have enjoyed working with him, and of course I am learning a lot.

Our task for the EVA is to translate equipment, using one of the station cranes (adjustable boom-type arm) from the Kvant 2 airlock to the other side of the station, where the damage to Spektr is located. I will be controlling the crane, manually, like a tank gunner does with handles, while Anatoli is on the end of it with the equipment. I will myself translate from the airlock hatch, along the lower, forty-foot length of crane, to its base at the Base Block, and then from there waggle Anatoli across a hundred feet or so of space to the work site. The boom is very springy and I have to be very smooth and slow in its operation.

Anatoli will work from the end of the crane, to which he is double-tethered (we always have at least two tethers hooked to the station), to install a lattice truss of metal poles and attachment fittings to the module's outer structure, after first cutting away segments of exterior insulation blankets. The site is very visible from the Base Block windows, and Pavel will be controlling us with TV com-munication as well, from there. The truss will end up about fifteen

....

feet by six feet, in two separate places, to enable future repair work on the module skin. We don't really know how hard it will be for Anatoli to work, unanchored, from the end of the crane, so I expect to have to be behind him, holding him the best I can, while he lays out the truss, and helping to hand off pieces from our very unwieldy platform of poles, tied on with bungees.

When cutting away the thermal insulation with a razor knife, serrated (I have one also), it is hoped that Anatoli will be able to see an obvious puncture, near a large external fuel tank, caused by a strut that may have been pressed into the pressure hull. Anatoli will also have with him an EVA TV camera, with a wide field of view, that will be sending back continuous live pictures to TSUP, while at the same time recording. This way a detailed picture can be built up of the extent of the damage, and location. I will also have with me an EVA camera, to take stills.

After the work on the truss is complete, or time no longer allows (more than five hours I am guessing), I will swing Anatoli back to Kvant 2, where he will tie off the crane, and then he will come back along the crane to the Base Block. There we will cut away more insulation, to install a vacuum valve cap which will be needed to enable the transfer of the CO_2 scrubbing system from the Kvant module to the Base Block, some time after the EVA. This may only take thirty minutes. Finally, we both move away from the Base Block, along the crane, back to the airlock, retrieving from the outside of Kvant 2 an American Dosimeter experiment that has been measuring radiation external to the station.

Next day, 2 Sept Just finished training run. Very successful. My suit feels good, and we are ready. I should say of course that we are also saddened about the death of Diana, which we learned of on Sunday. Messages from hams keep telling us how sad the world feels. The EVA will probably be over by the time the funeral services start.

Dad, I was really tickled that you were called by the Russian ambassador. What a twist of fate in your life, to have him calling you and congratulate you! Ten years ago it would have been unthinkable.

....

I love you all, and think of you very often, even if you don't hear from me.

Love, Mike

Spacewalking becomes an acceptable risk, because a number of controlled factors add up to a reasonable expectation of safety. The spacesuit has been recently checked and tested for being airtight, and the life-support system of oxygen and power fully charged for the duration of the exposure in space. A mistake or the collapse of any part would be hazardous. Then it is finally checked in the vacuum of the airlock, which in Pavel's case had been in the Node. A spacesuit is really only a small, man-shaped spaceship. It is vulnerable to exterior damage such as meteorite puncture or accidental cutting. Anatoli's energetic use of a sharp serrated knife for the removal of insulation covers was to give Michael continuous cause for alarm, and kept him hyper-watchful. A small puncture would not, like a balloon, be an immediate disaster, because the system's oxygen and pressurization surplus would, for a brief time, compensate for the loss of pressure. But the cosmonaut would need to re-enter the ship and repressurize the airlock very speedily.

The time planned to be spent outside in the vacuum is another safety limitation and must not exceed (including some spare) the life-support supply time of the suit. Pavel's leaking gauntlet would have fundamentally reduced the time available, perhaps to minutes.

Finally, there must be a foolproof system that will invariably tether the spacewalker to the ship. Weightlessness is seductive and floating movement is slow. Without a tether it is only too possible to drift, unknowingly, beyond the reach of a handhold for retrieval. Each movement of body or limb, no matter how gentle, imparts an equal force in the opposite direction, leading to a drift away, if the astronaut is not vigilant. Michael had three tethers for added safety which should have been, and proved to be, foolproof. Each one would need, in turn, to be released and reclamped as he progressed from one part of the station or crane arm to another. It looks like a pedantic process and it has to be, for safety's sake – it is easy to be distracted while on a spacewalk.

If the unthinkable happens and, for whatever reason, all tethers are

....

released and the hapless astronaut drifts into darkening space, all is not necessarily lost, but he still has a very complex situation on his hands. Theoretically he can release pressure from his suit as a mini-thruster, but must take care to have it thrust exactly in the opposite direction to where the station lies, and exactly from his centre of mass. Otherwise, the mini-thrust will impart rotation instead of line movement. There are other complexities. It is best to be certain never to let go.

Princess Diana's funeral was to take place on the same day as the EVA, but the latter was much earlier, starting at 02.05 UK time and lasting six hours. Mary and I have often said that, no, we do not lose sleep worrying about Michael in space, and in general terms this is true. However, on the morning of 6 September I happened to wake, pre-dawn, at about three am and I was immediately aware that Michael and Anatoli had already left Mir for external space an hour ago, and were now working hard to achieve their objectives. To try to sleep again seemed quite out of the question, so we got up and turned on the teletext, then rang the Sky News twenty-four-hour news desk. All was apparently going well and, with plenty of morning tea, time for us went quickly. We were almost startled soon after eight o'clock by our phone ringing. It was Michael's medical advisor in Moscow, Terry Taddeo, to tell us that both spacewalkers had completed their tasks and were safely back in Mir, hatches closed and spacesuits off.

For Rhonda, this occasion had been very harrowing. The unexpected calmness which she had felt, or mustered, at the time of the news of the collision in June had long since gone. Mir had continued to present the crew with new frights, times of helplessness and a need for calm endurance well beyond normal orbital experience. She was perhaps more aware than was good for her that, whatever the dangers are in space, they are much increased for those who are outside the craft, in spacesuits and working to a tight programme. Michael would be in a Russian suit, of the kind that might have killed Pavel. She felt that Michael had successfully dodged so many dangers that it was wrong and unbalanced for him now to be put in the firing line of a lengthy and exacting spacewalk. She was also conscious that he was beginning his last programmed month on Mir. Could he not now lie low, until he was safely brought home?

As the superbly balanced wife of an experienced astronaut, she knew

....

that her thoughts were unreasonable and, in any case, should never reach Michael or indeed anybody who loved him. The media with their natural nose for danger had asked her if they could be at her house during the EVA. She agreed, and continued to behave as normally as possible, although the action outside Mir would be over six hours long, covering her midnight in Texas time.

She never once broke, but the strain manifested itself in an enveloping body rash which she also wanted to hide. It was so severe that her doctor thought she must have rolled in poison ivy. The rash was directly associated with Michael's danger, and slowly disappeared in the days following the successful completion of the EVA.

Michael was clearly the least worried of us all. He sent a brief account the day following the EVA via Dr Dave Larsen, to 'ALL'.

7 September 1997

Anatoli and I had the pleasure of doing the EVA on Saturday, while most of the world was occupied with the sad loss of Princess Diana and her funeral, about which we are also very sad. During the EVA, Anatoli worked much longer than planned to be sure that under the buckled radiator panels there is no deformation of the pressure hull of Spektr. No deformation was found.

After moving to the area of the broken solar-array motor-drive foundation, we found that it was significantly out of alignment, suggesting that there could be substantial damage under the motor, and therefore to the pressure hull itself. More EVA will be required to investigate this area further. Anatoli was successful in manually aligning the working arrays properly to the sun, so that Mir can now fly in a power-efficient attitude without affecting the on-orbit resource of the Soyuz spacecraft. Previously the attitude required [by the station] caused a side effect of higher than desirable temperatures of the H_2O_2 fuel in the descent module.

Personally, this EVA was very rewarding for me, and was different in many ways from my first spacewalk on the shuttle. The Russian suit is well designed for working on Mir, and allowed me to use three attachment tethers for personal translation, the whole time.

On the shuttle I was mostly translated around on the end of the arm by others who were inside – this time I was the driver, moving Anatoli around on the end of the somewhat whippy Strela twenty-metre crane. We remained at work until the suit limit of six hours.

I will remember the views of the earth and the Milky Way, and of the station, in the light of the sickle moon, for ever. These exceptional night views were possible because, unlike the shuttle, the only external lights we had were those mounted on our helmets, and I could turn these off when appropriate. I hope that more people in future, and many more supporters of human space flight, will one day get the chance to enjoy these extraordinary experiences. I have been so lucky to have had them.

Michael has always been a spacewalking enthusiast. For him this necessary EVA had been the high point of his mixed time on Mir, to be remembered with gratitude and satisfaction.

The director of Phase I for NASA in Houston, Frank Culbertson, was quick to send his congratulations to the whole crew.

To Mike, Anatoli and Pavel,

My congratulations to all of you on two superb EVAs. Your performance has been an outstanding demonstration to the world of the reasons for which we are working together in space, and the potential for human performance in the most difficult of circumstances. Your teamwork with those supporting on the ground and with each other has been exciting to watch. I am proud of all you have done so far, and very grateful for the amount of effort you put into keeping this great adventure going so well. As for the recent search for damage, even though you did not find a specific puncture, I believe you did an excellent job of searching and working together, and increased everyone's knowledge of the conditions outside Spektr.

Again, congratulations on two outstanding EVAs and your consistent excellent performance. I look forward to seeing all of you again when you return.

Frank

An extensive NASA–Mir status report recounted the EVA triumph in detail, pointing out that it had been the second spacewalk for Foale, during which he had become the first person to have made a spacewalk in both the US and Russian spacesuits. The station appeared to be in a new era of stability. It ended with an editor's note:

> The next Mir status report will be on Friday, 12 September unless developments warrant otherwise. For further information, contact . . .

Michael with his Mir experience had found that it was rash to make assumptions too readily, particularly if they sounded more like a pious hope. Unfortunately, this was to prove no exception.

15

Final Uncertainties

The three men had gelled together as a crew. None of them commented on this, although it must have been satisfying for each of them. Pavel had been conscious from before his arrival that Michael would need listening to. He was equally conscious that Anatoli, while also accepting this, would find it odd. They had not exchanged views on the matter, but both Tsibliyev and Lazutkin had included Michael and his ideas in their handover briefings before their departure from Mir. The new crew and Michael had now been together, without Tsibliyev and Lazutkin, for three weeks. The period had been rewarding.

Since the tumble of the station on 15 August, Mir had been stable. An unprecedented IVA had been undertaken successfully, although not without a temporary terror. Almost normal station power had been restored and all aspects of living conditions improved. Within this apparent return to pre-collision normality of the incident-prone station, a complex EVA had been achieved by Anatoli and Michael. All three could well think that they had made a real contribution to the station's new-found docility.

The next blow was therefore felt to be well below the belt. The central motion control computer failed again. It happened soon after wake-up on Monday, 8 September, at nine-forty-five am Moscow time. It was even more of a shock than before, after three weeks of stability, particularly for the new

....

crew. The now familiar sequence of events followed: station tumble through space, misalignment of the solar arrays, a dramatic drop in solar-generated power. A frightening experience meaning the return of old dangers.

Anatoli seemed appalled and fearful at the effect, possibly because of the unfamiliarity for him, of feeling helpless. After so many laborious recoveries, Michael, on the other hand, found himself more dispirited than frightened. The recoveries had at least, so far, been successful. He said to Anatoli that, yes, it was indeed frightening, but that they should look on the bright side.

'We should be glad it did not happen three days ago, during our six-hour spacewalk while we were much more vulnerable. Can you imagine how you would have felt, trying to work on the end of a whipping sixty-foot crane, with me trying to control it, while the station and, for us, the surrounding universe, our only point of reference, went into a complex rotation around us?'

Michael's attempt at making light of the situation was not reciprocated, and Anatoli rather ungraciously continued to be surly with Michael. But eventually he did say, almost ruefully, 'You are, of course, right.'

Michael tried again to be helpful.

'And at least this time we're not power-critical, and we should be able to lead an almost normal existence while sorting it out.'

Now it was Michael's turn to feel rueful. He realized that it was he who was making all the effort to restore their morale and some semblance of high spirits, not Anatoli Solovyev, whose job as commander it was. And it *was* true that they did not this time have to switch off virtually everything to have a chance of recharging depleted batteries. The well-conducted IVA into Spektr and reconnection of its solar arrays had since kept batteries well charged in spite of the poor attitude. For Michael this alone was a huge step forward. But the station's attitude unreliability again rang warning bells in his mind about Atlantis making a successful docking in a month's time. Harbours and docks are meant to be in calm waters. This thought was indeed dispiriting.

Michael wrote on 9 September:

Dear Rhonda,

You probably know we had a GNC failure again today, and had to

....

replace a computer, but we have not yet lost power, and we even got to eat a hot lunch, so the day has really been quite pleasant and relaxing. I talked a lot with Anatoli about conditions in Russia, which is unusual. He is normally very hard to get to talk much about anything. Unlike Pavel, with whom I often have pretty frank discussions. We have started watching Russian films on the weekends, because Pasha found a player that Sasha had never managed to find, and we have seen *Man Overboard*, in Russian, with Goldie Hawn, and then two good Russian films, and two French films. The Russian films are pretty intense, and showed in one of them current conditions with the Mafia in St Petersburg. The other was historical, before and after the revolution, called *Life in Odessa*. The second one was quite disturbing, of course, and we watched it last night. It left me feeling even more convinced that it is time for me to extract myself out of this alien culture, and re-establish myself in the West. I am really hoping the promise of Hubble is a good one – I am sort of banking on it. I do need rehabilitating. Will send more.

Love, Mike

Michael was frankly expressing what had become over the past year a pent-up longing for his own kind and their values. He had not allowed himself the luxury of such bare personal examination for nearly two years, and had been a loyal and uncomplaining participant in the Russian way of doing things, carefully not dwelling too much on what he missed. Rhonda too tried hard. Russians probably did not understand or perceive the difficulties Western men and women go through in their wish to accommodate and understand their Russian colleagues. It will take time. When Michael and his family went on holiday after nearly a year in Star City, they flew from the grim, almost Gothic Moscow airport to Norway. They had to change aircraft at Copenhagen. Rhonda remembers the overwhelming joy and relief she felt on walking through Copenhagen airport, its carefree crowds, colourful shops, smiling faces, all like a voice inside her singing, 'You're in the West!'

Meanwhile, Michael was still on Mir, which needed attention. While attitude control was being regained, the recently re-established Elektron oxygen generator was switched off and 'candles' burned instead. Other items, including the attitude-control gyrodynes, were powered down, as without a computer to control movement they were redundant and could, as before, have become counter-productive. All the now well-tried measures were used to regain a proper attitude to the sun, from Soyuz thrusters to main station thrusters, until first attitude and then power generation were restored. Ground Control interrupted to tell them that they were experiencing a jubilee – the sixty-six-thousandth orbit of Mir's original Base Block! The crew were unresponsive.

A spare on-board motion-control computer system was located, and during a day of hard work its installation was completed, just before bedtime. Ground Control were then able to monitor the retention of the regained attitude until the following day, when the gyrodynes would be spun up again. Commander Anatoli Solovyev elected to stay up all night to monitor the efficacy of Ground Control measures personally, an action typical of his sense of responsibility towards control from the ground.

While this was happening, during the early part of our day, we in Cambridge awaited a visit at noon from a journalist, Angela Neustatter, who was with the *Daily Telegraph*. We had also received warning of a possible phone link with Michael at 12.28 pm, arranged through the Johnson Space Center ham shack in Houston. Angela Neustatter had already arrived, then the phone rang and we happily allowed her to listen in, as she hoped to write a family piece. Her article subsequently appeared in the weekend colour supplement, and we thought it was excellent, as did many of our friends.

When Michael came on the phone, we were again relieved to note the cheerfulness in his voice.

'Oh, well,' he said, 'it has happened before, five or six times. We have now restored attitude in the usual way. We have even got the computer back on line, but it will be tomorrow before the software has been fully re-established.'

He sounded weary and resigned but not tense. We talked about his epic Russian-suited EVA, and it was obvious how much he had enjoyed it, and *knew* that they had done a good job. I was reminded once again what a remarkable man this son of mine was, pushed to the edge repeatedly yet maintaining a warm and imaginative coolness, if that is not a contradiction. There he was, yet again responding to a vital equipment fall-down, yet making

....

all of us, safe on earth, happy by the way he spoke.

He went on to say that following his EVA with Anatoli, a Russian general at the Space Agency had asked him if he would be prepared to follow his success with another spacewalk, to take place before Atlantis arrived. Michael was very pleased to be asked but was obliged to say that NASA would have to be approached for authorization. This time NASA said no, almost certainly on the sound and prudent basis that Michael had in truth already done much more than enough. Michael felt that he would have been capable of doing it, and he wanted to, so he felt a pang of disappointment at the NASA decision. However, I found myself echoing the NASA view, and said that he ought to leave something for his successors to do. I also recalled the words of one of the less optimistic NASA advisers in Texas earlier, who said that the trouble with dodging bullets successfully so often was that you eventually felt bulletproof. This was dangerous.

The next day the attitude reference part of the replaced motion control system had been fully reactivated, and by noon ten functioning gyrodynes were spun up and once again began to control the station's attitude. This latest failure, no less alarming in spite of its familiarity, and the physical discomfort it caused to all, had been more quickly dealt with and resolved than previously. The increased power margins now available allowed the Kvant Elektron oxygen generator to work again, and repair continued on the generator in Kvant 2.

Michael was now well into his final month on Mir, if all went well, and he felt entitled to look forward to the time of Atlantis's docking and the transfer process. Like all spacemen, he could get a little impatient with the 'hands meeting in space' syndrome beloved of the world's media, which pictures a wide, clean docking area with astronauts emerging smiling from the shuttle and Russian cosmonauts meeting them from Mir in the Kristall module. He made what he obviously considered to be a somewhat heavy point, recorded for us in one of the NASA status reports.

NASA–Mir Status Report, 9 September 1997
Mike reported today that we've got to figure out as a crew what we are going to do with all the stuff that's around. All the French stuff that came up on Progress 35 is stuck on the wall. I have a list of

....

Russian return items – that's a big list, they're big-volume items. I also have the American list. My question for you is, must we clean out the docking module, or can we place stuff in the module? [They often had to, anyway.]

We've been putting all the pre-pack items on the floor in Priroda. I think we're going to be very short on space for the Russian and American transfer items, plus all the stuff delivered on Progress 35 that's still on the walls. Some of that will be put behind panels, we hope, but there is still water on the walls and we're trying to dry out the hull of Priroda. As a result, I have a very strong request, and Anatoli concurs, to use the docking module to pre-position return items. Is that going to be a problem? What it means is that we won't have a clean volume for the docking ceremony.

MOST [NASA representatives] informed Mike that both the Russian and US sides would be asked if this was an impact. They also informed Mike that a file was in work from Wendy Lawrence which summarized the hardware Dave Wolf would be bringing up with him.

Mike reported that he has returned to sleeping in Kvant 2 and that Dave Wolf will likely want to do the same.

ISSUES

1 Is it acceptable for Mir 24/NASA 5 to use the docking module as a staging area for their pre-pack items (both US and Russian items)?

2 Mike reported that they essentially had no way to print items on board any more – they had run out of ink cartridges. He requested that MOST make an effort to keep things sent to him short and succinct. MOST expects the Russian side to formally request additional ink cartridges be sent up on STS-86.

As ever, the problem of the accumulation of equipment led to concentrated thought on what they could and should do without. Progress 35, presently docked on Kvant in its stowage position until its departure into burn-up descent over the Pacific Ocean, still had space on board for rubbish. Permission was given to open the hatch for interior inspection. It was not left open for long – apparently the smell was not appetizing.

If the crew needed any reminder that troubles rarely come singly, they

....

received the first of a new batch on the evening of Monday, 14 September. Monitors at the USAF space command's headquarters in Colorado Springs had noticed a coming event of considerable interest. The path of a defunct US military satellite weighing 370 pounds was being monitored while it continued its normal stable orbit around the earth. Mir's orbit was also being monitored. Differences in orbital speeds were steadily and by chance bringing the two orbits towards a crossing path in space which appeared to be reducing in separation distance. The duty officer checked again, interrogating the computer to give a minimum miss distance. There was no doubt: at the closest miss distance calculated, the satellite would pass very uncomfortably close to Mir, at least for its occupants. He notified NASA of his concern. NASA felt rather more urgency than the officer had shown – his view had been that a miss is a miss, don't get too excited. NASA passed the information to their representatives in MOST who told Ground Control.

The Russians were alarmed. The calculated miss distance was well under a thousand metres. Calculations could be wrong. Computers could be wrong. Orbits could be less stable than calculated. A collision could not be ruled out. In the infinities of space, a mere thousand metres seemed dangerously inadequate. Ground Control called Anatoli. The controller's voice was carefully level.

'Anatoli, we have serious news of a possible conflict of path between Mir and a US military satellite.'

'Yes? When will this happen?'

'The best time we have got from the Americans is 19.33 Moscow time today.'

'How close?'

'They say less than a thousand metres.'

Anatoli thought about this and looked at his crew, who had heard every word of the warning. Michael found that both Anatoli and Pavel were looking at him, no doubt because of the American nature of the danger. He was careful not to appear uncomfortable, and said nothing.

'What will be the closing speed?' asked Anatoli.

'About sixteen kilometers per second [31,000 mph].'

If the 370-pound satellite hit Mir, the shock wave would cause a catastrophic failure and the station and its occupants would be destroyed. It

....

has been said that even a single grain of sand at this speed would have the impact of a .38 calibre bullet. Anatoli said, 'At that speed and size, we will not see it, whether it hits or misses us. If it hits us we are finished anyway. If it misses . . .'

The same thought came to Anatoli and Ground Control at the same time. Mir was so extensive with its modules and solar arrays, a hit had to be considered possible. But while catastrophic for the station as a whole if it hit centrally, it would perhaps not necessarily be so for the escape craft Soyuz if the crew were already in it. The decision was made.

Leaving nothing to chance, Anatoli and his crew quietly took up their escape positions in Soyuz at 19.00 hours, plenty of time before the event in case the time was wrong. They would stay there until confirmation was received from Ground Control that the satellite had passed.

It was a long wait. Michael thought how ironic, after all their dangers on Russian Mir, to be sitting ducks while an American satellite took a cockshy at them, taking its turn in a queue of troubles to send them all to oblivion. There was no point in looking out. There would be nothing to see, hit or miss.

He recalled Vasily's question, after all their tribulations: what else could now befall them?

Ground Control kept them informed of the decreasing time to the satellite's passage. The crew looked out, closed their eyes, looked out again. It was 19.30, 19.31, 19.32, tension increased, *19.33*, 19.34, 19.35, 19.36 . . .

'Rodnik, this is Ground Control. The satellite has passed, I repeat, the satellite has passed. Acknowledge.'

Grateful to be in a position still to acknowledge anything, Anatoli did so. They returned thoughtfully to the Base Block.

It was the Americans' turn to play down the incident, on the grounds that it was a known object in space on a predetermined path which would not have collided with Mir – the kind of thing that happens every month, said an official spokesman. Perhaps that was true, at least as seen from the safety of the ground. Not, apparently, in the eyes of Russian Ground Control or Anatoli and his crew, who together had had a truly concentrated ten minutes. It was, in the event, a closer encounter than previously calculated, and the miss distance was shown to be only 470 metres.

You do not have to be in space to have the same real fears when you

....

are fear-prone. It was easy to experience similar unease when I was flying low over Scottish and Welsh hills at a mere 160 mph, straining to see fast military jets which might hit *me*. One of my pleasant tasks with the Department of Aerial Photography for Cambridge University was frequently to fly my light little twin-engine Cessna to remote parts of the British Isles for the curator to photograph areas for the Nature Conservancy Council. Unfortunately for us, the wild places were also natural training areas for high-speed military jets, flying low at five-hundred-plus mph, such as I had formerly done when in the service. They would barely have time to notice me in my small, slow aircraft before it was too late, particularly if we were already on a true collision course, which makes each aircraft seem apparently still in the air, in relation to the other, while they are in fact getting steadily closer. It is the one you do not notice or cannot easily see that hits you. Or, you are frightened by a late sighting of a Tornado or Harrier jet, which, thankfully, passes – but you immediately think, where is his number two? (or three or four?). Collisions can and do occur, especially if you forget that they can.

The American satellite incident provided a general reminder of the hazards of space travel in an environment in which between six and eight thousand known, tracked fragments and pieces of debris regularly orbit the earth. The Russians have apparently never considered it worth while to have a 'dodging' capability, partly because accurate forecasting of miss differences was believed to be impossible. However, a Russian Ground Control spokes-man said that this was the closest brush Mir had had with an unrelated space object in its eleven years, a distance of barely five hundred yards. If two fully controllable aeroplanes pass each other at a thousand yards, it is officially considered to be a 'near miss', requiring international investigation.

Main computer crashes unfortunately repeated themselves. On 15 September the computer went down for the fourth time since July, and the recurring problem added fuel to criticisms of Mir's safety and viability. The crew had noticed that two of the three units in the main computer were behaving oddly, so decided as a precautionary measure to turn the whole computer off. Once again, all main non-essential electrical services had to be dispensed with, including the Elektron oxygen-generating systems, and attitude control reverted to use of the station thrusters. On this occasion, some spokesmen in Russia felt forced to observe that because of shortage of funds the programme had long ago stopped replacing items which had reached the end of their design life. Such items were now left in place until they failed, and it was then expected that they would be repaired in space, with a change of components should these be available. This could hardly have been news to the crew.

With further tinkering, the crew restored the computer to normal functioning yet again. Ground Control were reported as saying that a computer was stored and available on Mir, but did not say whether this one had previously failed and been serviced, or even if it had been stored satisfactorily, in view of the fluctuating conditions of heat, cold and wet which had been Mir's lot for many weeks. It was later said that the crew had changed the whole computer assembly. It seemed fairly clear that one way or another, the crew continually experimented with whatever they had (and could locate) in an effort to keep the computer viable. It was announced that a completely new computer would be sent up on the next Progress supply vessel in October. However, the world's press had noticed that this latest failure had taken place just two weeks before the scheduled docking with the space shuttle Atlantis, carrying Michael's astronaut replacement Dr David Wolf. A complete computer failure of the kinds recently experienced would make any docking attempt difficult if not impossible, and Atlantis was due to launch on 25 September.

Michael wrote on 15 September.

I am feeling a bit fed up today. Currently we have no hot water, hot food and no toilet running, for at least twenty-four hours. This power loss, and loss of control, is the direct result of a computer failure, the same which caused our problem a week ago. Then, we changed computers with an older one stored away, switched out from many years ago. It seems they switched it out back then for a good reason – it can fail! So now there are no more whole GNC computer blocks, and today Pavel switched subpieces of each bad block to make a whole one. We will see if this works later this evening. We are on the edge of being without flight control at all. I now realize I really do want to come home soon, because thinking this through, the lack of spares and new computers means that the chance of the shuttle being

....

able to dock with a stable Mir is becoming less certain. There is a very odd twist to the GNC system, which at first sight seems very clever: the gyrodynes keep spinning to keep Mir stable, if the computer works, using hardly any jets. But if the computer, or the gyrodynes, fail, then not only does Mir go into free drift, but then in the course of hours afterwards, as the gyros spin down, we start to spin in the opposite direction [a repetition of the plug-pull syndrome], and end up with a spin rate of about six degrees a minute. I am pretty sure the shuttle cannot deal with this without being totally heroic.

So I commented again to Anatoli that if Mir would only use its jets for attitude control, during docking, then if the gyrodynes and GNC fail, the Mir would just be in free drift, and remain so without building up rates due to the gyrodynes spinning down. That way, the shuttle can still dock. But Anatoli categorically said he would not propose this to TSUP, and that we are just executors, and it is TSUP's business to worry about such things. I feel that I have found a fundamental cultural difference between me and my crew. At the time, I just changed the subject and did not argue.

Michael was clearly feeling tired and jaded, and this had made him feel gloomy over the prospect of his timely retrieval. But he felt better the next day. He wrote:

Dear Rhonda,

I am sorry I sent you my last note, sounding fed up, but life is not always rosy up here. Things almost immediately after that started to get better. First I had a ham pass with w5rrr, and Dave Leestma, and Bob Cabana, and mystery guest Hoot Gibson all said nice things to me, which cheered me up, *and Dave Leestma heard my opinion about the gyrodynes, and said that discussions were already under way* [my italics]. Then Anatoli figured out a way to heat up our food cans, using the O_2 solid fuel generators [a welcome initiative], which we have been letting off because Elektron is not working while power is limited. And then the computer swap-out seemed to work, and there was enough sunlight on Kvant 2 for half an orbit to be able to

....

use the toilet successfully, and then we watched a pretty funny Russian thriller movie. And I received another letter from you. This morning Mir is back in attitude, and I am getting ready to plant a new batch of earth seeds and space seeds this afternoon.

Try and relax, read a little, sit by the pool a little. Soon I will be home and I promise to take the trash out, like I used to.

Love, Mike

Events on the station itself continued to provoke criticism in the United States of NASA involvement in the Mir programme. NASA officials felt it necessary to defend publicly their intention to include Dr David Wolf on the Atlantis mission later in the month, to preserve an American presence on Mir after Michael's retrieval. Everyone would consider it to be a surprising precedent if NASA reversed a decision in the face of political or public pressure. The dangers that had beset Mir in Michael's time had largely been overcome. The House Science Committee was scheduled to hold a hearing concerning Mir on Thursday, 18 September, at which the American NASA–Mir Phase I coordinator, Frank Culbertson, would be present. Meanwhile, in the wake of the previous few days' adventures, we received the following letter from Michael.

16 September 1997

Dear Mum, Dad and Susie,

Things are as usual up and down here. Thank you very much for your note, Dad. I enjoyed talking to you all on the ham radio. It is quite a different treat, compared to being on the shuttle. Although I always have to remind myself that many people are listening in when I speak. Your half of the conversation is much less likely to be heard, because the signal is directed out to space, whereas Mir's signal covers a two-thousand-mile radius on the earth.

The replacement computer failed this weekend, and pieces from the two bad units were taken to make a whole one, which may or may not work for a while longer. I got pretty fed up this last time, because it was my fifth time without a working toilet, hot food, light and hot water. But we're back up and running again today, and so my

....

mood is much better. I harvested all my plants of the second planting yesterday, and changed out the root module of the Greenhouse, and today plan to do a new planting with half earth seeds, half space seeds. If Atlantis comes on time, docking on the twenty-eighth, then the plants will only just be starting to flower, and I will have to harvest them prematurely for return. David Wolf will not be continuing this experiment, so Farmer Foale will be the only one who has done this. The space seeds produced this time are much bigger and healthier-looking than the first harvest, almost as large as earth seeds. This may be because I simply hand-planted them into the wick seed beds, rather than using sticky tape and a plastic screen, which was used to place them the first time.

I think Rhonda may have mentioned that we are hoping to get a work trip around the Christmas period, which would be ideal, or if not, then later on into January. I am sure an array of invitations for both me and Rhonda, some of which will be mandatory as far as NASA is concerned, will be waiting on my desk in Houston, and we will figure out what to do then.

Honestly I don't want to think about events after landing yet; I keep telling myself that the chance of Atlantis coming on time is still not that good, so I am keeping psychologically prepared for an extended stay here, if forced into it. After the preparation and sheer excitement of the EVA were over, I did experience a feeling of let-down, but have managed to get myself busy with experiments again, and the packing of equipment for return.

You have probably put the boat up by now, or you will soon [on 31 October]. I hope you had some good sailing this summer. You have all been so busy travelling around England, or studying. Susie, you mentioned you had heard my description of the sickle moon during my EVA. I don't remember telling you about it before our phone call – did you pick that off the Internet? I did write a short description as part of the Mir status report that I put on the ham mailbox here, that used those words. I know hams download and publish my updates on the Internet – do you find these little blips? Lots of love, Mike

I was moved by his continuing steadiness and entirely understandable and wise mental preparation for a possible substantial delay in returning to earth, although he was already thinking about Christmas. I felt that I had something to say to Michael about his return, so I sent him this letter in reply.

17 September 1997

We were so pleased to get your letter a few minutes ago, for all the usual reasons plus one. I rang Rhonda yesterday, and had a lovely conversation with her – we are all so glad that she joined our family, and are eternally grateful for your part in bringing it about – and she and the children were all fine and cheerful and looking forward so much to your return to earth. We uninhibitedly discussed you behind your back. Not so much your remarkable tenure on Mir, as the need to spoil you and treat you gently while you readjust to Seabrook and NASA and all the rest of us, your rehabilitation to gravity and indeed being with people other than your crew again.

Knowing you as I do, I don't expect you to *show* much sign of stress and neither, I think, would I wish to. I found that as a station commander with my three thousand people, there were many opportunities to express distress and disappointment, and the temptation was sometimes very strong to do so, and to give open rein to one's feelings. But in spite of the views of psychologists and counsellors, that it is best sometimes to do so, I never did. I actually think that for me it would have had a weakening and unproductive effect. So I kept smiling. However, I was aware always of the potential for breakdown because the strains of a flying command are very real. So I took Mountbatten's advice and never allowed myself to get too tired, catnapping after lunch for twenty minutes or at any time it seemed to be a good idea, no matter what, except that lunch hour when the Vulcan bomber crashed in flames on the town of Zabbar when people were killed. I suspect that you will find it equally useful to watch yourself carefully during rehabilitation, and do as *you* want. Not difficult for born autocrats like us. And I have been impressed with your ability to discard unwanted thoughts and emotions in favour of the real, important business at hand. You will now have to watch out for people who will want to demand of you and expect things of you as if you were Superman!

I take your point about ham radio telephone conversations, yours and our comparative random coverage. The report you made on Mir's status after your spacewalk, addressed to 'all', was relayed on to us by both Miles and Dave and we passed it on to Susie. Because of the way it was addressed, and because John Barraclough [Air Chief Marshal Sir John Barraclough] had just called me to congratulate you, I have copied it, slightly edited, to the Air League, who were very keen to have something from you for their newsletter. I also fully understand you about not wanting to anticipate your post-landing plans yet – I know what you mean, it is part of your personal survival kit.

We are off to Sussex tomorrow, and will visit the replica of Captain Cook's ship *Endeavour*, after which one of your shuttles was named. Rhonda has our address and telephone number. We will be back on Sunday evening – and as usual check the e-mail.

Lots and lots of love from us all, as always, Dad

His reply to these thoughts came briefly:

Dear Mum and Dad,

Thanks for your last letter. It was much appreciated, one autocrat to another. Please could you pass on the following note to David MacKessack-Leitch, by post if by no other means. [Michael this time gracefully refrained from the pejorative phrase 'snail mail'.]

There then followed a letter of deep gratitude for a gift which David had sent to him, at great expense and ingenuity, on a previous Progress supply vessel. There was no doubt that unexpected gifts of special food and other luxury items were appreciated by the crew well beyond the value of the items or even the trouble it had taken to get them there. No crew member could easily refrain from being interested in whatever arrived for another, and it was the normal practice with this crew to make something of a ceremony of the occasion, sharing with each other whatever the goodies were. Michael went out of his way to describe the scene for his godfather to pass on to his

Scottish friends, knowing that this would be appreciated. He said that times such as these were some of the few pleasant distractions from their rather laborious life on the station.

While the three of us were staying for a few days at the Barn House in Rodmell, Sussex, we unintentionally caused a mild sensation at our handsome guest house. We had not, by habit, revealed our connection with the now famous astronaut, but we had given the house telephone number to Rhonda for emergencies. NASA had lined up another ham radio phone link with Michael late on our second day, and Rhonda directed them to our Sussex phone number.

The telephone rang that morning and our charming hostess answered. She was surprised to be addressed thus: 'Good morning, this is Houston, may I speak to Air Commodore Foale, please?'

Our hostess matches intelligence with her charm, but Rodmell is a sleepy little village deep in the Sussex downs. She may be forgiven for assuming, if she did, that Houston was the American caller's name. She undertook to find one of us. The phone link took place successfully later that day and we thereby achieved immediate local celebrity status. But it would have been difficult for the house to show us more hospitality than they already had.

Michael had begun to feel that NASA might find his views on the continuation of Phase One useful in making any policy decisions. He decided to go formally on record and say why he felt that America should continue to cooperate on Mir. This coincided with the meeting of the House Science Committee.

Astronaut Michael Foale's Status Report from Mir
In an audio status report from the Mir space station, NASA astronaut Michael Foale summarized his spacewalking experience and scientific research. He also reiterated the importance of having an American astronaut on Mir as a precursor to the International Space Station, concluding:

'I'd like to summarize why I think Dave Wolf should stay on board space station Mir when I leave. I think it comes down to the fact that even though this flight, in particular for me, has been one of

....

the hardest things I have ever attempted in my life, I have to remember what John F. Kennedy said when I was about four years old. Forgive me if I get it wrong. He said, "We do not attempt things because they are easy, but because they are hard, and in that way we achieve greatness."

'I believe that out of this cooperation of America with Russia, which is not always easy, we are achieving some extremely great things, in sum, in the big picture. And for these reasons I have really valued my time on board space station Mir. I will always remember the last three or four months with great clarity and nostalgia. I count all that we are doing together, America and Russia, in space and on this endeavour, to be extremely valuable to future cooperation in space and on earth. Thank you very much.'

As if to rebuke him for this sally, on 22 September, three days before the planned launch of Atlantis, the main Mir computer crashed again. Even though it was retrieved a day later in the usual way and with further component exchanging, the international media leaped like hawks on this, yet another failure, and incorporated less important failures in detail for good measure. These included the failure of the main ventilation system (but the crew could manage without it for twenty-six days), the loss of the CO_2 scrubber or extractor caused by a 'worn' ventilator, and an unexplained brown cloud which was emanating from an 'escape' module.

Reading about the last item on teletext set strident alarm bells ringing in my head. In the pervasive uncertainty of Mir, indeed its regular, dangerous unpredictability, means of escape were of paramount importance, the factor which supported and justified otherwise untenable risks. And the computer failure was the third in three weeks, and the sixth since July. Michael would be drearily justified in avoiding counting the days because, so easily, the launch of Atlantis could be delayed. It was hair-raising to think that, with this situation, there could be doubts about their escape vehicle Soyuz.

Fortunately for our peace of mind on the ground, yet another telephone call from Michael to us had been arranged for 17.58 that evening, with all three of us, Mary, Susan and myself, on extensions in different locations. The NASA link reached Michael and told him that we were on the line.

M: Oh, really? Good. How are you?

Colin: Hullo, Mike. We're fine. How about you, we have heard a lot.

M: We have been working very hard and we're rather tired. We've had a lot to do since the computer problem.

Colin: Are you stable now?

M: Yes, we are regaining stability *but we are still tumbling*, and it takes time to get the computer back. We have been without a telemetry link with Moscow, voice only, for twelve hours, so that they can't assist us much or advise on computer rebooting.

Mary: Is the CO_2 scrubber restored?

M: We thought we had fixed it, but it stopped again. Pavel is working on it now.

Colin: What was the brown cloud? [I had to know.]

M: Something I first noticed during our previous tumbling, a brown substance streaming out of the Progress.

Colin: It was not Soyuz then? [Thankful.]

M: Oh, no, Soyuz is OK. [More thankfulness.]

Mary: Will you be ready for Atlantis?

M: I was told that if we were not able to get Priroda dried out and ready for Dave Wolf's experiments, the launch could be delayed. I told them that that was not a reason for delay. Control said that I should not be so clever. I said, firmly, that there *would* be power to Priroda by re-routeing.

[The twenty-second of September was Ian's third birthday. More conversation followed about birthday presents.]

M: I talked to Ian today. I am sure that he would like anything to do with his trains.

Susan: We have heard that decisions on the launch will be made on Tuesday.

M: It's bound to be at the last minute.

Susan: We read your frank statement about why America should go on with Mir.

M: [Chuckle] Yes, and I reread it ruefully when the computer failed again.

Mary: Something new every day ... Are you getting superstitious?

....

M: No, but it's best to joke about these events. Not much alternative.

He was still balanced and good-humoured, but he was tired and sounded so. On 24 September there had still been no decision about David Wolf or confirmation that the launch would take place on time. We at home imagined Michael hovering (literally) over the computer to ensure that Mir would be ready and steady for an eventual docking. On the same day, Tom Stafford, a great Apollo astronaut and a highly respected authority on space travel, announced that he and his team, having examined the Mir situation in Moscow and with NASA, saw no unwarranted risk in the US–Russian Mir programme continuing. Frank Culbertson lost little time in making the final decision that Atlantis would launch, with Michael's replacement on board, at 11.23 EST on 25 September, and plan to dock with Mir on the twenty-seventh.

Daniel Goldin, NASA's chief in Washington DC, said afterwards that he had always been prepared, if Mir was not safe, to pull the plug on the programme. But that if the world's experts told him now that it was safe, and they had looked at it four or five different ways, how could he have told the American people that it was safe to go up there, and we were still afraid? His view was essentially the same as Michael's and was formally supported by Jim Wetherbee, the Atlantis's commander, who said that the crew all knew it was a tough decision to make but that they thought it was the right one and they would stand behind him. An interesting example for the Russians on freedom of expression in America and people's readiness to use it.

Michael's trials and tribulations on Mir during his last few weeks brought him, and us, more attention from media and public. This was not all bad. We had had a new central-heating boiler installed at home nearly two years previously, and through its guarantee and insurance periods it had given us frequent trouble. It was clearly a bad piece, and to my mind deserved removal and replacement by the manufacturers, free of charge. I wrote accordingly to the company who sent a very intelligent engineer to examine the problem. He soon agreed that we had a good case, but he would need to consult his area manager. Could he use our phone?

After a few minutes on the phone, he rejoined us and said, 'The area manager was not keen to authorize a free replacement – too much of a precedent, he said. I told him that you were the father of the astronaut. He said, "Let him have it." '

It was installed forthwith.

Down to Earth

T he launch of Atlantis on 25 September was wholly successful and on time, but Michael would not know this because Mir was then on the 'dark' side of the earth from Cape Canaveral, and not in radio contact. Some of his generous American radio ham contacts called up another ham in Harrogate, England (a teacher at a girls' college), and asked him if he would like the privilege of being the first to give Michael on Mir the glad news of Atlantis's timely and successful launch. The teacher rose to the occasion, very early in the morning, with a dozen of his sleepy class. They made a call to Michael as Mir passed over northern England. Anatoli and Pasha were asleep at the time, but Michael was quietly awake, monitoring the frequencies in the hope of news. He was, of course, delighted with the call – and especially, he confessed, with the way it was relayed to him. His joy at the thought of returning to earth was tempered by an instinct not to appear too joyful or to cause unhappiness with his Mir friends, who still faced a four-month uphill journey on the station before they too would go home.

He knew now that events beyond his personal influence or control were in progress, all aimed, among other things, towards his retrieval from Mir and return to Rhonda, family and home. Still with a wary eye on the computer and the fitting of a precautionary air duct to keep it cool in case overheating was a problem, he attended more positively to packing up his experiments and his personal items. Long before the docking of Atlantis, the two vessels were within VHF radio range and communicated as the shuttle's approach closed the distance.

Mir's attitude held steady. When Atlantis reached a point two hundred metres below Mir, the commander, Jim Wetherbee, needed only a few small corrections to make a flawless docking with Mir's port on Kristall. First came the Russian phrase, *Kasanize e zakhvat* (touch and capture), then a few minutes later the 'hard mate', followed by gradual pressure equalization and leak checks. Then hatches were opened and the American commander entered the Mir hatch with something of a flourish. On his face he had an indulgent and satisfied smile. In his hands he had a new Russian computer. He shook hands with Solovyev and said in Russian, 'I thought you might like to have this first.' Wetherbee handed it to Solovyev, whose brilliant smile showed how he shared his crew's delight to receive it.

On earth, when hearing of this successful first phase of our Michael's return, the Foale family hugged, and went on watching and waiting. The day following the docking, Michael exchanged duties and accommodation with Dave Wolf, including the formal removal of Michael's seat liner from Soyuz and the installation of Dave Wolf's. On seeing his Mir accommodation, Wolf said, with some feeling, 'Talk about a room with a view!'

From this moment, Michael officially ceased to be a member of the Mir crew, and was accredited to Atlantis. But he found it hard to leave. He sent a brief farewell message to 'all', aimed at his many radio ham contacts throughout the world.

28 September 1997
To: All
From: ROMIR
STS-86 made its docking smoothly yesterday, and I must honestly say I am looking forward to seeing soon my wife Rhonda, daughter Jenna and three-year-old son Ian, who my shuttle crew tell me has grown twice his size since I last saw him. I will be sad to leave my good Russian friends Anatoli and Pavel here on Mir, but it is now time for me to say goodbye to them, and to all you radio hams in the world

....

who have spent time talking to me, and us. Thank you.

I will be showing David Wolf, my replacement, how to operate the PMS here, and I hope you will enjoy many contacts with him. For now, the seventy cm experiment is over, and MIREX will later post its findings.

Best wishes, Mike

Would Michael do it all over again if given the chance? a Canadian Internet questioner had asked. He wrote cautiously in reply: 'I am not sure that, if I was to be told that I was going to go through all that again as it happened, I would want to jump right into it.' He added later in a space-to-ground interview, 'It taught me something about how I handle dangerous situations, uncomfortable situations and, I suppose, over a period of time, stressful situations, when I'm not with the normal things that you look to for help, such as people on the ground and close relatives and friends.' It certainly had done all that, and he tells me that he will never forget it and that it has become a part of him.

On the same day, the world was further reminded of the risks of space flight when an out-of-control 65-million-dollar earth observation satellite burned up in the atmosphere, just weeks after its launch. The event was largely ignored by the media, who were more inclined to celebrate the imminent return to earth of their favourite astronaut, as no doubt he was too. 'Foale to catch the next spaceship home', said the BBC teletext, not forgetting to add, almost out of habit, that the troubled, ageing station he was leaving had suffered many mishaps, including computer malfunctions, air supply problems, an on-board fire and a collision.

Compared to the immediate past, life while docked with Atlantis was stable, but it was no laid-back picnic of mutual handshakes and smiles. There were many hundreds of pounds of repair gear to be transferred, scientific experiments, fresh drinking water, electrical batteries, tanks of air and a special cap designed to plug the leak in Spektr's outer skin, if the leak area could be located.

Michael too was caught up in the activity, with a residual but by now habitual proprietary attitude towards *his* Mir, in the face of all these interlopers. An Atlantis mission control officer observed that Michael was constantly moving about, like a shadow, not apparently eager to leave. But at the same time he kept looking out of the windows at Atlantis to make sure it did not go without him. He was of course anxious to brief his replacement as fully as possible, and he had a lot to tell Dave Wolf, if he could take it all in, in the time available. He repeated his general view that the science work on Mir is not always easy and is frequently interrupted by repair and maintenance work, sometimes just to ensure that the station and crew survive. But he was sure that the value of Americans and Russians working together with the same aims was priceless experience for the future.

Two Atlantis crew members, American Scott Parazynski and Russian Vladimir Titov, had been scheduled to execute a spacewalk during the docked period for NASA, not Mir purposes, and this was completed on Wednesday, 29 September.

By 3 October all transfers and interim work had been completed and Atlantis, with Michael on board, was prepared to depart. It had been agreed between the two commanders that as the two EVAs had not established precisely where on Spektr the air leak was located, Atlantis would fly around Mir in the best possible light, before departing, to photograph further and record the damaged areas. American Mission Control reported the event on 3 October at six-thirty pm CDT:

Mission Control Status Report, Friday, 3 October 1997 – 6.30 pm CDT
After executing a textbook fly-around to view damaged areas of the Spektr module on the Mir space station, Atlantis's astronauts separated from the Russian complex this afternoon, leaving behind US astronaut Dave Wolf and tons of logistical supplies and water for the next four months of scientific research.

Pilot Mike Bloomfield flew Atlantis to a point 600 feet beneath and in front of the Russian station to gather data from a European Space Agency navigation sensor in the shuttle's cargo bay. Bloomfield then brought Atlantis back to a point just 240 feet from Mir, where he began his fly-around of the station.

Aboard Mir, Commander Anatoli Solovyev opened a pressure valve in the station's Node, briefly blowing air into the depressurized Spektr module. Mission Specialist Vladimir Titov aboard Atlantis and

....

Flight Engineer Pavel Vinogradov aboard Mir both reported seeing particles seeping from the base of the damaged solar array on Spektr. Russian flight controllers suspect it is the most likely location for a hull breach, as a result of the June 25 collision of a Progress vehicle with Mir.

With the visual inspection of Spektr complete, Bloomfield fired Atlantis's jets to separate from the Mir for the final time at 3.16 pm CDT. The astronauts then settled down to several hours of off-duty time to relax following six days of joint docked operations. A second orbital adjust burn later in the afternoon opened the separation rate to more than a hundred miles per orbit. At 6.30 pm Atlantis was below and approximately a hundred and five miles ahead of Mir.

Atlantis astronauts are due to begin their sleep period at 10.34 pm, waking at 6.34 am Saturday for entry preparations. Bloomfield and Commander Jim Wetherbee will conduct a flight-control system checkout at 10.34 am, followed by a hot-fire test of the reaction control.

Having earlier pushed my luck a bit in presuming to give advice to Michael on stress-related reactions and his forthcoming arrival on earth, I felt emboldened to go further. He had at least acknowledged my letter in a friendly way. I knew well how much his little daughter Jenna had missed her daddy over the past months, and how she longed for his return. Like any healthy animal, she showed her deepest affection by running full tilt at the object of her love, invariably being caught and lifted high in the air in mutual jubilation. On Michael's return after his third mission in 1995, she had greeted him on the tarmac and sprung into his arms. She was only three then, and he caught her indeed – and almost dropped her with the unaccustomed enormous weight, after orbiting weightless for only fourteen days in the shuttle. All of us wanted Michael back in one piece, so I sent a cautionary note to Jenna by e-mail, to avoid the nightmare headline, 'Brave Returning Astronaut Broken by Little Daughter's Impact'.

3 October 1997
Dear Jenna,

Your mummy and daddy have told Grandma and me what a very good and helpful lady you have been since Daddy had to go away in space for over four months. It was a difficult and not pleasant time for you all, and a strain on your good nature and sense of humour. It must be impossible to find anything to laugh at, about your daddy being away for so long. But you have been good to your mummy and also helpful to little Ian.

Two things are true, though. One is that Daddy has missed you all every bit as much as we back on earth have missed him. The other is that he is *coming home* so very soon now, just over three days' time! What a wonderful moment that will be for us all, not just you at his landing but for all of us on earth, wherever we may be, like us in Cambridge and Aunt Susan in London.

Daddy too will be so *pleased*, it brings tears to my eyes just to think of it. He will not be as strong as he used to be, and won't even be able to pick you up to hug you, although he will want to very much. In fact he will need care and the most gentle handling you can manage until in a few weeks he gets his usual strength back. I just know that you have already thought about the need to be gentle, and to allow him some quiet moments as he gets used to being on earth again.

I think your daddy is a hero and he has done such a good job on Mir, everybody says so. He deserves a good rest. I hope that we in England will see you all here for Christmas.

Lots of love to Mummy and Ian, and of course especially to you, Jenna, from Grandpa. Grandma sends her love too, and all of us send it to Daddy to whom this is copied, with Happy Landings!

Jenna, nearly six, read the letter thoughtfully with her mummy and, on the day of Michael's arrival, was a model of longing, ladylike restraint. In fact, Ian, just three and without the benefit of my personal advice, ran full tilt to his daddy and was briefly picked up and quickly put down before the danger of collapse. There is a picture of this event with Jenna looking on, unwilling but necessary control written all over her little stance. I can get emotional over it.

The landing of Atlantis had been scheduled for shortly before midnight,

....

UK time, on Saturday, 5 October. Saturday was already a significant date. I had been approached many weeks before by our celebrated local butcher, Peter Welton of Wallers in Cambridge, who had invited me to be the final judge and arbiter of the Cambridge and East Anglian Federation's first annual sausage-making competition. I have always liked sausages and I was flattered to be considered a potential connoisseur. Perhaps I am, but I had of course been asked because of my fleeting celebrity status, conferred on me by Michael. Mary was to judge the hams. She tasted ten hams and I tasted thirty-six sausages 'small pieces', all excellent, and eventually the results were pronounced, followed by prolonged applause for the winner.

At the end, I was asked to say a few words. The company present knew, of course, who I was. I said, 'You all know how the press and TV have concentrated only on the black side of Mir. Some quotations are Troubled Mir, Ageing Mir, Mishap-stricken Mir, Crisis-hit Mir. After two most pleasurable hours of your company here, a new, even blacker phrase comes to mind, depressingly true but not so far used by even the least responsible representative of the press – Sausageless Mir!'

I had said the right thing.

After returning home and collecting our bags, we departed for London to watch the late-night landing of Atlantis in the studios of ITN. Our continued cooperation with various agents of the media was again to pay off, and this time ITN had invited us, with Susan, to London to watch the landing live at Cape Canaveral. We had gladly accepted, but the landing was delayed by twenty-four hours because of high crosswinds on the runway at Kennedy Space Center.

We are in the habit of welcoming any precautionary measure, whatever the inconvenience, and this has been a feature of both my RAF life and our family lives, particularly since we were with Michael at the time of the Challenger disaster eleven years ago. We had incidentally begun to receive many letters of relief and congratulation on Michael's imminent return, which pleased us, but also made me feel slightly uneasy. It is all to do with the superstitious side of being an RAF pilot (any military pilot will agree), and is concerned with avoiding the tempting of fate. Michael had shown this in his care not to rely too much on the planned Atlantis launch and docking dates. A letter which we received later from a very distinguished air vice marshal called Michael Lyne, who had known me since he was a squadron leader and I was a flight cadet at Cranwell, said it all, in a note to me: 'We know that a landing is not complete until your feet touch the ground at the bottom of the steps – and that a delayed landing is an additional hazard.' That was exactly what was in our minds. The shuttle's opportunities to attempt a safe landing had automatically been reduced by one. (We were saddened to hear of Michael Lyne's death after illness later that year.)

It was with more relief than we probably showed that, on the following night, we watched on the studio's enormous TV screen the great birdlike shape of Atlantis make its final steep turn in the early evening sky high over Florida. The winds had abated, the straight-in approach was steady and precise and, at the moment of flare as the nose was raised into the landing position, the fragile-looking wheels of the undercarriage assembly appeared and locked. A few seconds later there was the gentle kiss of each tyre, together, at 225 mph, touching on the Cape Canaveral tarmac. The wheels held, the braking parachute was deployed and the craft slowed to a stop. It was a moment of immense satisfaction for everybody. For us, the landing was indeed over in spite of not yet seeing Michael walk down the steps. In fact, like many spacemen who have been weightless for months, he felt nausea as the unaccustomed gravity of earth again took charge of his delicate balance mechanisms, unused for so long, and he needed several minutes to adjust before getting up.

Mary, Susan and I sat silently watching the now still Atlantis. He was back. Soon we would see him. But the transmission had ended. We had to wait until a later transmission before we saw him, rather gaunt and wearing a hat that was too big for him, but happy and surrounded by his family. The sight made all three of us very happy indeed.

He told us later that on rising from his prone position in Atlantis and reaching the door, he felt like a parody of Neil Armstrong arriving on the moon (a small step for man, a giant leap for mankind), except that for him the shuttle steps before him struck him as being the most enormous step he had ever had to make in his life.

He had been asked what he would like best to eat when reunited with his family. A cold beer, pizza and lasagne were, without hesitation, his express wish, and all were duly provided not long after he left the shuttle. That night

....

he was accommodated, under medical supervision, in the Kennedy Space Center crew quarters, shared after special arrangements had been made by his very contented Rhonda, Jenna and Ian.

On the following day, barely fourteen hours since his landing, he phoned us at home in Cambridge. There was a peculiar thrill for us to know that we were now talking with him on earth. There was a strange new feeling throughout the call. We probably looked no different nor sounded different. Neither did he. But in our heads seemed to be the warm, deep calming music of knowing that he had returned to safety. There were no longer occasional brassy discords to be pushed aside, no shrillness of alarm notes to be ignored, like those old-fashioned radio atmospherics. Just serious, emotional music in majestic cadences, a mental weightlessness to be enjoyed in its flow. We all felt it, looked at each other and knew that the others did too.

Yes, he was quite well now, but he had felt nauseated on landing. Yes, he had eaten the food he had asked for. His balance was still shaky, and if he shut his eyes while standing, he would fall over. His medical checkout had been satisfactory and as expected, and the children had both been thoughtful and kind to him. He regretted speaking of his first Mir crew commander, Tsibliyev, during his post-landing TV interview, which we had watched, because of the strong emotional reaction he had felt on Tsibliyev's behalf. I had of course noticed his difficulty, and told him that his emotion had come across with sincerity and friendliness, and it was perfectly all right.

Vasily Tsibliyev was later asked by a British television company what his feelings were now for Michael. He said, 'If you are a drowning man and Michael comes and saves you, you will remember him for the rest of your life.'

Michael asked us to call him at home in Houston the next day. He said that President Clinton had sent him a warm congratulatory note which he appreciated.

It was good to dial the familiar Texas number, knowing that he would be there. On his first day at home, he told us that both Jenna and Ian had been nauseous in the night, so poor Rhonda had had no sleep. While still in Florida, he had had a brief noonday swim with Jenna and found his muscles were very stiff. For twenty-four hours he still had no balance if he shut his eyes, and his ankle ligaments were very weak. He was well protected from intrusion at

....

home, and two police cars were permanently stationed outside. However, an overzealous builder had started to excavate the site next to his shoreline home in such a way as to threaten his house foundations. He felt that he had returned just in time.

I told him how pleased many people seemed to be over the way he had championed international cooperation in space. I had earlier written to the British government through our MP, Anne Campbell, about the need for more British government recognition of the existence, let alone importance, of space exploration and experience.

On 10 October I got a second friendly telephone call from the Russian ambassador, offering Michael his congratulations on his safe return and his excellent work on Mir. He understood that Michael was now enjoying terra firma with his family. He asked me to pass on to Michael and his family his congratulations, thanks and good wishes when I next spoke to him.

Over the next four weeks, Michael was encouraged to rehabilitate at his own pace. He was given two weeks of real leave, the first of which he spent quietly with his family in a secluded retreat in the Bahamas, which they could not really afford. Then followed nearly a week of media attention, when the scale of his impact on the world gradually sank in. Thankfully, NASA's plans for him made it possible for the whole family to come to England for Christmas at our home in Cambridge for two weeks, followed by a week for all of us to join his godfather up in Morayshire, beyond Inverness, for Hogmanay.

In the last week before their departure from Texas for London, arrangements had been made for Michael to attend meetings in New York with the editorial boards of several newspapers and broadcasting networks, to allow their members to ask penetrating questions. This formidable chore was to be softened. On 7 December, Jenna's birthday, Mary and I telephoned her home in the morning, Houston time, to sing Happy Birthday, which she gracefully acknowledged. Then Michael said that they had to hurry, because they would be leaving for Washington in two hours, not to attend any hearings, but to respond to an invitation for the whole family to meet President Clinton at the White House.

Michael had done more than just survive in space. He had brought honour both to England, the land of his birth and upbringing, and to America,

....

the land of his mother and the space organization that fearlessly and imaginatively continues to explore space. From 25 June there had been few days when he was not deeply involved in recovering from a crisis or weathering the effects of inadequate power and life support. With his fresh crew, he rose to the occasion and carried out unique internal depressurized power repair work and, later, a lengthy and successful external examination of Spektr, during the EVA with his new commander.

Mir and its international programme had been preserved against considerable odds. The Americans were staying in the Mir game to field at least two more astronauts. The possibility of future, wider international space cooperation and how it could proceed had been reinforced by Michael's show of dogged but inventive determination. He had been heroic. Two Russian crews had found that he would never let the unexpected deflect his aim to achieve what he thought was right. The Russians on the ground had been moved by his inspiration into a period of being more forthcoming with their space partner, and indeed the world. The Americans had been encouraged in their conviction that cooperation with Russia must continue, but perhaps in future they should expect answers to more questions. The world had been given a lesson in just how unexpected events in space could be, a timely reminder for the design of the International Space Station (ISS), and its construction and manning.

The last shuttle visit was in June 1998 and the Russians have announced plans for Mir's de-orbit and destruction in 1999. International attention should now appropriately focus on the construction and development of the ISS but there are many in Russia who are reluctant to see their flagship Mir cease to exist. Attempts in Russia have been made to find international investors to support its continuance, although the Spektr module is still in vacuum and general maintenance has remained a major preoccupation of successive crews to date.

We had our Christmas tree decorated and lit before our conquering hero and his family arrived quietly in England. When they got to Cambridge from Heathrow, it seemed most appropriate for them to be in the very large car which their London host organization had provided for them. The windows were shaded and it was difficult to see internal movement. The driver got out and opened the door. Jenna was the first out, quickly followed by Ian. Mary

....

and I were for the moment the subject of youthful jumping hugs. I stole a look at the car and was relieved to see not a giant, heroic figure but our own Michael and Rhonda alighting with their familiar relaxed and pleasing smiles and hellos. I am not sure, but I think that for some minutes we were all a bit self-conscious to find ourselves actually together and alive, normal and safe in one place. Tears were not far away. We had all been communicating in such different and difficult circumstances for such a long time. Our hugs made us real again for each other, but for the rest of the day we seemed continually to be caught out, just gazing wonderingly into faces – Michael too. A year ago we had welcomed them from Moscow for Christmas, but this time everything seemed so much bigger and more important, as indeed it was.

Michael had agreed to make a contribution to a forthcoming *Equinox* television programme about his time on Mir, and a brief meeting had been arranged in London with the Minister for Science and Technology and his parliamentary secretary, our MP, Mrs Anne Campbell. He was otherwise allowed to enjoy a much-needed private rest away from the spotlight. However, he had one presentation to give to an important group in the City of London, so we all spent a couple of nights in London before sliding contentedly into the festive season.

The City presentation was followed by some quite sharp questioning. One question was, 'Considering the real dangers that you face in your profession, are you philosophically adjusted to the possibility of death?'

'If I am killed,' Michael said, 'I have gone, and I don't think an adjustment will then matter very much.'

The questioner said, 'Yes, all right, but what about adjusting to the effect of your death on your family?' He replied, 'Yes, you have to adjust to that.'

Would he go to Mars if offered the opportunity?

'Yes', he said, 'with conditions. I want to be near my children as they grow up, so I want it to wait until then. I would like Rhonda to go with me.'

'What are the risks of shuttle operations?' asked another.

'We have had sixty launches since Challenger, so there may be a one in a hundred chance of disaster. Lloyd's puts it at a bit less. I can afford the insurance. I know that I throw the dice on these terms each time I go. But it is, of course, the launch which is the most dangerous part of a mission. So

....

much energy expelled in such a short time, on the forward edge of technology, is bound to carry risks.'

Our Christmas at home was predictably a lovely one, as good as the previous year. Michael took his family to the Cambridge University church, Great St Mary's, on Christmas Eve and Christmas Day and met some of the congregation who had remembered him in their prayers. He took Ian for a ride on the Nene Valley Railway twice. Then we all set out on the long train journey to Scotland, stopping for lunch in Edinburgh, where Mary and I had first met forty-five years before (it can't be). Then on to Inverness, past snow-laden mountains, to which Michael later drove his family, so that Jenna could try to make a snow 'cat'. (Jenna had seen our video of *The Snowman*, but she adores cats.)

My dear friend David has a large and beautiful family, mostly living nearby, and the eldest (my goddaughter Julia) and her family also joined us for Hogmanay. David and his wife Hilda were wonderful hosts to all of us, and Michael appreciated the hospitality so much – nothing could have been more different from Mir or from Cambridge and London. We all drew comfort, enjoyment and strength from it, while Michael held us all spellbound with his answers to our many questions.

At last, after three weeks of family company, Mike, Rhonda and the children returned to their home in Texas and Susan to London. There is a Russian saying about family visits – it's lovely when they come, and lovely when they go! We were not so sure now about the second part. We got so used to their being with us; it was even as if he and they had been with us all the time he was on Mir. The sharing of risk is a unifying thing.

Michael was allowed a week or two more to get his personal affairs in order before taking up a new post. At his request he remains an active astronaut, but his first job was to become astronaut adviser (with Jim Wetherbee) to the Director of the Johnson Space Center, George Abbey. It is a post well suited to his experience and flair, but he says that he has had to buy himself more suits. He also has his own telephone number and secretary; he is no longer just Michael Foale of the astronauts' office.

His unique experience on a space station has added to his responsibilities. Everybody involved with the ISS, from design to astronaut selection, wants his advice. He travels frequently to Moscow, Washington and London.

....

President Clinton continued to look upon him with warm friendship, and on the occasion of the visit by the British Prime Minister to the United States in February 1998, the White House included Michael and Rhonda on the guest list for the big reception and dinner (two hundred guests) given for Tony Blair and his wife. When Mike and Rhonda's turn came in the presentation line-up, the President grinned, took Michael's hand in both of his and, turning to the Prime Minister, said, 'Tony, I want you to meet *our* British astronaut.'

Michael's next scheduled mission, the shuttle visit to service the Hubble space telescope, has been brought forward to October 1999, when he will be part of the Hubble telescope maintenance team, involving many hours of EVA. So in addition to his advisory work with the director of the Johnson Space Center, and liaison visits to Russia and elsewhere, he has been training four hours a week for this mission which, in April 1999, became full time.

We, the English portion of his family, are finding more time now for a little reflection on the matter of space. We note that in Western civilization, it took over two thousand years, from the first recorded dreams of man flying, Daedalus and Icarus in Greek mythology, to the invention of an aero engine that made powered flight possible. There were various reasons why the wait was so long. For one thing, the Wright brothers and their hopeful predecessors had had to wait for the era of lightweight engine technology, from watermill through steam to the internal combustion engine. But since the first tentative flight of a few minutes in 1903, it has been barely one hundred years to the giant jets carrying hundreds of people and tons of cargo on intercontinental journeys every moment of the day.

A dream of space has been with mankind too. The enormous advances of technology, which permitted the phenomenal development of aviation, have encouraged us to think that the conquest of space lies just around the corner, like the conquest of the air has been for the ordinary person. Personally, I believe this to be unlikely. Getting people into the air and finding the means to keep them alive and comfortable has indeed led to bigger, faster, safer and more efficient air transportation, one development leading into another. But getting people into space is something else, something much more complex, and the problems of the effects of extended weightless-

....

ness and cosmic and other radiation on human physiology have barely yet been touched.

Evidence on which to base conclusions is of course growing, and perhaps weightlessness for a year or two during a journey to another planet will be shown to be survivable, for some people. Radiation is a more difficult problem to solve. Protection tends to require weighty materials, which presently have no obvious place in the design of craft dependent on explosive thruster power to get into orbit. Other safety measures need to be examined. The exposure during a four-month period on Mir was calculated to be half the amount of a person's tolerance to radiation for a whole lifetime before the threat of cancer becomes unacceptable. Michael was especially conscious of solar flare radiation, which penetrated every part of the station. He was aware of it even when his eyes were closed in sleep. The flashes would reach his brain regardless, whether through his eyelids or directly to his cerebral cortex he wasn't sure, interrupting and sometimes preventing sleep.

I think we need to face the fact that, unlike the conquest of oceans and the conquest of the air, breaching the frontier of space has revealed more problems than crossing the initial threshold might be thought to have solved. Humans will continue to dream and imagine what we would *like* to have, from anti-gravity devices to pro-gravity, anti-weightlessness devices, or the warping of space to allow a traverse from one part of space to another, which otherwise would require speeds many times greater than the speed of light. It is possible that the cost of sending people to Mars by current rocket technology would be better spent on serious research into these apparently unreal concepts. And like the ancient Greeks, we are not short of seductive storytellers to keep our presently extravagant dreams alive.

It is the dreams that drive us. Without much additional advancement in technology, we are already capable of building a new, larger space station, the ISS, the first of whose parts were launched in late 1998. If there really is water in significant quantities on our moon, a moon base is likely to follow. I think it probable that even with all the perceived dangers of extended weightlessness and radiation hazards, men and women will still wish to go to Mars and provision will be made for a few to do so. Some brave people may be lost, as they were so often lost at sea over the centuries, and more recently in the century of aeroplanes.

....

The dream of space travel is in fact not much different from our dreams in the past. Our imagination has always reached out, over the horizon, across the oceans, to great heights in the sky – or deep into space. Dreams are fuelled by our everlasting, insatiable curiosity. I see no diminishing in the future of our fascination for the unknown.

But it would be so nice eventually (ask Michael!) for the spaceship to have its own gravity for comfort, its own shields against radiation and space debris and, why not?, the facility to beam down, and then up, an away party to the nearby strange planet. The dream *is* alive; but perhaps we need another two thousand years. This should by no means be a disagreeable thought as we approach the start, and the challenges, of the next millennium.

....

Index

....

....

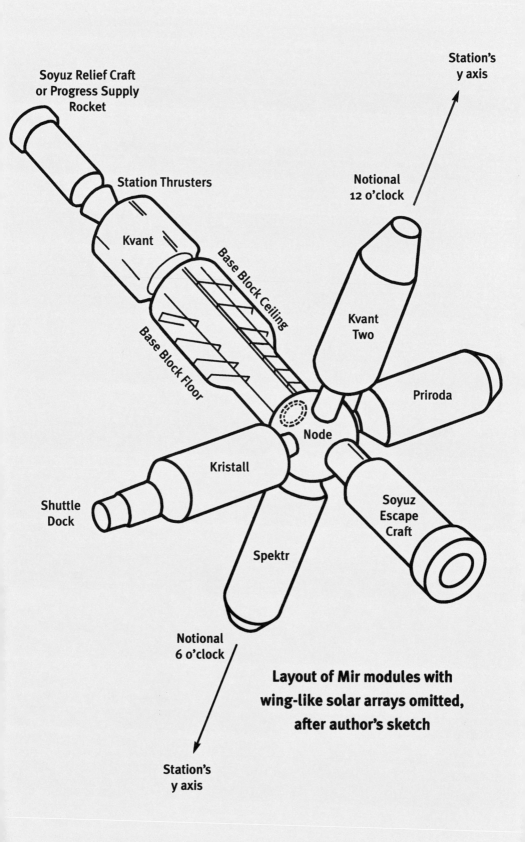

Station's
y axis

Soyuz Relief Craft
or Progress Supply
Rocket

Notional
12 o'clock

Station Thrusters

Base Block Ceiling

Kvant

Base Block Floor

Kvant
Two

Priroda

Node

Kristall

Shuttle
Dock

Soyuz
Escape
Craft

Spektr

Notional
6 o'clock

**Layout of Mir modules with
wing-like solar arrays omitted,
after author's sketch**

Station's
y axis